PRAISE FOR THE AGE OF DISCOVERY TRILOGY

A Secret Atlas

"High melodrama empowers a cunning tale."

—*Kirkus Reviews*

"Making maps can be gripping work, as shown in this sweeping novel of grand schemes, imperial machinations and brave heroes who seek new lands, the first in a new fantasy series from bestseller Michael A. Stackpole.... This satisfying story has it all—wild magic, the excitement of epic fantasy and the adventure of exploration in the age of sail."

—*Publishers Weekly*

"Stackpole creates a very interesting world that, while fantastic, mirrors our own in many ways.... The characters were quite alive, as was the world in which they live in and are discovering.... A solidly entertaining story."

—sffworld.com

"A story of adventure, but it also has intrigue, grandeur, alien cultures and lots of action.... The plot is tangled but fascinating, with politics, technology, love and ambition all threads being warped by past events and possible future disasters. The scenes of magic gone wild are very beguiling, with descriptions of lands where trees are living copper and sway like seaweed in water. New lands also add color, including a continent whose culture is obviously based on the great empires of Mexico and South America.... For the adventure, the magic, the exploration and the fun, you should try *A Secret Atlas;* it will be

l

"A story rife with political intrigue where everyone is vying to use his talents to get ahead. . . . Definitely a new series to watch." —*Affaire de Coeur* (4 stars)

"Michael Stackpole has done a fine and clever thing with the first volume in his latest series. He has married famous moments from our own history during the classical period of discovery—say, the 15th through the 18th centuries A.D.—with a strong fantasy milieu, whose elements in turn mirror cultures we know, mainly Confucian China. This strong resonant underpinning, combined with ingenious fabrications and Machiavellian plotting, forms a rousing saga whose lineaments we are only beginning to grasp when this book ends on multiple cliff-hangers. . . . Finding romance in exploration and the acquisition of knowledge rather than warfare—although plenty of the latter still intrudes—Stackpole's novel resembles science fiction almost as much as it does pure fantasy, lending it allure for readers who might not otherwise be tempted by a mere Tolkien-style trilogy." —Paul DiFillipo, scifi.com

"With *A Secret Atlas,* [Stackpole's] tried to do something a bit different with the fantasy genre. Does he carry it off? Well, judging by this, the first book in what will develop into the Age of Discovery trilogy, the answer's a yes. . . . A fairly rich and agreeable stew . . . There are enough hints, clues, depth charges and bombs on slow-burning fuses placed in the story that you know the second volume is definitely not going to be short on entertainment." —SFcrowsnest.com

Cartomancy

"Adventure aplenty for those who like their fantasies big and bloody." —*Publishers Weekly*

"Stackpole handles these machinations masterfully and makes his plotters fully as intelligent as their plots . . . a powerfully compelling page-turner." —SciFi.com

PRAISE FOR THE DRAGONCROWN WAR CYCLE

Fortress Draconis

"What a splendid story; it grabbed me and wrenched me full force into a gripping adventure. And the wonderful thing is, there are two more books to come."
—Dennis L. McKiernan,
author of *Once Upon a Winter's Night*

"I think that Michael A. Stackpole is incapable of writing a book that isn't imaginative, intelligent, and sympathetic. On top of that, *Fortress Draconis* is ambitious, even for him. It can hardly help being exciting and satisfying. When future readers name the writers who followed the Asimov-Clarke generation, and the Zelazny-Silverberg generation, they'll have to mention Michael A. Stackpole." —Stephen R. Donaldson

"A compelling and engaging escape." —*Publishers Weekly*

"With a deliciously evil antagonist and some truly remarkable supporting characters, this is a terrific read."

—*Booklist*

"A powerful epic fantasy that is wholly grounded in the gritty realism of battlefields and sacrifices."

—*Romantic Times*

When Dragons Rage

"Intriguing [and] complex . . . worth the wait."

—*Publishers Weekly*

"Addicts will devour [*When Dragons Rage*] swiftly and demand more."

—*Kirkus Reviews*

"Enough sex, love, bloody battles, and high adventure to keep reading lamps lit well into the wee hours."

—*Booklist*

The Grand Crusade

"This is fantasy on the most epic of scales, with plenty of bloody conflict and treacherous double-dealing."

—*Publishers Weekly*

BOOKS BY MICHAEL A. STACKPOLE

THE WARRIOR TRILOGY
Warrior: En Garde
Warrior: Riposte
Warrior: Coupé

THE BLOOD OF KERENSKY TRILOGY
Lethal Heritage
Blood Legacy
Lost Destiny

Natural Selection
Assumption of Risk
Bred for War
Malicious Intent
Grave Covenant
Prince of Havoc
Ghost War

THE FIDDLEBACK TRILOGY
A Gathering Evil
Evil Ascendant
Evil Triumphant

Eyes of Silver*
Dementia
Wolf and Raven
Once a Hero*
Talion: Revenant*

STAR WARS® X-WING SERIES
Rogue Squadron*
Wedge's Gamble*
The Krytos Trap*
The Bacta War*
Isard's Revenge*

Star Wars®: I, Jedi*
Star Wars®: Dark Tide
Star Wars®: Onslaught
Star Wars®: Ruin

THE DRAGONCROWN WAR CYCLE
The Dark Glory War*
Fortress Draconis*
When Dragons Rage*
The Grand Crusade*

THE AGE OF DISCOVERY
A Secret Atlas*

*published by Bantam Books

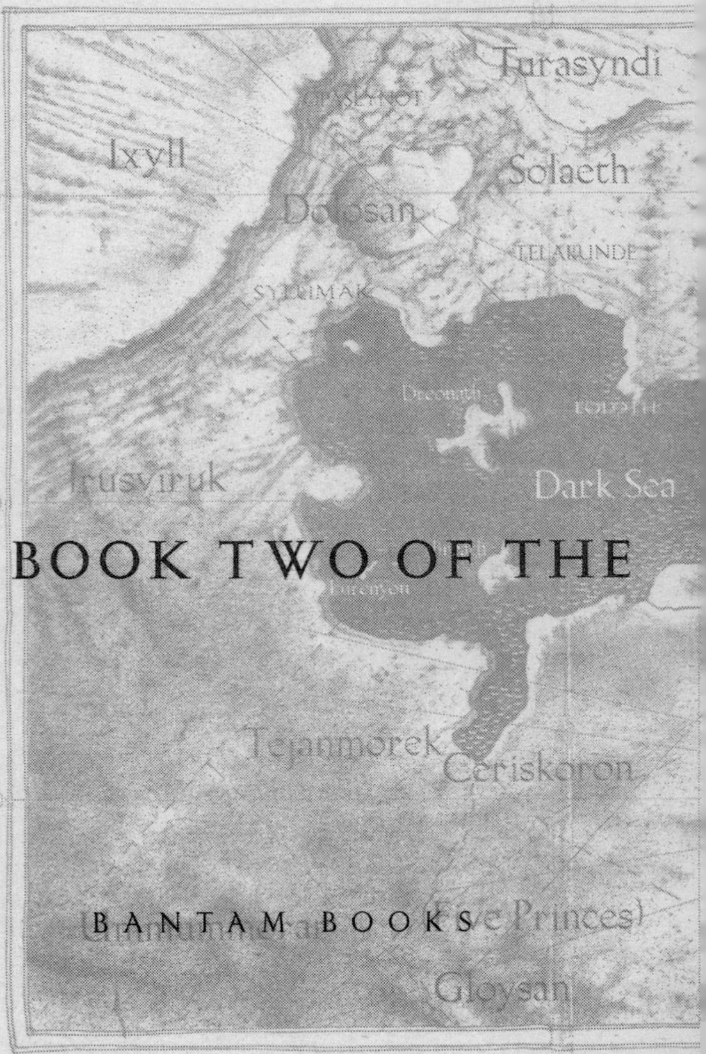

BOOK TWO OF THE

BANTAM BOOKS

Cartomancy

AGE OF DISCOVERY

Michael A. Stackpole

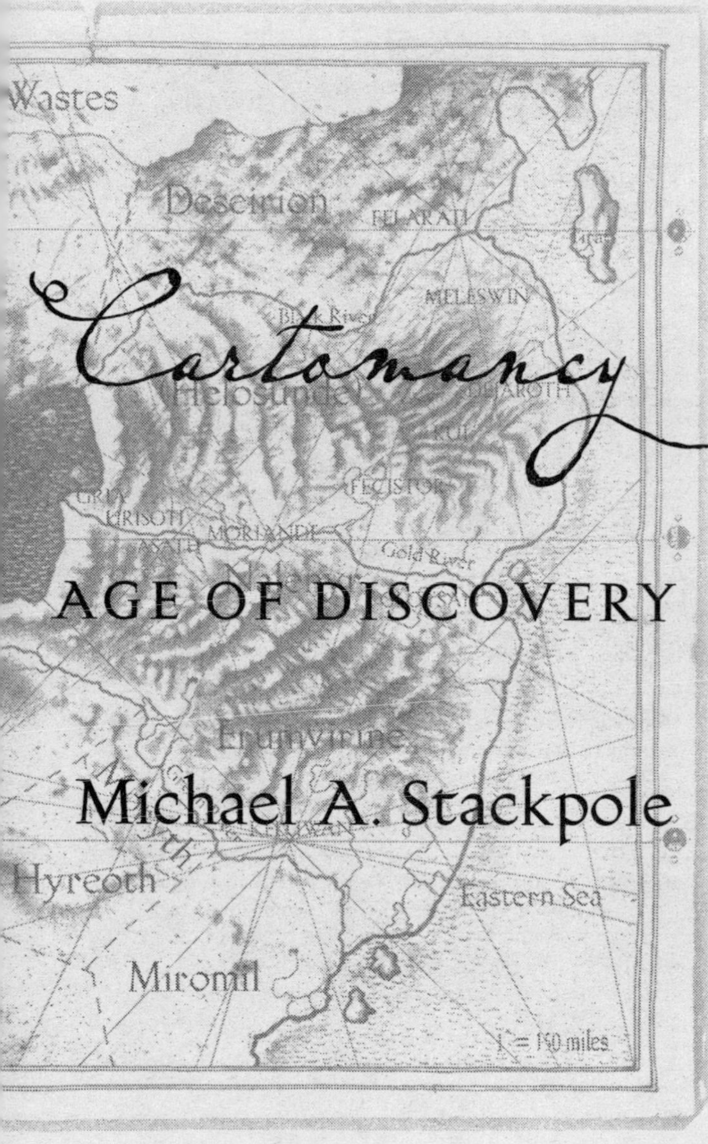

CARTOMANCY
A Bantam Spectra Book

PUBLISHING HISTORY
Bantam Spectra trade paperback edition published March 2006
Bantam Spectra mass market edition / December 2006

Published by Bantam Dell
A Division of Random House, Inc.
New York, New York

This is a work of fiction. Names, characters, places, and incidents either are the product of the author's imagination or are used fictitiously. Any resemblance to actual persons, living or dead, events, or locales is entirely coincidental.

Cover art by Stephen Youll
Cover design by Jamie S. Warren Youll
Map by Michael Gellatly

Book design by Glen Edelstein

Library of Congress Catalog Card Number: 2005054591

ISBN-13: 978-0-553-58664-0
ISBN-10: 0-553-58664-5

Printed in the United States of America
Published simultaneously in Canada

www.bantamdell.com
OPM 10 9 8 7 6 5 4 3 2 1

To Hunkie Cooper
A Mystic if there ever was one.

Acknowledgments

The author is deeply indebted to Anne Groell for her tireless work on *Cartomancy*. She knocked off all the rough edges and made the work literate. The author also thanks Kassie Klaybourne for her wisdom and support throughout the book's life. Howard Morhaim and Danny Baror are the best agents in the world, and if not for their business acumen and efforts, the author's work would consist of asking folks, "Do you want fries with that?"

Turasyndi
Ixyll
Solaeth
TELARUNDE
Dreonath
Ceriskoron
(Five Princes)

Wastes
Deseirion
FELARATI
MELESWIN
Black River
Helosunde
DEJAROTH
RUL
FECISTOR
GRIA
HRISOTI
MORIANDE
ASATH
Gold River
Nalenyr
GLOYSAN
Erumvirine
Moryth
Green River
KELUWAN
Hyreoth
Eastern Sea
Miromil
1" = 150 miles

Cartomancy

Chapter One

10th day, Month of the Wolf, Year of the Rat
9th Year of Imperial Prince Cyron's Court
163rd Year of the Komyr Dynasty
737th year since the Cataclysm
Derros, Erumvirine

Ranai Ameryne waited in the night, cloaked in shadow. She'd been living in the forest outside *Serrian* Istor for the better part of a week, becoming accustomed to its every aspect. Even in her days as a highwayman in Nalenyr, she had never become so attuned to her surroundings. As an outlaw she found fear and resentment of society constant companions, and they barred her from a union with nature as much as they did from society itself.

Here, in the forest, she found peace. She watched life surrounding her, studying the drama of predator and prey. Growing up, she'd had a basic education designed to allow her to fill a role within the vast governmental bureaucracy. That education had taught her that there was an order to all things, and that as long as it remained undisturbed, life was idyllic and perfect.

Her teachers had such information on very good authority. Grand Minister Urmyr had codified things with his books of wisdom in the earliest days of the Empire. As he was oft quoted as saying, "The wind is wise, and water wiser still, for none who oppose them can stand. Yet those who travel with them do so at ease and swiftly."

And more often than not, such quotes are used to caution one against challenging a more powerful foe. She smiled, aware but uncaring that the scar on her left cheek twisted the smile awry. For those she awaited and would hunt, she would be the wind and the water.

She glanced up at the sky. Fryl, the owl-moon, had half its white face hidden by a black crescent. Its position confirmed what she knew in her heart, that the night was nearing its midpoint. Her opponents would soon be released. They would seek her, thinking they were the hunters, but they would be proven wrong.

She shivered as the faint echoes of fear ran through her. Up until the previous year's Harvest Festival, she had proven other hunters equally wrong. Her name had been Pavynti Syolsar and, with her companions, she'd preyed on travelers in Nalenyr. The Festival had brought many people onto the road and she'd robbed most of them. She had stood against all of their defenders—including some very good swordsmen—and had defeated them all.

Save for Moraven Tolo. She'd not taken him for anything special at first. He had appeared to be nearing middle age—at least middle age for most men—though his long black hair had not been shot with white. He moved easily and without fear. He identified himself as one of the *xidantzu,* and she'd thought he was just one more of the wandering warriors she'd have to cut down before harvesting whatever gold his traveling companions possessed.

Then he told her to draw a circle.

A cold trickle ran down her spine even after four months. As good as she was, he was better. He was a Master of the Sword—a Grand Master and beyond. He was a Mystic, capable of making magic with his blade. *He would have been the wind and water; I could have been earth, fire, and wood, and I could not have stood against him.*

By rights she should have been dead, but he had chosen not to kill her. He put her through her paces and determined she had some skill with the sword she bore. So he demanded she travel south, to the Virine coast, to join *Serrian* Istor. Once Master Istor released her, she would spend nine years traveling as *xidantzu.*

She'd undertaken the journey south even though she could have run away at any time. While she had been a highwayman, she had clung to the honor of the swordsman. It was not fear of Moraven Tolo that kept her on her journey. It was the knowledge that she should have been dead—and complying with his command gave her a chance for a new life.

She embraced that new life and made her way quickly to *Serrian* Istor. She had been received immediately into the small cadre of students, most of whom were, at the closest, a decade her junior. Master Kalun Istor made no comment as she told him her tale and why she had come. She had expected derision or contempt, but got none.

Master Istor had listened; then, without a word, he took a brush, dipped it in ink, and quickly wrote. Setting the brush down, he turned the piece of paper around so she could read it. "You do know what it says?"

She'd nodded. "It can be read two ways. One is 'the tiger's young kitten.' The other is Ranai Ameryne."

The wizened swordmaster slitted his eyes and nodded. "For you it is both. You *are* a tiger yet to grow into your claws. You are also now known as Ranai Ameryne. Who and what you were before are gone. Welcome to my school, Ranai Ameryne."

Master Istor proved to be as relentless as he was wise, pushing her constantly. He gave her responsibility for the adolescent students. They, in turn, pushed her, frustrated her, and, in retrospect, taught her to curb the anger that would otherwise have had her lashing out mercilessly at them. Her care for them did not excuse her from her duties as a student, however, and often her personal studies lasted well into the night.

In her studies she came to grips with the conflict that had driven her to become an outlaw in the first place. Having been raised to believe that the wind and water swept all away before them, she spent her life waiting for retribution because she had chosen to defy convention. She had abandoned her early training and left home to study swordsmanship wherever she could find a school willing to take her in. She seldom stayed long with them—no more than two years and often much less—preferring to find a new school instead of dealing with the responsibilities and frustrations the old school thrust upon her.

Her life had become one of defiance, and she waited to be punished for it. Yet through Master Istor, she came to understand that she could be one who defied wind and water... or she could *become* wind and water. It was not a matter of finding accommodation with the world, but becoming strong enough that the world had to accommodate her.

That might have seemed a license for megalomania, but Ranai's training and Master Istor's guidance carried her beyond that. Just because she *could* destroy all those who defied her, it did not mean she *must*. She remained very aware that Moraven Tolo could have killed her but had stayed his hand. Following his example, she sought even the tiniest spark of potential in an individual. Were there no such spark, she could kill without compunction.

She also realized that part of the reason she had been assigned a small group of students was to learn to spot such sparks. While she was almost positive she would not have struck at any of her charges had she encountered them in her past life, the fact that she could not be absolutely certain bothered her. So she did restrain herself—and admired Moraven Tolo more for the restraint he had shown in the face of her far more serious provocation.

And now she waited in the darkened woods for her students to come hunt her. She had no doubt that one or the other of them would have tried to organize the group efficiently. She was likewise sure that several of the students would strike out on their own in an attempt to reap the glory of her capture by themselves.

While her easiest course would have been to locate those individuals and defeat them before facing the pack, reversing that strategy would be best. The exercise was meant to be one in which everyone learned that working in a team was preferable. If the group captured her, the value of teamwork would be shown. If it failed to do so and she subsequently hunted down the others and took them, the folly of striking out on their own would be proven.

Her awareness of the forest life sharpened her focus. Winter on the Virine coast did bring colder weather, but warm currents prevented snow from falling. Instead, misty rain prevailed, often producing fog. The forest creatures still thrived, but they had suddenly fallen silent. Curiously, the quietest quarter lay in the direction of the sea, not due south from Derros and the *serrian.*

Is it possible they thought I'd secure my eastern flank with the sea? And since I expected them to come from the south, they chose to come in from the sea? While the coastline was not very hospitable, little smuggler coves would allow a dozen students to bring in a small boat. Scaling the thirty-foot cliff would be no problem for them.

She slowly slid her scabbarded blade from her sash. Her black robes blended with the night, and her cowl only had holes for her eyes and ears. She'd blackened her exposed flesh with charcoal. Down by the shore she'd found bits of torn fishing nets from which she made an overshirt. Into it she stuffed branches ripped from trees. If she went to ground, she looked like a small shrub.

Moving with the silence her intimate knowledge of the area permitted, she headed east. The most obvious trail—a smuggler's trail—wandered through small depressions, beaten flat by the tread of thousands. She hurried to a point where she could ambush the group, going to ground in the hole at the base of an uprooted tree.

Yet the silence continued, which surprised her. Tillid, the smallest of her students, had never remained quiet for so long. Still she heard nothing, save the wind's whisper through the trees and the creaking clack of branches as they swayed.

Then, from above, came an awkward and surprised squawk, followed by a crunch. Something dropped onto the wet leaves beside her. A seahawk looked up at her with a golden eye, its mouth opened wide in a silent scream. The head, however, had been severed; the bird did not realize it was dead.

Even before she was consciously aware of danger to herself, Ranai bared her blade. The seahawk's killer dove from the branches above and her sword arced up and around in a backhand slash. The blade bisected it. The lower body, legs pumping, fell into the wet leaves. Tree roots snared the upper torso, having already punched through the thing's batlike wings.

She peered closely at it. It strongly resembled the tree frogs native to the area. *Save for the wings.* The moon's dim light revealed hints of color in the stripes streaking its wet flesh.

The dying thing opened its mouth, revealing rows of triangular shark's teeth. She pulled back at the sight, but not quickly enough. Its tongue flicked out and lashed her face. It cut through her cowl, and a barb sank into her flesh. Fire poured into the wound and she stumbled back. The creature died before its tongue could completely retreat, so it just dangled there, bright with her blood.

She raised a hand to her face. The barb had gone in over her cheekbone. Half an inch higher and she'd have been blinded. As it was she could feel the swelling start and already tears poured from her eye.

Ranai fought the first instinct to run. She wanted to credit it to courage, but it was nothing more than logic.

Whatever the creature was, it could fly, so she couldn't outrun it. If that had been the only one, she was safe. If there were more, they'd eventually find her and kill her. She was too far from Derros to give anyone warning and, as silent and nasty as that thing had been, only a handful of the students and staff had the skill to fight them.

And if they come in hundreds or thousands...

She shivered and pushed forward toward the sea. This thing—or it and companions—had been what had silenced the forest. She made her way along cautiously. Her right eye had already swollen shut, so she had to repeatedly turn her head to scan for danger. It took her half an hour to cross the thousand yards to the cliffs, but she arrived without further incident and crouched there.

The moon splashed silver over the water, which allowed her an easy view of the coastline all the way down to Derros Bay. Things wallowed there like huge barrels, but they were too long and slender. The length and breadth of a moderately sized open-ocean trader, they bobbed innocently in the dark water. As she watched, some sank out of sight and others rose like some sort of marine crocodile.

One that had just risen opened its mouth, revealing puff-adder-white flesh. Then black dots speckled it, hiding the white in shadow. The next moment the blackness rose vaporously. It twisted and curled in the sky, then turned and dove toward the sleeping town of Derros.

That is a cloud of the frog-things. In her mind's eye she could see them clinging to rooftops and walls, squirming under doors and between shutters. They'd slip into barns, dive into cisterns, and crawl up under the eaves of every building. The city would be covered with a wet pulsating blanket that would consume everything in its path.

She did not ask herself *why* Derros was under assault because the answer was immaterial. That it was under attack was enough. She realized she could do little to stem the tide but, if she was careful, she might be able to help those who would have to deal with it. The frog-beasts, as vicious as they might be, would hardly allow an invader to hold the territory.

Ranai Ameryne looked out toward the deep ocean. Something else was going to come, and something yet again after that. She could feel the things lurking out there. She didn't know what they were, but if she *was* careful, she'd be able to survive long enough to find out.

And once she had that information, she could help others figure out what to do.

She glanced toward Derros and saw the first sign of a building in flames. Beyond it, somewhere, Master Istor waited. She nodded silently in his direction. *I think you intended I have more years of training before becoming* xidantzu. *It's not to be. I just hope what I have learned is enough.*

Chapter Two

8th day, Month of the Wolf, Year of the Rat
9th Year of Imperial Prince Cyron's Court
163rd Year of the Komyr Dynasty
737th year since the Cataclysm
Ixyll

Ciras Dejote awoke in a world that had become unrecognizable. His head throbbed, though not as painfully as before. Memories of how he had gotten to the dark cavern—where he lay next to his unconscious master—came only in fragments. They'd been traveling in Ixyll and there had been a storm of wild magic. He remembered nothing substantive after that, save for the pounding of horses' hooves and a strong hand keeping him in the saddle.

His master, Moraven Tolo, twitched and groaned beside him. What little light there was glowed from his sweaty face. Ciras sat up and turned to get Moraven some water, but a wave of dizziness washed over him and he sagged back, groaning. Then, moving more slowly, he got a waterskin and crawled over to Moraven.

His master's jerks and moans made it seem as if the man were having a fit. Still, no foam flecked his lips; no blood ran from his nose. In the dim light, Ciras saw nothing to indicate what his master's injuries might be.

"Master, you must drink." Ciras slowly pulled himself into a kneeling position and slid a hand beneath Moraven's head. Sweat soaked the man's long black hair. Ciras raised his head and prepared to give him water. Then Moraven's body stiffened.

His eyes opened.

Moraven Tolo's eyes ran from the deepest sea blue, to a pale, icy color which missed white by a hair and back, cycling both fast and slow. Color flowed fluidly like the undulations of a silk scarf dancing in a mild breeze. Sometimes a lightning pattern shot through his eyes in dark, jagged lines.

When the lightning played, Ciras felt a tingle in his hand. A painful tingle that grew as the lightning flashed more intensely.

Torn between duty to his master and the increasing pain, Ciras did not know what to do. He wanted to comfort and care for Moraven, both because that was his duty and because Moraven had cared for him on their journey. To leave him alone would be wrong—but the tingle swiftly became a shooting agony that numbed his arm.

"Leave him be, boy. You can't help him."

Ciras looked toward the voice's source. A small ivory creature crouched on a bier. He would have taken it for a child, save that its oversized head held seven eyes. Two, which were black with gold pupils, lay where expected. A third lay in its forehead. Four more, smaller and gold with black pupils, dotted its face at cheekbone and forehead, above and below the normal eyes.

It's a Soth Gloon, harbinger of Disaster! Ciras eased Moraven's head to the floor, then came up on one knee to ward his master from the creature. His right hand reached down to where his sword should have been, but found nothing.

The Gloon laughed. "I am no threat to him. Come, you are needed to help Tyressa."

Though Ciras remained confused, the words "need" and "help" prompted an instant response. He staggered to his feet and trudged after the ghostly creature as it leaped from bier to bier, deeper into the cavern. It slowly dawned on him that he was in some sort of tomb complex, and he did not take that omen as anything save fell.

With each step Ciras' attention abandoned the dying pain in his head. From the darkness he heard an odd grunting and wheezing, which was about as strange a sound he could recall.

A thickset figure emerged into the light, dragging something heavy. A horrid stench hit Ciras. He recognized the object as Tyressa before he realized the man pulling her along was Borosan Gryst. Ciras darted forward and grabbed her ankles, holding tight despite the slimy muck coating her boots.

"Over here. Put her up on this bier."

Both men carried her to a flat bier and struggled to lay her down. Her heels hung off the end of the marble slab. Despite the bat guano streaking it, there was no mistaking the pale blonde hair gathered into a thick braid. The exposed flesh on her arms and legs showed abrasions, but how serious Ciras could not tell because of the shit covering her. Those cuts, no matter how deep, were not her major problem.

A crossbow quarrel jutted up just beneath her navel. The head had disappeared in the muck coating her tunic.

Ciras supported himself by bracing his hands against the bier. "The bolt is rising and falling with her breath. That's good. It's not stuck in bone."

Borosan looked up at him. "What are we going to do?" The man's mismatched eyes remained wide. "We have to do *something* or she'll die."

"I know." Ciras shook his head to clear it, and instantly regretted it. "I am not thinking straight yet. Keles will know. Where is he?"

Borosan shook his head.

The Gloon, perched on a nearby bier, pointed a slender finger back into the darkness. "They went together. He is alive. This much I see."

Ciras nodded toward Tyressa. "How about her? Soth Gloon can see the future. Will she live?"

"That will depend, Ciras Dejote, on what you do."

Ciras closed his eyes. His entire life had been spent in training as a swordsman. His masters had insisted on his understanding the human body and its parts. He knew where and how deep arteries lay. He could thrust through organs without a second thought. He'd even been trained in ways to deal with cuts and wounds. But all of this left him far shy of being a healer.

Part of him wanted to reject the Gloon's statement, but he could not. He had trained as a swordsman in order to be a hero. He had grown up listening to the tales of ancient Imperial heroes, wishing he could equal their skill and daring. Many of them faced challenges that did not require mere sword work as a solution. *If I reject this task, she will die, and I will never be a hero.*

He opened his eyes again and touched the quarrel

lightly. He didn't try to move it, but just felt the fletching brush between his fingers as she breathed. He slid his hand slowly down, doing his best to estimate how deeply it had penetrated. While archery had never been his focus, the quarrel's thickness suggested a length, and that gave him hope that it had not penetrated far at all.

Then his hand reached her belly, and he smiled. He scraped away some of the muck, then a bit more. His smile broadened, and he looked up at Borosan. "It is not as dire as we feared."

"What do you mean?"

Ciras straightened up. "The Keru, like Tyressa, wear swords, but they prefer to wield a spear. Because of that they wear their swords in a scabbard, which they belt on, not in a sash as a swordsman would. The archer who shot her hit her belt buckle. The quarrel penetrated, but not very far. Probably just an inch, through her skin and the muscle beneath."

"So we have to yank it out?"

Ciras nodded slowly. "The difficulty is that it's going to hurt her a lot. If she jerks, she'll do more damage to herself."

"That shall not be a concern." A hulking form moved forward from behind Borosan. Hunched as he was, the Viruk appeared barely taller than Borosan, though his broad shoulders and muscular body made him far wider. Black hair hung to his shoulders and ran down his spine between bony plates covered by dark green flesh. His skin tone lightened from throat to groin, and along the insides of his arms. Thorns thrust up through his hair, as sharp and strong as the hooks at his elbows and the claws that capped his hands and feet. His black eyes seemed to be holes in his face, and needle-sharp teeth glittered in his mouth.

He reached the bier and studied Tyressa for a moment. "Get water. Wash around the wound. We will cut her belt away so all we need deal with is the buckle."

Borosan fetched water, and they were able to wash the muck from her clothes. Following the Viruk's directions, Ciras used a small knife to cut away Tyressa's thick leather belt, then slice open the canvas tunic she wore. More water cleaned her skin, and very little blood trickled from beneath the buckle.

"What now, Rekarafi?"

The Viruk raised a finger, pressing his thumb against the uppermost pad. Moisture began to gather, hanging from the claw's sharp end. "First we ready her. Borosan, hold her ankles. Ciras, her shoulders."

The two men did as they were bidden. When they were in position, the Viruk slowly scratched a line above and below the wound, then to either side of it. The woman groaned at his touch. Just inside the square, Rekarafi plunged his talon into Tyressa's flesh and a jolt ran through her. Ciras almost lost his grip, but held on tightly. Tyressa had stiffened, but after a third puncture, her body began to relax.

Ciras' eyes narrowed. "You're not using magic, are you?"

The Viruk's huge head turned slowly toward him. "Not in any sense you would recognize, *Lirserrdin*. Do you not remember how Keles Anturasi had been poisoned by my claws?"

"Yes. He said that was very painful."

"You have spittle and you have tears; you have other fluids which use the same conduits to flow. Why should

I be different?" Rekarafi returned his attention to Tyressa and continued to puncture her stomach. "This will numb and restrict blood flow. There, that is done. Give it a minute."

The swordsman raised an eyebrow. "Are you going to draw it out now?"

"No, you are. She might yet move, and neither of you would be strong enough to hold her down." The Viruk rose up and laid one hand over her thighs. Then he settled his other forearm against her collarbone and leaned forward. "Proceed, Ciras Dejote. As you would feel a sword going into a target, feel the bolt coming out."

Ciras moved opposite the Viruk, then held his hands out for Borosan to wash. He shook them dry, then closed his eyes. The Viruk's words, delivered with just the hint of contempt, helped focus his mind. He had trained so well with a blade that he could think it through a joint, twisting and curving his cuts so they severed muscle and sinew without ever touching bone. Here he would have to do the reverse.

Curiously enough, it did not occur to him that he might fail. He was young enough yet to have confidence in his abilities, and scant few challenges had defied him. He reached for and grasped the bolt in both hands, as if it were the hilt of a sword. He concentrated, letting the shaft move in his grip. As his hands tightened, they moved with it.

He got a sense of how shallow the wound really was. The bolt had continued to twist after it entered, but not too much. The buckle had warped the broadhead, limiting the damage. He sensed its path of entry, felt how much play it had, and slowly began to reverse its course.

It came—not easily or fast, but it came—sliding from

the muscle and flesh. Tyressa cried out and batted a hand against the Viruk's abdomen, but Rekarafi held her down tightly and nodded at Ciras to continue. He did, working gently, feeling the shaft come free. Then it hung up—catching on something—so he pressed down, sliding a corner of broadhead beneath the impediment. Another twist, a little tug, and he plucked it free.

Ciras reeled back, half-faint from exhaustion, half-propelled by Borosan. The other man washed the wound, then pressed a bandage down over it while he threaded a needle. He carefully sewed the wound shut, then bandaged Tyressa's belly. Only when he'd finished did Rekarafi lean back.

The Gloon nodded from his perch. "She will survive. At least a little longer."

It took six hours for Tyressa to awaken, but in that time Borosan and Ciras had traveled deep enough into the cavern to find the narrow crack through which Keles Anturasi and Tyressa had climbed. Darkness had fallen by the time Ciras emerged on the top of a hill, but he used a small lantern to inspect the place. Though dust on the rock had not been too deep, it yielded enough tracks to let him puzzle out what had likely happened to their companion.

Back in the cavern, washed clean of muck and changed into cleaner clothes, Ciras sat near the Viruk, with his back to a bier. "It was three men. They'd stopped and had a small fire burning. One of them shot Tyressa. There were signs of a fight, but it appears Keles lost. They also had horses. I don't know who they are, really, but in their haste to run, they left a small pouch behind."

Rekarafi caught it when Ciras tossed it to him. The Viruk sniffed. *"Saamgar."*

Ciras nodded. "Moon-blossom tea. We have it on Tirat and use it when real tea is not available. The Desei live on it."

Borosan squatted beside him. "You think the men who took Keles are from Deseirion?"

"It's a logical conclusion."

"Then you revere logic not at all." Rekarafi let the pouch swing slowly, trapped between two talons. "You had decided the raiders we chased through the Wastes were Desei. You have now decided that those men and the kidnappers are one and the same."

"You have no proof they are not."

"No, *Lirserrdin,* I do not. Nor have you any to suggest they are. However, would you think Prince Pyrust such a fool as to task raiders with both collecting *thaumston* and relics *and* capturing Keles Anturasi? Were you he, would you not give the latter task to those you knew could do it well?"

Ciras started to argue but held his tongue. The Viruk's words made good sense. Moreover, if Pyrust had known the details of Keles' trip, he would have dispatched many teams to find him since the Wastes were so vast.

"Your point is well taken." Ciras bowed his head respectfully. "In the morning, if you will open the cavern, I will take a horse out, find them, and bring Keles Anturasi back."

The Gloon laughed, rolling back on the top of a sarcophagus. The Viruk smiled, a brief glimmer coming to his eyes. "You will not be going after Keles."

"But it is my duty. My master and I were charged with keeping him safe. I must."

"But you will not. Ask Urardsa; he knows. The thread of your life and that of Keles Anturasi may again intersect, but it is not in the immediate future." The Viruk examined his claws. "I will be going after him. I know he yet lives, and I know the direction they are traveling."

Ciras frowned. "How?"

"You've forgotten. My claws have drunk of his blood." Rekarafi's hand curled into a fist. "Because I struck him in error, it is my duty to find him and save him, so I shall."

"And what of me?"

The Gloon recovered himself and perched once again on the edge of the marble box. "Yours is the most perilous journey. With Borosan Gryst, you will travel north and west, deeper into Ixyll."

"But they are going the other way. No matter who took him, they are going back to civilization, not away from it."

"You will find, Ciras Dejote, that the fate of Keles Anturasi is a minor thing. The fate of the world will depend on how successful you are on your mission." The Gloon looked away for a moment, then all of his eyes closed. "There is a chance—slender and fleeting—that you will succeed."

Ciras swallowed hard, hating how his mouth dried with fear. "And what is my mission?"

"You will go into the heart of Ixyll and beyond." The Gloon's eyes opened and fixed on him. "You will find where Empress Cyrsa has lain sleeping for seven centuries. If you are able, you will waken her. If you are persuasive, you may even convince her to save the world she left behind."

Chapter Three

10th day, Month of the Wolf, Year of the Rat
9th Year of Imperial Prince Cyron's Court
163rd Year of the Komyr Dynasty
737th year since the Cataclysm
Dolosan

His horse's rapid descent of the hill pounded Keles Anturasi into his saddle. The jolts hammered his body and started his right shoulder throbbing again. It had been two days previous that he had broken his collarbone, but it seemed like forever. Once his captors had him, they had bound his arm tight to his chest and started riding hard.

The pain had distracted him, so he couldn't be sure of his actual location, but it seemed deeper in Ixyll than he thought they'd gone. He smiled. *My grandfather would have my hide if I admitted I was lost. Such a thing would be unthinkable.*

The Anturasi of Nalenyr were the unquestioned and unrivaled masters of cartography. Qiro, Keles' grandfather, oversaw a workshop of cousins, nephews, nieces, and grandsons that turned out the finest charts in the world. Ships using Anturasi charts almost never ran into navigational problems, and returned from their voyages with treasures beyond imagining. Keles and his brother, Jorim, had engaged in some of the most comprehensive and difficult survey operations ever mounted, returning with information that improved those charts and filled the family's coffers to bursting.

Anyone but Qiro would have been happy with the family fortunes, but the patriarch desired mastery over the world. He wanted to know everything about it, and so had dispatched his grandsons on dangerous expeditions. Jorim had sailed the *Stormwolf* into the Eastern Sea to discover what lay there. Keles had been sent to Ixyll, to survey the land of wild magic to see if the path west had finally opened.

Keles' survey had been successful as far as it got. Through his mystical link with his grandfather he had been able to communicate information that expanded the maps being drawn back in Moriande, Nalenyr's capital. Though the link hardly promoted full communication, Keles had been able to sense his grandfather's pleasure at the information he had gleaned.

At this point, even his grandfather's ire would have been welcome, but Keles had not been given a chance to communicate with him. His captors—admitted agents of Prince Pyrust, the ruler of Deseirion—had pushed him hard in the ride from Ixyll. They met up with other small bands—some in Desei employ, some just scavengers in the Wastes—trading for horses and supplies. The four of them had already killed a horse apiece through hard riding, and between exhaustion and the pain of his shoulder, Keles had been unable to concentrate enough to open the link with his grandfather.

Once they'd crossed into Dolosan, Keles had been able to orient himself. They bypassed Opaslynoti and turned southeast. Instead of riding straight east through Solaeth, which would have taken a very long time, they would head to the port of Sylumak and ship east. While the journey would be longer, ships made progress from dawn to dawn, as they did not have to stop for sleep.

The horses trotted onto a level, arid plain. Dalen, the leader, held up a hand. The horses, well lathered, welcomed the respite. Keles did as well. Slowly the throbbing in his shoulder grew quiet. *Quiet enough that now I can feel how saddle-sore I am.*

Dalen stopped his horse and waved one of his men forward. Cort—short, squat, and swarthy—rode up beside him. Dalen pointed further ahead, to where the trail narrowed and carried past a little crest into what Keles assumed was a valley. The feature was hardly unique in Dolosan, but nothing here could be taken for granted because the land had labored beneath centuries of wild magic.

When warriors, or anyone else, became sufficiently skilled in their vocation, it was possible they would become Mystics. Then they would become supernaturally better than lesser-trained men. Moraven Tolo, a swordsman who had been traveling on Keles' expedition, had been a Mystic. In one fight he'd torn through a half dozen or more foes with less effort than Keles would use to sketch a street map of a one-road town.

When any two Mystics clashed, the display of skill would be staggering—at once beautiful and terrible. It would also leave a residue of wild magic. Circles could contain it—hence the circles often worn as charms against magic, or the stone circles outside town and villages where challenges could be fought. There the wild magic would be trapped. But, left to its own devices, it could be used for good or ill.

Over seven centuries before, Turasynd nomads from the desert wastes had gathered legions of Mystic warriors and invaded the Empire. Empress Cyrsa gathered to her the greatest soldiers and Mystic warriors in the Empire. To forestall political chicanery in her absence, she split the Empire into the Nine Principalities, then took the Imperial treasury and headed west. The nomads and her armies fought several skirmishes in Solaeth and Dolosan, but their grand battle took place in Ixyll.

By all reports, the armies annihilated each other—and the wild magic they released nearly annihilated the world. The magic changed things in wonderful and horrible ways, and its mark could most easily be seen in Dolosan or Ixyll, where it still raged. On his survey, Keles had recorded living pools, valleys that breathed, trees bearing glass foliage, and so many other oddities that it hurt his head to think of them.

His mind shifted to the journals he'd kept, now back in Ixyll with the rest of his companions. *And Tyressa, poor Tyressa.* Just thinking of her made him feel even more alone. With her gone, some of the color had flowed out of the world.

Cort, the man riding forward to the hillcrest, had been the one who shot her. And it wasn't just that act that made Keles hate him, but the eager leer on his face when he'd done it. And the way he chuckled about it afterward.

I hope you die.

The man crested the hill and started to ride down into the valley. Then he reined back hard and his horse reared, but not before something had wrapped itself around the horse's front legs. The horse came back down, squealing, eyes wide with terror, then it and Cort disappeared.

"Cort, damnit!" Dalen reined back on his horse. Asbor, the third man, drew his sword and started galloping forward, but Dalen called him back. "Don't be foolish."

Asbor gave him a puzzled look. "But we have to help him."

"There's no helping him. He never even had time to scream." Dalen turned to Keles. "Have you seen anything like this before?"

"Tough to answer since I don't know what it is." Keles dismounted and would have fallen save for a quick grab at his stirrup. He got his legs under him, then started forward.

"You should ride." Asbor glanced nervously at the valley. "You can escape."

"Cort didn't." Keles kept his voice even, betraying neither his satisfaction at Cort's death nor his fear. He began the trudge up the rise.

"Asbor, get his horse; take my reins." Dalen dismounted behind him and quickly caught up. His eyes narrowed as he looked over at Keles. "I would not have thought you to be so adventurous."

"Adventurous is my brother. I'm just curious." Keles pointed toward the plant tendrils Cort had ridden over. "I think I saw something green binding the horse's hooves. I intend to avoid anything green."

Dalen nodded, then the two of them cut off the trail

and up through some rocks. The Desei agent helped him negotiate the steeper parts, then they both rounded a large boulder and looked down into the valley.

Dalen shivered. "Who could have imagined?"

Keles shook his head and squatted. The valley had widened into a basin that he believed might once have been the home to a fair-sized pond nearly a hundred feet deep. The red rocks around it and the grey-red sediment in it contrasted sharply with the green of the plant. Tendrils—hundreds of them, perhaps even thousands—lay like webbing throughout the basin. Where they lapped over its edges they were little thicker than a finger. Deeper down, closer to the heart, they were fully as round as a man and stiff with rough bark festooned with sharp thorns.

Centermost sat a grotesque blossom, corpse white with scarlet veining. It pulsed and quivered in time with the pain throbbing in Keles' shoulder—a fact he found rather unsettling. At its heart lay a darker patch the color of liver, which opened and closed slowly, producing a faint sound reminiscent of snoring.

They spotted most of Cort, but his horse had almost ceased to exist. Small tendrils reached out to pull the carcass forward. The sharp thorns sliced through flesh and sinew, taking the animal apart as it slowly slid toward the plant's heart. Hunks of dripping tissue and steaming organs moved more quickly, dropping into the maw between snores.

Cort soon joined his mount in a sharp slide to feed the plant.

Keles narrowed his eyes. "No, I've never seen anything like this before. Not this size. My brother said there are flesh-eating plants in Ummummorar, but the samples he tried to bring back died. Even so, those were only big enough to eat insects."

Dalen frowned as he watched the plant. "I would have been ready for monsters. You know, the things we hear about in stories—bears with six legs and mandibles, steel serpents, giant spiders. Not this."

"This isn't something bards would sing of. Its only prey is that which blunders into it." Keles frowned. "That doesn't make it any less horrible, though."

"In some ways it makes it more so."

Keles considered for a moment, then glanced up at his captor. "What are you going to do? I'm not sure you can kill it."

"Kill it? No." The man smiled slowly. "My job is to get you to Deseirion. We'll just go around it. I can recruit more men later, so you'll be safe."

"You mean so I won't escape."

Dalen snorted. "Even if you were whole, you couldn't escape. You could kill me and Asbor in the night, or kill our horses and take off with as many supplies as you wanted, and you'd still not escape."

"Give me a horse and provisions and I'll prove you wrong."

Dalen snorted again and started leading the way back. "You may know where you are and even where you want to go, but you know the world as a map. But a map is like the world in the same way sheet music is like a song. It merely describes it. You don't know enough about this world to survive it."

Keles said nothing. It wasn't the first time he'd heard that criticism. Tyressa had leveled it against him on the expedition, and he had taken strides to correct the problem. In Dalen's opinion, however, he had not gone far enough.

But that didn't really surprise him. He'd been in pain and had been traveling swiftly, neither of which gave him the time to get to know much about the places they were passing through. More important, however, he'd shut himself off to such learning because it reminded him of Tyressa; and to think of her was to have his heart feel as if it were sliding into the plant with Cort.

Tyressa had saved his life several times over, and when he was sick in Opaslynoti, she had tended to his needs. She was always honest with him, willing to hurt his feelings if it awakened him to realities he had to deal with.

And now she is dead.

Tyressa had been pulling herself out of a crack in the earth when Cort had shot her. She had gasped loudly, then slipped from sight. The last glimpse he had of her was the flash of her golden hair.

Numbly he remounted the horse and followed Dalen as the Desei sought a new path south. Tyressa had confused Keles, because most of the time she had been brusque and gruff. That had been part of her Keru discipline. Being that tough, she had lived up to the Keru legend—implacable, unapproachable, and incorruptible.

By just being strong and beautiful, the Keru—a select cadre of Helosundian women who served the Naleni royal house as bodyguards—had long been the object of fantasy for many a Naleni youth. Everyone had heard tales of liaisons between Keru and nobles or heroes—young Keru had to come from somewhere, after all. Boys dreamed of a Keru falling for them, or even just using them; but such things were fantasy alone.

And yet, for Keles, Tyressa had shown some tenderness. It wasn't a melting of her resolve, but as if their association had disarmed her heart. At the last, even as they crawled through the cavern and muck to reach the place where he'd been taken captive, they'd joked companionably, as if she were his friend.

Keles refused to consider the possibility that he loved her. He had great affection for her, but if he admitted to love, then the grief he was holding at bay would consume him. But as determined as he was to deny love, he couldn't deny the possibility that it might have grown into love; and having lost that was just as bad.

Keles frowned and swallowed past a lump in his throat while his horse plodded along in Dalen's wake. The sun would be setting soon, and what little warmth it had created would be stolen away.

It occurred to him, as Dalen signaled a stop for the night in a hollow that would shelter them from the wind, that he could have pitched himself into the plant. But, no, that would never have done. His suicide would dishonor Tyressa's sacrifice, and he would not write that epitaph to her life. She deserved more, and he would see to it that she got it.

And suicide would have prevented one other thing. Prince Pyrust, the half-handed tyrant, had caused her death. He'd once offered Keles a new home, and the cartographer had refused. Pyrust, clearly, had not accepted his refusal. He wanted Keles' service, and no price was too great to pay for it.

He'll find that's not true. Keles would travel to Deseirion and give Pyrust all the help he wanted. *All the help he needs . . . to put his nation into the grave.*

Chapter Four

10th day, Month of the Wolf, Year of the Rat
9th Year of Imperial Prince Cyron's Court
163rd Year of the Komyr Dynasty
737th year since the Cataclysm
Wentokikun, Moriande
Nalenyr

Though Grand Minister Pelut Vniel appeared quite calm as he delivered his reports, something about his manner set Prince Cyron on edge. Pelut's predecessor had always insisted on a formal setting for their discussions, so Cyron had taken it as a good sign that his new Grand Minister was willing to join him in his private chambers. Pelut did evidence some lingering traces of stiffness in the Prince's presence, but that seemed to be largely affected.

Which means he is using it to hide something. Cyron's shoulders sagged slightly as a great weariness washed over him. He remembered well how sitting on that same throne had aged his father so quickly. *And Father ruled during a time of prosperity, with no enemies actively seeking his destruction.*

Muted light glowed gold from the room's wooden floor and Pelut's shaved head. "Because of the relatively mild winter, my lord, we anticipate both a bountiful harvest of winter crops and an early planting season. We have no sign of drought and no reason to expect anything less than the abundant harvest with which we were favored last year."

Cyron nodded, an unruly lock of brown hair falling over his forehead. "This may be true of crops, but if the winter is mild, both the Helosundians and Desei will be free to campaign early. Prince Pyrust would take great delight in attacking during the month of the Hawk."

"Your Highness' perception of the political climate is, as always, stunning."

Cyron held up a hand. "You have no need to gild gold with me, Minister. Your predecessor raised empty praise to an art form, which is why I found dealing with him rather tedious."

"I understand, my lord." Pelut bowed low enough to touch his forehead to the floor. His golden silk robe, trimmed in yellow with small red dragons embroidered on it, shimmered and shifted. It allowed Cyron to imagine that his minister was not human at all, but some nightmare creature sent to torment him.

Cyron narrowed his light blue eyes. "You have been monitoring the shipments of rice to Deseirion. For every *quor* we send north, how much actually reaches Deseirion?"

Pelut straightened. "Minister Kan Hisatal is overseeing the shipments, Highness, and he has been most efficient. He reports to me that ninety-five percent of what we send to Deseirion reaches its intended destination."

"Really?" Cyron leaned forward, not quite menacingly. "We were going to send a million *quor* north, so this would mean nine hundred fifty thousand *quor* will make it. And yet, you told me that forty thousand *quor* were destroyed in a warehouse fire in Rui."

"That is true, Highness."

"You might wonder why I mention this fire. Prince Eiran had ridden to Rui, to meet with other Helosundians and urge them to forestall provoking the Desei in the spring. I had a note from him in which he said he admired our people for their industriousness. He could not believe how quickly they had rebuilt Rui, after the fire."

Pelut blinked, but Cyron could feel it was forced. "Highness, the destruction was confined to a warehouse."

"Your informant on that matter was incorrect, Minister." Cyron rose from his chair and began to pace crisply. His heels clicked sharply with each step and his robe—black, trimmed with gold, embroidered with brightly colored dragons at breast and back—whispered ominously. "A single *quor* is enough rice to keep a man alive for a year. It occupies roughly six and a third cubic feet. It would take a warehouse one hundred sixty feet on a side, rising to ten stories, to hold it all. Rui may have grown in the past nine years, Minister, but it hasn't a building over four stories. The fire that consumed that much rice would have consumed the whole of the town."

"I can see that, Highness."

"But can your man, Hisatal? Does he think we are blind and stupid? Knowing Eiran would be going to Rui, I asked him to look for fire damage. I had already done the math."

"Highness, you should have brought your concern to

me. You did not need to send Prince Eiran as your personal spy."

Cyron stopped and glared at Pelut. "My personal *spy*?"

Pelut's face tightened, then he bowed to the floor again. "Forgive me, Highness."

"No, Minister, this bears discussing. Have I not the right to information about my nation? You are the chief of all my ministers, from the grandest to the lowliest clerk. Shouldn't any information I want come through you?"

"Yes, Highness."

"I believe that, too, Minister, but I believe you have served me poorly in this matter. What disturbs me more than Hisatal's fraudulent reporting—and we both know he is diverting grain into markets where he can benefit—is that you saw fit to provide me with the raw reports he sent to you. You did not even correct so elementary an error. Could it be you wanted me to catch it and therefore demand his removal or punishment? Did you want him caught because you had not approved his theft, so therefore the proceeds of his crimes never benefited you? Or was it merely that you saw his actions as a way to undermine a program you never liked?"

"Highness, if I might explain . . ."

"Can you?"

"I believe so, my lord."

Cyron folded his arms. "Please. This will be fascinating."

Pelut sat back up, but kept his head bowed. "I had noted the anomaly, Highness, and had begun my own investigation into the truth of the matter. I did not mention it to you because I did not want to cast aspersions on Minister Hisatal without just cause. If it were his subordinates who were stealing and he was just being sloppy in his reporting, he *would* have to be dealt with—but in quite a different manner than if he were actively stealing."

"Your explanation makes sense, but I think that is only half of it, or *less.*"

"You misjudge me, Highness."

"I don't believe I do. You have never approved of the idea of our sending rice north to keep the Desei from starving. You see the Desei as a threat, and if they starve, there are that many fewer to descend upon us. The diverted rice, if not being sold on the black market, could certainly be waiting as provisions for Helosundian troops this spring. Not only would it not have fed Desei, but it will strengthen those who would kill more of our enemy. That means the chances of disruption to *our* society is minimal—and that goal is exactly what you have been trained to promote."

"Highness . . ."

The Prince shook his head. "You need to be *listening* right now, Minister. As your own Urmyr would put it, 'The chittering of the *dulang* masks the approach of the wolf.' "

Pelut nodded silently.

"You must remember that Empress Cyrsa, lo these many years ago, divided her Empire among the princes and entrusted it to *them,* not the Imperial bureaucracy. Do you know why? Because a society that is perfectly ordered is a society that becomes stagnant. It becomes inflexible. You would have it such that every family is a man, a woman, and two children—preferably one of each gender—for it keeps things perfectly stable. But life is *not* stable. Families change for any of nine thousand different reasons. No planning can encompass them all, which means circumstance is reduced to a controllable number, everything is lumped together, and the society frays because the needs of individuals are not accounted for."

Pelut's head came up and fire flashed in his azure eyes. "But, Highness, a society that caters to each individual is one that descends into chaos. It has no stability. No one knows how to act since all acts are valued equally."

"Nonsense, and you know it. Your society of anarchy is as much a dark fantasy as is mine of perfect stagnant stability. You deliberately miss both of my points. The first is this: by rising to deal with challenges, a society gets better. Look at our current prosperity. Remember how my father and I fought to get ships built for exploration. Doing something new and different has been of a great benefit to the nation. It promotes our long-term welfare and provides us with the resources to deal with new threats."

Cyron spread his hands. "And my second point is this: the Empress entrusted the nations to the nobility, not the bureaucrats. It is true that I could not administer the nation without you and your people. I acknowledge that and thank you for it. There may well have been princes past who were content to let the ministries do everything for them. I am not among their number. I need information. I need good information, and I will get it from you, or I will get it some other way. It is not because I resent or dislike the ministry; it is because Nalenyr's welfare is *my* responsibility. And nothing will prevent me from acquitting it."

Pelut bowed sharply. "Yes, Highness, I understand."

"Good." Cyron returned to his chair. "From now on, I want only accurate information. If you have suspicions, I want them brought to me immediately. How much do you think Hisatal has stolen?"

Pelut's momentary hesitation told Cyron his answer was a lie. "I suspect him of diverting roughly six percent of the grain into other destinations. As you suggest, some is going to the Helosundians; he has ties to that community. Some has been sold—price fluctuations in some of the northern provinces could be the result of his selling stock off. There are, over all, indications of eight percent shortages. The difference is pilferage by workers, grain consumed by pests, spoilage, and circumstance."

"I see." Cyron turned away from the minister and crossed to a pair of doors that opened onto a balcony overlooking his gardens and animal sanctuary. They'd been shuttered for the winter, but still the winds howled faintly through them. He very much wanted to push the doors open, vault from the balcony, and wander through the snowy enclosure, but doing so would be an escape from the very responsibility he'd used to chide the Grand Minister.

He glanced back over his shoulder. "You are dismissed, Minister."

"But, Highness, there is much more to report."

"I am aware of that, but I am granting you time to check your figures before you waste more of my time."

"Yes, Highness. Strength of the Dragon be with you."

"And you, Minister."

Cyron again stared at the doors until he heard Pelut slide the room's other door closed behind him. Convinced he was alone, Cyron raked fingers up through his hair and stifled the urge to scream. He'd had great hopes he could trust Pelut Vniel, and having them dashed was almost more than he could bear.

He took a step forward and rested his forehead against the chill glass in the doors. The secret of Naleni prosperity had been the charts made by the Anturasi family. Qiro, their patriarch, had been a venal, cantankerous, moody man, but his genius with charts had compensated for that. Cyron had indulged the old man as much as he could. As long as Qiro produced the charts that kept Naleni ships safe on the high seas, there was no end to their prosperity.

The difficulty was that Qiro was now missing.

The sheer impossibility of his disappearance would have baffled Cyron, save that he'd been through Anturasikun himself and found no sign of the man. The tower had been a magnificent cage for a genius, and Qiro had only occasionally chafed at his imprisonment. It was almost as if his having supreme knowledge of the world was freedom itself.

What disturbed Cyron most was the map on the wall in Qiro's personal work space. The world had been drawn in with care, every detail exact. Cyron had always marveled at it and many details had been added since Keles and Jorim had been sent off on their quests. The Prince had no doubt that it represented the world as accurately as possible.

The difficulty was that it showed a new continent to the southeast, occupying what had previously been an unexplored portion of the ocean. The continent had been labeled *Anturasixan,* and showed all the signs of being a land populated by diverse and ancient cultures.

Cultures of which no one in the Nine Principalities had ever heard.

Worst of all, it had been drawn in Qiro's blood. And

the legend beneath it simply read, "Here there be monsters."

A shiver skittered down Cyron's spine. Qiro, genius that he was, arrogantly assumed that his place was rightly among the gods. If he had discovered this land—or, worse, *shaped* it through magic—there was no telling what sort of creatures lurked there or what their intention would be toward the Principalities.

He would have every right to want revenge! Qiro's granddaughter, Nirati, had been horribly butchered by a murderer who had gone unidentified and uncaptured. The Prince had ordered a full investigation, but nothing had borne fruit so far, and he was doubtful it ever would. The murder would go unsolved, and Qiro's wrath would be limitless.

Cyron had wanted to confide the news about Qiro to Pelut, but the man's willingness to lie meant he could not be trusted with so delicate a bit of information. And yet, without telling him about the possible threat, there was no way the nation could be prepared to handle it. *If I dole out just enough information, I will be playing the same sort of game he is.*

The Prince straightened up, then ran a hand over his face. Pressure from the north, pressure from the south; rumors of discontent among the inland Naleni lords—it was all slowly crushing him. He crossed to his chair and dropped heavily into it.

Perhaps I should *let Pelut just run everything. Better his collapse than mine.*

He smiled, then threw his head back and laughed, trying to keep a note of hysteria from it.

A tiny tapping came at the interior door. It slid open enough to reveal a kneeling servant with his head pressed to the floor. "Does his Magnificence require something?"

"No, Shojo, I am fine."

"Yes, Master." The older man began to slide the door shut again.

"No, wait, don't go." Cyron drew in a deep breath and exhaled slowly. "Send a runner to the Lady of Jet and Jade. If it would not be an inconvenience, I would enjoy the pleasure of her company this evening. I have need of relaxation."

"Yes, Highness, of course." Shojo lifted his face enough for the Prince to catch the hint of a smile. Not because the Prince was summoning the nation's legendary courtesan to attend him; Shojo found no scandal in that. He smiled because he didn't think Cyron did it frequently enough.

"Shojo."

"Yes, Highness?"

"Don't send a runner. Convey the message yourself. All arrangements will be in your hands."

"I shall see to it, Master."

"Thank you." The prince bowed his head as the man slid the door shut again. "If only Pelut would serve me as well as you." Cyron slowly shook his head. "But he does not, which is why the burden of the nation's future rests squarely on my shoulders. But for how long?" Cyron could sense doom lurking. "And from what direction shall destruction come?"

Chapter Five

12th day, Month of the Wolf, Year of the Rat
9th Year of Imperial Prince Cyron's Court
163rd Year of the Komyr Dynasty
737th year since the Cataclysm
Kunjiqui, Anturasixan

Nirati Anturasi rather liked being alive. She dwelt in a paradise that had been a childhood fantasy she'd shared only with her grandfather. Somehow he had shaped it for her and put it at the heart of a vast continent. In Kunjiqui, flowers always bloomed, clouds never cluttered the sky, and water ran cool in streams. Whatever foods or refreshments she desired would be borne to her by small fanciful creatures that, if the expressions in their large eyes could be credited, worshipped her.

The only thing that disturbed her was that she seemed to have remembered dying. Lying naked on the grasses at the edge of a stream, with one toe dipped into the water and fat goldfish nibbling at it, she tried to recall the circumstances of her death. They would not come—though it seemed to her that she had shed her old body the way she shed clothes, and had come to Kunjiqui newborn, innocent, yet a bit wiser and more perceptive than before.

Dying certainly was unpleasant business, and she felt no impetus to dwell upon it, save from time to time when nothing distracted her. These moments of pure peace came seldom on Anturasixan, for much was being done and, she had been assured, much also needed doing.

As her grandfather had shaped her sanctuary, so he shaped and reshaped Anturasixan. From where she lay, she could see him silhouetted as a dark speck against the dying sun. She knew he faced north, but only because along what would have been the line of his vision, a sharp mountain range rose slowly and inexorably, its grey teeth piercing the sky. In one heartbeat snow capped the peaks, and in the next had melted and flowed down into valleys she could not see.

She had not puzzled over how he could do this because, in a sense, he always had been able to do it. When Qiro Anturasi added features to a map, it meant they truly existed. Qiro had defined the world for countless Naleni merchants and sailors. Here he defined his own continent, revising and reshaping it as he would have in changing the details on a map.

Nirati heard a delighted squeal and brought her head up. A tiny creature—barely the size of a two-year-old child, yet with the body and well-formed limbs of an adult human—came bounding through the grasses. Takwee would have appeared to be entirely human, save that a soft ivory down covered her body. Her head, which was slightly large for her body, held big gold eyes, a slightly protuberant muzzle, and was crowned with a glorious golden mane that ran down her spine and matched the tuft at the end of her tail.

Takwee had been born in one of the Anturasixan provinces. Nirati did not know if she was the only one of her people in Kunjiqui, but Takwee did not seem to suffer loneliness. She seemed content to spend time herding the serving creatures or washing and braiding Nirati's hair. She would chitter and whistle away gaily—Nirati could not understand a thing she said—but the squeal usually presaged one thing only.

In the tiny creature's wake, a man crested the hill to the north. Quite tall and powerfully built, he descended toward her with a casual confidence. His long black hair danced at his shoulders. The hue matched his beard and the thick mat of hair on his broad chest. His loincloth and eyes both were a deep blue, and Nirati felt joy rising in her at his approach.

She sat up, but made no attempt to cover herself. She and Nelesquin had become lovers. In fact, he had taken her within minutes of their meeting. The memory of it still shocked her—not so much because she had never given herself to a man so quickly before, but because it had seemed the most natural thing in the world. It was as if upon meeting him, she had discovered the lover she had always been meant to have.

Nirati smiled. "My lord, you have been away much today."

"And every moment away from you has been as if a year under the lash." He came and sat at her feet, then leaned over and kissed her. He pulled back after only a second, stared into her eyes, then smiled before kissing her again, more fully and deeply.

Nirati broke their kiss but lingered with her forehead pressed to his. "And why was it you were away so long?"

A little tremor ran through him, and it surprised her. He straightened up and pulled away, his eyes half-closed. "Memories come back slowly, Nirati, and not all of them are pleasant. I collected scrying stones and have consulted them—this helped, but also revealed a number of things to me. I had to sort through them to help me focus. Your grandfather and I will work well together, though his lack of focus hurts us."

"I am not sure I understand, my lord."

Nelesquin smiled and caressed her leg. "Take your dear Takwee here. A delightful creature, with many uses, but not suited to the tasks we need to accomplish."

Takwee, upon hearing her name, looked up from the stream bank where she crouched. She smiled, baring all her teeth, then returned her gaze to the stream. She barked harshly, then dove deep, scattering a small school of bright green fish.

Nirati laughed at her antics and Nelesquin joined her. "I think your grandfather modeled Takwee on the Fennych. He worked from memory, and had not heard the true tales, or sought to forget them. It seems much of the truth of the world has been lost."

She smiled indulgently. "I have no doubt it is as you say, my lord."

"And I am chastened for telling you my conclusions without sharing my full thoughts." He nodded. "Indulge me, please, Nirati."

"As you desire."

"Tell me what you know of Empress Cyrsa."

Nirati frowned, not at all certain what the last empress had to do with anything on Anturasixan. "I only know her from the tales told to children, my lord. At the time of the Turasynd invasion she gathered together all the greatest heroes of the Empire. She took them west, along with the Imperial treasury, so the barbarians would follow her into the far provinces. There they fought a battle that released much wild magic. It devastated the provinces and created the Time of Black Ice. Millions died as magic and years without summer ravaged the land. Some say she was killed in the battle, others say she waits in far Ixyll for a threat to the Empire to rise, whence she will return with her army to restore peace and order."

"I thought as much." Nelesquin shook his head. "She is a hero."

"Yes. She saved the Empire."

"But she was the one to split it into the Nine Principalities, wasn't she?"

"Yes, but only to prevent the power-hungry from tearing everything apart while she was away." Nirati frowned. "Is this not true, my lord?"

"In some ways I suppose it is, Nirati, for any tale that survives the generation that lived it becomes the *truth*. It is not what *I* remember. It is a story that masks a monster, and it is against that monster your grandfather and I will strike."

Nelesquin turned his head from her and gazed northwest, toward the land once known as the Empire. "Cyrsa has, no doubt, been counted as one of the last emperor's many wives. He did have quite the harem, for along with a love of peace, he loved women and spirits. He was, by all accounts, weak-willed. Still, we hoped, he would someday be able to pick an heir from among his many sons. I eventually attained that position, but that is somewhat beside the point.

"Cyrsa was not one of his wives of long standing. She was a common whore, gifted to him by a noble who sought his favor. She infatuated him and distracted him at a time when distraction was the last thing we needed."

Nelesquin's eyes narrowed and his expression darkened. "When the Turasynd invaded, we all beseeched the Emperor to act. We were ready to gather an army, but with each report of their attacks, the Emperor withdrew a bit more. He knew what fighting them would do to the Empire and could not bring himself to order such destruction. Yet his good intentions doomed the Empire.

"Cyrsa acted. She murdered the Emperor in his bed and was found naked and blood-spattered by Soshir. He should have slain her outright, but he did not. He wanted to be her consort, clearly, so he supported her claim that she was now the Empress. She issued orders to gather an army and head west. She sundered the Empire, looted it, and fled the capital."

Nelesquin looked at her, his expression opening. "I tell you in truth, dear Nirati, that I was prideful in my youth, but I was not stupid or untalented. The whore's division of the Empire made me the Prince of Erumvirine, the Crown Province. Perhaps that should have satisfied my ambitions, but it did not. I gathered my loyal retainers and went with her. I suspected treachery, and was rewarded with it. I died in Ixyll because of her. She was so afraid of the esteem in which I was held that she split my army off and offered me as a sacrifice to the Turasynd."

Nirati closed her eyes tight as memories of pain

washed over her. She drew her legs up and hugged them to her chest. Then she slowly opened her eyes. "But if you died, how is it that you are here now?"

Nelesquin, gaze focused distantly, shook his head. "I do not know, but the how of things does not concern me. It is the *why* that intrigues. And from our conversations, from what I have learned from your grandfather, I think I know the answer. If I am correct, the world may face a challenge yet greater than the Time of Black Ice."

"How so?"

"Consider this. Cyrsa was never a stupid woman. She knew the sort of catastrophe her battle would unleash. She had no idea if the world would survive or not, but she was certain it would be devastated. She planned, therefore, to deal with the world after it had been healed. She planned her return then, when things would be closest to what they were when she departed."

"But how would she know when that time was?"

He smiled grimly. "It is simple, Nirati. She created a sanctuary in Ixyll, where she could wait out the years of wild magic. The Turasynd have a different understanding of it than we do, and she captured and tortured enough of their shaman to learn their secrets. She creates her sanctuary and waits, like a spider tucked safely in her web. When the wild magic has receded enough, explorers will come. All she has to do is capture them, learn from them, and plot her return."

Nirati's eyes grew wide. "But my brother, Keles, is bound for Ixyll."

"I know. Your grandfather has told me this. Still, it could have been worse. If Qiro had succeeded in finding her earlier, Anturasixan would not exist. We would have no base from which to fight her."

"Can we fight her?"

"Oh yes, most assuredly." His smile warmed. "With my help, your grandfather is preparing an army that will oppose her. His initial efforts have had modest results—he learns quickly, but has no background in warfare. But the mountains he raised today are full of iron, and I have shaped creatures that will mine and refine it, creating steel for armor and weapons. In other provinces we will raise warriors worthy of the name, whose skill at combat will be finely honed. We will be ready."

"But Ixyll is a long way from here."

"Agreed, but we have our second purpose to consider, as well as the first. We will need a base of operations, so our armies will first return to me my birthright. I shall be Prince of Erumvirine again. After that, we shall consolidate our position and wait for her arrival."

"And your second purpose?"

Nelesquin smiled softly and drew her into his lap. "Do you not remember my telling you that you would be avenged, Nirati? I know what they did to you there. I don't know who did it but I know there is punishment to be meted out, and unruly princes to be brought to heel. Order shall be restored to the lands of the Empire, so we may face Cyrsa with a united front. To do otherwise would be foolish."

"Yes, my lord." Nirati reached up, sinking fingers into his black hair. "And once she is destroyed, we can go home again?"

"Yes, Nirati." Nelesquin nodded solemnly. "I shall return the world to the perfection that was the Empire, and together we will make the world into paradise."

Chapter Six

12th day, Month of the Wolf, Year of the Rat
9th Year of Imperial Prince Cyron's Court
163rd Year of the Komyr Dynasty
737th year since the Cataclysm
Nemehyan, Caxyan

For at least the third time that day, Jorim Anturasi wondered if all the gods had gotten their start this way. He sat on a circular stone platform set in the bottom of a bowl-shaped room. It had been buried in the lower reaches of the largest ceremonial pyramid in Nemehyan. A star-shaped stone had been fitted into the ceiling about twenty feet above him. The Amentzutl *maicana*—the ruling magician class—had shaped and set the stone with magic. They'd pierced it with tiny holes, so the stone wept. Its tears poured down on him.

The water soaked him, pasting the golden robe with the black dragons embroidered on it to his body. He found its clinging an annoyance, but on this, the fifth day of his ritual cleansing, at least he would actually get clean.

He'd endured one ritual for every day of the Amentzutl creation story, with each rite centering on that day's symbolic element—although the sequence ran in reverse. The first day, he dwelt in a tree because the rain forests were the final bit of creation. The third day, for earth, he lived in a cave. He'd survived that and the ordeal of fire, which brought him to water.

The relentless dripping was enough to drive him mad, so he did his best to shut his mind to it and concentrate on his predicament. By agreement with Anaeda Gryst, the *Stormwolf*'s captain, Jorim had communicated nothing of his discovery to his grandfather. No one in Nalenyr knew where the expedition was or what it had discovered. Besides, in his most recent attempts to reach his grandfather, he'd been unable to make mind-to-mind contact. He knew that his grandfather was out there—and his brother as well—but both of them were distracted enough that he couldn't even be certain they noticed his attempts to reach them.

It would not have mattered much if they had, because he still could not have gotten across the whole of his experience. As part of the *Stormwolf* expedition, he'd sailed on Nalenyr's largest ship into the vast Eastern Sea. At its far edge they'd discovered a continent no one in the Nine knew existed. The people who lived there called themselves the Amentzutl, and believed Jorim was the incarnation of their god Tetcomchoa, who had returned to save them in a time of dire peril.

To complicate matters, the Amentzutl identified the threat as the rising of a demon-god, Mozoloa, in the west. Iesol Pelmir, the *Stormwolf*'s ship's clerk, had noticed a curious linkage between one of Mozoloa's secondary names and that of an old Imperial prince,

Nelesquin. Iesol said there were stories that Nelesquin, like Empress Cyrsa, would rise again from his grave and return to the Nine—but only to wreak havoc.

A howling shriek broke his concentration. He turned his head and saw a small, stout creature spinning and sliding down the inside of the wet bowl. For a moment, he reminded Jorim of a small bear he'd once seen playing in Prince Cyron's sanctuary, especially when he abruptly sat down with a splash and glided right into the puddle at the room's base. The creature looked up, his tufted ears rising. He leaped up, fur dripping, and tackled Jorim.

"Jrima, Jrima, glad, heart-glad."

"Me, too, Shimik." Jorim grabbed the Fennych and held him up much as a father might a child. "How much have you changed since I last saw you?"

The Fenn wriggled free of his grasp, then stepped away and slowly twirled. The fur that covered his sturdy body had once been all shades of brown, but had changed significantly during his time with the Amentzutl. The fur on his head had become mostly gold, but striped with jade. Likewise, gold and jade twisted into a pattern reminiscent of the dragon crest decorating Jorim's robe. Finally, two tufts of hair rose from his forehead; tiny twins of the sorts of feathers the Amentzutl used to decorate their masks of gold.

"A bit more gold. Not unexpected."

"Actually, Jorim, it's surprising he remains that much the same." A tall, slender woman with dark hair and hazel eyes walked along the bowl's edge. She wore the robes allowed her as the captain of the *Stormwolf,* this one of deep blue with white wolf's heads embroidered on them. "He was fairly frantic when they took you away, and went hunting in the jungles to find you."

The Fenn nodded slowly, his dark eyes growing wide. "Lost, Jrima lost."

"Not lost, just away."

"Jrima *found*!"

The Fenn's elated shout made Captain Gryst smile, and the small man who trailed in her wake laughed. Iesol Pelmir looked every inch a clerk, from his bald head to his ink-stained fingers. Though he wore a ship's robe—this one of white with black wolf's heads much smaller than those on Anaeda Gryst's—no one could have mistaken him for a sailor.

Jorim looked up at his visitors. "You wouldn't be here if the *maicana* had not allowed it."

"No, they agreed. They're an interesting lot." Anaeda sat on the bowl's lip and let her feet dangle. "While they all profess agreement with our plans to leave inside a week, they are doing little to see my ships provisioned. Day after day they agree that things will be finished in a week, but that week shows no sign of ending."

"Really?" Jorim frowned. "We were very clear on our intention to leave. I wouldn't think they would deceive us this way."

The clerk raised a hand. "I don't believe, Master Anturasi, they are being deceptive. As the Master says, 'A tree is tall save when the eagle passes over it.' "

"You're quoting from Urmyr, not the Amentzutl Book of Wisdom?"

"No, but there are parallel sayings."

Anaeda raised an eyebrow. "And, Minister Pelmir, your thoughts about deception are?"

The clerk stiffened. "Forgive me, Captain. It is just that a week for us and a week for them may be different."

Anaeda shook her head. "I've seen their calendar. Their weeks are nine days long, just like ours."

"But, Captain, we are in *centenco*. We are outside their calendar."

Anaeda frowned. "In what way?"

Jorim sighed as Shimik wandered around the platform, head back, tongue out, trying to catch droplets. "The Amentzutl figure time on a cycle running seven hundred thirty-seven years. After that they enter a time called *centenco*. It's like our festivals."

"But our festivals last a week, then we are back to another trimester."

"Right. For the Amentzutl, *centenco* lasts only a week, but may have many more days than nine. It lasts however long it takes for the new cycle to begin. I gather there have been times when it has lasted years."

Anaeda scowled darkly. "So when they agreed they would train you and give you back your divine powers 'in a week,' they meant by the end of *centenco*."

"Right."

"That is not acceptable." She shook her head. "We are on an expedition for Nalenyr. Just having discovered the Amentzutl and their continent is of very great importance. I cannot allow my fleet to be bound up here for an undetermined length of time. The considerations of our mission are paramount, over and above concerns about the threat they report from the west. If the threat exists, Nalenyr may have no idea it is being threatened, and we have a duty to inform the Prince of his peril."

Jorim stood slowly. "I don't disagree, but we have two other considerations to keep in mind."

"Such as?"

"The original reason we agreed I would not inform my

grandfather about what we had found is because knowledge of it could create chaos back in Nalenyr. Countless ships could be launched toward Caxyan without reliable charts, and those who made it might well cause harm to the Amentzutl." Jorim hooked his hands behind his neck. "Other nations might see this as something that will make Nalenyr so rich it cannot be opposed, so they will strike. To bring back knowledge of the Amentzutl before learning as much as we can about them would be foolish."

"But, Captain, if I may, we have a greater difficulty."

Anaeda and Jorim both looked at Iesol, so he continued. "If this threat is real, then the Amentzutl believe that Tetcomchoa-reborn is the only way it can be dealt with. Jorim must be trained to accept his powers, else all the warning in the world will be to no avail."

"But they could be wrong."

"True, Captain, but you are picking and choosing which parts of their beliefs you will validate, with no information to help you make that decision." Iesol shrugged. "The understanding I have of their history, meager as it is, suggests they are not wrong."

She snorted. "I know."

Jorim smiled. "Anaeda, you just don't want to be stuck here doing nothing. I can feel the restlessness in you."

"It's not just me, it's the whole expedition. While we were exploring, we had a purpose. Without purpose, the crew will fragment. It has already begun."

"Really?" Jorim frowned. "What's been going on while I've been going through these rituals?"

She raised her chin, her face an impassive mask. "Ships' crews are superstitious. Rumors have flown that you are to be made *maicana*. You'll be learning to use magic, and many tales are being told of the *vanyesh*."

Vanyesh. The word sent a trickle of fear down Jorim's spine. The Cataclysm that brought the Time of Black Ice had been the fault of Nelesquin and his *vanyesh*. While anyone who trained hard enough in any endeavor could hope to become a Mystic, the *vanyesh* worked to harness magic by working with magic. Tales of the *vanyesh* were vile and used mostly to frighten children—but men can easily rekindle that fear in themselves.

"So, they think I'll become a new Nelesquin?"

"Not all of them. Some know of the last *vanyesh* trapped in Moriande. They know Kaerinus heals people during the Festival, and they say the Amentzutl *maicana* don't seem to hurt anyone. Still, they've seen strange things on this journey. They're a long way from home, and unusual things make them uneasy."

"I know." Jorim looked down and watched water drip from his braided side locks. "They're not the only ones afraid of my training. But it really doesn't matter if they are afraid that I'll become like Nelesquin or not. That's what *I'm* afraid of."

Surprise widened Anaeda's eyes. "You, afraid of something?"

"Only myself." He looked up at Iesol. "What does the Master say that is relevant?"

"Many things, Master Anturasi, but Book Nine, Chapter Five, Verse Nine speaks most to your point." The clerk knelt and his voice became very solemn. "And the Master said, 'Wisdom often begets power, but the child often destroys the work of the father.' "

A jolt ran through Jorim. "Yeah, that pretty much covers it."

"You are afraid of power?" Anaeda grinned. "That's not possible. You have been raised in one of the most powerful families in Nalenyr. Your grandfather's merest whim is something the Prince treats like a command. You can't fear power."

"I don't fear power, I fear what I might do with it." He looked up at her. "You know of my grandfather, but you don't know of my uncle, and my cousins and their children. You've not seen how my grandfather's use of power has left them. Uncle Ulan was once his equal, but years of Qiro's belittling have worn him down. I can barely remember a time when Ulan did not quake in my grandfather's presence. Yes, I grew up around power, and I know how it can twist someone."

"It doesn't have to be that way, Jorim."

"No? Urmyr's opinion seems to be that there is no other result."

Anaeda glanced at the clerk. "No disrespect to Urmyr, but this is not always true. Power distills and concentrates what is already there. I sail for the Prince of Nalenyr, and I have sailed under captains both good and bad. Aboard ship their word is law, to be obeyed without question. Some captains are cruel and live in fear, and it consumes them. Others are smart and brave, and their crew thrive with them.

"If what Urmyr said was an absolute, we would have no navy. We would have no leaders because the moment anyone rose to power, it would consume him. This isn't true; we've all seen that."

Jorim bowed his head toward her. "You're a fine example, Anaeda. You are firm and fair, quick to discipline, but quick to praise. You'll punish, but you'll forgive and you listen to reason. I can accept you as proof of what you say. The question then is, how do you *know* how you will handle power?"

She laughed quickly. "It distills, remember? Look at how you handle everything, Jorim. Look at your life, at times when you have had to lead, or chafe under the leadership of another. How you act and have acted will tell you."

He smiled, but she raised a hand. "One thing, however, will be very important. You need to think about the consequences when you're wrong."

"With the powers of a god at my command, they could be catastrophic."

"Of that there is no doubt." She stood and beckoned to Shimik. "We will leave you now, so you can reflect. Imagine the worst you can possibly imagine, then double and triple it. Then you might begin to see the first glimmers of how bad things could be."

Jorim's shoulders slumped. "You're making this very hard."

"No, I'm just helping you define the challenge." Anaeda Gryst regarded him with sharpened eyes. "If you think that challenge is something you couldn't handle as a man, you don't want it as a god."

"I don't think I have much choice."

"Perhaps not." She took Shimik's paw in her hand. "But then you better find it in yourself to answer that challenge, for failure to do so may be the greatest catastrophe of all."

Chapter Seven

15th day, Month of the Wolf, Year of the Rat
9th Year of Imperial Prince Cyron's Court
163rd Year of the Komyr Dynasty
737th year since the Cataclysm
Moriande, Nalenyr

Count Junel Aerynnor shifted stiffly on the daybed in his modest suite. He even forced a grimace for the benefit of his guest. While the knife wound he'd taken a week previous had not yet fully healed, it did not hurt him nearly as badly as he would have his guest believe. There was an advantage to appearing weak. He'd been trained in such deception as an agent of Deseirion, so Junel easily adapted his role to suit his mission.

Lord Xin Melcirvon had cast his sword onto the rumpled bed and pulled up a rough-hewn wooden chair. The chair did give him a slight height advantage, which he would have surrendered were they both standing. Junel wore his black hair shorter than his visitor, and his body was of longer, leaner proportions than that of the inland lord. They both had light eyes—blue for Junel and hazel for Melcirvon—but the visitor's were set a bit too close to suggest intelligence or inspire confidence.

Melcirvon smiled almost sincerely. "I was dispatched here as soon as word reached us about your injury. I was told to assure you that any aid you require will be rendered. I will be making arrangements—discreetly of course."

"This is most welcome news, my friend, but quite unnecessary." Junel passed a hand over his face as if fatigued. "Prince Cyron has seen to it that I am being cared for. He was most solicitous and, had I desired it, I would now be ensconced in Wentokikun as the Prince's guest."

Melcirvon failed to hide his reaction. Blood drained from his face. "His outrages become more . . . outrageous!"

"What do you mean?"

The man from the western duchy of Gnourn waved a hand at Junel. "The instant we heard of what had happened to you, we suspected—we *knew*—the Prince had laid you low."

Junel suppressed a laugh, but then decided to abandon pretense. "My lord, please do not lie to me. I doubt your mistress sent you here with that intent."

"I never . . ."

Junel raised a hand. "Your mistress does not believe I am stupid. Please do not measure my intelligence by yours. The reason you were sent here was to determine if I have betrayed your mistress and her confederates to the Prince. She wants to know if, as I lay ill, I spoke of the things we discussed earlier this month, when I visited Gnourn. And were you apprehended by the Prince's

Shadows either upon your arrival in Moriande, or after you leave me today, she would know if I had. She would then be prepared to disavow any knowledge of you and your treason."

Melcirvon blinked. "But if you had betrayed us to the Prince, he would have already sent troops out to destroy us."

"Indeed, he would have. And he has not, so you are safe."

"Then it was not the Prince who had you stabbed?"

"Not Cyron, to be sure. Prince Pyrust might well have done it. He has agents in Moriande and he slaughtered the rest of my family. It may have been my turn."

The Gnournist nodded slowly. When he had visited Gnourn, Junel had represented himself as a conduit through which a number of disgruntled Desei nobles could liaise with the Naleni inland lords. Neither loved the regime in the capital and would have been happy to see it overthrown. The Desei would be willing to funnel money, weapons, and some troops into Nalenyr. When the time was right, the western portions of each province would revolt and close on the western half of Helosunde. It would be a bold stroke and both Princes Cyron and Pyrust would be powerless to stop it—because the first man to turn his military might to the war for the interior would leave himself open to invasion by the other.

The Naleni inland lords welcomed him because the wealth being made by the merchants and traders in the capital was not heading up the Gold River in any significant proportion. Cyron, citing the Desei threat, still taxed the inland provinces for defense, then spent the newfound wealth on provisions for exploration, the benefits of which the inland lords would never see. Once they declared their independence, they could sell their harvests to Nalenyr at greatly inflated prices, enriching themselves and addressing a host of grievances that ranged from petty to significant.

What the westron lords did not know, and would never know until far too late, was that Junel represented only *one* Desei noble: Prince Pyrust himself. His mission was to stir up rebellion among the inland lords, forcing Cyron either to divide his strength or lose half his nation. Either decision would cripple Nalenyr, and Prince Pyrust would be able to sweep in.

Melcirvon's eyes narrowed. "Then Prince Pyrust had the Anturasi woman killed, too?"

"Of course—and he had another woman here slaughtered after she and I became betrothed." Junel looked down, letting sadness veil his face, and his visitor accepted his grief in silence. It took all Junel could do to keep from curling his lip in a sneer, so he contented himself by imagining what it would be like to take Melcirvon to pieces as he had both of the women.

"No wonder, then, that your masters want to be independent of him." The Gnournist shuddered. "As bad as Cyron is . . ."

Junel laughed. "A moment ago you felt certain Cyron had his agents stab me. Do you think he would pause for thought before he ordered someone slaughtered? His spies are everywhere—I was told this often in my visit."

"Well, of course . . ."

"No, my friend, there is no 'of course' about it, and I'll tell you why. As much as you hate Prince Cyron, you hate us Desei more. Not your fault, mind you, for the Komyr

Dynasty has long used the threat of Desei invasion to keep everyone in line."

"But Deseirion *did* invade Helosunde."

"There is no disputing this, but you are a fool if you do not think things run deeper than that." Junel smiled slowly. "Think back to what you thought I would be before you met me. You had decided I would be weedy and thin, an idiot at best, ignorant of history and custom. You viewed me as a stable hand with a title, and you thought I would be an easy dupe to further your aims. Admit it."

Melcirvon sat back as his face reddened. "I may have had my misconceptions, my lord . . ."

"You didn't have *misconceptions,* you had *prejudices,* and you allowed them to blind you. I will admit to having had similar prejudices, but I have overcome them in service to a cause greater than you or I. You must do the same, Xin, or your prejudices will destroy you."

He lowered his voice and leaned forward, forcing the Gnournist to do the same. "In my youth, I believed all Naleni to be lazy, fat, indolent, and stupid. You live in a lush land. The green hills and valleys of Gnourn are unknown in my nation, where life is hard. I have learned, however, that you Naleni have an inner steel. You have wisdom and courage. You can determine right from wrong and are willing to fight injustice."

Melcirvon's expression went from confusion and anger to one of pleasure and pride. "Thank you, my lord."

Junel nodded. *You are stupid and lazy. Flattery is the first trap for a moron, and you've fallen full into it. A bit more spider silk spun, and you shall be mine.*

"You know, Xin, I am pleased that your mistress sent you. It had to have pained her greatly to risk you, but she also knew you could be trusted. She is a very smart woman, and her trust in you is well placed. It promises great things for you, and I hope you will permit me to recommend you to my masters. In the unfortunate event that anything might happen to your mistress, we need a brave man who could step into the breach and accomplish our mutual goals. Would you allow me that honor?"

Again Melcirvon blinked, then nodded slyly. "You honor me, friend."

"You are much too kind." Junel again averted his eyes for a moment, then looked up. "How is it that I may be of service?"

That question baffled the visitor. "I was sent to see how you were and to see to your well-being."

"And you brought funds with you to accomplish this end?"

"Yes. I was going to arrange a way to get money to you covertly, but if the Prince is paying . . ."

"He is, my friend—and we should make him pay double."

"What do you mean?"

Junel slowly swung his legs over the edge of the daybed and sat up. He could feel the stitches tug in his back, but other than a mild desire to scratch at it, the wound was easy to ignore. "Your mistress gave you money, but I do not need it thanks to the Prince's generosity. You might return that money to Gnourn, or you might do something more profitable with it. There are ventures in this city—commercial ventures—where such money could be doubled or tripled in a month. If you could do that, you would have more money to use against the Prince."

Melcirvon nodded slowly. "I'm certain my mistress would approve such a plan."

"She would, *if* you were able to inform her of it."

"But . . ."

"Follow me, my friend, for this is your future." Junel coughed lightly, then gestured to a pitcher and cup on a side table. "Water, please."

The Gnournist quickly fetched him a cup and waited anxiously as Junel drank it. He refilled the cup, then sat again, clutching the pitcher in his lap. "Explain, please."

"Your mistress already counts that money as gone, so she will not miss it. And it is not as if you are stealing it, since you will be using it in her cause. Most important, it will become a hidden asset. If the worst were to overtake this enterprise, you would have a ready sum of cash available for your escape, or for the continued financing of the rebellion. Taking this precaution speaks well of your foresight and initiative."

"There is no denying what you say." Melcirvon glanced down into the pitcher as if the water might offer some oracle to aid his decision. "This investment would be safe?"

"You would be using the people I use for my investments."

Melcirvon looked up, a smile growing on his face. "If you trust them, then I shall as well."

"Good. You'll take the money to Bluefin Street, number twenty-seven."

"A good omen, that."

"I thought so. There you will ask for Tyan, a small man with a crescent scar on his chin. Use my name, and tell him to invest the money as he would with mine. He obtains excess cargo from ships and moves it into markets where those who truly appreciate its value pay well. You will agree with him on a code sign that will let you or your agent withdraw the money. Tell no one what that is, not even me."

"A code sign, yes."

Junel smiled and almost warned the man not to use his mother's name, for that would surely be the case. "Once you've done that, you should go to ground, lose yourself in Moriande for a couple days. There are houses where your gold is more important than your name. Come see me in three or four days. I will have messages for you to take back to your mistress. While you are relaxing, you will keep your eyes and ears open, of course, and get a sense of the capital. I hope you will learn things that my present infirmity prevents me from discovering."

"Yes, of course." Melcirvon frowned. "How much longer do you expect to be stuck here?"

"A day or two. The Prince's own physician is seeing to my care. I hope, within two days, I will be pronounced fit enough to pay my respects to the Anturasi family and meet with the Prince."

"Isn't that dangerous?"

"The former, no, but the latter . . . Perhaps just a bit." Again Junel shrugged. "If the Prince suspected me, he would not have his doctor here, nor would he want to speak with me. And having me close will mean I can learn much that will aid us. It's a risk I must take."

"Of course." Melcirvon stood, found himself holding the pitcher, then set it down and bowed. "Our success will be assured."

"It will indeed, thanks to your brave efforts." Junel

smiled as the man slipped his sword back into his robe's sash. "I look forward to seeing you in several days."

Junel sat again on the daybed and watched through the window as Melcirvon hurried off toward Bluefin Street. If the time were right, documents found at 27 Bluefin Street would show Tyan to be a Desei agent, or perhaps a Virine agent, and would link the westron lords with money spent to buy weapons and mercenaries. If the inland lords could not be convinced to stage a rebellion on their own, Junel would reveal their plot.

The difference was negligible. In either case Cyron would be distracted and forced to act. His nation would be torn apart and his dynasty would become weakened. It would collapse of its own accord, or Prince Pyrust would descend and crush it.

The seeds of Nalenyr's destruction had been sown.

Chapter Eight

17th day, Month of the Wolf, Year of the Rat
9th Year of Imperial Prince Cyron's Court
163rd Year of the Komyr Dynasty
737th year since the Cataclysm
Muronek, Erumvirine

Dunos shivered, hugging his good arm around his skinny chest. Goose pimples rose on his flesh, and he would have given anything to pull the barest scrap of blanket over his naked body, but even that comfort had been denied him. He had to sit on the rickety wooden stool and stare at the fat black candle guttering at its center. It gave off weak light and no discernible heat.

Nor was he shivering just because of the cold. The crone's gnarled left hand and the way her thick, uneven talons scratched at the sheet of rice paper puckered his flesh. Her bony fist knotted around the brush in her right hand and, despite her tremors, she managed to paint words that were as beautiful as she was ugly. Dunos could only read a few of them—the ones with a half dozen strokes at most—but the words made no sense, scattered over the square sheet as they were.

Part of Dunos wanted to run from the witch's hut. After all, he was ten years old now, and barely a child. He'd made the long walk north to Moriande. He had met a Mystic swordsman and undergone a healing in the Naleni capital. He'd been touched by the magic of the last of the *vanyesh,* Kaerinus. If that master of *xingna* could not heal his arm, how could this woman do it? She was nothing compared to a sorcerer who had survived the Cataclysm.

But he didn't run. Just as with the people of Muronek, his fear of her tightened his chest and made his legs weak. She was hated by many, and yet they came to her in times of need. With a potion or tincture, she could bring down a fever or ease pain. As much as people feared her—forcing her to live on the outskirts of the town, in the dark woods—they needed her.

More important to Dunos, his parents wanted him to remain. His father had been hopeful when they'd gone to Moriande, but Dunos' left arm had remained withered even after the healing. With their greatest hope dashed, his parents had turned him over to the ministrations of Uttisa, the witch-woman who had haunted his mother's dreams since her childhood in Muronek.

What Dunos dared not tell his parents was that, as they had grown more desperate that he be made whole, he had become less worried about it. Moraven Tolo, the swordsman he had met, had been at the healing. Dunos' distress that his arm had not been cured was obvious, but the swordsman had calmed him. "The magic promised only to heal us, not to give us what we wanted. It gave us what we needed."

That remark had confused Dunos, but he had thought hard about it on the long walk back to the mill his family operated. True, his left arm was fairly useless. If he had to haul water from the well, he could only carry one bucket at a time—but the simple fact was that he could make two trips, and the difference mattered very little.

It had hurt that his infirmity meant he could never be a swordsman, as he had once dreamed, but it hurt even more that his father now thought he could not even be a miller. Moraven had said that perhaps he could become a swordsman, but to his father he seemed doomed to a life of beggary. They'd even taken in another boy as an apprentice, valuing his oxlike strength, even though it came with oxlike stupidity.

And so Dunos sat there, cold and afraid, in a hut steeped in magic, hoping his father's wishes would come true—and determined to show that even if he couldn't be all his father wanted, he could be loyal and obedient.

The crone laid her brush down and blew on the paper to speed its drying. She turned to look at him, her right eye squinted almost shut, the left preternaturally large. Wrinkles scarred her face like cracks in muddy earth. Her hair had become brittle and crinkled, its unruly white locks escaping the leather-and-wood clasp.

A thick tongue wetted her lips, and when her mouth opened, the few teeth he could see were mottled with decay. "You have a busy mind, boy."

"Yes, Grandmother."

"Can you read what I have written?"

"Some, Grandmother."

"Doesn't matter. It's good that you can't." She lifted the paper and extended it toward him. "Take it."

Dunos' right hand came up, but the witch hissed. "Not *that* hand, stupid boy. Your left hand! You can use it a bit, can't you?"

Dunos slowly raised his left arm. He didn't like looking at it, for it looked inhuman. His bones were twigs, and the flesh rough old leather. He concentrated, forcing his hand open and his elbow to bend. He pressed his lips firmly together, determined not to cry out no matter the pain. *But it doesn't hurt as much as it has, does it?*

He didn't let the idea that maybe his arm *was* getting better distract him. His thumb and forefinger closed on the white sheet and she released it. The document's weight alone started his arm dipping. A corner of the rice paper dove toward the flame, but he managed to pull it away, his eyes tightening with the exertion.

The crone nodded slowly. "Very good. Now you are to crumple it. Make it a ball, with your left hand. Do it, boy. Now!"

Her sharp bark jolted him. He began to comply, wondering how all that paper could fit into the palm of his hand. As he gathered it, however, he felt a tingle in his arm. The sensation echoed what he'd felt during the healing, and what he'd felt over a year before, when he'd found a glowing blue rock. He'd reached for it, stretching, and touched it. He'd remembered nothing after that until he awoke, a mile downstream from where he'd found the rock.

His fingers slowly gathered in the rice paper. It felt dry to the touch—as dry as his skin. His fingers brushed the words and crumpled them. The paper crackled. Though the tightness never loosened, his fingers seemed to possess more power as he worked. Gradually the paper disappeared into his fist—that pathetic, withered fist—and he tightened it down as hard as he could.

He said nothing. The only sound came from the rustling of the trees outside and the crone's wheezing. He hung on, willing the paper to get smaller and smaller—smaller than the rock, smaller than anything. He wanted it to be so small it disappeared.

"Open your hand, boy. Give it to me."

His fingers snapped open as if they were mechanical devices. The paper dropped into her waiting hands. She picked at it, slowly teasing it open. Dunos let his hand fall to the table and left it there, no longer hiding it by his side.

The crone smoothed the paper against the table, nodding and mumbling as she did so. With a dirty fingernail she traced the wrinkle lines, pouncing first on triangles, then linking them to squares and diamonds. Her nails skittered faster over the document, sounding like dry leaves scuttling over paving stones.

She looked at him again, both eyes wide and rimmed white. "What are you, boy? Why will you kill a god? Why have you come to destroy us all?" She punctuated her questions by pounding a fist on the table. The candle tottered for a moment, and wax spilled onto the paper.

Then it *flowed* over the paper, up through the wrinkles. The black wax added strokes to some of the words and erased strokes from others. Dunos could read very little, but one mark—the month mark—stood out clearly.

The mark of Grija, the wolf. The god of Death.

"Answer me, boy!"

"I don't know what you mean!"

She reached out, grabbing him by his hair, forcing his

face toward the paper. "Look, the death god's mark! The lines, all conflicts. Triangles within triangles, disasters all, squares showing no resolution! It is all death and destruction. Death, ruin, for everyone."

Her voice shrank into a harsh whisper as her hand tightened, and long nails sank into his scalp. "For everyone but you, Dunos. What are you?"

"I don't know!" Dunos' left arm came up somehow and batted her away. He heard something snap and she screamed. The crone tottered back and almost fell off her stool, then stood and tried to lift her broken arm. She couldn't.

The paper began to move, drawing itself up in folds. It collapsed and opened, twisting and narrowing, then straightened out. In seconds, it formed itself into a folded paper wolf, its flesh decorated with all the words Uttisa had written.

The crone fished in her robe for a circular talisman, which she raised to her left eye. "You're *his* thing, Dunos. You belong to Grija. You're death's pet and he's come to claim you."

"No, no I'm not." Dunos grabbed the paper in his left hand and fed the wolf to the candle flame. "I won't be his pet!"

The flame caught and the wolf vanished in a bright flash of light. Yet instead of hearing the hungry snap of flame, the lonely howl of a wolf echoed as smoke drifted up into the dimness. And though his hand remained in the flame, he felt no pain, no warmth, and somehow wondered if the god of Death had not claimed him anyway.

Suddenly, the hut's door exploded inward. Shattered planking gouged the dirt floor. The door's remains hung from one twisted hinge and, in the moment before the night's breeze extinguished the candle, Dunos caught sight of hulking forms bursting into the hovel. Broad shoulders smashed the doorjambs, and harsh, clicking, guttural sounds filled the hut, as if the creatures were gargling sharp stones.

Uttisa screamed, but her cry ended abruptly. Something warm and wet splashed over Dunos. He closed his eyes, then wiped blood from them. *They've killed her!*

He didn't want to open his eyes again because he didn't want to see what the creatures were doing. The crack of bones and the wet sucking scrape of teeth stripping flesh communicated more than he could have seen. He decided that seeing would be better than imagining, so he opened his eyes and found he was half right.

He should have been in complete darkness, but his left arm glowed with a pale grey light that cast no shadows. Other parts of his body glowed as well—the parts that had been splashed with Uttisa's blood. Most curious of all, the glow around his left arm showed him a limb both hale and hearty.

The three squatting creatures gorged on the crone, ignoring him entirely. They were completely hairless and, though he could see that their flesh was scaled, the ghostly glowing imparted no hint of color. The triangular teeth that filled their maws made short work of the witch. They lifted their chins when they swallowed, but had no discernible necks, and their powerful shoulders hunched above the rounded domes of their heads. He saw no ears, and their large round eyes had the flat black quality of wet river stones.

They squatted on short but powerful legs. Their long arms easily snapped the witch's bones, and their long talons dug marrow from the hollows. They sucked the grey jelly from their fingers, gurgling with delight.

Dunos had no idea what the creatures were, and didn't want to remain to find out. He darted for the doorway before any of them had a chance to react, then he ran as fast as he could. His left arm almost felt as if it were moving normally. He glanced back once to check on pursuit. He didn't see anything, but that didn't slow him a bit.

He ran down the forest trail toward Muronek, thinking that he could raise the alarm. Then, as he neared the forest edge, the light of multiple fires alerted him to greater danger. The town was under attack, and somewhere his mother and father were in danger.

Or are already dead!

No! Dunos poured his anxiety and fear into his running, and sped through a ruined gate. All around him monsters abounded, dragging shrieking people from their homes. Many bled from small wounds, others had lost limbs. People collapsed in the street, their lives pumping into puddles, screaming until death took them.

Fierce fires lit the town. Burning people ran through the streets until they fell and roasted. He could feel the heat, but it remained distant somehow. He ran on, leaping human pyres, rejoicing as one of the *vhangxi* staggered from one inferno, the beast's upper body on fire. He'd named the creatures after a demon from the Third Hell, and darted aside as the burning one reached for him.

Up Green Dragon Road he sprinted, then cut north on Seamster Lane. He refused to look west, toward the home his grandparents inhabited, but as he turned west on Gold Dragon, nothing but fire remained of the houses on either side. He continued running, his gait faltering only when he came to a body lying in the roadway. The fire's heat had already scorched the gold robe, and the person's head had been ripped clean from her body, but there was no mistaking his grandmother.

He stared at the golden-white flames blazing through the house. The fire roared and wood popped loudly. Somewhere within lay his parents. A lump rose into his throat. His knees quivered and he would have fallen, but then he heard another sound. It came from within and, though it could not possibly be, he heard his mother calling his name.

Heedless of his own danger, Dunos dashed into the fire. On his third step into the building, a floorboard gave way beneath him. As he fell into the shallow space beneath the house, timbers above cracked. The last thing he saw as he looked up was the house's main beam splitting in half and crashing down upon him.

Dunos had no idea how long he lay in the ashes that had been his grandparents' home; the ashes that had been the town of Muronek. Night had flowed into day, and he guessed several days had passed, since the ashes from which he emerged had long since grown cold. Ash tiger-striped him in grey and black.

He moved cautiously through the ruins at first, then more boldly. Skeletal dogs and feral cats skulked through the town. More majestic, and more numerous, carrion birds perched on the highest points available, descending in flocks to chase dogs away from the choicest bits of food.

Dunos didn't want to see what they were eating. As he

explored he picked up a battered pot here, a blackened knife there and, toward the outskirts, he stripped robes and sandals—all oversized—from half-eaten corpses. He washed the clothes and himself in the river outside the town, then dressed and started walking.

He had no more idea where he was going than he did why he survived the attack and fire. All he knew was that he had gotten away, and had to get still further. He had vowed he would not be Grija's pet. The more distance he put between himself and such slaughter, the closer he'd be to keeping that vow.

Chapter Nine

20th day, Month of the Wolf, Year of the Rat
9th Year of Imperial Prince Cyron's Court
163rd Year of the Komyr Dynasty
737th year since the Cataclysm
Ixyll

Though barely a week and a half away from the tomb complex in which he had awakened, Ciras Dejote found himself faced with yet one more challenge. The ever-changing land that was Ixyll made many demands on him. He scarcely dared sleep, lest his concentration slip for an instant. Even the most benign-appearing scene could hide virulent peril, and always having to be alert wore on him.

But no hero would shrink from a quest such as ours!

He glanced out over the lip of the bowl-shaped valley. It stretched off to the north in an ellipse, the dying sun reflecting warmly off the fluid gold flesh coating the whole of the landscape. The muted forms of trees and bushes pushed up from beneath it, but remained as hidden as if thick snow covered them.

The only anomalous bit of color in the valley skittered about from bush to tree to boulder like a ball sliding on ice. Borosan crouched at the valley's edge, watching his *thanaton* try to find purchase with its spidery legs. When it finally bumped up against something, slowing its momentum, it could raise its spherical body on its four legs, but would only manage a step or two before its wild sliding would begin again.

Borosan shook his head, then made a note in the book opened in his lap. "This is not good. The measurements Keles wants will be useless. Pacing out the distance won't work here."

Impatience tightened Ciras' belly, but he slowly exhaled and calmed himself. "Perhaps, given the hour, we should make camp."

Borosan scribbled another note without looking up. "Perhaps this will be like the plain two days ago. At night it will change."

"Gods forbid." Ciras shivered. That plain had been a paradise while the sun had shone. They'd been able to eat their fill of fresh fruit, the water ran sweet in small rivulets, and small animals—related to rabbits as nearly as Ciras could make out—gamboled peacefully. They'd decided to spend the night there, but the moment the sun went down, everything had changed. A wave of wild magic pulsed up from the ground, as if the land were shrugging off the day's warmth. With it went the glamour of the place, revealing a dark land full of corruption. The half-eaten apple in his hand suddenly writhed with worms. The streams ran with blood and the rabbits became *rabids*.

They'd sacrificed one of their packhorses to them and barely escaped with their lives.

That incident had been just one of many along their journey. There would be more because they were in Ixyll. Over seven hundred years before, the forces of Empress Cyrsa fought and defeated a Turasynd horde from the northern wastes. That battle had unleashed enough magical energy to warp the land and trigger a Cataclysm that nearly destroyed humanity. While the wild magic had retreated from civilized land, here in Ixyll it still held sway.

So much variety, and so much to see, made it impossible to catalogue it all, but Borosan Gryst seemed determined to do just that. Though he was a practitioner of *gyanri*—the mechanical magic that Ciras found an abomination—he'd adopted the role of a cartographer, too—continuing the work that Keles Anturasi had begun. His painstaking devotion to exact measurements reduced their progress to almost nothing.

And impatience to find the Sleeping Empress rose in inverse proportion.

Abandoning Borosan, Ciras descended the hillside, relishing the crunch of gravel beneath his boots. He reached the small grassy circle they'd use for a camp. It and the nearby tree to which they'd tied the horses were the only relatively normal bits of landscape they'd seen in the area—and the tree sprouted clusters of crystal acorns that chimed as a light breeze shook the branches.

He moved to the circle's center and closed his eyes. He listened to the chiming and the way it shifted. At times discordant and at others harmonious, he sought the core pattern. It had to be there, since the branches were limited in the distance they could travel and the breeze remained fairly constant. Listening as intently as he could, he found it. And, once he had it, he slid his sword from the sash at his waist.

Still blind to the world, he moved through all the sword forms he had learned. He flowed from Scorpion to Wolf as he imagined a sharp peal as an overhand stroke. He parried it, then thrust beneath a subtle chime into what would have been his foe's heart. A twist and flow into Dog, then a Cat leap and slash took him above another desperate attack and beheaded his foe at a stroke.

As the sounds were limited, so were the abilities of foes. The human form could only move in so many ways and do so many things. The men he'd faced before had all had their limits. Speed and strength, the length of a limb, and the knowledge of forms made them different, but there were some things none of them could do. In those limitations lay the opportunity for victory.

And then there were those who had reached *jaedunto*.

He had seen some of those very special Mystics, whose skill with a blade transcended the natural. Normal limitations did not apply. The Mystics were able to go beyond what any other mortal could manage.

Ciras hoped he had the seeds of such greatness in him. He'd arrogantly assumed it to be true when he'd come to Moriande and *Serrian* Jatan, demanding to be trained. Phoyn Jatan had apprenticed him to Moraven Tolo, which Ciras had first taken as a dismissal. But slowly he learned that Moraven himself was a Mystic, and the lessons he had for Ciras encompassed more than the Art of the Sword.

Again Ciras had taken this as a dismissal, but contemplation—for which he'd had plenty of time in the last week and a half—had led him to consider that what he was being taught were the disciplines he'd need *if* he reached *jaedunto.* Enduring patience seemed to loom large among them, and he fought daily to embrace it.

Tolerance seemed to be another, and being paired with Borosan Gryst demanded he learn that as well. Magic was a great and powerful force in the world. Only through studying a subject and perfecting one's skill at it could magic be touched. A Mystic would have the wisdom and strength to be able to handle such power. And with magic limited to those who had worked so hard to achieve it, civilization was safeguarded from another Cataclysm.

Gyanri defied this logic and, therefore, seemed an abomination to Ciras. A *gyanridin* created devices that obtained their motive energy from *thaumston,* a mineral charged with wild magic. A *gyanrigot* could do anything. On far Tirat, his home island, he'd seen the blue *gyanrigot* lights that had become fashionable among the merchant class. Borosan's *thanatons,* which came in a variety of shapes and sizes, could crawl about, measuring things, carrying things, and even killing things—that latter trait making them even worse in his mind.

Of course, Ciras did prefer to have a *thanaton* slipping and sliding about in that valley to doing it himself. And the fact that you could set one of the smaller ones to kill and fetch edible game did make travel easier. And they could even be made to stand watch and raise an alarm if something odd was happening.

But while he wanted to hate the creators of such machines outright, Borosan really wasn't that bad of a person. He had no concept of physical discipline, but he wasn't one to quit or complain when put to a physically demanding task. His wide-eyed wonder at the world was something Ciras found almost childlike—and though he'd not have admitted it even under the most dire torture, it was something he regretted having lost during his own childhood.

If I had it, I'd not be so impatient.

"Ciras."

The swordsman spun to a stop, crouching in Fourth Scorpion, with his sword above his head, pointed forward. Sweat dripped down his face, but he did not wipe it away. It soaked into the beard he'd grown on the road and the breeze cooled his face. Slowly he opened his eyes and glanced up the hill toward Borosan.

The *gyanridin* closed his book and waved Ciras toward him. "Ciras, come here."

Ciras straightened up. "In a moment."

"No, I really think you should see this."

"Boroșan, I need to finish my exercises."

"But I . . ."

A gold apparition reared up above Borosan. A long-fingered hand closed over the man's head and shoulders, then tugged him backward. Golden arms closed around Borosan, and metal flesh poured over him. When the apparition opened its mouth, flashing fangs defiantly, Borosan's scream echoed from its throat.

Ciras sprinted up the hill. Sword in his right hand, he scrabbled with his left for purchase. He tripped only once, but got back up instantly and reached the hillcrest a couple of heartbeats later.

The apparition—flesh flapping as if a golden robe were sheathing its legs and arms—was flowing down toward a large, dark hole which had opened in the heart of the valley floor. Ciras assumed the *thanaton* had already been sucked down into it. Between him and the apparition, a trio of golden warriors had risen and advanced. One bore a sword like his own. A second had the curved blade of a Turasynd. The third carried no sword, but the golden flesh outlined the form of a Viruk warrior. Its claws and size alone made it lethal.

Though it occurred to him that Borosan was most certainly lost, and that chances of his own survival were negligible, the thought of retreating never came to mind. A friend was in trouble. To know he had abandoned him would have been to live in shame. It would not have been a life worthy of living.

Not a life to be sung of.

Into the valley he leaped, and from the moment his heels touched the golden surface, he realized there were times it was not possible to be heroic. His feet sailed out from under him and he crashed down on his back. Somehow he maintained his grip on his sword, but he'd already begun sliding toward the hole, and his foes flowed toward his path to slash at him as he sped past.

Ciras jammed his heels hard against the slick gold surface. His spurs dug in, ripping through it. Golden fluid welled up to heal the rifts, but he slowed. Smiling, he reversed his blade and tucked it back beneath his right shoulder. Pulling up on the hilt and pushing down with his shoulder, he used his sword like the rudder on a ship. He cut a path through the gold, steering at a large rock.

Braking hard with his heels, he slowed enough that he didn't slam too heavily into the rock. He scrambled about, steadying himself, and got to his feet. Then he pressed his back to the rock and crouched as the first warrior reached him, swinging its scimitar down.

Ciras shifted his body right and the blade clanged off the stone, ripping away a patch of the golden flesh. Even before the gold could ooze out to close the wound, Ciras whipped his blade around in a forehand slash that took the Turasynd through the neck. Its head popped off, exposing white bone. Gold covered it quickly as the head spun, the masked expression revealing surprise.

But the body did not collapse. Instead, it reached up, caught the head, and plunked it right back down on its neck. Lips peeled back in a feral grin and the jaw vibrated as if it were laughing triumphantly.

It was in midlaugh that Ciras' return stroke caught it again. With both hands on his sword's hilt, he split the Turasynd from crown to pelvis, crushing each vertebra. The body sagged left and right. Gold tried to cover the bones, but they turned black after only a second or two's exposure to the air. Their decay tarnished the gold flesh, and it fell from the bones in a spray.

Though he might have acted foolishly leaping into the fight, Ciras Dejote had learned enough not to presume that he knew exactly how things were working—but he had enough information to make some educated guesses. As the second swordsman came toward him, Ciras pushed away from the rock and slid toward it. He dropped to his left knee, controlling his path ever so slightly, ducked a slash, then returned it.

His cut sliced through the gold flesh over the warrior's left thigh. When he pared it down to the bone, the femur decayed immediately. The warrior flopped over, and with a quick slash Ciras laid its face open. The black rot ate through the skull and the head collapsed like an overripe melon. With that, the gold flowed from the skeleton and the black bones melted.

Ciras stabbed a spur into the gold and kicked back. He slid from beneath the Viruk's slashing claws. Flipping his sword about, he stabbed it down, anchoring himself. Then using his momentum, he whipped his legs around and snapped a kick through the Viruk's right leg. Gold splashed as the shin parted.

The Viruk toppled, but bounced up and around onto its belly. As Ciras pulled himself up to one knee and turned to face it, the creature lunged. Ciras dodged, then drew his blade and slashed. He missed the hand, but cut deeply into the gold flesh covering the valley floor. He opened a deep, wide wound, exposing the ground and the thick mat of pale grasses that lay beneath it.

Gold oozed to close the opening, but not before the grasses took on color and sprang up. The wound closed, but a half-dozen green leaves poked up through it. Beyond them, the Viruk came up on its knees and slashed with both claws—at the grasses.

Ciras' eyes narrowed, then he whipped his sword around and cleaved another gap in the gold flesh. More grasses sprang up and a flower with a brilliant red blossom burst through the opening. He bisected that cut with another and the corners of the cross drew back, opening a larger green patch. Another crossing cut and another, and he isolated a patch of gold flesh that quivered and deflated. Spiky grasses thrust up through it, and the earth below drank in the gold.

Rising to his feet on the greensward, Ciras slashed the Viruk's head off and sent it whirling toward the hole. He began advancing in its wake, crosscutting a green path into the basin.

Before he could get too far, a pair of objects shot from the hole and spun toward him. The *thanaton* reached the path and immediately sprouted legs, checking its momentum. Borosan, who tumbled after it, rolled a bit more when he hit grass, but came up in a sitting position with his notebook still clutched to his chest.

He coughed, then spat out a lump of golden phlegm. "I think it was alive."

"I think it still is, Master Borosan. It just discovered you to be about as tasty as a few of the meals we've had on the road."

The *gyanridin* struggled to his feet and Ciras steadied him. "On my map, I'll mark this place as very dangerous."

"Or mark it as a place for farmers." Ciras cut a furrow through the gold to open a trail back to the hilltop. "As menacing as it found a man with a sword, I think it far more vulnerable to plowshares."

"You're probably right." Borosan smiled. "We should move on. We've got a few hours of sunlight left and can be far from here before we camp."

"No, we'll stay the night." Ciras returned his smile. "Knowing how fast it heals is something you'd find useful. The Empress has been waiting a long time. I trust another day will not try her patience."

Chapter Ten

25th day, Month of the Wolf, Year of the Rat
9th Year of Imperial Prince Cyron's Court
163rd Year of the Komyr Dynasty
737th year since the Cataclysm
Thyrenkun, Felarati
Deseirion

Despite the roaring fire in his chambers, Prince Pyrust wore his cloak. He found the room uncomfortably warm, but the visitor he expected would be half-frozen and exhausted. The warmth would be welcome, and he had every hope Keles Ánturasi would feel welcome as well.

The Prince had made the decision to meet Keles in his personal chambers rather than any place more grand. Pyrust suffered no illusions about the Naleni cartographer and where his loyalties lay. In their previous meeting, Pyrust had made overtures to him, and Keles had politely but firmly rebuffed them. Pyrust actually respected him for that display of familial and national loyalty.

The fact that Deseirion's need would require that to be crushed was another matter entirely.

A gentle knocking came at the door. Pyrust glanced in that direction. "Enter."

The door opened silently. Pyrust almost didn't recognize the young man framed in the doorway. Since they'd met he'd acquired a puckered scar on his forehead. He'd lost weight on his long journey. Exhaustion rimmed hazel eyes with red.

Though he was clearly tired, Keles' eyes still sparked with intelligence and surprise. He even half made to bow, but caught himself with a hand before he sagged against the doorjamb. As it was, he grimaced when his right shoulder hit the doorway.

Pyrust crossed the distance between them and took his left elbow and shoulder, steadying him. "I did ask them to convey you here as fast as possible. If you were hard used, I will have the men beaten. Killed even."

Keles shook his head slowly. "I've no love for them. They murdered a friend of mine, but they did their duty."

Pyrust guided him to a seat beside the fire. Keles slumped in the blocky wooden chair. He cradled his right arm against his chest and his head lolled toward the left. He stared into the flames. "You know I will not work for you."

"You made that clear in Moriande." Pyrust walked to a sideboard and poured two pewter goblets of dark wine. He brought both and offered them to Keles. "It is customary for us to welcome guests with wine. Rice and cheese will follow. You may choose which goblet you prefer."

Keles looked up at him, then reached out with his left

hand and took the goblet from the Prince's half hand. "If I am a guest, will I be permitted to leave when I desire?"

Pyrust stared down past his wine. "You know that is not possible. Nor will you be allowed to communicate with your family. I know you can reach your grandfather and brother through your mind. I could have you drugged to prevent that, but I would prefer to have your word that you will not attempt it."

Keles drank, then frowned. "You would accept my word?"

"I would." Pyrust set his goblet on the mantel over the hearth. "You are a smart man and you know the way of the world. If your grandfather learns you are here, Cyron will threaten war. And, quite likely, blood will flow before you are returned to Moriande. On the other hand, news of your presence here will slowly be communicated through the ministries. They will inform Prince Cyron in a manner that demands diplomacy. We will negotiate, and what he would have had to win through blood, he will pay for in time—time you will spend here."

"What good will that do you?" Keles pulled himself upright and gingerly rested an elbow on the chair's arm. "I've said I won't work for you."

"I hope I can convince you otherwise." Pyrust smiled. "You think I want the Anturasi charts of the world? Everyone does—and if they were offered to me, I should not spurn them. Those charts have allowed Naleni ships to sail far and wide, reaching new nations and new trading partners. Those charts have brought Nalenyr a prosperity that may let Cyron buy the provinces back into an empire."

"And you'd like to stop that."

Pyrust nodded, his green eyes narrowing. "I have

never hidden my ambition to become the Emperor. Ambition, however, is hardly a virtue that is easily sated. Believe me when I tell you that I do not desire the Anturasi charts of the world, nor will I ask you for them."

"I am too tired for that to make any sense." Keles slowly shook his head. "If it is not that, what do you want?"

Quicker to the question than I would have imagined. Pyrust took Keles' wine and placed it on the mantel. "Please, come with me."

Keles stood. Pyrust removed his cloak and settled it around the young cartographer's shoulders. Gently taking his left elbow in hand, the Prince guided him to the chamber's external wall, opened the door, and ushered him onto the south balcony.

The sun had just set, leaving the cloudy sky streaked with grey. Around them, from the Prince's tower to the Black River and beyond, Felarati stretched out. Pyrust knew the city well and loved it, but he saw it as it truly was, not colored by romance or nationalism.

"Tell me what you see, Keles Anturasi. Tell me about my city."

Pyrust could feel the tremor running through Keles' body. The cartographer slowly studied the city, starting with the western precincts, following along the Black River, and ending east, at Swellside, where fog was already beginning to grow like fungus over dark buildings.

"I will compare it to Moriande, and you know it will suffer." Keles looked at him. "And you know that is not just national pride talking."

Pyrust nodded solemnly.

"Felarati has grown without much planning. It started

near the bay, on the north side. The south was farmland and benefited from spring flooding. As the population grew, you constructed levees and buildings, but you still have flooding there and the sewer system is constantly in disrepair."

Keles pointed to the factories spewing smoke in the middle of the city. "You can see that the water above those factories is cleaner than that below, which means the people living closer to the sea have poor water. You have a lot of sickness there. Upriver is not much better, because of the silt in the river. If it were flooding into fields, once again your land would be more fertile, but now it is wasted. The air stinks of smoke and sewage. The city is dark, and the people clearly suffer from melancholy."

Pyrust raised his chin. "Is that all you can tell me?"

Keles frowned again, then continued his survey. "Your development of the riverside is insufficient to handle the sort of trade the Anturasi charts would bring to you. I already know the Black River is not navigable for any significant distance. We were constantly riding overland between one river station and another to get here. Your ability to get wealth to and from the interior would be limited to cart traffic. Even if those factories can turn out *gyanrigot* capable of moving freight, the cost of taking it very far would eat up any profit.

"And I will tell you this, Highness. I kept my eyes open as I moved through your nation. Your people work hard, but they are living skeletons working a harsh and unforgiving land." Keles hesitated for a moment. "Yet, as little as they had, they offered us everything once they learned I was bound for your court. Your people have nothing, still they love you and would do anything for you."

"Perhaps they fear what will happen if they displease me."

"Some certainly, but most I saw spoke of you with great affection. Some even call you Little Father. How is that possible when you have so much here and they have so little?"

"You really mean to ask me how I can care so little for them when they care so much for me."

Keles nodded.

"Come back inside." Pyrust waved Keles past him to the chair by the fire. He waited for his guest to resume his seat, then clasped his hands at the small of his back. He looked into the flames, then began speaking in a low voice.

"You know the Desei are a hard people. We survive on pride. We have always been a frontier people, eschewing the comforts of the south. The south is weak—this we tell ourselves again and again—and yet we harbor secret dreams that someday we shall know the pleasures of its existence.

"I am seen as a hard man—cruel to the point of barbarism. It's convenient for the southern princes to characterize me thus. It serves me to let them. While none of them truly believes I can mount an invasion, they fear what I would do to an invading army. Their image of me keeps their ambitions in check, and this simplifies my life enormously."

Pyrust walked to the hearth and passed Keles his cup of wine, then recovered his own. "The truth of the matter is less than the illusion. I have dreams, Keles, in which I see how my nation can change. All these things you pointed out—things you saw in an instant—haunt my nights because I feel the devotion of my people and yet find myself powerless to save them."

He sipped wine, relishing the dry taste. "What you said of the southern shore is correct, but how do I deal with it? If there were a solution, I could implement it, but solutions elude me. If you were me, what would you do? What would you do if you could do anything at all?"

Keles blinked, then pursed his lips. *"Anything?"*

"Your fantasy."

"I would return it to farmland. A mile to the south, in the hills, you could build housing and put a sewer system in place. An aqueduct could bring water from further upriver."

"I would have to move the factories as well?"

Keles nodded. "They're fouling the river. You could divert part of the river to feed a small lake. They could draw water from it. I'm not sure that would work, but it could be explored."

Pyrust smiled. "Very well. It shall be done. I shall start tomorrow." He pointed his goblet toward the balcony. "You'll come back here tomorrow evening and you will see how your plan is working."

"What? You can't do that!"

Pyrust frowned. "Of course I can, my friend. This is my realm. What you have said will improve it. All of it will be done."

"No, no, no. Wait!" Keles winced as he pointed to the south. "You would have to make sure drainage was right. You have to have a plan that will work with the land."

"Ah, you see, Keles, that might be the way it would be done in Nalenyr, but there you have the luxury of having those who can draw such plans. If we had such people, do you not think we would have done this sort of thing?" Pyrust slowly shook his head. "This is why I brought you here, Keles Anturasi. You saw—the Anturasi charts would be worthless to my people because we could not profit from them. But you did the Gold River survey. You know how my city can be changed to benefit trade and the people. That was what I asked you about in Moriande."

Keles' head came up. "It's true, you did."

"Please understand, Keles, that my dream for Deseirion is not that it become the new Imperial capital, but that it becomes a nation the new Emperor would welcome in his Empire. The changes you have described bring me much closer to that reality. We may not have the skills to accomplish it as efficiently as you would in the south, but my people are strong and willing to endure hardship for their Prince and their nation."

"But if you do things quickly, without sufficient planning, it will make for unnecessary hardship. Can't you see that?"

Pyrust shrugged. "I see the hawk fly, but I do not have wings. Therefore, I walk, even though my feet may complain. The journey, though swifter by wing, must begin regardless."

Keles glanced into the fire, then up at Pyrust. "How long will you hold me here?"

"I haven't decided."

"Then I'll make you a deal. Four months. I'll do some surveys, I'll draw some plans, I'll teach some people."

"That's what you offer me. What must I offer you?"

"You'll abide by my plans and my timetables."

"Are these things subject to negotiation?"

Keles nodded. "I won't be unreasonable. I'll give you

my best estimates. You'll return me to Moriande for the Harvest Festival."

Pyrust raised an eyebrow. "And if your work is incomplete?"

"I will grant an extension of my time here. Another two months."

Pyrust closed his eyes for a moment, then glanced down at Keles. "Can you transform my nation in six months?"

"I can blaze a trail. You'll have to make the journey."

"Done." The Prince raised his cup. "You will have the best of my nation while you are my guest. If you have a need, it shall be fulfilled. If you have a desire, it shall be granted. And you will always have my nation's gratitude."

Keles smiled, raised his goblet, then drank.

Pyrust nodded to the servants who opened the door and brought in trays with cheese and rice. "Eat and drink, Keles. We wish you to feel very much at home."

"Thank you, Highness."

Pyrust smiled, hiding it behind his cup. *Yes, enjoy our fare, Keles Anturasi. From this day forward, and for the rest of your life, Deseirion shall be your home. You give us your thoughts now, but soon you will surrender your secrets. This is how it must be.*

Chapter Eleven

26th day, Month of the Wolf, Year of the Rat
9th Year of Imperial Prince Cyron's Court
163rd Year of the Komyr Dynasty
737th year since the Cataclysm
Wentokikun, Moriande
Nalenyr

Prince Cyron sat on the Dragon Throne, making no pretense of polite pleasure as Grand Minister Pelut Vniel approached with shaved head bowed. The Prince had endured two weeks of meetings in which Vniel had told him there was nothing to worry about—a continuance of his previous behavior. Though the Prince pressed him for more details, Vniel had not been forthcoming. Then he surprised the Prince by asking for a meeting in the audience chamber.

This cannot be good.

The Prince had not donned formal state robes for the meeting. He couldn't abide the suffocating folds of silk, and relished the freedom of more utilitarian garb. He had chosen black silk trousers and robe, with an overshirt of gold. Dragons had been embroidered on the robe and overshirt—in gold thread on the black, and the reverse on the gold. A gold sash held everything in place and the Prince had refrained from wearing a sword.

I might have been tempted to use it.

Vniel shuffled forward with his head lowered. His gold robes flowed out and obscured his body. The man could have been a snake slithering forward, but Cyron dismissed that image. It would have made Vniel too close to a dragon, and this Cyron would not grant him.

Finally, the man knelt—though "coiled" would have more accurately described his motion—and bowed deeply enough that his forehead touched the floor.

The Prince answered with a nod. "What is it you have to report? Have you come to the bottom of the embezzlement of grain shipments north?"

"Would that what I have to report were so trivial, Highness." The man's voice wavered, and that further surprised Cyron. He had no doubt Vniel could be a consummate actor, but he was also an egotist and fear was not a big part of his repertoire. "I have grave news."

Does he know Qiro Anturasi is gone? "Tell me."

Vniel's head came up and he visibly paled. "News has trickled north from Erumvirine. The nation is under attack. Hideous creatures, worse than the demons of the Nine Hells, have launched themselves from the ocean. Poisonous toads that fly and odd ape-things have attacked. They are pushing inland from the coast toward Kelewan."

Cyron's pale blue eyes narrowed. "Poisonous flying toads?"

"Your tone mocks me, Highness, but what benefit would there be in bringing you such a fanciful story were it not true?" Vniel actually sounded offended. "You have accused me of hiding information, so my credibility has suffered. Were this not true, my credibility would be utterly destroyed, and you would have me removed. And I would deserve it."

Cyron leaned forward, scrubbing his left hand over his jaw. "What proof is there?"

"Of the creatures? None other than stories from refugees. But something is happening in eastern Erumvirine. None of the wood harvested near Derros is reaching Kelewan. Market taxes from that region have not been brought to the capital. A squad of troops sent to determine what delayed them has not reported back."

"Signs that something is wrong there, certainly, but is it an invasion? There are many other explanations. The eastern lords could be in revolt. There could be a plague . . ." Prince Cyron's recital tailed off as he recalled a dream he'd had, in which a dragon lay shattered and a carpet of black ants devoured a bear as they made their way north to feast on him. The dragon was the Naleni national symbol, and the bear represented Erumvirine.

And the ants?

The Prince shivered. Qiro Anturasi's map added a new continent, home to monsters. If they had launched an attack, they might have made landfall in Erumvirine. It would have made more sense for them to have sailed directly up the Gold River, especially if Qiro was bent on avenging his granddaughter's murder. But while an error in navigation might have put them in Erumvirine, Cyron refused to countenance that as a possibility. *There is no way troops associated with Qiro Anturasi could have ever made an error in navigation.* Either they were not associated with him at all, or they had a purpose in taking Erumvirine first.

He glanced at the minister and saw hope blossoming in Vniel's eyes. "You would know if it was a revolt because the bureaucrats would know. So, you really don't know what it is, do you?"

Vniel slowly shook his head. "I only know what I have told you, Highness."

Cyron sat back in his throne and felt as if a hundred *quor* of rice had just landed on his chest. As much as he had hated the bureaucrats, they had always protected society. No matter how depraved a ruler might become, they insulated the people in the same way they insulated the ruler. They provided stability and assured that when destruction came, it would only go so far.

But now even they didn't know what was going on. The invasion—or whatever it was that was eating up eastern Erumvirine—was beyond their control. They had for so long used their tools of deception and diversion to control events that they knew no other way of doing things. They were not prepared to handle emergencies; they'd just done everything they could to prevent them. And this they had taken to be one and the same thing, which it was not.

Cyron's growing horror encompassed more than just the events in Erumvirine. If the bureaucracy failed there, it could fail elsewhere. Previously, the bureaucracies had been largely immune to harm, since everyone needed them to maintain order. But once they lost that power and began to panic, entire nations would fail with them.

"What would you have me do, my Prince?"

"Give me time to think." Cyron forced himself to

stand, then glanced down. "What word have you of the Virine military reaction?"

"Most of the Virine troops are in the western and central districts, Highness, guarding the borders with Moryth and Ceriskoron. They are moving troops east, but slowly. Prince Jekusmirwyn has always prided himself on being deliberate. He has not called up his populace to defend the nation."

"Ministers have raised the alarm and he is not receptive to their message?"

"As you are, my lord, he is suspicious of them." Vniel shrugged. "There was the Miromil misunderstanding."

"Ah, yes." Cyron nodded distractedly. "The negotiations to marry his daughter to the Crown Prince of Miromil were unnecessarily contentious, with each set of ministers misquoting their master to slow things down."

"Errors in transcription . . ."

"Spare me, lest more errors cause needless delay here." The Prince frowned heavily. "When did you first have word of this?"

"A week ago, but then it was nothing but horror tales." Vniel opened arms swathed in gold silk. "By the time I began to see fire where there had just been smoke, so many reports were coming in that I could not group them into any cogent story."

"And you were worried that members of the bureaucracy were in jeopardy, especially those staffing our legations in Erumvirine?"

The minister's eyes tightened. "Fault me for that, Highness, as you wish, but without them we are blind."

Cyron held a hand up. "Spare me your ire and I shall do the same, Minister. Something is attacking Erumvirine in the east—something you do not understand. The chances of success are incalculable and immaterial. Refugees will flee north, west, and south. Those who come north will take refuge in the mountains. If Kelewan falls, they'll come north on the Imperial Road or head south. They'll cause a panic, and that will *not* do. There are those in the Five Princes who will become ambitious."

As he spoke, Cyron envisioned the world as a giant game board. His grandfather had used toy soldiers to wage imaginary wars, and the education he obtained from that allowed him to depose the previous Naleni prince and establish the Komyr Dynasty. *Would that I had followed your example more closely, Grandfather.*

What happened in the Five Princes really was immaterial. Each of those nations balanced the other. Had they ever been united, they might have posed a threat to the four larger nations. Efforts such as the dynastic marriage Jekusmirwyn had arranged had long helped play one nation off against the other. But even if the five of them united to attack Erumvirine while it was weak, they would still have to face whatever was attacking Erumvirine. And even if they succeeded there, chances were their alliance would fracture before they ever moved north through the mountains and set one foot on Naleni soil.

Cyron could not rely on Erumvirine to defend itself. And even if it did beat back the invaders, the refugees would cause serious problems in the south. Cyron would have to send troops to maintain order and be ready to defend his nation if the invaders moved north.

Unfortunately, the troops he would move south would have to be pulled from his border with Helosunde. He'd be forced to move some of his Helosundian mercenaries south as well, which would leave his northern border vulnerable. While he doubted Prince Pyrust would strike south and attack him, the Desei ruler might take the opportunity to solidify his grasp on Helosunde. Since Cyron's troops acted as much as a brake on Helosundian adventurism as they did on Desei ambition, to pull troops south was to invite chaos on his northern border.

In his mind, he could see soldiers moving from one point to another, with troops of other nations drifting in to fill the vacuum. The amount of time it would take to move the troops, and to raise others to put in their place, would become critical. If he could keep Pyrust unaware of what he was doing for long enough, he would be able to get troops from the interior in position to defend the nation.

Yet, try as he might, he couldn't see the maneuvers working. Desei troops advanced too quickly, and Helosundian units evaporated. Besides, Pyrust had married Jasai, Prince Eiran's sister. If he used her influence to convince the Helosundian ruling council to agree to a truce, the Desei could pour into Nalenyr while Cyron fought to keep his southern border inviolate.

The Prince exhaled heavily. "Does this terrify you as much as it does me?"

"I am worried, Highness, but I am sure I do not see things as you do."

Cyron clasped his hands at his waist. "I have no choice but to send troops south and they must be drawn from the northern garrisons, as those are our best. I can and will call up troops from the inland lords and send them north. Unfortunately, I have little control over what your counterparts in Helosunde will do. If past conduct is any indication, they will make the least intelligent move possible, which will invite Deseirion to descend.

"I cannot let them know the threat we are under from the south, because they would use that pressure as a bargaining chip. You can see that, yes?"

"Plainly, my lord."

"Good. I am then given two other choices. One is to confide in Pyrust. He might be convinced to send troops to aid Erumvirine, but that is unlikely. He does not have the shipping needed to convey them there quickly. Like me, he will look to his southern border, which means a push to my northern border and, if it is seen as weak, a further push to the Gold River, which is the next logical line of defense."

The minister nodded. "And your other option is to tell him nothing?"

"Exactly. I tell him nothing and hope he learns nothing until it is too late for him to profit by the news."

Vniel closed his eyes for a moment. "The latter choice is the only viable one."

"I agree, but its success hinges on maintaining the secret." Cyron stared hard at his minister. "You cannot allow this news to leave Nalenyr. You cannot allow it to leave Moriande. There is to be no informing the network of bureaucrats. I know you have skills at hiding information, but now you must hide it from others of your kind."

Vniel's lips quivered. "But, Highness, to do so undermines the stability of the world. If the bureaucracy fractures, all is lost."

The Prince sighed. "You're a fool, Vniel. The bureaucracy is already fractured. You don't know what is going on. Even with your agents in the south, you're still blind. What will you do when your Virine brothers beg you for help—help you know will do nothing to save them? Will you send it, or will you keep it to arm and armor our people and save Nalenyr?"

"I serve our nation, Highness."

"Don't give me the answer you think I want to hear. Think. Know in your heart what you would do."

Vniel lowered his head. "I would save Nalenyr."

Cyron nodded, having heard the truth from the man for the first time. "Do you expect your brethren in Deseirion and Helosunde will react any differently? You may all work to preserve the power of the world, but when the world is being devoured, you will fight to save your piece of it. That's not a vice, but a reality. You must pledge to me, on your life and those of your children and their children, that you will do whatever is needed to keep knowledge of the invasion a secret for as long as possible. If you do not, all will be lost."

Vniel nodded solemnly. "It shall be as you desire, Highness."

"Good. Go now, bring me all reports you have on the readiness of my people to deal with an invasion. And I want real numbers, not figures intended to make me happy. I'd rather shed tears now before I defend my nation, than shed them in its ruins."

Chapter Twelve

28th day, Month of the Wolf, Year of the Rat
9th Year of Imperial Prince Cyron's Court
163rd Year of the Komyr Dynasty
737th year since the Cataclysm
Nemehyan, Caxyan

Jorim Anturasi stood alone in the dark as the heavy gold door closed behind him. It shut out all light, leaving him blind in the subterranean chamber. Even when it had been opened, the weak light coming through had let him see little more than the end of the walkway a dozen feet into the room.

He moved forward, cautiously, feeling for the edge with his toes. He could hear water splashing and echoing through the cavern, but the faint sound did not help him navigate. Instead, the dripping reminded him of how the chamber had been formed, and while the Amentzutl had clearly worked portions of it, they had left most of it untouched.

His toes reached the edge of the walkway. *One more*

step and I am on the path to becoming a magician. That very thought sent another chill through him, but in its wake ran a thrill. He had always been an adventurer and explorer, and now he would be the first man from the Nine to explore magic. It might have ruined men like Nelesquin and his other *vanyesh,* but the Viruk clearly used it, as did the *maicana.* Or in a more controlled manner, every Mystic.

All the terror tales of the *vanyesh* crowded into his mind, but then he remembered Kaerinus. He had survived since the Cataclysm. He now resided in a prison in Moriande, and during the Harvest Festival conducted healings. *If that is not a good use of his power, what would be?* His sister Nirati had even been healed in the last Festival, and while he saw no obvious change in her, she had been happier afterward than he'd seen before.

He rolled his shoulders to loosen them, then took a step forward into the darkness. His left foot hit something solid where nothing should have existed, and this surprised him. He took another step and, this time, his right foot encountered emptiness and he began to fall.

Upward.

Panic arced through him as he ascended faster and faster. He pulled himself up into a ball, utterly confused, then his body splashed into water, headfirst. Cold and bracing, it closed around him. He started to sink, but it still felt as if he were rising, which was impossible. Without light, he had no way to orient himself.

Then, ahead of him, a golden spark blossomed and began to grow. He stretched out and started swimming toward it. As he grew closer he could see it was light pouring down from above. *But it's coming from a direction that should be below!* Still puzzled, he struck for it and twisted himself through a narrow tunnel that ended in a heavy wooden grate.

Jorim gathered himself beneath the grate and braced his arms and legs against the tunnel's sides. He pushed up, ignoring the burning in his lungs, and slowly the grate began to rise. Kicking hard, he rose through it, feeling the edge scrape down along his back.

The light from above vanished, but Jorim swam hard for where it had been. He broke through to air again far more quickly than he had expected, and his feet found solid purchase at the tunnel's edges. He stood there for a while, head and shoulders above the water, catching his breath.

He remained in the darkness until his breathing returned to normal. Then he looked around and, at first, could see nothing. Then, off to his left, a soft green glow began. He turned toward it and found the light growing to illuminate three individuals—two men and a woman. They all wore loincloths and golden masks. Though he could not see their faces, he recognized them as three of the eldest *maicana* by the serpent images on their masks.

The woman, who stood flanked by her companions, raised both hands to shoulder height. "In your birth into this place, you have experienced all of the elements. It is through them you reach *mai*. The recovery of what you entrusted to us, Tetcomchoa, shall begin here."

Her companions likewise raised their hands, then all three brought them together, quickly, in the same motion one might use to strike flint against steel. And as if their hands were made of such, sparks flew. They danced in the air as if rising on a column of smoke, then congealed into one spark that arced over Jorim's head.

He spun to see where it landed. A small flame began

to burn in an earthenware lamp. It rested on a small island in the lake, created by concentric stone disks, stepped like the pyramids the Amentzutl raised. On the uppermost, on the opposite side from the flame from him, a slender young woman knelt, her hands on her knees, her head bowed, her long, dark hair hiding her breasts.

Nauana. Jorim smiled, not having seen her during his ritual purifications. What he knew of Amentzutl beliefs came from her. She had served as his liaison with the *maicana,* and through her the orders needed to destroy the invading Mozoyan had been issued.

He turned back toward the elders, but their light had already vanished. Given no other alternative, he slowly approached the island and mounted the steps. Water dripped from his beard and hair, down his lean body. He did not hesitate as the water exposed him, for the Amentzutl did not share his people's taboos concerning nudity. Reaching the penultimate step, he slid to his knees on the top platform and faced Nauana.

Her dark eyes flicked up. "Welcome, Tetcomchoa. The *maicana* have chosen me to teach you the ways of magic. If it pleases you, we shall begin."

Jorim nodded in accord with the formality of her words and manner.

She looked down at the flame for a moment, then back up. A tremulous note entered her voice. "I would ask of you one favor, Lord Tetcomchoa. I am returning to you what you gave the *maicana.* Please do not humiliate me for showing you what you already know. Do not patronize me. Guide me and all I possess will be yours."

Jorim let the corners of his mouth twitch back in the

hint of a smile. "I would never humiliate you, Nauana. I know nothing and am anxious to learn."

She remained silent for a moment, then pointed a finger at the flame. "You will learn the most important invocation first. You see the flame. Which of the elements does it possess?"

Jorim concentrated. The Amentzutl had developed an interesting cosmology, which was all tied up with their six gods, half of whom had two aspects. The three singular elements or aspects of anything were solid, fluid, or vapor. Tetcomchoa, the serpent god, ruled the aspect of vapor, since smoke rose and twisted in most serpentine ways. Three other gods, with their dual aspects, covered the paired elements of light and shadow, heat and cold, and destruction and healing. In the Amentzutl world, anything could be described as a mixture of those elements.

"I see it as having four elements: heat, light, destruction, and vapor."

She nodded. "It also heals, for in destruction new things are created. Recall that Omchoa, the jaguar, slew his twin Zoloa and consumed him, so he is two that are one. This flame has five elements, all in a balance that allows the flame to thrive. At the same time, the elements of shadow and cold have been unbalanced."

"I see the sense in that."

"Good, then we shall have you see the sense in something else." Reaching back, she dipped a finger in water and then allowed a droplet to drip onto the lamp. It hit close to the flame, sizzled, and rose in a puff of steam. "Here you see water that is fluid become water that is vapor. You know that water can also be solid."

"Ice, yes."

"But you know it cannot be those three things at the same time, yet it is always water."

Jorim nodded. He'd not thought about anything in that manner before, but could instantly see that most everything could be found in those three states. He'd seen metal turned fluid in a furnace, and had no doubt that were it hot enough, it might rise as steam.

Nauana half closed her eyes. "The very nature of a thing's being—that which makes it what it is regardless of form—this is how these things exist in the *mai*. *Mai* is like the light from the sun, but there are many suns and they always shine. *Mai* is everywhere and defines everything. That which we see and touch and taste and experience are all *maichom*—you would call it magic-shadow. Only through *mai* may we see the thing as it is, and as we know it through *mai,* we can use and manipulate it."

She reached a hand toward the flame, palm out. "Use a hand to feel the flame. Feel the heat. See how the light plays over your flesh. Watch the flame dance. Encompass all of it."

Jorim took a deep breath, then slowly exhaled. He raised his right hand and stretched it toward the flame. The light did play over it, wavering shadows as it twisted and flowed. He brought his hand close enough to feel the first hints of warmth, then closer. The heat intensified and where his hand eclipsed it, some of the light glowed red through his skin. He watched the flame, matching its undulations to the rise and fall of heat and the sway of shadows.

Her directive to "encompass" the flame baffled him for a moment. What she wanted was for him to take physical aspects—things he could sense—and to carry them into the theoretical realm of the *mai*. He knew magic existed, but only in the way that he accepted the existence of things he'd never seen. While he *had* seen Mystics duel and otherwise had seen evidence of magic, he had still been insulated from its reality. She wanted him to push past that.

He could identify the aspects of the flame and sought to keep all of them in his mind, according none of them ascendance, even as the light flared or the heat rose. By opening himself to all of them, embracing all of them, he would not be doing what most people did, which was to diminish things. Most people, while they knew all the elements that went into fire, tended to concentrate on one or the other. If you needed light, you lit a torch. If you were cold, you kindled a fire. If you wanted to clear brush or get rid of debris, you burned it, then spread the ashes on the fields as fertilizer. Fire was thought of not as what it was, but as a means to an end.

Jorim refused to allow himself to be so lazy. He forced himself to experience the flame as an amalgam of his sensory experience. He listened for it, watched it, felt it. He brought his hand through the flame and back, feeling the way it caressed his flesh. He caught the acrid scent of hair singeing on his hand.

And then he found it. Just for a heartbeat, there was something more. A fusion of everything that surrounded its true essence like a shell on a nut. He sensed the thing within. It existed, the truth of fire. The second the concept of *truth* struck him, he knew that was how his mind would classify the essence. It was truth. It was distillation. It was that without which the thing did not exist.

His head snapped up. "I felt it. I saw it. The truth of fire."

Nauana smiled. "Very good. My lord recovers his

knowledge quickly. The truth, as you call it, is part of the secret teaching. When you realize that, you have the key. That which defines the truth is *mai*. The *mai* is what you use to change the truth, to redefine it. For this first lesson, however, you only need a trickle, and you only need to modify two aspects of this particular flame."

"Which two?"

"The flame exists because enough *mai* was used to stabilize an imbalance. Where the flame exists, cold and shadow are held at bay." She looked into his eyes. "You will touch the *mai* and rebalance things."

Jorim found himself nodding matter-of-factly even though his hand trembled and his stomach began to tighten. His first brush with magic, just sensing the truth of flame, was passive, learning to see things in a new way. He'd had that experience countless times before. As a cartographer, he saw the world quite differently from others.

He steeled himself. He did not know if he truly was Tetcomchoa-reborn or not. He did not know if he could use magic—at least not beyond how it would be used as a Mystic cartographer, if he ever became that good. His learning *how* to use it, however, did not demand that he *would* use it. The learning itself did no harm; it was only in how it was used that could do harm.

And if the Amentzutl are right about centenco, *to refuse to learn could be a disaster.*

Jorim calmed his mind and reached out to find the truth of fire again. It took work, but he retraced the steps that had led him there before and found it. Reflected from it, like sunlight from a mirror, he found the *mai*. In his mind it was soft and resilient, like a porridge that had not hardened, but was not fluid either.

When he tried to grasp it, it squirted away from him. So he stopped trying to grab it and, instead—as if it were a living thing—teased it forward.

He wove it through the shadows of his fingers and bound into it the sense of cold he felt from his wet hair against the nape of his neck. He used the *mai* to strengthen shadow and cold, to embolden them. He brought them forward and they lapped at the flame the way water flows and recedes on a beach. With each successive wave, the cold dark tide rose and the flame shrank.

And finally, it was smothered, instantly plunging the chamber into darkness.

Nauana's voice filled the room with soft, steady tones. "This, then, is the first lesson. It is easier to restore a balance that has been disturbed through the *mai* than it is to unbalance something. Balance is the key. As you become stronger, you will be able to use more the *mai,* but you must beware attempting to unbalance too many things."

"What happens if I do?"

"*Mai* is everywhere, even in us. It gives us life." Her voice became colder. "If you attempt too great an invocation, a balance will be maintained. *Mai* will be drawn from the nearest source: you. It may kill you. It *will* exhaust you."

"How do you know if what you are trying to do is too much?"

"When you fail to waken from the attempt."

A spark sprang from her fingers and the lamp ignited again. She looked at him solemnly. "Now, my Lord Tetcomchoa, you will restore the balance again. And again. You will do this until you are satisfied you have mastered this invocation, and then you will do it again."

He smiled. "My sense of sufficiency is not good enough?"

"It is, my lord, but such are the decrees you laid down when you gave us the gift of your knowledge." Nauana nodded toward the flame. "Begin, please. *Centenco* is a time when the world is out of balance. Only you, a god, can restore it to the way it must be."

Chapter Thirteen

28th day, Month of the Wolf, Year of the Rat
9th Year of Imperial Prince Cyron's Court
163rd Year of the Komyr Dynasty
737th year since the Cataclysm
Ministry of Harmony, Liankun
Moriande, Nalenyr

Pelut Vniel knelt at a small table. The brush in his right hand hung high over the pristine sheet of rice paper. Ink hung in a pregnant drop at the bristle's end. He did not know if it would grow fatter and drop, splattering over the paper, ruining it, or if somehow it would remain there, where it should, waiting for him to apply brush to paper in a flash of inspiration.

How like the problem the Prince has presented me.

His face tightened slightly. The Komyr, grandfather through grandsons, had never understood the way the world worked. They were great ones for giving lip service to how valuable the ministries were; they praised how well the ministries worked and urged them to do more. In private—but what in the world was ever truly private?—they railed against sloth and inaction, as if they were bad things.

What they missed was that the bureaucracy was the foundation of the world. Emperor Taichun had seen this when he organized and formalized the ministries to administer his Empire. Urmyr, the most celebrated of his generals, had been placed at their head. He gave them the directives that ordered their lives and set their mission. From the beginning it all had been very clear: the bureaucracy was not a means through which revolutionary ideas and practices could be efficiently spread through the Empire. Quite the opposite: it was the brake on reckless fads that might be a cure for an immediate ill but would prove fatal to society in the long run.

Pelut Vniel needed look no further in the past than to the Viruk Empire and its history to know the consequences of failure. The Viruk had employed the Soth as their bureaucrats, and the Soth functioned perfectly. Since they were a subject people, however, and as much slaves as the humans who supplied muscle to the Viruk Empire, the Viruk ignored their counsel when it came to matters of internal politics. As a result, doctrinal differences split the Viruk population, and the resulting civil war destroyed their homelands and broke the Empire's power forever.

He studied the drop of ink and found in it a correspondence to the world's black moon, Gol'dun. Legends cast it as the last resting place for all Viruk evil, and while historical conflicts had proven that to be a lie, every minister knew that if he failed in his duty, another black moon would rise to the heavens to mark the passing of mankind.

And Prince Cyron hastened that outcome.

Pelut Vniel did admire Cyron on one level, for he had managed to motivate the ministers to speed up their work in ways no one else ever had. Of course, outright bribery had been tried in the past with a modicum of success, but the Komyr Dynasty's expansion of trade required internal distribution of wealth. This was overseen by ministers, and the opportunities to enrich themselves had gone neither unnoticed nor unexploited. Ministers acting in their own best interests had moved quickly, and this had created a great deal of internal strife, both within Nalenyr and the wider bureaucracy.

The haste with which ministers moved to facilitate the expansion of trade created many problems, too—not the least of which was ambition among the lowest ranks and a desire to rise more quickly. Ministers who felt threatened sought to reinforce their own positions by grabbing as much wealth as they could, then bribing subordinates or buying the loyalties of others. This destabilized the bureaucracy and had to be stopped.

What the Komyr had never truly appreciated was that bureaucracy was the true nature of the world. Flocks of birds would fly in formations that mirrored the bureaucracy's organization. The heavens had countless stars organized into constellations that had their own hierarchy and yet were all ruled by the whim of the sun. Even the Nine Heavens and Hells were ranked, and progression through them was all but impossible. And the gods, with minor spirits beneath them, had arranged supernatural hosts as a bureaucracy.

That was simply the way things were.

Disasters of epic proportion could be seen in the natural world when this hierarchy was abandoned. When farmers wiped out wolves in a district, rabbits ran wild and destroyed their crops. That was divine retribution for failing to recognize the natural order and attempting to subvert it.

What Cyron had asked him to do was an even more heinous crime against Heaven. Cooperation throughout the bureaucracy was the way things were meant to be. It had always been thus, even after the Empire had been split into the Nine. It had been reinforced since then that only by cooperating could the nature of the Empire be preserved even though local political events might shift the people on the thrones. Whereas the Emperor might remove a provincial governor, now the bureaucracy permitted the removal of a leader who was a threat to stability. It was just part of what the bureaucracy had to do.

Pelut Vniel did see Cyron's point. This new invasion was overturning the whole of the nature of society. It did threaten everything, and he did fear what would happen if Erumvirine fell and the invaders moved into Nalenyr. Unlike Cyron, though, who feared being overthrown because his dynasty was the product of usurpation, Pelut knew that the bureaucracy was more resilient than the Prince could imagine. While the invaders might have swept into eastern districts, he was certain that ministers were already organizing things in the occupied lands to ensure that life continued as normal.

The Viruk had needed ministers. Men had needed them. Why would not the invaders need them? There was no question they would. In time, they would come to rely upon them and, once again, the way of the world would be restored and life would continue as it had been meant to.

But Prince Cyron threatened the natural order. By ordering Pelut to keep silent, he raised the Naleni bureaucracy above all the others. He was asking Pelut to create a new level of bureaucracy, which was something only the Emperor could do. Cyron was arrogating power and position he had no right to—trying to change the natural order by way of a most unnatural whim.

While Pelut Vniel did acknowledge that he, himself, was certainly the best candidate to be the Grand Minister of a new empire, he knew that the consequences of abiding by Cyron's request would be swift, disastrous, and inescapable. Cyron would immediately set each nation's bureaucracy against one another. The invasion would face a fractured enemy. Their advance would be certain, and the demise of each nation would be just as sure. Only by remaining united in the face of the threat could humanity survive.

Cyron missed a key point in his analysis of events. Dynastic revolutions came and went. Hot blood would earn a throne, but in time it would temper even the most vigorous bloodline. The bureaucracy could rein in even the most ambitious. It could thwart alliances or halt armies, all by misplacing dispatches or rerouting supplies. The invaders, unless possessing their own bureaucracy, would need the ministers.

And, in time, they will come to be dependent on us, and we will become their masters.

Only for the briefest of moments did Pelut Vniel feel guilt at suggesting collaboration with an enemy that likely was not human and clearly sought dominion over mankind. Collaboration with such an enemy was no vice. The farmer whose field was overrun with rabbits killed and ate them, preserving his family for a time of no rabbits. So it would be with the bureaucrats. They would save mankind for a time when the enemy would be weak and could be overthrown.

This left him, of course, with the problem of Prince Cyron. Here he had a twofold dilemma. The first was not that great a problem. Getting rid of Cyron was simply a matter of choosing someone to replace him. Countless of the inland lords would be happy to take his place. Because Lord Melcirvon had never been proficient with letters or ciphering, he entrusted all of his confidential correspondence to a clerk who, in turn, made copies of them available to the ministry—in hopes of currying favor. Providing information to the ministries had forever been the means of advancement, and one Pelut much preferred over the buying of position with newfound wealth.

Melcirvon's letters revealed a rather extensive network of treasonous lords in the interior. All that their success would require was the raising of an army and an opportune moment to strike. Cyron had actually supplied the reason for the former, and Pelut would see to it that a call for troops went to the interior. It would be rebellious troops who would secure the northern Naleni border.

The lords of the interior could actually supply Pelut with the solution to his second problem. Cyron especially, but even his father before him, had encouraged the merchant houses in their trading ventures. As they grew rich, they created newer and bigger ships. The taxes they paid allowed Cyron to create even bigger ships, and to send them off on expeditions, like the one the *Stormwolf* was engaged in.

It would be tricky to manage, but Pelut could engineer a revolution that would replace Cyron with a trio of lords acting as corulers. They would impose taxes to enrich themselves and their home realms, which would beggar the merchants and slow the economic expansion. They would cancel Cyron's current shipbuilding programs and discontinue funding any exploration. With a few well-placed hints on devoting oneself to security matters at home, he could also divide the trio into warring factions and they would collapse.

Giving him the opportunity to rise at the head of a ruling council that, unlike its counterpart in Helosunde, would not be foolish.

The brush descended and caressed the paper swiftly. Black ink bled out over the white surface and Pelut began to smile. He lifted the brush again and nodded. In a moment of inspiration, he had stroked the glyph for serenity, which is exactly what his plan would bring.

He lifted the paper from the table and realized, too late, that he had acted in haste. One droplet of ink trailed down, adding a stroke which changed serenity into ambition. Then it continued its waving trail down the page, cutting across another stroke.

Ambition became chaos.

Pelut set the paper back down again, then laid his brush beside it. A superstitious man might have read doom in the omen he'd witnessed, but Pelut Vniel prided himself on being free of superstition. He knew exactly what the drippings meant, and his smile broadened as he nodded.

Haste will be the undoing of all good. He knew Master Urmyr had written that in one of his books. *And I must use better ink.*

Chapter Fourteen

28th day, Month of the Wolf, Year of the Rat
9th Year of Imperial Prince Cyron's Court
163rd Year of the Komyr Dynasty
737th year since the Cataclysm
Ixyll

The moment I awoke, I knew who I was *not*. Moraven Tolo I had been, or, rather, he had been a part of me. He was an aspect of who I was, and perhaps a glimmer of who I could have become. He had been useful, and doubtless would yet be useful, but he and I were separate individuals.

I had no sense of how much time had passed, and the place in which I found myself served only to heighten my confusion. I had access to Moraven's memories, but they had a dreamlike quality to them. I could not be certain which parts of them were true or which might be his dreams. I had, after all, been somnambulant while he controlled my body. Yet, even in that state, I knew time had passed.

But this place—a tomb complex clearly—showed little signs of decay, and all the signs of Imperial construction. Gathering myself, I slowly stood. I wavered as dizziness washed over me, then rested against the wall until the world stopped spinning.

When it again turned normal, I stepped forward to the nearest sarcophagus. A woman's effigy had been raised on the lid, and the artisan had done an admirable job. I recognized Aracylia Gyrshi and caressed her cold stone cheek. Her name I knew, and her loss I felt as keenly as a fist tight around my heart. I likely could have even picked her voice out of a chorus. I definitely remembered stitching up the wound that gave her the serpentine scar on her brow.

I could not, however, remember who I was.

"Awakened, I see."

The voice did not surprise me, though it should have. A note of the familiar ran through it, too. I looked slowly to the right and found a Soth Gloon perched on another sarcophagus. "Seven eyes do not lie. I am awake. You were once known as Enangia."

"An old name only whispered by ghosts." He canted his maggot-white head. "I am Urardsa now. And what shall I call you?"

"Call me the name you know me by."

"Most recently this is Moraven Tolo."

I refused to take the bait in his game. He knew who I was, but he would not tell me. Soth logic demanded he withhold that information, and I had neither the patience for his game nor need for the information. Names and identities meant nothing—labels at best, masks hiding doom at the worst.

"Then I shall be Moraven Tolo for a while yet."

The Gloon fell silent, which is what they preferred to do rather than cackle insanely, as a man might in a similar situation.

"You have been trapped here for how long?"

"Long enough for empires to be forgotten and the world to be made anew."

I shook my head. Though I did not know who I was, I did know better than to ask a Gloon questions that did not demand specific answers. I thought about the last memories Moraven Tolo had and formulated another question. "Tell me please of the disposition of my companions—their suspected locations and intentions."

The Gloon's gold eyes closed. "Your apprentice and the *gyanridin* are bound northwest on the Spice Route, hoping to find the Sleeping Empress and awaken her to save the Empire. They have no sense of what lurks out there, but one is inventive and the other desires to become a hero, so they will stumble on."

I arched an eyebrow. "You see the future. How far do their life-strands extend?"

"Far enough for them to wish they did not." His face tightened. "They will not emerge from their trials unscarred."

"Keles Anturasi?"

"Gone. It is presumed Desei agents have him. Ask me not about his life-strand, for it is tangled and one loop has already been threaded through death. It is a knot I have never seen before, nor one I can untie."

I nodded. "The Viruk and the Keru, they have gone after him?"

"As best they can."

"And they left me with you." I crossed from Aracylia's bier to the small bundle of possessions that had been left for me. Rough canvas clothes meant to protect me against the magic of Ixyll had been neatly folded. Road rations, a canteen, and a small pouch of coins had likewise been left behind. All in all, it looked like meager offerings at some half-forgotten godling's roadside shrine.

And then there was my sword.

More correctly, Moraven's sword. I picked it up and slid the blade from the lacquered wooden scabbard. It came out clean. Single-edge, sharp, and polished until it seemed to glow all by itself, it was a pretty piece of metal. The balance was perfect, the hilt comfortable, and an unconscious smile came to my lips as I wove it through circles and loops. A single blade was not to my preference, but if I were limited to one, this would do very nicely.

I returned the blade to its scabbard and slid it into place over my left hip. "Did they leave me horses, or am I stuck here forever?"

"There are no horses." The Gloon leaped from the bier and stood upright. "You will not be here much longer."

"Have you foreseen that I'll walk, or something else?"

The Gloon looked hard at me with all of his eyes. A flutter began in my stomach, but I refused to let my nervousness show on my face. His eyes narrowed, then opened again. He frowned heavily.

"There are simple people whose lives are a single, slender strand. Others have knots, or become interwoven with one or two others. Still others have many strands, many years. You have pieces. Broken pieces that pick up and leave off. They tangle with others, foul them, and there are points where your life makes the future incomprehensible. There is no predicting for you."

I would have made to question him further save for a glow that began deeper in the mausoleum. It started as a dark blue spark, violet even, then cycled down to red. It vanished for a moment, then reversed itself, growing larger with each cycle. After five or six cycles it had become a sphere twenty feet in diameter within which I began to discern the shape of a man.

The sphere collapsed to reveal a man standing on an oblong wooden platform rimmed with gold. Around its circumference a railing ran about three feet high, and gold disks attached to the sides of the base, one at each of the eight cardinal points. Most remarkably, in front of the man sat a large globe on a gimbaled stand. While I could not see the six-foot globe clearly, I knew it had a map of the world spread over its surface. This told me I'd seen it before and, as if in confirmation, the man on the platform looked at me and smiled.

I bowed to him, respectfully, and he returned it. "I am Moraven Tolo, and though we have met, I do not know your name."

"When we met, you were much worse for the wear. I'm glad to see you've recovered from your injuries."

"Yes, the scar on my chest and back." My left hand brushed over it. "Then the last time we met was over two hundred and fifty years ago?"

"It depends upon how it is measured." He stepped toward me, then kicked one of the disks down parallel to the wooden base. "This time, I think you can hang on to ride."

"Ride?" I questioned his comment, but still scooped up the coins and the traveling rations. "Obviously you got in. Presumably you can get out. Where will you be going to?"

"Where doesn't matter quite as much as *when.*" He kicked another disk down on the other side and nodded to Urardsa. "You're coming, too."

The Gloon eyed him with a bit more consternation than he'd looked at me. "Who has told you this?"

"You did, or you will." The man took my bundled goods and set them on the platform at his feet. "I'm Ryn Anturasi, by the way. Just hang on tight. This won't take long."

I grabbed the rail with my right hand.

"Try holding on with the other one. When we get to where we're going, you'll want your sword free."

I nodded and shifted the blade to my right hip.

Urardsa got on the other side of the thing. He held on with both hands and winced.

Ryn fiddled with the globe. I recognized some features on it, though the map of the Empire had been split into many different nations. I knew of that from Moraven's memories, but I still found it disconcerting. The regions themselves were represented by inlays of stone and wood, each bit of which, I assumed, was native to the location from which it came.

Ryn removed two carved bits of stone that appeared to be the front and back end of a dolphin. They must have been made of lodestone, for they stuck together and, as he put them down, they adhered to the globe itself. The front half he placed in Ixyll, roughly where we were now. The other piece he planted in the Empire. He slipped a lever to the right of the globe and slowly began to spin it. The rotation he imparted would have had the sun rising in the west instead of the east.

"Brace yourself." He spun the globe so quickly the

landmasses became blurred splashes of color, then he drew back on the lever and locked it into place.

From Moraven's mind, I pulled the memory of the ball of wild magic exploding, and this felt much the same. Instead of a thunderous detonation, however, a wave of magic pulsed off the globe and took my breath away for a heartbeat, then two. A shifting sphere of red and blue surrounded us. All of a sudden the sphere evaporated and the wild magic moved back through me, canceling the vibrations it had started.

And even before I was certain our journey had begun, it had ended, and the familiar sound of battle again rang in my ears. I leaped away from the disk, bringing my sword to hand. Turning toward the sounds of battle, I found myself on a modest landing halfway up a small hill strewn with dead. The Soth Gloon crouched on a pile of bodies, and a new, diminishing glow heralded Ryn's departure.

I did not wonder at his haste to be away. A quarter turn around the hill a steady stream of hulking beasts with long arms and scaled flesh scrambled upward. They clawed their own dead and wounded down in limp piles that slithered to the hill's base. At the hill's zenith fought a trio of people, two of whom I recognized.

Without a second thought I entered the battle. I did so without screaming out my history or any challenge, nor did I inform those above of what I would be doing. I merely flowed into it, became one with it, and began to change the nature of the fight.

There are those who will say that to be a Mystic is to use magic to make yourself better than others. It is true that this is the effect, but the means is almost unknowable. It is not so much that I move faster than others, but

I perceive them as moving slower. I see the flows of energy in the battle. I know which way they will move, which ways they can move, and by which means I can most easily stop them.

And, for me, that means killing them.

The hulking creatures stood on powerful but short legs. Their knees, a fine creation of bone and sinew, parted easily as I swept a blade through them. Because they had no necks, I could not decapitate them, but a swift stroke across the throat slashed arteries. Blood geysered and bodies collapsed. Their heads, while massive, had little in the way of bone structure to protect their large flat eyes, and their braincases proved as brittle as sun-dried mud chips.

My first pass through their line harvested a full rank of seven and brought me an unexpected prize. A man, his face clawed to ribbons, had fallen and his sword impaled one of the beasts. I kicked the corpse off him, then tugged the sword free of its belly, before turning to face the things pursuing me.

Coming about, I realized none did pursue me, so intent were they on overwhelming those above. I knew I should have felt some relief at that. Moraven would have, but I was not Moraven. I did not feel what he felt.

And what I felt was insulted.

On my return I did not sweep through their line, I strode into it, boldly, head high, defiantly. One blade flicked out, then the other, plucking eyes, opening throats. Double slashes had sufficient force to spin a disemboweled beast so its entrails could snare others. I inflicted cuts here and there, not fatal, but painful—and it took some learning to find something those beasts considered painful—so their wails would inspire fear in their companions.

It seemed, however, they knew no fear, and in that their creator had doomed them. Someone unschooled in the art of war would think the perfect warrior should know no fear, but that is wrong. A fearless warrior continues forward even though death is inescapable. The perfect warrior is not one with no fear, but one who does not allow fear to overwhelm his judgment.

I slashed and cut at them, at once happy that Moraven had taught my body so many new things, but annoyed that he had abandoned the fighting styles I so much enjoyed. Because the creatures kept coming, each so like the last, I was able to practice and regain my skills. I learned to thrust just deep enough to explode hearts and shred lungs, or to open arteries or hole their stomachs. I fought as I had not fought for ages.

The trio from the hilltop descended and joined me, stealing my prey, but I did not mind. They'd already slain many, and so had the knack for it; but they had been running and relished a chance to regain ground they had lost. The woman I knew from Moraven's mind and the scar on her cheek. She wore no crest, just simple robes long since scavenged, and had the look of having been on the run for weeks. She used her blade well and killed without remorse.

The second swordsman I had not seen. He wore the crest of a leopard hunting, but his robe and overshirt had been a long time without laundering. Neither he nor the woman would have been thought older than their thirties, save for the age that fatigue, blood, and grime put on them.

The boy, however, there was no mistaking. A mail

sleeve had been tied onto his withered left arm, and a spike thrust out where his fingers should have been. In his other hand he carried a sword that had been snapped in half, then resharpened. The hardness of his eyes bespoke much of what he'd seen despite his youth. He was just entering his second decade of life, that I remembered from Moraven.

And his name. Dunos.

The beasts—which Dunos had named *vhangxi*—came until there were no more, and out of deference for my companions, I did not go hunting. With Urardsa joining us, we moved into the night and toward the west. They slept for several hours, and then at dawn we pushed on. When we reached a road we joined a flood of refugees. Thus began the long journey to Kelewan and what they hoped would be a stronghold that would not fall.

Chapter Fifteen

29th day, Month of the Wolf, Year of the Rat
9th Year of Imperial Prince Cyron's Court
163rd Year of the Komyr Dynasty
737th year since the Cataclysm
Ixyll

It surprised Ciras Dejote to realize he didn't hate Borosan's *gyanrigot* anymore. He respected the *gyanridin*'s skill at fabricating the machines. During the one day they'd remained in a cavern while a torrential rain fell—which had the added effect of melting a mountain in the distance—Borosan was able to modify one of the skull-sized mousers, create another duplicate of it, and get the larger *Nesrearck* working. It resembled the smaller ones in that it had a spherical body atop four spider legs, but boasted more substantial weaponry. Whereas the smaller ones could shoot darts sufficient for impaling vermin, the larger *thanaton* carried a crossbow and a small sheaf of bolts.

Originally, the magic machines had been nonfunctional in Ixyll, which Ciras didn't mind at all. The excess of wild magic rendered them unreliable, so Borosan continued to tinker with the devices as they traveled. He eventually figured out that if he sheathed what he called their "difference engines" in the protective cloth men wore in Ixyll, they would be insulated from the wild magic. Another modification let the *thaumston* recharge overnight, so the *gyanrigot* functioned better than ever.

With three *gyanrigot* conducting the survey, they were able to move more quickly. Even Borosan had become anxious to push on, and Ciras found no reason to complain. While he respected Borosan's decision to collect data for Keles Anturasi, the new mission they'd been given was to find the Empress and bring her home. Both men realized it took precedence over the survey, so they picked up speed.

As much as he came to appreciate the utility of *gyanrigot,* he still was not comfortable with one aspect of *gyanri.* The discipline of mechanical magic could impart skills to people. A *gyanrigot* sword would make a warrior formidable—at least while the *thaumston* held a charge. Once that wore off, the soldier would likely die.

Ciras had trained daily for years to gain his mastery with a sword. If men were able to get results with no work, then the very discipline of swordsmanship would wither. If success required no work, no one would work and the very means of accessing magic could be lost.

Ciras was fairly certain Borosan couldn't see any of that. His machines went about their tasks faithfully, pacing off distances to landmarks, scaling cliffs, measuring depth. They did so many things that men could do, but could only do at great risk to themselves, that the benefit of their utility couldn't be denied. Keles would be overjoyed to have the data they had collected.

But there would come a point where someone who did not have the Anturasi skill at cartography would be able to use *gyanrigot* to gather data for his own charts. The need for exploration would evaporate because men could soon just dispatch machines. Even if a few of them were eaten by things like the goldwort, losing a machine was better than losing a man.

As long as the machines cannot make judgments, men will always have to explore.

Yet even with his reservations, he became quite glad the *gyanrigot* existed. As they traveled northwest, they cut across the trail of another party. Ciras recognized the tracks. The men had been part of a bandit group they'd trailed through much of Dolosan. They'd lost track of them when they entered Ixyll, but before that had seen evidence of the men having defiled graves and slaughtering *thaumston* prospectors.

The tracks revealed that the men were three days ahead. Moving swiftly, they shortened the lead significantly and found them sooner than expected. Had it not been for the bandits lighting a fire, Ciras and Borosan might have ridden into the small valley where they had made camp. Forewarned, they dismounted, approached on foot, and dispatched the *gyanrigot* to reconnoiter the bandit camp.

While he waited for the devices to return, Ciras crept up to the valley ridge and peered down. He saw only three of the bandits, but a round hole had been pounded into a stone stab, so he assumed Dragright was somewhere in there. Bigfoot, an unkempt giant of a man, rested beside the heavy steel sledge he'd used to make the hole. Tightboots sat on the other side of the hole, a couple of yards from where a bow and quiver lay. Closer to Ciras, with his back to the swordsman and the fire between him and the hole, Slopeheel squatted and held his hands out to the fire. He wore a sword in his sash, but squatted as a peasant would, so Ciras dismissed him as any real threat.

Something crashed from within the hole, jetting out a dusty gust. None of the bandits reacted with anything more than idle curiosity. Then a long, narrow cylinder sailed out. Its lower half split on impact, revealing an aged sword with a stained hilt. The blade rang when it hit the ground, but none of them moved to retrieve it from the dust.

Dragright emerged from the hole, dirty enough for him to have lain there since the Cataclysm. He coughed, pounding on his chest with a fist while hoisting a prize into the air with his left hand. Bits of flesh fell from the skull he lifted, but much of the shrunken scalp remained in place. Ciras even saw a white ribbon woven into one brittle lock.

Dragright hurled it to the ground. It shattered on impact. He stomped on it, reducing the skull to dust. He laughed, the others joined him, then he squatted and sifted the dust with dirty fingers.

He took a pinch of the dust and brought it toward a nostril.

Tightboots tossed a pebble at him. "Don't. Save it. It's worth more than you are."

Dragright shrugged. "Just seeing how good it is. We've enough. There's a dozen more in there. Swords, too, maybe even a bow for you."

He snorted the corpse dust.

His head snapped back and his eyes widened. His body shook violently and he should have toppled onto his back, but somehow he came upright, as if being lifted by his throat. Dragright sneezed once, hard, and thick green ropes of mucus dripped from his nostrils like wax. He coughed again, then shook his head spasmodically, four times.

He smiled, all gap-toothed and happy. "This is the best we've found."

Tightboots lofted another stone at him. "You say that with every tomb."

The man's hand swept up fluidly and snatched the pebble from the air. "And this time I'm right."

Ciras rose and began a casual stroll down into their camp. He angled to keep Slopeheel on his right and the fire between him and the other three. He forced himself to walk loosely, never betraying the revulsion he felt at finding breathers of the dead.

Nor did he let his fear show. If *thaumston* could animate machines, so corpse dust could power others. A Mystic weaver's dust could impart her skill to someone who breathed it. Likewise the dust of a warrior. Just how much skill no one knew. The practice was proscribed and the only source of knowledge about it came from stories whispered around campfires.

Slopeheel turned to look at Ciras. "Who in the Nine Hells are you?"

Ciras' blade cleared its scabbard in a draw-cut that caressed the man's throat front to back. It parted his spine and only left a small flap of skin and muscle beneath the man's right ear intact. Slopeheel's head flopped onto his shoulder as blood geysered from his neck, then he collapsed, thrashing.

Tightboots cursed as he dove for his bow. "Damn the *xidantzu*!" He rolled and came up with the bow, but by the time he nocked an arrow and started to draw it, Ciras had reached him. The archer began to turn toward him, but the swordsman's blade descended. It swept through his right elbow. The forearm whipped away, propelled by the bow. The archer stared at the stump in horror, then a second slash blinded him.

As Ciras turned to the right, the giant ran into the darkness and Dragright kicked the antique sword into the air. He caught it deftly. He dropped into a fighting stance, with his left hand wide, his right jabbing with the sword, and his body open. He stood the way an unskilled brawler might, a casual cut away from death. In fact, tired, dirty, and snot-stained, he looked more dead than alive anyway.

Ciras did not attack. He took a step away from the dying archer, then bowed toward his opponent. He held it for a respectful time, then straightened up again.

Dragright frowned. "You're a strange *xidantzu*. You slaughter two, then do me honor?"

"Not you. The warrior whose skull you crushed, whose sword you bear."

"Heh." The man half smiled, then convulsed again. He spun the sword up and around, easily, as if he had been trained to it all his life. "He was one of the best, you know. Out here. Better than you could have ever hoped."

"Of this, I have no doubt." Ciras waved him forward with his left hand. "But you are not he."

The bandit attacked and the twin effects of the corpse dust and the sword made themselves readily apparent. Ciras had tracked the man and named him because he dragged his right foot a bit. In his attack, he moved more fluidly and with more precision. He flowed down into Dragon, whipping the sword down and around, then up in a cut meant to slash Ciras' right flank.

Ciras slipped to the left, then pivoted back on his right foot and backhanded a slash aimed at the bandit's spine. Steel rang on steel as Dragright spun back faster than possible and parried the slash high. Snapping his wrist around, he attacked back.

Pain scored a fiery line through Ciras' armpit. He leaped away, feeling blood already dripping. He'd never seen an attack like that, and he knew the Dragon form well. Moreover, he felt a tingle in the air, much akin to what he'd felt when the magic storms played in Ixyll.

Magic! It wasn't possible, but the bandit had accessed magic.

Ciras' realization prompted him to take another step back. His right foot landed on the archer's severed forearm. His ankle twisted and he went down. He landed on his right elbow, striking it against a stone. His sword twisted from numbed fingers and clanged against the ground.

Dragright strode boldly to him, kicked the archer's arm away, then raised the sword in both hands, as if it were a dagger. Firelight played over the expression of glee on his face and, for the barest of moments, Ciras could see hints of softness there, as if the ghostly likeness of the dead warrior overlaid his features.

The man laughed. "It feels so good to fight again."

He raised the sword higher, his back arched, his mouth open in a fearsome snarl. Then his body shook and a crossbow bolt burst out through his breastbone. The force of the shot sent him flying toward the tomb.

He bounced once, hard, and rolled, coming to rest on his chest near the hole.

With delicate little arms setting another bolt in place, *Nesrearck* skittered forward and crouched.

Ciras smiled and scooped up his sword. He stood, gingerly testing his ankle, then bowed to the *gyanrigot*. Beyond it Borosan entered the firelit basin, skirting Slopeheel's body. "Where's the fourth one?"

"He ran."

"How badly are you hurt?"

The swordsman shrugged his right arm out of his robe and checked. "He got flesh, nothing else. If he'd cut the artery, I'd have been dead inside a minute. As it is, I'll live."

"So will I, *serrdin*."

Ciras spun as the corpse flopped itself onto its back. It grabbed a handful of corpse dust and stuffed it into the gaping hole in its chest. The body jerked and the spine bowed violently enough that the bandit bounced upright. It set itself, then waved him forward with its left hand.

This is impossible! Fear coursed through Ciras. Dragright had been faster and more skilled than he. He had used magic and cut him. He couldn't stand against such a creature, especially when it clearly couldn't be killed. To remain and battle against the unbeatable foe was suicide.

Panic seized him, and he almost turned to run. He knew what would happen if he did. The thing would catch him like a hawk stooping on a rabbit. It would cut him down. He'd die with his face in the dirt, his spine slashed open to prove that he'd died a coward.

Though he might not be a master or Mystic, Ciras was

no coward. Shifting his sword to his right hand, he wrapped the sleeve of his robe through his sash so it would not flop around. He wiped blood from his hand, then took up the sword again.

He waited. It had used the Dragon form, and the best forms to counter it were Tiger and Wolf. *But it will expect that.* That meant it might shift to Eagle or Mantis, perhaps even Dog. The various permutations of the battle ran through his mind. As fast as Ciras could adapt his tactics, the creature would be faster, and the outcome as dire as if Ciras had run.

Ciras squared around and reversed his grip on his sword. He brought it back so it ran up along his forearm with the tip appearing at his right shoulder. Instead of using the blade to shield his body, he used his body to hide the blade.

"Borosan, get out of here. Take *Nesrearck* with you."

"I don't understand."

Ciras began to move back slowly, easily. "Dragright is dead, but his body is linked to this place. You know the stories of corpse dust. Imagine how powerful it would be if the corpse had lain here since the Cataclysm."

"Oh, oh, I see." The inventor began to trek back up the hill. "What are you going to do?"

"I'm going to kill it." He set himself and nodded to the corpse. "If I don't, remember to mark this place as very deadly on your map."

The corpse laughed. "I'll hunt him down, too."

"No, you won't." Ciras pointed toward the hole in the tomb entrance. "Leave here, and someone else will despoil your comrades. You can't allow them to be dishonored."

"No, I can't." The thing launched itself at him. The

Dragon form shifted into Tiger, but Ciras kept his sword where it was. He cut to his left, working back against its right. The slash meant to decapitate him whistled just past his face. The blow opened the creature to a counterattack, but even as Ciras feinted with his right shoulder, the sword cut back to parry a low slash.

Again, Ciras danced away, working always to the right. The creature might no longer be Dragright, but whatever had caused him to drag his leg still affected it. Ciras moved with calculation, slowing to draw it into attacks, then cutting to the right. The creature darted around to head him off and trap him, but he just ran in the other direction.

The corpse, backlit by the fire, hunched its shoulders. "So this is what the Empire has come to? Unskilled cowards who run rather than fight?"

Ciras nodded. "The Empire you died to save is dead. The Nine Principalities have risen in its place. You and yours are all but forgotten.

"In fact," Ciras added as he began to spin to the right, exposing his back to the creature, "you're beneath contempt. *Nesrearck,* shoot it again!"

The creature had already begun a forehand slash at his spine, but glanced off up the hillside. Its blade rose with the distraction, and Ciras' spin brought him down onto his left knee. As he spun, he shifted the sword around into a double-hand grip, directed by his left hand. As the corpse's slash whipped past an inch above his skull, Ciras' sword bit into the back of its right knee and continued out through the front.

The corpse continued its spin and began to fall. Shifting his blade to his right hand, Ciras rose and cut down. As the corpse hit the ground, his sword clove its skull in two.

It thrashed on the ground, then reached out and clawed the stone. It slowly began dragging itself back toward the white stain of corpse dust. Ciras could imagine it trying to pack its shattered head and come at him again.

He would have hacked it into pieces, but he had no desire to dishonor the warrior. He just let the corpse keep crawling, because between it and the corpse dust lay the fire.

He moved downwind so he'd not breathe any of the smoke rising from the body. Borosan appeared at the edge of the basin and smiled. "I'm glad to see you won."

Ciras frowned. "You should have been a long way from here by now."

"I couldn't have left you behind." *Nesrearck* strode up beside him. "I was refitting the *thanaton*. We would have gotten it."

Before Ciras could ask, a panel slid up on the machine, revealing the crossbow mechanism. Instead of a bolt, one of the mousers was set to be launched.

The swordsman nodded. "It would have taken him apart from inside?"

"That was the idea."

"Better than what I had, which was just a lot of hope." Ciras smiled. "It showed me a move I didn't know, so I showed it no fighting style at all. That confused it."

Borosan frowned. "But that left you vulnerable and could have gotten you killed."

"True, but it did not. Not this time." Ciras returned his sword to its scabbard. "Next time I hope I have a better plan."

Chapter Sixteen

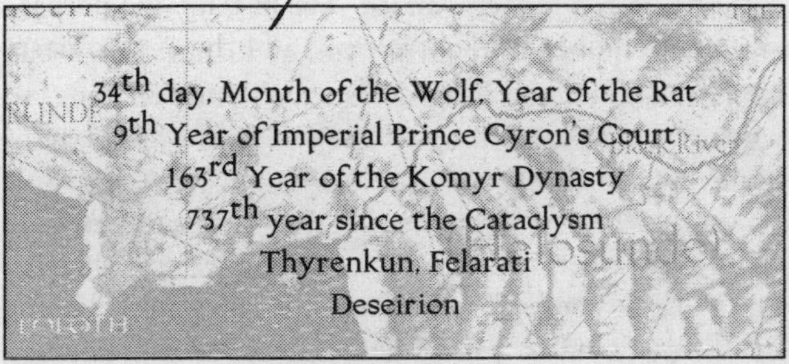

34th day, Month of the Wolf, Year of the Rat
9th Year of Imperial Prince Cyron's Court
163rd Year of the Komyr Dynasty
737th year since the Cataclysm
Thyrenkun, Felarati
Deseirion

Keles Anturasi rubbed his eyes, then looked out from the tower library's balcony at the Black River's southern shore. In less than a week, the transformation of Felarati had begun, and had begun in a way Keles would have thought impossible. The day after he'd spoken with the Prince, he rode south to the hills. It took him a full two days to do a preliminary survey—largely because he had a cadre of eighteen people following him. They hung on his every word, aped his every move, and generally got in his way.

The Desei surprised him. Living in Nalenyr, he had grown up with stories of bloody-minded savages who slaughtered innocent Helosundians for sport. Many Naleni thought the Desei were slope-headed dullards who labored happily in a nation devoid of color because they were all inbred. While it was true that the two images could not easily be reconciled, Keles acknowledged that people seldom had trouble maintaining the veracity of multiple stereotypes as long as they were all derogatory.

But the Desei he worked with were hardly homicidal or stupid. While they did not benefit from some of the formal training people obtained in Nalenyr, they were clever and quite resourceful. And as Prince Pyrust had suggested, they had long done much with nothing, so when they had something to work with, they adapted to it quickly and used it well.

Sooner than he thought possible, his students were able to work with minimal supervision. He set them to the more simple tasks of laying out roads and aligning buildings. Some of his students were water-witches—one of them approaching near Mystic status. He had them locate sites for wells and lay out the sewer lines. By the second day, a whole new district for Felarati had been laid out. It would be able to house twice the number of people as the section of the city it was replacing.

On the third day, Pyrust gave the order for the construction to begin. Keles had argued against it, pointing out that they had none of the building material they needed. But Pyrust had simply said, "It is Deseirion, Keles. We have what we need."

Soon people began to stream through the southern city gate, bringing with them the stones and wood that had once been their homes. Every man, woman, and child carried something to the new site. A third of them stayed to work, and the others headed back for more.

Even now, almost a week into the project, the lines of

people stretched north to south and back again. They looked almost like ants, and they certainly worked with a similar single-mindedness. And, from off to the west, another stream of farmers arrived to make the vacated city land productive again.

It was so unlike his home that he could not feel homesick. There was not enough of Moriande there to remind him of the south. While Deseirion was hardly as colorful or fecund as his home, it all seemed new and amazing.

Very clearly, had Prince Cyron attempted what Pyrust was doing, Moriande's streets would have been flooded with people protesting his actions. The whole of the city would have been in an uproar. The inland lords—ever resisting any directive from the capital—would be threatening open revolt. And yet, if put to the question, every citizen would say they loved Cyron as much as the Desei loved Pyrust. If called to it—with the possible exception of the inland lords—they would willingly fight to protect Cyron and his nation.

Keles clearly had misjudged the Desei, and found his reeducation rather harsh and chilling. The Desei were content to move their homes, brick by brick, a couple miles south. He had no doubt they would have moved them as far south as Moriande if so commanded. While many Naleni feared invasion from the north, he doubted any of them understood how complete an invasion that could be.

However, the Naleni were not the only ones who underestimated foreigners. Pyrust clearly underestimated Keles, because the renovation designs had problems that would take years to solve.

Problems that will pay them back for Tyressa's murder a thousand times over. The close-set side streets would let fire rage through the city. The broad main roads would allow for a lot of traffic, and the traffic on those main roads would one day be Naleni troops!

The biggest problem was not one Keles had designed on purpose. While the people were able to bring their homes with them, Pyrust could not allow them to tear down the city's southern wall. The new city sector would be outside the walls, and until Pyrust could get enough stone to build new walls or expand the old, that district would be vulnerable. Granted, the risk of invasion was low, but if Cyron decided to come north, Pyrust would have a huge problem.

And if he moves the factories outside the walls, he loses even more.

To solve such problems, Pyrust needed Keles. The Naleni cartographer had been under no illusion that Pyrust was ever going to let him go. Like his grandfather before him, Keles had too much information ever to be given his freedom. Pyrust would build him a tower and keep him in Felarati, trading privileges for plans. If Keles became uncooperative, Pyrust would have him killed.

Keles didn't like either one of those alternatives, which meant he had to escape—though an acceptable method eluded him. It was not that slipping away was impossible, but that Pyrust would likely torture those who should have prevented his escape. Until he could find a way either to insulate people from Pyrust's retribution or steel himself to accept it, Keles was trapped.

It did strike him that his willingness to design a city that would allow a conqueror to slaughter thousands conflicted with his reluctance to expose those Desei he knew to danger. He blamed the Desei for Tyressa's death, but the people he knew clearly were innocent of that crime. It would make sense to try to reconcile those two points, but if he let his desire for vengeance slip, he would be losing a connection to Tyressa. No matter how much that connection hurt him, he couldn't let it go.

So thousands of Desei were doomed.

"They are remarkable, aren't they, Keles Anturasi?"

Surprised, Keles spun and found himself looking at a petite blonde woman with icy blue eyes. He'd have thought she was very young, but there was a wariness in her eyes that was ageless. *More like ancient.*

"Please, you have the advantage of me."

"I do. Should I press it?"

"That would be your decision." Part of him wanted to send her off, telling her he was doing the Prince's work, but there was something hauntingly familiar about her. "And you are right, the Desei people are remarkable."

She nodded slightly and moved to the balcony railing beside him. She wore a blue silk robe of a darker and richer hue than her eyes. On the breasts, sleeves, and back, hawks on the wing had been embroidered. Their left wings lacked two feathers—an emblem marking her as part of the Prince's household. The hawk was less surprising than the robe's color—most Desei wore bright colors only on very special occasions, since the dyes had to be imported from the south at great expense.

She peered out at the shifting columns of people. "We attempt to belittle and disregard them, and yet they are capable of picking a city apart. As irresistible as the tide, aren't they?"

"They bend to the will of their master."

"Do you as well, Master Anturasi?" She faced him, appraising him openly.

"I am his guest. Can I do otherwise?"

She smiled and turned back to look to the south. "I have no doubt you have found many ways to comply in appearance, but resist in substance."

Keles said nothing.

"Tired of our game already, have you?"

"Is it a game we're playing? Because I am working." He pointed back to the library table with drawings scattered on it.

"So am I, Keles." She turned and caught his arm. "What if I were to tell you that I am tasked with seducing you and seeing to it that you desire to remain here forever?"

Keles shrugged. "I'd say you're too late for that, or too early. Had the Prince poisoned me to mimic illness and you nursed me back to health, I might have fallen in love with you."

She smiled. "That's how your parents met, wasn't it?"

Keles jolted and she laughed. "You see, Master Anturasi, we knew you would find it suspect. And, as you suggested, I am too early, because the time to find you companionship will be in a month, during the planting festival. You do know that here in Deseirion we will *all* be in the fields, plowing and planting? It is backbreaking work, and you'll find yourself in the fields working with a Desei noblewoman. You'll talk, she will laugh and be punished for it. You'll feel guilty and try to make amends. She will tell you that you are different, a dream come true for her. She may not even know her part—though I doubt that. Chances are she will be one of the Mother of Shadows' special operatives. I doubt you're a virgin, but she will be unlike any woman you've ever slept with."

He frowned. "And what am I to make of you telling

me all this? If you're even halfway truthful, I have to assume the Mother of Shadows has me watched at all times. She will know we have spoken, and probably know what was said."

"She might, but at the moment she is distracted." The woman smiled and glanced back at the library door. "And the people tasked with watching you right now are not going to report anything about our meeting. After all, I have leave to consult you."

"You do?"

"From the Prince himself."

Keles leaned back on the balcony's railing. "Now I *am* tired of this game. I don't know who you are, and I really don't care. Leave me be."

"I can't, Keles Anturasi." She studied his face for a moment, then looked down. "Then again, if you are not intelligent enough to figure out who I am, perhaps I waste my time even talking to you."

He studied her. She clearly wasn't full-blooded Desei. She'd not referred to them as "my people." She was in the Prince's household, had Helosundian coloring, and... *How could I have missed it?* Her voice. She spoke with a Naleni accent—which he'd not noticed because it was so familiar to him. That, combined with her intelligence and arrogance, led to one inescapable conclusion.

"You're the Prince's wife."

"I am Jasai of Helosunde."

"In Newtown, the rumor is going around that the Prince will have a son before the year is out."

"No, Keles Anturasi, *I* will have a son." Jasai stared up into his face. "It is up to you to decide if he will be born here, or you will help me see to it he is born in freedom."

Chapter Seventeen

35th day, Month of the Wolf, Year of the Rat
9th Year of Imperial Prince Cyron's Court
163rd Year of the Komyr Dynasty
737th year since the Cataclysm
Moriande, Nalenyr

Junel Aerynnor slipped into the opium den's dark, dank depths all but unnoticed. His clothes, which he had taken to wearing while hunting, had long since been stained with things noxious and unknowable. The splotch over his right elbow, in fact, contained a virulent poison. Driving that elbow into a mouth with enough force would guarantee that whomever he hit would be dead within a minute.

Though the Dreaming Serpent was located in the older portion of the docks—one where Naleni nobility was seldom found—he felt no trepidation about passing through the nearby precincts. Footpads and cutthroats abounded and the sense of danger gave him a thrill. Granted, it was one that was fleeting, but he sought it on those nights when he was not yet hunting. His game came to be one of avoiding trouble, and if he failed there, he played at killing the troublemakers as quickly as possible.

This night, however, he had not come to hunt or flirt with danger. A message had come to him, summoning him to a meeting. It alluded to certain facts that told him someone had been studying him. Clearly they'd sensed that he was hiding something and had concluded it was an addiction to opium. Hardly a surprise, given that he'd lost two lovers to most horrible slaughter, and had been wounded himself, not the sort of thing that had an appeal for the families whose daughters he might want to woo.

At least they have not penetrated to the truth. While the lords of the interior knew he was willing to promote revolution to overthrow Prince Cyron, they stupidly assumed he was motivated by greed. If he succeeded in aiding them, they would clearly reward him with lucrative trading concessions. Of course, this was because their own thinking was colored by greed, and they failed to look beyond it.

He really didn't know how they would react if they knew he was an agent for Deseirion. Some of them would not care, as long as he could help them overthrow Cyron. That a civil war would split their nation and leave it easy prey for Prince Pyrust seemed beyond their consideration.

Junel slowly picked his way through the low-ceilinged basement. Pallets had been stacked three high with barely two and a half feet of clearance between them. An addict would slide onto a filthy pad while an attendant brought them a pipe and a small pea of brown opium.

Most would lie there for hours, until their money ran out and the thickly muscled guards ejected them.

Following the instructions he'd been sent, Junel passed to the back and into a curtained passageway. Here the ceiling rose a bit, though the passage narrowed. The ability to wield a weapon in such tight confines would be severely limited, giving the guards a great advantage over anyone who might cause trouble. Junel had no doubt that somewhere further along, in one of the side rooms, a trapdoor opened into the sewers and those who expired from their addiction or some other violence were unceremoniously disposed of.

The fourth door on the left stood slightly ajar. He opened it and entered, closing it behind him. The small room had been richly appointed, with a thick, colorful carpet from Ceriskoron in the center, countless tapestries shrouding the walls, and exquisite bronze lanterns burning on pedestals in three of the corners. A table and single chair sat in the center of the carpet, so Junel seated himself and turned to look at the four-paneled screen in the room's fourth corner—the one without a visible lantern.

The image on the screen struck him as chillingly prescient. Painted on golden silk, it showed the Naleni Dragon and Desei Hawk descending on a pack of Helosundian Dogs. That would mean the screen dated from before the Komyr Dynasty, when the previous Prince had allied with the Desei to put down a Helosundian threat. Not only was the screen impressive for the power of the image and its antiquity, but for its survival beyond the Desei conquest of Helosunde.

And the person behind it was clearly one who was intent on surviving a long time as well.

Though a lantern burned behind the screen, no silhouette presented itself. Not only would it hide his patron's identity, but the padded screen and all the tapestries would help mute and disguise his voice. *He is not someone who can chance discovery, and may only be an agent of some more powerful master.* Junel knew immediately that it was no one associated with the westron lords, since they neither understood subtlety nor the need for it.

"You honor me by accepting my invitation." The voice, which came in a whisper, betrayed little more than the speaker's gender. "You have our sympathies over the tragedies you have suffered. How are you recovering?"

"My flesh heals, but my heart is slower to mend."

"Yes, those things that wound the soul are slow to heal. But these are times that require drastic remedies."

Junel nodded. "Your wise advice shall be remembered."

"We hope it shall be acted upon. We hope you will be able to help us steer events in a way that precludes great suffering for all."

Junel's eyes narrowed. "It would be my pleasure." Either the speaker would want him to cease his relations with the inland lords or expand them. Having another player enter the contest could make his goal much easier, or it could complicate things.

"You have the failing of youth, Count Aerynnor, for you name as a pleasure something that will be difficult and offer freely that which should be valued highly." A mild note of disdain made it through the whisper. "Or you seek to beguile us with false innocence."

"It had best be the latter, or I should not be the person with whom you desire an alliance."

"Very true. We shall proceed from that assumption. There are lords of the western provinces who are not pleased with the Prince's policies. They believe the Komyr Dynasty has outlived its usefulness. They would prefer to see it ended, with one of their number taking control. You are well aware of this."

Junel made no reply.

"There are three among the westrons who most desire the Dragon Throne. The duchess of Gnourn would be the most capable but, sadly, the fruit of her loins show a penchant for idiocy and dissolution. While she might have the strength of character and quickness of mind to take the throne, her dynasty would die with her.

"Count Linel Vroan of Ixun is likewise older. He has two grown sons and two daughters, and his new wife, the Helosundian, has just given him another daughter. He might be seen as more sympathetic to Helosundian issues and thereby favored by the Keru—though their loyalty to Cyron is unshakable. He has standing in the nation and is known to many because he fought beside the Prince's older brother and was a chief mourner at his funeral."

Junel smiled. "Known is not the same as beloved."

"True. Would that rumors of his first wife's death were stripped of such ugly suspicion. In that case he might be a tolerable choice."

The man behind the screen cleared his throat, then continued. "Finally, we have Count Donlit Turcol of Jomir. Young and dynamic, even charismatic, he could win the people. Alas, he has no children by his wife, a scattering of bastards by his many mistresses, and does not appear to want to rein in his sexual proclivities."

"You see no other candidates in the west?"

"It matters not what we see, but what you see, Count Aerynnor. Have we missed someone?"

"The duchess' fourth son, Nerot, has been underestimated." Junel leaned back in his chair. "While in Gnourn, I played him at chess. He plays the fop to amuse his mother and distract the court, but I am not so easily distracted."

"But is he not frail?"

"A broken leg never healed properly, true, but it has not affected his mind." Junel shrugged. "I am not saying he would be the sort of prince who could face down Pyrust, but he would not ruin Nalenyr."

Silence came from behind the screen, then the whispering began anew. "It pleases us to have this news. Perhaps if one of Vroan's daughters was married to Nerot, the prospect of a grandchild on the throne would strengthen the alliance."

"I was under the impression that both of his daughters were married. Isn't one Count Turcol's wife?"

"True on both counts, but life is uncertain. If one were widowed, an opportunity might present itself."

And in the civil war, the three Scior heirs between Nerot and the throne might meet with accidents.

Junel frowned. "The question for you is this. Do you mean to have me believe you did not know about Nerot, or do you merely wish to ascertain that I do?"

"Immaterial, for now we both know the possibilities he provides. And your mind is racing ahead, so we shall anticipate you. With our knowledge of the people of the interior, we could aid or end their plans. We have reached out to you because you have already gained their trust, and are already facilitating their activities. You have made yourself into the lever that will allow them to shift the Komyr Dynasty from power. This makes you critical to our plans."

Junel nodded. "I'm pleased you believe I will be of use to you. Shall I surmise you wish to learn what my cooperation will cost?"

"Is it gold? Or were you thinking that one of the widowed daughters of Vroan would come happily to your bed, positioning you as her consort when she ascends to the throne?"

That latter idea sent a jolt through Junel because he had never considered it. He had been trained in the way of the shadow, to be a spy and assassin, with loyalty to the House of Jaeshi and Prince Pyrust that superseded loyalty to blood. Indeed, his whole family had been accused of treason and slaughtered. He'd betrayed them to his masters and their murders provided him with the perfect reason for fleeing south.

Never in his life had Junel had any ambition other than to become as good at *vrilri* as possible—perhaps even becoming a Mystic, as was the Mother of Shadows. He'd never even entertained the idea of supplanting her—though such an honor was one he would have willingly accepted. But here, now, he found himself wondering what it would be like to become more than the Prince's agent—to become his equal. It could happen, and he could influence events to guarantee it.

"Gold is always welcome but, as you have noted, there are scant few candidates who could sustain a dynasty. I am not a puppet, but by no means am I a puppet master. I understand power well enough to flow with it, and to know that moving against it is ruin."

A richer note entered the whisper. "This we hoped might be your reply. Rest assured, gold beyond dreams of avarice shall be yours. What more remains in your future shall depend on your conduct. If predictions of your intelligence prove true, a new dynasty may rise from the graves of the Aerynnor family. With the proper alliances in place, you might even find yourself on the Hawk Throne, on your way to becoming Emperor."

"A dizzying height."

"But one attainable, nonetheless."

And you have gone a step too far. To tempt him with being a Naleni prince-consort was within the bounds of reason. Imagining that he could inspire a nation stepped well beyond it. It seemed more likely that once he had ascended, anti-Desei sentiment among the Naleni would be mustered to unseat him. His birth would forever be his weakness.

So when I reach the throne, I'll simply have to cede it all to Prince Pyrust. Junel kept his face impassive, then nodded—certain his hidden patron had been watching through the screen.

"What would you have of me, my lord?"

"We would have you continue your negotiations with the westrons. Unify them. Court Nerot and, if possible, acquaint yourself with Turcol's widow. That will be enough to start."

"Do you want reports?"

"If necessary, another meeting like this shall be arranged. We have other sources of information that should be sufficient." The hidden man paused for a moment. "We urge you to be very careful. Betrayal would be unfortunate and the consequences regrettable."

So if I am found out and captured, I shall not live long enough to reveal anything. Junel smiled. "I shall bear that in mind." He almost added "Minister" to the comment, but being too wise would not be good. Intrigues such as this could not be undertaken without the complicity of the bureaucracy. And for a minister to dabble so directly meant the bureaucrats found Cyron a risk. Their support could make even the most haphazard plan succeed.

"I bid you a farewell, Junel Aerynnor. If things go well, I shall not greet you again until I have the honor of addressing you as 'my Prince.' "

"Then peace to you until then."

The lantern behind the screen went dark, and the tapestries on that wall shifted. But Junel did not get up, for even if he located the switch that operated the secret door, his patron would be long gone. Who he was did not matter, after all. What mattered was that Junel's plan now had backing of a strong Naleni element. Success merely awaited implementation.

He stood, stretching, and felt the urge to hunt slowly come over him. *No, not yet. Delay it. The gratification shall be so much more.*

Besides, I have much to think on now, and much more to plan. To plan, as a prince would plan.

Chapter Eighteen

1st day, Month of the Dragon, Year of the Rat
9th Year of Imperial Prince Cyron's Court
163rd Year of the Komyr Dynasty
737th year since the Cataclysm
Kunjiqui, Anturasixan

The growing sense of dread within her surprised Nirati Anturasi, for she generally loved surprises. A lover's surprise—making manifest the desire of another to please her—had always seemed a testament of love. This alien apprehension urged her to remain by her stream, but she defied it.

Bearing Takwee in her arms, she had begun the trek to the western reaches of Kunjiqui. She knew that the place to which she was headed was many miles distant—further, certainly, than from Moriande to Kelewan—yet her walk would take no more than minutes. Such was the nature of the paradise her grandfather had created that she never needed to be far from the heart of it and never had to tire herself while journeying away.

Not that she ever went far, or for long. Days melted one into another, to the point where their passage meant nothing. Night lasted as long as she wanted, and likewise day. If her desires shifted quickly enough, they could change with an eyeblink. She'd made time pass that way once, but she didn't think it had been for long. Then again—as she had laughed at the time—how would she have known?

Such miracles were not uncommon in her grandfather's world. He had raised mountains and sunk land to create an inland sea. He split the land with a wave of his hand and joined it again with a simple caress. He made places where years passed in heartbeats, and others where an hour would take nine years to be spent. All this he did with purpose, consulting with Nelesquin, who, in turn, sought counsel from his scrying stones.

And all for me.

As she walked west, it occurred to her that she had not seen Qiro Anturasi for a while. Instantly she regretted this, then composed her face in a smile. He loved it when she smiled. He had ever been tender in his care of her, and she owed him every possible kindness.

So with Nelesquin's surprise and a chance to see her grandfather again, she had no idea why she felt such dread. *This is paradise. What could go wrong?* Of course, anything could go wrong—everything. As her brother Keles once told her, "Just because you have flipped a coin a dozen times and it always comes up sun, the thirteenth time it could come up moon."

She heard his voice as if he were walking with her. Nirati turned and saw the washed-out, ghostly image of her twin matching her strides. "Keles, is that you?"

He looked at himself, then at her curiously. "Is it, or is it how you desire to remember me?"

His question caught her off guard. She let him move ahead of her and glanced at his back, but she saw no scars from Viruk claws. "It's you, but not as you are. Where are you? Are you a dream, or are we communicating in the manner you do with Grandfather?"

"I must be a dream. Communication with Grandfather has never been this clear, nor have I ever been able to reach you, Nirati."

She nodded, certain he was correct. Then Takwee grabbed for Keles' nearly transparent arm. *Can Takwee see my dreams?* "Where shall I dream you are?"

"In Felarati, a guest of Prince Pyrust."

Nirati laughed. "Is that possible? I'd rather dream you in Ixyll. But if you are there, don't go to the Empress. She will only torture and deceive you."

"The Sleeping Empress? Why would she do that? She waits for us to reach her so she can help reestablish the Empire." Keles smiled at her and Takwee cooed delightedly. "As long as you are dreaming, will you tell me where you are?"

Nirati opened her arms—letting an alarmed Takwee dangle from her right wrist. "I am in Kunjiqui. Grandfather made it for me. He created it and he . . . he brought me here when I died." *Is that right? Did I die?*

"You cannot be dead, Nirati. The dead do not dream."

Oh, but I think they do. I think they dream of being alive again. She brought her arms in over her chest and shivered. "You're right, Keles; I am certain of it. But dreams are never certain, are they?"

"No. What of Grandfather and Jorim and Mother?"

"I've no news of Jorim, but no worries for him. Were

I to dream him in Felarati, he would dream himself away again. With Mother I have no contact. Grandfather is well and happily at work. Are you not in contact with him?"

"The situation here is complicated enough that I don't need him interrogating me. I can't risk being distracted by his ire. When I am done, he'll have a complete map of the new Felarati. Maybe that will please him, though my failure to complete the Ixyll survey will not."

"He loves you. He loves us all." She reached out to caress his face, but her fingers just moved through the image. Still, his face turned to her hand, and he would have kissed her palm had his lips not passed through it.

"Nirati." Nelesquin's voice boomed from high atop a distant hill. "Quickly, darling!"

With the echoes of his voice, the image of her brother evaporated. Takwee mewed sadly—the first real sign of any discontent on her part. Nirati's heart sank a bit, but she salvaged the memory of Keles' smile. She created its twin on her face, then, in three long strides, reached Nelesquin's side.

He rested his hands on her shoulders and turned her back around to face whence she had come. He kissed the back of her head, then settled his large hands over her eyes. "Who was that I saw you with, Nirati?"

"My twin, Keles. I dreamed him."

"Ah, I look forward to meeting him."

"I warned him of Cyrsa."

"Better he should warn her of me." He laughed easily. "Now, my love, the surprise I promised you. Let me just turn us about."

Neither of them moved. Instead, the whole top of the hill spun slowly. With his hands over her eyes, he hooked his elbows in front of her shoulders and drew her tight against his broad chest. He held her there for a moment, then rested his chin on her head.

"Behold, beloved, what we have wrought."

His hands fell away and she opened her eyes. She blinked, quickly, for so much sunlight glinted from thousands of pinpoints that she almost shifted day to night to protect her eyes. *But they would shine just as brightly in the dark, I am certain.*

Below her, the land had sunk between two mountain ranges. Vast plains isolated the foothills from the slender finger of deep blue water thrust deep into the land. On that narrow ocean bobbed dozens of ships—none as large as the *Stormwolf,* but each large enough to carry hundreds of soldiers. Other ships waited next to quays or in dry docks, ready to be launched.

At the hill's base, nine formations—nine ranks deep, nine men wide—stood tall and proud in silver mail, with glowing silver helmets. The sunlight reflected from their weapons—and Nirati knew that each ship could carry just such a unit. They reminded her of the ranks of the Naleni army and the Keru, save these men had a blue cast to their flesh, jet-black hair, and—if the two nearest them were models for their race—amber eyes like those of a cat.

The two men approaching them differed from the others in that their armor and helmets had been washed with gold. At twenty feet each dropped to a knee and pounded his right fist to his left shoulder in a salute. They bowed their heads and held those bows for longer than she had ever seen before.

Beyond the time required for a Prince. Then it occurred to her that she *had* seen such a bow held before. *In a temple, when one sought the favor of the gods.*

Their heads came up and they both rose as Nelesquin beckoned them forward. They still stopped a respectful distance—just out of reach—yet they had an arrogance that she found both attractive and frightening.

Nelesquin waved a hand toward the one with a snarling ram crest on his helmet. "This is Gachin. He is Dost of the Durrani host. Keerana is his second-in-command."

Gachin's eyes narrowed, and the sharpened tips of his ears were visible through hair as he doffed his helmet. Still, he gave her a respectful smile. "The goddess honors us by visiting as we embark. The invasion of the Empire has already begun, but we shall consolidate it, as you desire, goddess."

Invasion? As I desire? She vaguely recalled Nelesquin mentioning a need to position himself to defend against Cyrsa, but invasion had not been part of it. And yet while she tried to remember what exactly had been said, a part of her knew that invasion was the only way his goals could be accomplished.

Keerana watched her closely. "The goddess is not pleased?"

She shook her head quickly. "It is only the thought of your departure so quickly after our meeting that displeases me. I am certain you will be successful with your endeavor."

"We shall, goddess, then you shall come with our Lord Nelesquin and reside in Kelewan. We shall raze Quun's home and build you the most beautiful temple." Gachin bowed his head confidently.

"Though no temple," offered his subordinate, "could ever approach your beauty, goddess."

Nelesquin laughed, then dismissed the two of them with a wave. "Go to your ships. You will take Kelewan and secure all of Erumvirine. From there we shall march north."

Gachin bowed again, but Keerana raised an eyebrow. "My lord, I would ask your consent on a matter."

Nelesquin folded arms over his chest. "Speak."

Though Nelesquin's tone had not been inviting, Keerana did not quail. "Lord Nelesquin, once we have had the glory of returning Kelewan to your possession, I ask permission to take a third of our force and range south. I have studied all you have made available, and I believe that the Five Princes, in their jealousy and envy, will rise. I wish to punish them swiftly so my lord's further plans shall not be hampered."

Nelesquin contemplated the request, then he nodded. "Very well, you have my leave, provided those troops are not needed to consolidate our holding."

"As you command, lord." Keerana bowed deeply, then withdrew with Gachin.

Nelesquin smiled down at Nirati. "They are perfect, are they not? Clever, respectful, ambitious, resourceful. They will do well."

She frowned. "But will not an invasion unleash the same destruction as happened during the Cataclysm?"

"No, not at all. This is the brilliance of Anturasixan." He opened his arms to take it all in. "I was schooled in the ways of magic, and as your grandfather created this place, we altered reality. We have placed magic both in the land and in those who people the land. None of the Durrani will ever be Mystics, but they do not need to be. Here, in this valley, we bred generation after generation of them, pitting them against each other. You saw it, with Keerana and Gachin. Keerana would replace him in an instant, save Gachin's clan was ascendant in their last war. The Durrani are brilliant at war, and those who do not fight are gifted as healers, helping keep their companions alive."

Nirati shivered. "You have re-created the *vanyesh*?"

He stepped to her and enfolded her in his arms. "Do not believe the tales of the *vanyesh*. We did not seek magic for power, but merely so we could undo that which wild magic unleashed. We were always mistrusted, but this is because such vast power can be difficult to control. Not here. You yourself control it. Look how you make the day and night pass as you will. You are not evil, nor is the power."

"Lord Nelesquin has it correctly, Granddaughter."

Upon hearing Qiro's voice, she turned and managed to keep a smile on her face despite the horror running through her. Her grandfather had been eternal and unchanging. Tall, slender, proud beyond arrogance, with thick white hair, a white goatee and moustaches, Qiro Anturasi had always been an image of power. He ruled Anturasikun as would an emperor, and was treated by many as something more.

But now he had become something less. Deep bags, dark and heavy, hung beneath his eyes. His hair had become matted and his beard had grown unkempt. He still held his head high, but his shoulders were slumped. As he walked toward her, his left leg moved stiffly, as if that hip refused to work. And his eyes, his icy blue eyes, which had always been keen, now somehow focused past her.

She tore herself from Nelesquin's grasp and ran to her grandfather. She hugged him tightly and could feel him quake within her grasp. He returned the hug, weakly, and leaned heavily upon her.

"It has been far too long, Grandfather."

"No, girl, no time at all. Much has been done." A palsied hand stroked her hair. "My Lord Nelesquin has given me many tasks, but when I am done he has told me I am free to indulge myself. Soon I shall."

Nirati looked at Nelesquin. "I think he needs a rest, a long rest. I will take him back to Kunjiqui and tend to him. Will you permit that, my lord?"

Nelesquin laughed. "That is an excellent idea. You have done wonderful work, Grandmaster Anturasi. I knew I was right to choose you. You have repaid my faith many times over."

Choose him? Nirati frowned, then got under her grandfather's right arm and looped it over her shoulder. "Come, Grandfather, I shall tell you stories. I shall tell you of Keles and his adventures."

"Keles?" The old man's voice softened and became almost wistful. "He was a handful, just like your father."

"No, you're thinking of Jorim, Grandfather." She put her left arm around his waist and was shocked to find him so thin. She could have easily lifted him and borne him to her sanctuary like a child. "I dreamed of Keles, and he said he was in Felarati. Can you imagine?"

"A grandson of mine in the Dark City? No, this will not be permitted. I will stop it."

Nirati tightened her grip. "Later, Grandfather, when you have rested. You always said you did your best work after rest."

"Yes, yes, and this will take my best work." Qiro kissed Nirati's head. "I will always do my best for you."

"And I for you, Grandfather." She smiled, genuinely this time, and led him off.

And, after he admired his fleet sailing northwest, Nelesquin joined her.

Chapter Nineteen

3rd day, Month of the Dragon, Year of the Rat
9th Year of Imperial Prince Cyron's Court
163rd Year of the Komyr Dynasty
737th year since the Cataclysm
Nemehyan, Caxyan

Jorim Anturasi had progressed so quickly in his studies that the *maicana* took it as a sure sign he was Tetcomchoa-reborn—and even he began to wonder if it was not true. He kept telling himself it wasn't, but the sheer joy he felt in learning magic made him question many of the convictions he'd held his entire life. He still accepted that magic was a bad thing, but perhaps only *out-of-control* magic was bad—the same way anything done without respect for tradition, and without discipline, was bad.

He knelt in his private chamber's anteroom across a round wooden table from Nauana. She had proven an apt teacher and he'd quickly moved from simple to more complex invocations. The key to it all, as she had insisted the first day, was to find the *mai* that defined things.

The truth was the link to magic, and could be used to call it forth and shift the balance of things. And shifting the balance of more than just the elements was also possible; one could use magic to alter objects physically. Best of all, while there were traditional methods for doing anything, there usually were multiple ways an effect could be created. As he learned more complex magics, he came more quickly to the desired ends. And, often, the more refined methods, while requiring more concentration, exhausted him less than the crude methods.

Nauana's dark eyes sharpened as Jorim took a small wooden bucket from Shimik and poured golden sand in the center of the table. He tossed the empty bucket back to the Fenn, then scratched him behind an ear. Shimik fell over backward into a somersault and rolled away toward Jorim's bedchamber.

"Tetcomchoa, I do not understand why you have this sand here. The lesson for today does not require sand."

"I know, Nauana, but I had an idea and wish to try something." Jorim touched a fingertip to the sand, then brushed away all but a single grain. "If this works, I think you will see something completely miraculous."

She smiled, but slid back from the edge of the table. "As my lord wishes."

"Thanks for the display of confidence." He forced himself to relax, then concentrated on the grain of sand. Because it was so small, he found it difficult to identify at first. Solidity was the easiest aspect to grasp, with a hint of light. As he located it within *mai,* he found a strong connection between it and the rest of the sand, which did not surprise him too much. He had already learned that like was connected to like, and part of one thing was always connected to the other parts.

Slowly, he began to play with the balances of reality. First he used magic to make it light enough to float. That was not difficult given how little it weighed. The hard part was in retaining enough weight so it didn't shoot up to the ceiling. After a few ups and downs, he centered it a finger length above his fingertip.

Then he began to play with heat. He channeled the *mai* into it and felt it begin to warm. Knowing his goal was within reach, he pumped more in. The grain of sand warmed, then became incandescent.

Then it exploded into a puff of vapor.

Nauana blinked, then leaned forward. "Are you all right, my lord?"

The barest hint of fatigue washed over him, but he nodded. "I'm fine, Nauana."

"Was that the miracle, lord?"

"No, not quite. Watch." He picked up a handful of sand, raised it to face height between them, then slowly let it drift down. Using the *mai,* he caught the falling sand and held it suspended as a small sphere in the air. "Nor is this, yet."

She said nothing, but watched the sand intently.

Again Jorim located the sand through the *mai,* and this time used the connectedness of it all. He slowly began to rebalance it so it would become warmer and warmer. As it began to heat up, he recalled his previous error and used the *mai* to alter another balance. Very carefully, while allowing the heat to continue to rise, he shifted the balance of the sand from solid to fluid.

When he'd first arrived on the *Stormwolf* in the land of the Amentzutl, he'd noticed a number of things which were common in the Nine, but nonexistent among the Amentzutl. One was horses, and the other was the wheel—at least as something to be used for more than a toy. While some on the expedition wanted to brand the Amentzutl as hopelessly primitive, wheeled transport was highly impractical in their rugged, mountainous land. When the expedition's military had used war chariots against the Mozoyan, the Amentzutl had been impressed and even credited him with a miracle in their production.

One other thing the Amentzutl lacked was knowledge of glass. Jorim's knowledge of it was not much more than basic, but he did know that sand, if heated enough, would become a thick, viscous fluid that could be shaped. While he had none of the skills of a glass artisan, *mai* and his ability to control it did give him some tools to manipulate the glass.

The sand sphere began to glow and give off light, easily illuminating the joy on Nauana's face. Even Shimik keened with delight from the doorway. As the glow built, Jorim kept careful control of the sand, slowing the flow of *mai* into heat and pushing more into making it fluid. Curiously enough, it continued to get warm, which made sense. *It is melting, which requires heat no matter what. By shifting that balance, I force it to become hotter.*

The sand melted into glass and hung there, a miniature sun, blazing away. Using *mai* he constricted it around its equator and split the glowing yellow mass into two teardrops. He rounded both of them off and saw a look of pure wonder and joy on Nauana's face.

And now to see if I can do the last of it.

Ever since he had noticed that things had a truth to them, he had been drawn to studying it. Though he was restricted from using magic outside the training sessions, he did spend a lot of time sensing the truth of things and defining them in *mai*. As he learned to see them, he began to understand the Amentzutl cosmology and could identify things by their sense in *mai.* He'd even had Iesol hide common items in a sealed wooden box and he'd been able to pick out what they were sight unseen.

Concentrating, he drew the truth of the table into his mind, then projected that into the glass. The twin orbs merged, then flattened out into a low disk. Three small legs dripped down and froze in place.

Nauana gasped and covered her mouth with a hand.

Jorim smiled and reached out to touch her essence with *mai.* As he did so he realized he'd not tried that with any living creature before, and he didn't know what to expect. From the surface he felt her physically. Much as he had done with the table, he projected that sense of her into the glass.

The glass flattened itself into a thin disk that rotated between them. Though it still glowed, it remained thin enough that he could see her through it. The glass molded itself over the image of her features, sculpting itself to her face. The high cheekbones, the straight nose, the full lips. The glass flowed back to define her jaws and her ears. It even followed the shape of her head and flowed down over her neck and shoulders to become a perfect bust, save for her eyes.

The glass could not capture her eyes, so it thinned and holes opened, allowing him to look through it and to her.

And in doing that, he pushed past the surface and found her truth.

Heat pounded back through him, part blush, part fear, his and hers, and joy and delight and . . . so many emotions he could not catalogue them all. They flowed in a vast river of rainbow colors, with eddies and shoals, swift currents and places where the water remained almost still. While the river and its flow remained strong, the composition of it shifted.

Barely aware of what he was doing, he lowered the glass to the table. Setting it atop the remaining pile of sand, he reached past it with a hand. He gestured and she rose, as did he. Jorim came around the table and took her in his arms. He brought his mouth to hers and they kissed.

The instant their lips touched, all he had felt through *mai* intensified. Physical sensation flowed along the same routes as the magical, confirming what he knew. Then it grew as he caught her sensing him through *mai* and he opened himself to her, showing her who he was, what he was.

Unaware of moving, but realizing they had moved, Jorim found himself lying down with her on his bed. Neither of them wore much, and slipping a couple of knots relieved them of their loincloths. He stretched out beside her, his right hand drifting about an inch above her skin. From shoulder, over her breast, past a tight nipple and down the swell, over her flat stomach to hip and upraised thigh, he could feel her in the *mai*. He lowered his hand to her flesh, on top of her thigh, and slowly slid it back up, inch by inch. The smooth warmth of her skin, the pulse of blood beneath it, the twitch of muscles, the silky caress of hair, all of it combined with what he could sense. He caught the thrill running through her both in the *mai* and the way she lifted her chin as he stroked her breast. He let a finger circle her nipple and could feel the sensations ripple through her body.

He wanted her intensely and furiously. He had always found her beautiful beyond imagining. Her gentle teaching, her faith in him, had always represented a greater sense of who she was. But now, linked to her through the *mai,* he could see so much more.

She looked him in the eyes, but said nothing. Then new sensations pulsed through the *mai.* He closed his eyes and watched as she opened herself to him. He had been able to read her physically before, then emotionally, but he never could have seen who she was in her mind. He could not have found her secrets without destroying her.

But what he would never take, she freely offered. He saw her as a child, born into the caste of the *maicana.* She had gone through the lessons she had shared with him. He saw her teachers in the way she had taught him and learned she had been terribly gifted. *As much as I have learned, she learned faster, and before she was even nine years old.*

He watched her in other studies as she learned about the end of the calendar cycle. Her teachers warned her of the horrors of *centenco.* From them he heard of the promise which was Tetcomchoa's return. He caught her firm conviction that only Tetcomchoa could save them from whatever was coming, and her resolve to be the best she could to help him.

She spent hours praying to Tetcomchoa. She offered sacrifices. She created prayers and songs. She rebuffed suitors, not because she did not like them, but because courting, marriage, and family would all be distractions from what she knew would be her life. She was prepared for Tetcomchoa's return.

The day of his arrival floated through her mind. Jorim entered the chamber at the Temple of Tetcomchoa's apex. The sun backlit him, so all she saw was a silhouette at first. She had expected him to be taller. The braids in his hair confused her for a moment, then she stepped from the shadows and took a closer look at him. His robe was decorated with the coiled serpent, the god's sign.

Then, for the first time, she saw his face. Handsome, in a way no Amentzutl man had ever seemed to her. But it was the expression on his face—one of wonder and humility, tinged with anxiety and fear—that told her everything. He was Tetcomchoa, come to save them, ready to undertake all that was necessary, provided the Amentzutl would return to him the powers he had shared with them.

She had trained her entire life to do just that. And now, on the eve of her task's beginning, she learned one more thing about herself and Tetcomchoa. She learned she had loved the god since before remembering. She had never pictured him in her mind, and yet he stood before her and could have been nothing else. The others might take convincing, but for her there was only knowing.

She knew this was Tetcomchoa.

Nauana caressed his face. "If it pleases my lord."

He turned his head and kissed her palm. "You please me, Nauana."

She blushed, then rose on her side and pressed her body to his. She rolled him onto his back, then rose above him. She straddled him, accommodating him. "I have loved you . . ."

Jorim nodded. "I know, Nauana." He slipped his hand into her hair, grasping the back of her neck, and drew her mouth down to his. They kissed again—a kiss tasting of sweet fruits and the sea. They lost themselves in that kiss, and in each other.

And thus lost, created another magic altogether.

Chapter Twenty

5th day, Month of the Dragon, Year of the Rat
9th Year of Imperial Prince Cyron's Court
163rd Year of the Komyr Dynasty
737th year since the Cataclysm
Wentokikun, Moriande
Nalenyr

Prince Cyron found the two men kneeling before him a study in contrasts, though more for their demeanor than their physical appearances. Count Donlit Turcol did have the advantage of size and muscle over both Cyron and Prince Eiran of Helosunde. Cyron and Eiran shared light brown hair and blue eyes, though Cyron's were icier by far; whereas Turcol had dark brown hair worn in a thick braid and flat grey eyes. Turcol had always struck Cyron as being predatory, and he meant that on a level far above the legends of the count's womanizing.

Both of his visitors also shared relative youth with the Prince—Eiran was the youngest, and most new-come to his responsibilities. Cyron had trained all his life for the throne and Turcol had schemed for the same, eclipsing an older brother to become his father's heir. That naked ambition, which he made no effort to clothe with even the most flimsy of artifice, made for the biggest difference between him and Eiran. Eiran had not yet learned ambition; he had barely learned to aspire.

Cyron frowned. "I believe I am having a difficult time understanding you, Count Turcol. You were delivered a copy of the orders sent to your father in Jomir and your father-in-law in Ixun. You have told me you will be placed in command of the soldiers my provinces will supply, in compliance with the order. Is this not all true?"

Turcol nodded stiffly. "It is, Highness."

"You protest your troops' assignment to our northern border." Cyron opened his right hand to indicate Eiran kneeling on the other side of the red carpet strip running from throne to audience chamber doors. "You will be there to help protect Prince Eiran's people. I do not understand your difficulty with this."

Turcol stirred, his agitation betrayed by the way his hands slowly curled into fists. He had chosen to wear robes of forest green edged with gold, displaying his family's crest of a small dragon coiled for sleep. He clearly meant it to remind Cyron that the Turcol family had once occupied the Dragon Throne.

His hands opened again. "It is a matter of honor, Highness. You summon us for your service, then exile us to the northern hinterlands. At the same time, in Moriande, you are surrounded by Helosundian mercenaries. You ward yourself against your people as a conqueror would against those he oppresses."

Eiran bowed his head for a moment, and Cyron nodded to him. "If you please, my lord Turcol, Highness, perhaps I could explain that when I heard of the unit being raised from Jomir and Ixun, I requested they be stationed among my people."

Turcol's eyes narrowed. "What?"

He senses the trap, but cannot avoid it.

The Helosundian Prince continued. "My people have learned much of the Naleni way in our time as your guests. The Keru who serve as the Prince's bodyguard do so out of personal devotion to him only. They acquit a debt to the Naleni nation by warding their beloved leader, much as the nation guards us. And Count Vroan has likewise taken a Helosundian bride, honoring us, and we are grateful to him for his part in fighting for us. He even recovered Prince Aralias' body from Helosunde."

Eiran kept his voice soft and his delivery slow. Turcol's impatience etched itself on his face in deepening lines. Had not six feet of carpet separated them, Cyron was certain the westron lordling would have slapped Eiran. *I would have him slain for his insolence.*

Turcol's nostrils flared. "If my lord would come to his point?"

Eiran, feigning surprise, ducked his head obsequiously. "Please, forgive me. Owing so much to Count Vroan, and having heard so much of your valor, wisdom, and courage, I knew having your people among mine would be exactly what was needed. Our younger generations only hear bitter stories of what we have lost. You, my lord, and your men, would remind us of what we can win again."

The westron frowned. "But the troops on the border now are drawn from your ranks, Prince Eiran."

Cyron smiled. "I would not have my brother Prince be forced to utter what must be said. You know, Count Turcol, that his Highness led an assault on Meleswin.

His troops took the city, only to be overwhelmed by the Desei. His sister was taken and forced to marry the Desei tyrant. We have made much of this."

Turcol nodded. "We have heard even in the interior."

"Good. What you have not heard is that the Helosundian troops were broken. Their best generals were slain, their armies scattered. The simple fact is that while the most elite of the Helosundians become my Keru, the state of the other troops is deplorable. If the Desei knew the quality of troops on that border, you would be meeting with Prince Pyrust, not me."

And he would have your guts for a sash and throw your smirk to street curs to fight over.

Even if he had made an attempt to hide his feelings, Cyron doubted the visiting nobleman would have accomplished much. A light enlivened those grey eyes. Cyron could almost hear thoughts clicking in the man's mind, as if his brain were a *gyanrigot* construct of gears, springs, and levers. Turcol was measuring the Dragon Throne for himself, realizing that if the Helosundian troops were so weak that they could not stop the Desei, he might easily lead a force to the capital that could begin a new Turcol dynasty.

"Highness, if the situation is as dire as you suggest, then this is even more reason for my troops to be brought here to the capital. We are no match for the Keru, this is well known, but we could keep you safe while the Keru warded their homeland."

Cyron nodded slowly. "This was the plan I considered at first, but then I realized that such a move would alert the Desei to the sorry state of affairs among the Helosundians. No, I will move the Helosundians south, to the Virine border, where they will face no threat and may be trained. I will put your troops in their place and raise other companies from the western marches to help. Pyrust will imagine I am shifting troops around just to annoy him, and shall not look further than that—even if he were to dream the path south was open."

Cyron waited a moment or two, then smiled. "Which, with your troops in place, my dear Count, will not be true."

"We would make it a nightmare for him."

"Indeed, you would." Cyron's smile broadened. "Thank you for accepting this mission so prettily. 'Nightmare.' I shall remember you said that."

Turcol stiffened. "But, my lord . . ."

"Fear not, Pyrust shall never hear of your brave boast. If he opposes you, I want him surprised at how facile you are."

The westron lord shifted on his knees, but Cyron snapped open a silk fan, hiding his face. Though he could see through it, all his two visitors could behold was the snarling visage of a dragon. The audience had ended, and with it the discussion.

Eiran bowed. "My lord Turcol, I have the maps and provision lists you will desire. Please, come with me."

"As the Dragon wills it."

The two men bowed toward the throne, then withdrew, remaining crouched until they reached the door, and never turning their backs on him. Once they opened the doors and passed through, two tall, blonde Keru shut them again, and Cyron closed the fan once more. He tucked it down into the little hidey-hole on the chair's right arm, then stood and slipped through a side passage.

He thought he might remain in a foul mood, but the faint hint of jasmine made him smile involuntarily. He hurried along the passage, loosening the ties of his formal purple robe. He mounted the circular stairs, and the scent grew stronger. He imagined he was within steps of catching his quarry, and even thought he could hear the whisper of slipper on stone step ahead of him. Then he reached the panel leading into his personal chambers, slid it open, and stepped into a room redolent of jasmine.

Across the blond wooden floor, she knelt at a low table, pouring him a cup of golden tea.

Scented with jasmine.

Cyron would have been happy to cast his robe into a violet puddle, scoop her up, and carry her to his bed, but doing so would desecrate the aura of peace she'd fostered. In his absence, she had even rearranged the furnishings. His antechamber had always been spare, so she would not have needed much help, and he knew her to be stronger than she appeared. Ultimately it was less what she moved than how and where she moved it.

He, by preference, had kept table and chair edges parallel to walls and the line of the floorboards. She twisted them. The sword stand had been moved from beside the bedchamber door back toward the corner where a chair half hid it. The low table at which she knelt preparing tea had moved closer to the room's center, but not quite there. The furnishings, which before had been positioned with an eye for maximum utility, now had become islands in an ocean teased by a jasmine breeze.

And on the table, in a slender vase, was a single branch from a jasmine shrub with three blossoms remaining on it. The white petals from the other blossoms had been scattered haphazardly from window to table, as if the branch had floated in all by itself. And while the scattering appeared random, Cyron had no doubt the Lady of

Jet and Jade had placed each petal deliberately. They were glyphs in a language he would never understand and yet, even like ballads sung in dialects he did not know, he found it beautiful.

Her silver eyes flicked in his direction, then she set the teapot down and bowed deeply. "Forgive me, Highness, I did not hear you arrive."

"You are kind, for my tread on those stairs was as loud as a chariot's wheels on cobblestones." He approached the table and slid to his knees opposite her. As he did so, the jasmine branch lost a single petal, which fluttered to the tabletop. He did not know how she had managed that, but he knew she had. "I apologize for surprising you."

"To their regret, there are many who find you surprising, no, my lord?"

Cyron smiled, then lifted the small ceramic cup. He let the tea's steam caress his face and fill his nostrils. He drank and, for the time it took for the tea to warm his insides, he pushed the world away. A sense of peace washed over him and soothed his heart. He exhaled slowly, then drank again before setting his cup down.

"You were prescient in suggesting how Count Turcol would approach negotiations. He *did* rely on his honor, and Prince Eiran did all I asked of him. He flattered, then fell silent, so I was able to take over. I offered Turcol the dream gambit, and he replied with the nightmare comment. I thanked him for accepting the mission, then ended things. He was trapped." Cyron studied her soft, seamless face. "Your reading of him was flawless."

The Lady of Jet and Jade shook her head. "It was not my reading of him, for I have never spoken to him. I only know of him through others."

"You have never watched him when he has been at the House of Jade Pleasure?"

She did not reply, but instead raised her own cup and drank. Her silver eyes flashed at him over the cup's edge, and her fingertips caressed the gold dragon crest facing him. She lowered the cup slowly, then smiled. "The House of Jade Pleasure is discriminating in whom it allows within its precincts. Count Turcol has not been admitted."

"No?" Cyron raised an eyebrow. "I imagine that has pinked his vanity."

"Your Highness is most assuredly correct." She fell silent, then poured more tea.

Cyron smiled. While the Lady of Jet and Jade presided over the House of Jade Pleasures, her apprentices were present in all strata of Naleni society. Some of her students became concubines as she was—and some had even left to form their own schools. Other of her students had come to her covertly, were trained, and returned to their lives feeling indebted to her. Cyron had no way of knowing how far her web of influence extended, but given that she had been in Moriande far longer than the Komyr had been on the throne, it could easily be vast. While he doubted it rivaled the bureaucratic tangles of the ministries, he had no doubt it might be more effective in gathering certain types of information.

"If I might ask . . ."

"Anything, lord."

"Have you heard much from the Virine?"

Her eyes half closed. "Very little comes from the south these days. Warriors are heading east quietly so no alarm will spread, but the army is being mobilized. They seem to be moving so quickly that families and camp followers cannot keep up. Many have been warned to move west."

He nodded slowly. "And of the east?"

She plucked the fallen petal from the table and brushed it against her cheek, then set it back down again. A single tear glistened there.

Worse than I could have imagined. He felt a sudden urge to tell her what little he knew of the invasion and his precautions against its spread. Given how she had suggested he deal with Count Turcol, she might well have guessed at some of what was going on. While everything had been kept very quiet, soldiers ordered to move south would have bid farewell to their loved ones, and doubtless that news had made its way back to her.

He looked at her and his fingertips tingled with the memory of how soft her flesh was beneath his touch. He nodded slowly, then smiled.

She returned the smile. "My lord?"

"I choose to trust you."

"Is this wise, Highness?"

"Wise and necessary. You have eyes and ears where I do not, and you have a mind capable of understanding and communicating subtlety. I need you. Nalenyr needs you."

"You do me great honor with this trust, Highness."

"And I give to you a great burden." In low tones, Cyron explained all he knew about the invasion. She, in her subtle way, provided him with more information. When he noted that the invaders had reached at least as far as Muronek, she gently corrected him. "I believe, your Highness, you meant to say 'Talanite.' "

She took his recital of facts well and seemed no more alarmed than she would have been if he suggested it would rain that evening. When he finished, he looked at her and fell silent. He drained his cup and returned it to the table.

She refilled it. Setting the pot down again, she rested her hands on her thighs and faced south, as if she could see all the way to Kelewan.

"The Virine, Highness, have ever been secure in their history as the Empire's capital province. They have more people, more crops, more of everything save the spirit which the Naleni possess. For a long while I resided there, in the Illustrated City, but I moved north seeking the future. Their complacency will be their undoing. They may already have been undone."

Cyron's stomach began to tighten. "Then the invasion will take us, too?"

"I am not a fortune-teller. Your precautions are wise. They must be taken in stealth, lest panic reign." She slowly rotated her cup a handful of degrees. "There will come a point where the news will spread, and you must be positioned to respond. This is reminiscent of the Turasynd invasion: all must be called to service, and you must guarantee that no Cataclysm will follow."

He blinked. "Is that a claim I can make?"

She shook her head. "No, but does it matter? The Cataclysm *may* kill, but the invaders *will* kill. The dead will not hold you to account, and the survivors will praise your name that things were not worse."

"For someone who says she is not a fortune-teller, this is a dire prognostication."

She fixed him with a stare that made him shiver. "A fortune can be ignored. My warning cannot. Accept that and act accordingly, or the Komyr Dynasty will not live out the year."

Chapter Twenty-one

6th day, Month of the Dragon, Year of the Rat
9th Year of Imperial Prince Cyron's Court
163rd Year of the Komyr Dynasty
737th year since the Cataclysm
Princes' Road East, Erumvirine

When the Soth Gloon and the one-armed boy first sought to join the caravan of refugees my warriors were shadowing, voices had been raised against them. Their addition did bring the group's number to twenty-seven, which should have been seen as auspicious. But those who feared the Gloon said that he should not be counted and that the boy wasn't even half a man. Urardsa made hopeful pronouncements, and he even sounded sincere—though I was not certain if he believed what he was saying or if he was trying to command me to make it come true.

Moraven had known Pavynti Syolsar before, but her new name, Ranai Ameryne, suited her much better. Her time at *Serrian* Istor had given her a direction and purpose, and Dunos' presence had reinforced it. He had remembered her, and she distantly recalled him. She had set about training him to be a swordsman, though a long knife was all he could wield at the moment. Despite that, he'd done much damage in the skirmishes we'd fought, and was able to creep about silently enough to be *vrilridin.*

Swordsmanship's loss would be a gain to the art of assassins.

The other person I'd rescued from the hill had immediately prostrated himself before me when he learned who I was. He'd called himself Deshiel Tolo and told others he was a cousin of mine. He begged forgiveness and I granted it—he was a very skilled swordsman and welcome to the name. When not on his belly, he stood as tall as I did, though he was lighter. His long black hair and grey eyes contributed to our similarity, and it was easy enough to believe we could be mistaken as cousins or brothers. The crest he wore, the leopard hunting, and his penchant for the southern dialect, marked him as someone from the Five Princes.

Given his skill with a sword and our needs, I forgave him.

The knot of refugees *did* find themselves very lucky. Though they made as much haste as they could, the Princes' Road was not meant for speed. Most commercial traffic passed up the river because the road twisted a scenic path between the capital and the coast. The Virine Princes traveled to the coast on it each year before the monsoon season, so they had beautified it. In places they had hills created, streambeds shifted, and even forests planted for shade. It had been an ambitious project, which had killed many of the peasantry in its making, and now was killing more.

As fast as the refugees tried to travel, they could not outpace the enemy. This suited us well, for we used them as bait. The enemy would send out scouts to locate stragglers—though they attacked them more out of hunger than any apparent desire to halt word of their advance.

Along the Princes' Road, their scouts disappeared.

The three of us were not alone, and before the fight at the Singing Creek, we actually outnumbered the refugees. My scouts gathered the hale and hearty regardless of their combat experience. I did not bother to learn their names, which saved me the bother of forgetting them when they died, but a couple of our number were worth the effort.

As dusk fell on the sixth day I knew the balance of things had begun to shift. Four people fleeing east joined the group, numbering them at thirty-one. Try as I might, I could not manipulate numbers to discover any sign of good fortune. Then came the first reports from my scouts that a group of the *vhangxi* approached. They appeared more numerous than the other scouting cadres and in better order, leading me to believe they had become more intelligent or cautious. I wanted to believe the latter, but any commander who bases plans on his enemy's stupidity is himself a fool.

We watched and waited in a grove of flame-leafed trees as our party made camp. The refugees who had joined them had reported no sign of the enemy to the west, and our bait took that as a good sign. So instead of taking up defensive positions, they all gathered to gossip and exchange news.

If we could not hold back the *vhangxi,* they would all be slaughtered. And as much as I detested their foolishness, I still needed them. I briefed Deshiel and Ranai, then took command of a dozen men who, prior to our meeting, had only threshed grain and gigged toads. The two of them took their squads out into the darkness, and we waited as we had so many nights before.

This night, though, we did do one thing that we had not done before. In the past, I would block the road as a highwayman might by felling a tree across it. The *vhangxi* would stop to move it. While they were thus engaged, we would fall upon them from the front and both sides of the road, slaughtering them mercilessly.

This time we set up a bit differently. My group hid on the north side of the road just past a thicket of thornedberry bushes. Ranai positioned her people, including the handful of archers we had, twenty yards down on the south side. Deshiel set up further to the east and back, ready to circle around north to cut the road behind the scouts. Since Ranai's people would launch the attack and thus be most vulnerable, we had sharpened stakes and driven them into the ground before her position, in the hopes that rampaging *vhangxi* would impale themselves as they attacked.

The enemy crept up the road, taking great care as they went. In the past, they had jostled each other like boys at play, but now they came with flat eyes wide, watching the forest. With such huge eyes I assumed they could see well at night, but how well I could not guess. In the past it had not mattered much and, as we would engage them closely, I didn't think it would matter to us either.

Ranai let a half dozen get past her position, then black arrows sped from darkness and scythed through the *vhangxi.* Four went down, stuck through their chests. A half dozen sprang off the road toward Ranai's position, but an equal number leaped the other way. Attacking an ambushing force head-on was the only way to defeat it, but the *vhangxi* had never done that before. Moreover, their action suggested they had analyzed our tactics and, anticipating a trap, planned a counter.

More arrows flew, dropping another pair of *vhangxi.* Those who had been following loped forward. Some cut into the woods almost immediately, but others came past the point of ambush, then drove in, looking to encircle Ranai's force. This revealed tactical thinking on a level unseen before. They knew what we did and had figured out how to counter it.

Which meant it was time to do something else.

Without even bothering to draw my swords, I broke from cover and sprinted down the road. A heartbeat later—or a half dozen, given how their hearts were pounding—my troopers followed me. They came as quiet as death and when I pointed south, they poured into the woods and hit the *vhangxi* in the flank.

Further east, from the darkness, someone shouted a command, and more of the hulking beasts came running.

I had no time to consider what I had heard. The enemy who had gone north now emerged from the woods to attack south—only to find me in their way. My first draw-cut opened a *vhangxi* from hip to shoulder. His guts gushed out in a wet rush, and he collapsed atop the steaming heap. Drawing my second sword, I bisected a skull before spinning away from slashing claws which, with one circular cut, I amputated at the wrist.

A quick thrust finished that one, then crosscut slashes beheaded the next. Dropping to a knee, I allowed a leaper to pass above me. His claws raked through air while my right blade raked through his stomach. He landed hard, bounced, and rolled, entangling himself in his entrails.

Coming up, I stepped back. Claws passed within an inch of my face, but concerned me no more than the touch of a spring breeze. The missed blow twisted the creature, exposing his back to me. I whipped the sword in my left hand up and snapped it flat against his body. The tip bent, spending its energy against a vertebra just below the juncture of neck and shoulders. Without breaking the skin or even loosening a single scale, the blade shattered that bone, severing his spinal cord.

The *vhangxi* collapsed, only able to open and close his mouth as he struggled for breath that would not come.

From the south came the sounds of battle. *Vhangxi* grunted as they struck or were struck, and only the abrupt cessation of the sound differentiated between circumstances. Men screamed, all of them differently. From the quality of those screams, I could tell who would live or die. My mind tallied the sounds and I knew we were giving better than we got, but that this ambush was the last we'd be doing for a long while.

Then a man rode up the road. At least he looked like a man, and wore a man's armor. He reined back as he saw me standing amidst the slaughter. I read no fear on his face and this I welcomed.

The *vhangxi,* having no discernible facial expressions, had been unsatisfactory foes.

The armored rider looked at me and spoke. He addressed me in a dialect I'd not heard in a long time. Moraven had never heard it. By the time he had come to be in Phoyn Jatan's care, such formal and precise language, as well as the special dialect in which it was delivered, had long since passed from vogue. Those who had used it the most had died, and it had died with them.

I stood there, my swords dripping, then bowed my head. Though my mouth had difficulty with the words, I answered him in kind and stepped back down the road to a clear spot. With the tip of my right blade I scribed a circle. Its diameter was the road's width. When I reached the point where I had started it, I spun on my heel, presenting him my back. Then I marched to the opposite side, resheathed my blades, and turned to face him.

He'd removed his helmet, then doffed his breastplate and gauntlets. He did not bother to remove the armored skirts or mail and greaves on his legs—the rules of the formal duel he offered precluded slashing legs. His robe and overshirt bore the crest of a bear's paw, which would have marked him as a simple citizen of Erumvirine.

A blind man could have seen he was neither. Sharpened ears poked up through his black hair. His flesh had a blue tint to it, which made him very dark in the night. His amber eyes, however, glowed like those of a cat. I assumed he could see as well as one in the darkness, and likely had reflexes to match. Though he did not seem hurried in anything he did, he was ready to strike.

He bowed in my direction, holding it for a respectful time, but hardly as long as I was due. I returned the bow and held it for as long as befitted a peasant new-come to the sword. Though he covered his reaction well, his eyes tightened enough to tell me I'd drawn first blood.

Sounds of fighting in the woods tapered off. More important, I still caught tingles of *jaedun*. The strongest came from Ranai, and some came from Deshiel. The weakest came from Grieka—but mastering the wasp-flail had ever been difficult. I even caught a hint of Luric Dosh and the havoc he wrought with a spear, scribing his own circle with the blood of *vhangxi*.

My foe drew his sword and struck the first Crane guard. With his forward leg lifted and that foot planted against his right knee, his left arm drawn up and his sword high but back, it looked dramatic, but was seldom practical in actual combat. While it countered the Tiger and Wolf forms well, he'd not paid attention. I might wear the black tiger hunting, but I'd killed his troops as an Eagle. He should have adopted a Snake form to face me, but my slight had stung him and he wished to show he understood some of the more complex forms.

I understood them as well, so I stood there and waited. I did admire how he maintained his balance. His arms did not tremble or otherwise betray fatigue. He didn't sway at all. He waited, knowing he had chosen a form that invited an attack. Given my arrogance, he clearly expected one and, had I had any way to measure his skill, I might have obliged him. With him being an unknown quantity, the only invitation I would accept was the one to join him in the circle.

I don't know how long we waited, but my people slew the last of the *vhangxi* in the interim. A storyteller would have measured the duration in days. Some of my companions, and all of his, measured it in lifetimes. All sounds of battle ceased and my companions—half the number they had been earlier—stopped well outside the circle. Some watched and others—those wiser—drew their own circles for protection and peered through the lenses of amulets meant to ward off magic.

My foe, still without exhibiting any fatigue, slowly

extended his left leg and lowered himself into a crouch on the right. His sword remained high, but came down to point toward me. His left arm curled down, forearm parallel to his waist as he finally adopted Cobra third position—though those watching likely identified the form as Scorpion.

I drew my right leg up, touching my foot to my left knee. My sword I held high in my left hand, higher than he had. My right arm mirrored his left. I allowed myself a smirk and curled my ring and little fingers in—hardly the perfect Crane form he had displayed. I mocked him and he knew it; and I did it while daring to invite an attack.

He did nothing to conceal his consternation. If he waited as I had, he was just aping me. If he attacked, he would be less patient, more impetuous, less mature. *Less worthy*. Then again, if he killed me, none of that would matter.

He attacked.

As he came in, I read how he expected the exchange to go. He would lunge at my throat, and my sword would come down in a parry. I would bat his blade aside, but he would flip his wrist and use the momentum I imparted to slash me from nipple to hip on the right.

He came in, extending his blade, lunging. His right leg pushed off, his left bent. His blade's point, without a quiver to it, flew at my throat. His eyes watched the target and also watched my blade, waiting for it to fall, waiting for the first contact. At that vibration, he would flip his wrist and open me. His slash would also hit my right arm, slashing tendon and muscle, perhaps even breaking bone. I would be sorely wounded and the duel's outcome would be decided.

But in his planning and anticipation, he had not found

the path to victory. He did not really thrust *at* my throat, he thrust *toward* it, knowing his blade would never find it. He had planned for my counter, and when it did not come—though he struck with the swiftness of a Cobra—he had no true target.

As he attacked, I lunged forward. My right leg slid down and planted itself just past his left heel. I leaned to the right and his blade shot over my left shoulder. My sword, held high, never even began to fall.

As we came face-to-face, I read his fear.

And he read my triumph.

My right hand closed on the hilt of my other sword and I drew it in an instant. The razored edge slashed up beneath his skirts and sank deep into the junction of thigh and groin. I drew it up in a long cut and it came free with a hot splash of femoral blood.

He began to fall backward slowly.

A heartbeat for me, forever for him.

He did try to flip his wrist and cut my throat as he toppled, but my robe's collar blunted his feeble strike. I watched shock and betrayal blossom on his face as he fell, and knew it would melt into a mask of disdain.

My other sword whipped down and his head rolled away to spare me his opinion.

Ranai, standing closest to me, dropped to a knee. Her expression and the tone of her voice betrayed confusion and mild offense. "What have we just witnessed, Master?"

"An enemy who believes that by mirroring our forms, using our blades and ancient formulae, they are worthy of respect and honor." I pointed a sword to the east. "Has anything they have done so far been honorable?"

She shook her head. "No, Master."

"No matter how they appear, that is their nature. Do not forget it. Do not be lured in." I kicked the sword from my foe's lifeless hand. "They are not what they pretend to be, and we cannot be what they assume us to be. As Taichun once taught, one must know his foe to defeat him. This is true. We have one path to victory."

She looked up. "Learn as much about them as possible?"

"No, Ranai." I wiped my blades on the dead man's robe, then slid them home again. "We will make ourselves unknowable, then they can never win."

Chapter Twenty-two

7th day, Month of the Dragon, Year of the Rat
9th Year of Imperial Prince Cyron's Court
163rd Year of the Komyr Dynasty
737th year since the Cataclysm
Ixyll

Try as he might, Ciras Dejote could not shake the feeling they were being watched. He saw no one in the Wastes; he found no footprints—even old ones—to indicate that anyone else was out there. But, regardless of an utter lack of evidence, he knew they were being watched—and Borosan didn't help matters by agreeing with him.

He would have been happy to ascribe it to paranoia, or the influence of the sword he now bore, but it was rooted in something far more substantial than that. After killing whatever Dragright had become, he'd trailed out after the giant. At first the man's panicked footprints were easy to follow. He'd run past where the looters had hobbled their horses and conveniently stepped in manure. That petered out eventually, so Ciras returned to the camp and waited for daylight to continue the pursuit.

In camp, they cleaned up the bodies and piled rocks over them to slow down whatever scavengers might lurk in Ixyll. They contented themselves with a cold meal that night, and both wrote out prayers on strips of cloth, which they left as streamers over the tomb entrance.

When they awoke, the streamers were still in place, and the hole in the tomb's slab had been repaired fully. Ciras had run his hand over it and not only could feel no seam around where the repair had been performed, but could not even find any stray scars from where the sledge had hit off target.

To make matters worse, after they collected the looters' horses and continued west, they found the giant's body—or what was left of it. Something had stripped most of the meat off the bones and scattered them, but both men were able to reconstruct enough to determine this had been their quarry. More important, their work allowed them to make a rough guess at the cause of death.

Something, it appeared, roughly a foot in diameter, had punched through his chest, pulverized his spine, *and* powdered the rock upon which he lay. Borosan guessed he'd have to have been impaled by a wharf piling heaved by a ballista. The utter absence of so much as a splinter cast doubts on that explanation, but Ciras couldn't come up with anything better.

But still, both events could have been dismissed as some sort of magical retribution for disturbing the grave. The problem with that explanation—aside from the fact that no one in the Nine knew how to lay such an enchantment since the Cataclysm—came from the fact that the sword had been left with Ciras. Even before they cleaned up the corpses, and even before he'd taken care of his own sword, he'd cleaned and oiled the blade. He'd slept that first night with it beside his own sword, and couldn't imagine why it had been left to him.

As they rode around a hill, his left hand fell to the ancient sword's hilt. In studying the blade he'd learned a lot about it. Though he did not recognize the maker's mark stamped into the blade, the general form indicated it was of Virine manufacture.

The sigils worked along the blade defied deciphering, though both he and Borosan made attempts. They'd been written in the old Imperial script. While both men were literate, and had even been exposed to Imperial writing, in the time since the Cataclysm the Ministries of Harmony had revised and streamlined the six thousand, five hundred, and sixty-one characters one needed to know to be considered educated. Clerks would be required to learn nine times that many—and ministers, it was said, could command even more.

But the true difficulty with picking out the message was that it seemed to change. Ciras had noticed that effect, but had said nothing. Borosan, without telling him, had written down the inscriptions, then found they changed. They tried to pin it to time of day, weather, and direction they were heading, but if there was a pattern, they couldn't discern it.

Both of them reached the same conclusion about the sword: it had belonged to one of Prince Nelesquin's *vanyesh*—although they each acknowledged knowing next to nothing about the *vanyesh*. Down through the years any truth about them had been lost. Aside from knowing they were sorcerers who traveled with an evil prince, neither man had any information.

Ciras reined his horse to a halt beside Borosan's mount. They'd crested a hill that overlooked a vast but sunken plain, which angled off to the northwest between two lines of mountains. "We'll be two days on that plain if we just strike out across it, don't you think?"

Borosan nodded. "If we keep close to one set of mountains or the other, we should find water. All the green veins running into the plain indicate water, but I would just as soon avoid as many valleys as we can."

"Agreed. And I believe you're right. The wild magic flows like water and seeps into the low points. Every valley we've seen is more alive with it than elsewhere."

Borosan nodded as if he'd only half heard. Ciras had become used to that. The inventor leaned back, pulled a journal from his saddlebags, and made a note. "Shall we camp here?"

"Back down the hill, yes, by the spring."

They retraced their steps and made camp. Neither knew what Ixyll had been before the Cataclysm, and anticipating what it would be from day to day was impossible. The wild magic had scoured the world down to its stony bones in some places and yet, in others, grasses formed meadows and trees grew into groves. Granted, most often the trees were odd—like having gorgeous blossoms that became fist-sized fruit in a matter of hours, only to burst into flame shortly thereafter. The grasses seemed more normal. Though they were seldom a simple green, the horses ate them with no apparent ill effects.

They made camp on a bluesward and collected deadwood—first making sure it was truly dead and truly wood. Borosan made a fire and Ciras stepped well away from it before he started his exercises.

Borosan looked up after Ciras had stripped himself to the waist. "Finally decided you will use it?"

The swordsman nodded and slipped the ancient sword into the sash around his middle. "A swordsman is a union of sword and man. The blade I have carried with me has been in my family for generations. It is not enchanted—it's not one of your *gyanrigot*—but it helps me focus. It is hard to explain."

Borosan warmed his hands over the fire. "I've heard it explained that it is easier to walk in boots that have been broken-in rather than those that are brand-new."

"But you scoff at this."

Borosan shook his head. "Not at all. You think a blade that is well used helps you to focus. If I were to use *gyanri* to build a blade, my purpose would still be to aid the warrior. The difference would be that the focus and guidance would be stronger because the person using it would know little of fighting."

Ciras' expression soured. "That would be terribly wrong."

"So I have come to learn through my association with you, Master Dejote." Borosan smiled. "If I venture into designing weapons, I will work on armor, to keep people alive."

"But that's no better than . . ."

"Isn't it? Your objection to my *thanatons* is that they could kill without reason. The same would hold true for *gyanrigot* swords and spears. They would make anyone capable of fighting and killing without training. I agree that helping people kill without discretion is wrong. The reverse of that, however, should not be true. I would be saving people from dying."

The swordsman folded his arms over his chest. He didn't like Borosan's turning his argument back on itself. There was something wrong with what he was saying, but on the surface it was hard to argue with. *If I say it is wrong to stop people from dying, I am as foolish as those who would kill without discrimination. Death is death, and if one believes it should be limited, one cannot pick and choose cases and be consistent.*

"If you make someone invulnerable, Borosan, then he will be as dangerous with a simple knife as he might be with a *gyanrigot* sword."

"But he will likely do little harm *and* the armor will work only until the *thaumston* is exhausted. Facing someone such as you, he would do no harm. Your attacks would wear the *thaumston* down and you would kill him eventually."

"What if someone else supplies him a *gyanrigot* sword?"

That question contorted Borosan's face. "I'd not thought of that."

Ciras nodded. "It should be considered." Then he turned away from the inventor as the chubby man went digging for his journal. Ciras took a deep breath, exhaled slowly, and began his exercises.

He drew the sword and dropped into the third Dragon form. Closing his eyes, he imagined a foe in fourth Wolf across from him. Ciras stamped a foot and the man came in, slashing low. The swordsman easily leaped above that strike and was ready to land in sixth Dragon. Instead, his right foot flicked out and caught his enemy in the face, snapping his head around.

Ciras landed in a crouch and spun, aware of another foe coming in at his back. This enemy was a Turasynd of the Tiger clan. Strips of orange fur covered his arms and chest. The Turasynd's heavy saber whistled down in a cut that would bisect him, but his own sword came up and around in a double-handed circular parry.

Ciras would have slashed back across the Turasynd's body, but for awareness of another attack at his back. He stabbed back over his right shoulder and could feel the blade punching through breastbone and heart. He looked up and saw his imaginary Turasynd foe looming over him, transfixed by both the blade and surprise. The enemy had raised his sword over his head with two hands and it still descended, but Ciras caught his wrists and pulled, flipping the man forward and into the other Tiger.

Ciras came up and whirled, slashing blindly at waist height. A third Tiger folded over the blade's edge. Ciras slid his blade free and continued the spin. He dropped his blade's tip, then slashed up, catching the first Tiger beneath the chin as he threw off his dead comrade. Both of them fell back into a tangle of limbs, allowing Ciras to leap over them and turn to face other enemies.

The supply of Turasynd seemed endless. Endless and eager. They rushed forward, two coming for each one fallen. Ciras retreated, then lunged, slashed, then parried and riposted. He beat blades down, then cut above them, or ducked a blow and stabbed deep through an enemy's vitals. His blade licked out, opening armpits and groins, throats and bellies. He had no time to employ the fine cuts that would all but sever a head or cleave wrist from arm.

Scenes blurred as foes came faster and faster. Some he

saw as whole and normal, others appeared far larger than they ever could have been. Some even appeared in degrees of decay, as if they had clawed their way from a grave to have a second chance at the man who had killed them. Regardless of how they looked or moved, Ciras fought each back, ending their lives again and again.

Then he spun to the right, coming about in the same cut he'd used to take Dragright's leg off. His blade bit deep into his enemy's left side. It carved through his robe and overshirt, the blade's forte all but reaching his spine. It would have, too, had Ciras not stopped, had he not let go of the blade.

But he did, and sank to his knees. The visions he'd been fighting melted. The sword thudded to the ground before him and sweat stung his eyes. He'd have been happy if the sweat burned them completely from his head, but he knew that even that would not steal the vision of what he'd seen.

Borosan knelt at his side and pressed a waterskin into his hands. "What's wrong, Ciras?"

The swordsman didn't answer. He raised the waterskin and directed the stream over his face and head. He shook his head, spraying water, but Borosan did not complain. Ciras drank a bit of water, spat it out, then drank again and swallowed. He waited a moment to see if he would keep it down, then opened his eyes but stared straight ahead, down the length of the blade.

"How long was I exercising?"

"Nine minutes, perhaps eighteen, no more than that." The inventor shrugged. "I didn't really pay attention until you started mumbling."

The swordsman glanced at him. "What did I say?"

"I don't know, but I didn't like it. Once you started

speaking, strange things began to happen." Borosan pointed to Ciras' left.

Ciras followed the line of his finger. The bluesward showed signs of where he'd been. His feet had depressed grasses but, more significantly, his footprints had filled with blood.

"What happened, Ciras?"

"I don't know. I began my exercises as always, then they became something more. My foes became Turasynd. They came in an endless stream." The swordsman looked around, baffled. "I think, perhaps, they all died here. The man who owned that blade met them here and killed them. Their ghosts recognized the sword and wanted revenge."

Borosan's mismatched eyes widened. "I'll start packing now."

Ciras smiled. "That would be wise."

He remained on his knees and looked at the blade a little longer. He would help Borosan pack, but for the moment was glad for the other man's preoccupation. He knew the inventor would ask the logical question at some point, and wanted a chance to think about the answer before he ever gave it.

Why did I stop?

The image of the blade slicing through a robe came again. The robe had been white save where blood began to seep into it. The red line spread slowly upward, toward the crest embroidered in black on the overshirt's back. A tiger hunting.

A crest he had seen before.

And recognition of the crest prompted recognition of the man he was attacking. The size, the shape, the length of his hair. Ciras even knew the man had a scar on his left side that matched the cut perfectly.

He looked down at the blade. "Why would I see you plunging into my master's back?"

Neither the blade, glinting red and gold in the firelight, nor the sigils slithering through shadow, provided him an answer.

Chapter Twenty-three

7th day, Month of the Dragon, Year of the Rat
9th Year of Imperial Prince Cyron's Court
163rd Year of the Komyr Dynasty
737th year since the Cataclysm
Thyrenkun, Felarati
Deseirion

Prince Pyrust sat in the very chair Keles Anturasi had used as he listened to the Mother of Shadows report. The fire blazed at his left hand, snapping and popping. He stretched his legs out, forcibly ignoring the heat.

"This report is difficult for me to hear, Delasonsa. From here, I can see the great work Anturasi has accomplished. Returning this much land to cultivation will not solve our food shortage, but it will help. He's guaranteed Felarati can continue to grow beyond my lifetime. His value to me is considerable."

The crone bowed her head. "This I understand, Highness. But his conduct with your wife is unacceptable."

"To whom?"

Her head came up. "To me—for one, and it should be to you. She carries your child."

Pyrust's eyes half lidded. "Her child will be born as my heir. She knows this. We all do, and there is nothing she can do to make things otherwise. Even rumors of the child having been fathered by Anturasi will not matter. Besides, you tell me they have not slept together yet."

The old woman's grey cloak closed and shrouded her form, making her seem smaller than before. "It is not for your wife's lack of trying, Highness."

"Then the fault is hers."

"But she cannot be slain. Anturasi can. Our people found him in Ixyll, very ill. They did all they could for him, but he succumbed to some illness. We can return his body, or burn him and return his ashes. We could even send Prince Cyron the heads of the fools who did not get him here quickly enough."

"Those are plans that shall be held against the future." Pyrust rose and turned his back to the fire. "My ambitions aside, my purpose is to make my nation stronger. Anturasi aids that. As for my wife . . . he is never leaving Deseirion. He may have her all he wants as long as she gives me another child or three. I know this is a matter of honor for you, and I appreciate your devotion to my family. But recall that the children are my blood, and to them goes your allegiance."

Delasonsa's head came up, her eyes hot. "Beware her frustration, Highness. You may see her as a broodmare, but she sees herself differently. She could do you harm."

"And this is why you will continue to watch her. You will also find someone else to seduce Anturasi."

"Done and done." The old woman held his stare as a

web holds a fly. "And if they seek to escape, do I kill them?"

"Her, certainly. Anturasi is too valuable to let go so easily."

"As you desire, Highness."

"Thank you." Pyrust clasped his hands behind his back. "Now, my Grand Minister reported to me on the state of international affairs, and I have noted a curious lack of information about Erumvirine. He suggested couriers have been delayed by bandits in Helosunde. I've heard no other reports about bandits. You would have told me of them, wouldn't you?"

"If they existed in more than your minister's imagination, of course, Highness." The Mother of Shadows shook her head slowly. "Something is happening in the south. Cyron is moving Helosundian mercenaries and Naleni Dragon Guards south to the Virine border. He's raising troops from the inland counties to hold the north. This works well for us, as our agent has been fomenting revolution among the same, and Cyron has just given them reason to draw closer to the capital while fully armed."

Pyrust arched an eyebrow at her. " 'Something is happening in the south'? That is hardly your usual precision in reporting, Delasonsa."

"True, Highness, but it is also the truth. My Virine assets are unusually quiet. There is enough limited communication that I know they still exist, but they have no credible information to offer."

The fire roared for a moment, then a log exploded into a shower of sparks and embers that scattered well past the Prince's vacated chair. The two of them jumped back, then stepped further back as the sparks began to spin, sweeping the embers into their tight embrace. Fire whirled into a column, then congealed into a humanoid form with the head of a wolf. The fiery creature appropriated the chair, dragging it closer to the hearth as it sat.

Pyrust stared for a heartbeat at the creature, then dropped to a knee and bowed deeply. "Greetings, Grija, Lord of Death. You honor me."

"I do no such thing, Pyrust. I give you an opportunity. You are bound to my realm—all mortals are—and the only question is how many of your fellows you have sent to me. Your dead shall be your slaves in my realm."

Delasonsa, who had remained standing, snorted. "The Prince is too wise to be seduced by your lies. Thousands may slave under him, but he will slave beneath the one who slays him. What is the benefit of a few or many?"

Grija laughed lightly, jaws agape. "I shall enjoy continuing this discussion in my realm, Mother of Shadows. You shall not." A fiery hand flicked in her direction and Pyrust's assassin collapsed.

"You do right to value her, Pyrust, for she defends you as a hawk would defend her own young. Yet she thinks she could defend you from me, which is foolishness. She would prolong a discussion that is best brief."

The Prince nodded. "When you spoke to me before, you said I would drive many through the gates of your realm."

"That was true then, and will be more so now. I have seen great things from you but the circumstances have shifted. Two who were meant for my realm have eluded me. They have died, yet they live in defiance of all that which is ordered in the heavens. This is an omen that heralds the arrival of a tenth god."

Pyrust, who had never given too much thought to the gods, found that prospect surprising. "Can there be a tenth god?"

"You might as well ask if there can be ten more or ten fewer. There have been countless gods. The Viruk had their gods, and the Soth the same. Even men have different gods. We warp mortals, and they change us. It is all the stuff of endless and tedious discussions among priests—and I restrict it to the Sixth Hell."

The flaming god leaned forward. "It is also immaterial to you, Pyrust. All that matters is this: two people meant for my realm have eluded me. They have accomplished this because the tenth god is invading heaven. And, as go the heavens, so goes the earth—for the tenth god's terrestrial forces are invading Erumvirine."

The Desei Prince slowly stood. "And this is why no news flows north."

"And why the Son of the Dragon Throne throws his troops south. His intent may be good, but his means and timing are not." A flaming tongue licked flickering fangs. "The initial invasion sent many to my realm, and perhaps was meant to distract me from those who are missing. Now a second wave has come, and Virine defenses cannot hold it."

Pyrust's jade eyes narrowed. "Where are they attacking? Show me."

"Show you?"

"Yes, damn you. You're a god. You conjured a body; conjure me a map."

Grija lunged up, then reached an oversized hand back into the hearth. He scooped up fire as if it were sand and let it pour over the floor, where it puddled inches away from Delasonsa's limp form. The flames became incandescent fluid, then dark lines ran through them marking the rivers and borders. Flames danced up for mountains, then, on Erumvirine's eastern edge, the flames died completely.

Pyrust's stomach began to knot. *A quarter of the nation is gone. The invaders are driving straight for Kelewan.* A momentary flash of jealousy ran through him. His dreams of marching triumphantly into Kelewan died, for he knew the city he might take now would never match the city he had lusted after for so long.

"How long since they invaded?"

"A month."

"And they've come that far? I am impressed."

"You should be afraid."

"Fear avails me nothing. Respect for my enemy is vital."

The death god squatted and peered down at him. "Do not be disdainful of me, Pyrust."

He met Grija's gaze without fear. "If I am to be your scythe, do not complain that I am sharp."

The god sat back and chuckled. "You are not the only scythe."

Pyrust nodded. "I shall consider well what you have told me."

"And act on it?"

"You will know one way or the other."

Grija stared at him for a moment, then nodded curtly. "Make your decision wisely, Pyrust. If there is a tenth god, there will be a Tenth Hell, and I shall reserve it especially for you."

Before the Prince could reply, the fiery avatar imploded and flowed back into the hearth. Aside from Delasonsa's body and the little flames licking at his chair, no sign existed of the god's visit. Pyrust waited, thinking he might awaken, but he did not.

The Desei Prince frowned. When Grija had first spoken to him months ago, it seemed that his dreams of becoming Emperor would come true. Certainly, any campaign would have resulted in many deaths. Succeed or fail, his effort would swell the population of the death god's realm.

This manifestation, however, betokened something entirely different. If the god of Death was powerful enough to intervene in the affairs of men, he could have simply slain the tenth god's troops. But the fact that people had escaped death meant his power was waning. War was being waged on the earth as it was in heaven, and Grija clearly needed a terrestrial ally. *Or allies. After all, I am not the only scythe.*

Divine politics aside, the information he'd been given was useful. He'd known Cyron was moving troops, and now he knew why. The troops on Nalenyr's northern border were unreliable, and perhaps even rebellious. Punching through Helosunde and into Nalenyr would hardly be bloodless, but it now seemed possible.

It is also necessary.

Grija had said it, but Pyrust knew it even before the death god had provided the details. Cyron might well be a genius in organizing his nation and accumulating wealth, but he was not the military leader any of the other Komyr princes had been. If he were, he would not be sending troops south to his border with Erumvirine; he would be sending them straight into Erumvirine. It would be far better to fight any wars on someone else's territory—whether you intended to keep it or cede it back later.

Pyrust had choices. He had Helosunde between his nation and Nalenyr. Even if the invaders chose to turn north and come up the coast, their supply lines would be stretched beyond all imagining by the time they reached Deseirion, and Pyrust could guarantee they'd find not a single morsel to eat in his realm. His troops, though not as numerous as other nations', were well trained and would fight hard. He could hold the enemy in Helosunde and keep his realm safe.

Or I can fight them further south. While part of him still dreamed of taking Moriande and Kelewan, a greater part of him now contemplated their defense. *If we are divided, we shall fall.*

But no one would agree to be united beneath the Hawk banner. Even if Cyron realized this was the only chance for his realm to survive, he'd not agree. Surrendering command of his troops to his Desei counterpart would spell the end of his dynasty.

"But I shall need his troops and his nation to defend us all." Pyrust frowned. If the tenth god's invasion had inspired fear in the death god, there was no way to see that as anything but a disaster for mankind.

Pyrust sank to a knee beside the Mother of Shadows and shook her shoulder. She jerked, then rolled away. He felt certain she'd come up with a dagger in hand, but she kept it hidden beneath her cloak.

"Highness, I have failed you."

"No, Delasonsa, you have not. We have much work to do."

"What, my Prince?"

Pyrust stood. "You will send word to your agents in Nalenyr. They will encourage an open break between the inland lords and Moriande. I want the former armed and ready to join me. I will also need you to slay the leaders of Helosunde's dissident factions, though you will spare my wife's brother. In her name, a message will be sent to the Council of Ministers offering an alliance and peace between Deseirion and Helosunde."

"They will not believe it."

"You will tell them I will grant Helosunde full autonomy when my heir is born."

She looked at him closely. "Are you well, Highness?"

"My next order will answer your concern, Mother of Shadows. I want every unit possible to head south. This includes the training cadres and the garrisons on the Turasynd borders. Any man or woman fifteen to thirty will report to a unit unless their occupation is vital to the war effort. Find me some cowards of whom I can make examples and crucify them at crossroads."

"As you wish, my lord."

"Within a month, Mother of Shadows, we march south." Pyrust pointed in that direction. "It's not empire we seek, but if we repel the invaders, it is empire we shall have."

Chapter Twenty-four

10th day, Month of the Dragon, Year of the Rat
9th Year of Imperial Prince Cyron's Court
163rd Year of the Komyr Dynasty
737th year since the Cataclysm
Vnielkokun, Moriande
Nalenyr

Pelut Vniel waited until his servants had poured tea and withdrawn before he bowed his head to his visitor. "You honor my house with your visit, Count Turcol. I apologize for not having been able to see you earlier, but my household has been in an uproar as we prepare to celebrate the anniversary of the Prince's ascension to the Dragon Throne. If you are here on that blessed day, please accept my invitation to be your host."

The westron lord returned the bow, but without grace or sincerity. "I believed, Minister, that I had communicated the urgency of my business with you to your subordinates. Perhaps they do not serve you well."

Pelut did not immediately reply. Instead, he sipped his tea. "In Miromil they train monkeys to climb to the highest reaches of the tea trees and to pick only the most delicate leaves. This variety is called Jade Cloud, and my servants have been given specific instruction in its preparation. I believe you will like it."

Turcol did not so much as glance at the tea on the little table beside which he knelt. "I appreciate your hospitality, but I have little time for it."

"There is always time for being hospitable, my lord."

Turcol might have caught a hint of warning in his voice, or had remembered he had come to ask a favor of Pelut. So, he did not reply and instead sipped the tea—far too quickly—then offered thanks.

Pelut returned his cup to the table beside him. "You were fortunate to be in Moriande when the request for troops was issued. You will, no doubt, be joining them at the Helosunde border very soon."

"I will be joining them, yes." Turcol's eyes slitted. "I thought to seek your advice on a matter of protocol."

"And what would that be?"

The inland lord squared his shoulders. "Given that our Prince will be celebrating his anniversary, I thought a parade of troops to honor him and the occasion would be appropriate."

Pelut hesitated but let no surprise show on his face. "The Prince eschews such displays, save during the Harvest Festival. His celebrations are usually private. Often he takes a group of courtiers into the countryside for hawking and other pursuits."

"Of this I am aware, Grand Minister. I am also aware that he has sent most of his Keru south, so he is without his customary retinue of bodyguards. I imagine this will cause him to remain in Moriande." Turcol attempted to layer pity onto his expression but, never having felt it before, the effort was transparently false. "I had thought that, since my troops would be in the vicinity four days hence, the Prince might come with us, enjoy our hospitality, and see just how well we will guard the border. It would be a blessing for my troops to see their Prince as well."

Pelut smiled. *Ambition, Count Turcol, is always impatient.* "Your concern for the Prince's welfare is noted and appreciated. Shall I communicate your invitation to His Highness?"

"I would be in your debt. What would you have me do to repay you?"

"I have no idea what service you can perform for me, Count Turcol, beyond that of faithfully securing our border."

His reply clearly frustrated Turcol. Pelut had seen it for what it was: an invitation to suggest killing Cyron and supplanting him. The plot would be obvious to everyone, but Turcol arrogantly believed that his celebrated rise to the throne would blind everyone to the means by which he obtained it.

Turcol nodded. "I am certain you will think of something, Grand Minister, for your wisdom is celebrated throughout Nalenyr."

"Again you honor me." Pelut sipped tea once more, then glanced past his visitor. He'd caught the hint of a shadow against one of the rice-paper-panel walls. He knew Turcol would never spot it. If he did, Pelut already had a stratagem in place for dealing with the situation. His eldest daughter would be found hiding there, claiming she wanted just a glimpse of the famous noble. Pelut would let the man use her as he would, and Turcol would forget any other suspicions.

His vanity would never allow him to believe I had a clerk transcribing our discussion.

Such precautions would have been unnecessary, but Turcol's repeated demands for a meeting had forced Pelut to take them. Even a blind and deaf man who had been clapped in an iron box and sunk to the bottom of the Gold River for fifty years would be aware of the westron's desire to speak with him. Pelut had to assume Prince Cyron knew already, and while Pelut feared no spies in his own household, he assumed the streets outside his small tower would be choked with them by the time the interview had been concluded.

"I should tell you, my lord, that I think it unlikely the Prince will accept your invitation. In fact, I should think the chances of it would be negligible . . ."

"My pleasure and generosity were he to join me would know no bounds!"

Pelut continued speaking, making no response to the outburst. ". . . unless you were perhaps first to invite Prince Eiran and suggest to him you dearly wished Prince Cyron would join you. If you were to say that you would have asked the Prince directly, save that you felt certain he would look down on an offer from such a lowly noble as yourself, I am confident Prince Eiran would use his influence on your behalf. He and Cyron are quite close."

Turcol glanced down, then nodded. "Of course. I should do it that way, yes."

"I would be happy to arrange an audience with Prince Eiran for you."

"If I may ask it of you, please." Turcol tried to make his next question sound casual, but the enthusiasm in his voice betrayed him. "I do have one question—spawned by the desire for continued stability in Nalenyr."

"Please."

"If the unfortunate were to happen . . ."

" 'The unfortunate'?"

"If the Prince were to fall victim to an assassin, a Desei assassin, what would happen next?"

Pelut smiled and shook his head. "Do not concern yourself, my lord. There are no Desei assassins who could penetrate Wentokikun."

Turcol frowned, dark and deep. "No. What if it were *assassins,* a group of them, and they fell upon the Prince while he was coming out to join my troops? What would happen? If he died, I mean."

Though Pelut knew exactly what was being asked, he chose to misunderstand a bit more. "This is all highly unlikely, my lord. Prince Pyrust is quite wise, so any assassins would not be revealed as his agents. I mean, in such an unthinkable scenario as you describe, a band of assassins would need to be at least twenty-seven in number and likely would be disguised as bandits. In fact, we would find nothing to indicate they were not bandits. About the only chance they would have, I should think, would be to attack while you, the Princes, and a few other of your most trusted and brave warriors are relaxing at Memorial Hill, as is the Prince's wont. Then and only then might they kill the Prince. As for the rest of you, if you were able to fight your way clear, well, recall how the people love your father-in-law for having brought Prince Aralias' body back from Helosunde."

Turcol nodded and sipped at his tea again.

Pelut bowed his head. "I hope this does not alarm you, my lord, for I know you would give your life to protect our Prince. You might be wounded even, but his loss would cause you greater pain than any physical wound."

"Of course it alarms me, Grand Minister, and if I thought bandits could harm the Prince, I should never offer my invitation. That is not possible, however, so I shall use the route you suggest."

"I am pleased to be of service."

"My original question, however, dealt with the aftermath of such a grand tragedy. The Prince has no heirs, and his brother died without any as well. In the event of the Prince's death, who would lead our nation?"

Pelut took a long drink of his tea before answering. "You present me with a question for which there is one of many answers—but one that should not be shared outside this room. I trust I have your confidence in this?"

Turcol nodded slowly in agreement. "I understand."

Pelut canted his head to the right. "You must understand that the Prince's lack of an heir by blood or declaration is a situation which I, as Naleni Grand Minister, must address. I look to Helosunde, with its Council of Ministers, and see how their deliberations have been a disaster. I will not have a government of ministers, for we are not of ruling blood. Few people are, and fewer still manifest their blood's full promise."

The count could not conceal a smile. The fact that his family had once been on the Dragon Throne clearly proved he had the bloodlines that could lay claim to it. *And he is certain his bloodline's promise has blossomed full in him.*

"It has struck me, my lord, that to maintain stability and promote the future, we might be required to take extraordinary methods. It has been my thinking that a triumvirate made up of your father-in-law, Duchess Scior, and yourself would provide the proper mixture of wisdom, charisma, experience, and, in your case, vitality to lead our nation into the future. The three of you would have to cooperate, of course, sharing power."

"Yes, yes, I can see that." Turcol's curdled expression made his opinion clear. "Still, we would have to come down to one Prince if our nation was to maintain its legitimacy. While both of the others are wise and powerful, neither of their houses predates the Cataclysm. As with the Komyr, they have risen since the Time of Black Ice."

"Their houses were not unknown before the creation of the Nine."

"But they were not Imperial nobility."

"Very true." Pelut nodded solemnly. "The question for you, my lord, is how best the ministries would serve the ruling triumvirate?"

That comment gave Turcol pause, and his clenching fist did not escape Pelut's notice. "I should think, Grand Minister, that the ministries would serve best to consolidate power in the hands of that one individual best qualified to lead the nation. The duchess, while wise—even if it is a fishwife's cunning—and my father-in-law are both too long in the tooth to provide the sort of continuity needed to carry Nalenyr into the future."

"I should agree with you, my lord, save that both of them have progeny who can carry on. You could well be Count Vroan's practical heir, but if you had heirs of your own, things would be even better."

"True, but were my wife pregnant now, Count Vroan might designate my child his heir, and I would be reduced to a regency. I find this unacceptable, and you should as well."

"I seek only that which is best for our nation."

"And I believe the Grand Minister should see that I am Nalenyr's future."

"*If* the unthinkable happens."

Turcol halted for barely a heartbeat. "Yes, of course, if the unthinkable were to happen. Bandits. It would be terrible."

"So it would, my lord." Pelut glanced down at his cup and the tiny bits of tea leaves gathered at the bottom. "Were that to happen, I think your guidance would be invaluable to our nation. You clearly have thought of this, and such foresight is a value that shall not be discounted."

"And you, Grand Minister, have a clarity of vision, which will guarantee our future."

"My lord is too kind." Pelut bowed to him. "I should not take up more of my lord's time, as I know he is busy. I shall speak with Prince Eiran myself. You will have his answer in a day."

"And the Prince's after that?"

"I believe you shall."

Count Turcol bowed. "Your hospitality is appreciated, and your wisdom even more."

"Be well, my lord. May the gods smile on your future."

"My future is nothing, Minister; the future of my nation is everything." Turcol slid a door panel open and withdrew. He did not close it after him, which Pelut found irritating; but this alone did not decide Turcol's fate.

The Grand Minister drank until his cup was all but empty, then swirled the last of the golden liquor around.

Quickly he inverted it and clapped it down on the small table. He lifted it away from the small puddle and set it down again in a dry spot.

The object of Turcol's visit had been obvious. The Prince's order to gather troops had been the only pretense he needed to consider open rebellion. Pelut had expected him to demand the ministers throw open the gates of Moriande and deliver the Prince to him—which would have been a grand show, to be sure. The assassination attempt was not something he'd expected, and clearly not something Turcol had spent too much time thinking out. His willingness to adopt the blind of bandits showed a flexibility that could be useful, but his comments about succession revealed the difference between flexibility and malleability.

Were he malleable, he would be far more useful. Clearly he desired to be Prince, and considered himself the obvious choice. Pelut had no doubt that Turcol entertained dreams of being welcomed openly by his adoring people—merchants opening their coffers to him, and women opening their thighs. During his reign, the fantasies about the Keru being the Prince's harem would come true, or a Cyrsa would arise from among the Keru, with Turcol's blood on her hands.

Which might not be a bad choice. Marry her to Eiran and we could join two realms.

Still, while that would be an interesting expedient, like as not Eiran would die at the same time as Cyron. While he doubted Turcol had approached the Helosundian ministers, they would seek him out as soon as word got out that he was leading troops on the border. Their need to have Eiran dead would lead Turcol into further plots.

While the prospect of Turcol being prince did not excite Pelut, the idea that he could be rid of Cyron did. He would have preferred a method with more refinement, but dead was dead and a bludgeon worked as well as poison. Cyron posed more of a threat to Nalenyr than Turcol did, and certainly a more immediate one. He had to be dealt with.

Pelut turned his cup back over and read the leaves. Their positions and shapes communicated omens for the future. While they were not as clear as he might have liked, they were sufficient.

The fate of Turcol's effort had been decided.

And with it the fate of Nalenyr itself.

Chapter Twenty-five

12th day, Month of the Dragon, Year of the Rat
9th Year of Imperial Prince Cyron's Court
163rd Year of the Komyr Dynasty
737th year since the Cataclysm
Blackshark, Caxyan

Any hopes Jorim had harbored of keeping the changed nature of his relationship with Nauana secret died very quickly. Shimik had always been happy to spend time with Nauana, but now he doted on her and defended her. He growled at anyone who got too close to her—save Jorim—and sailors bored with life onshore had no trouble figuring out the reason behind the Fennych's behavior.

The Amentzutl accepted this change readily, and Tzihua, the gigantic warrior who had been raised to the *maicana* caste because of his skills in combat, confessed that they'd all expected it to happen. While the interaction of the gods with mortals was not common in their mythology—or history, as Jorim reminded himself—it wasn't unknown. For the most part, everyone had just hoped Tetcomchoa would find his time with the Amentzutl pleasurable.

And Jorim did find it pleasurable. Nauana had been beautiful and exotic, and he'd felt attracted to her when he first saw her. His interaction with her had strengthened that attraction, but he had not thought she had any interest in him. The care with which he undertook his training amplified his feelings for her, and yet he did not read into her actions any emotion.

But reaching out to touch her essence and her willingness to open herself in return revealed all. It was as if he had known her all his life, and the reverse. Curiously, their likes and dislikes, their experiences—though all shaped through cultures that knew nothing of each other—meshed effortlessly. It felt as if they were each half of a coin that had been divided and now had come together again.

Jorim had been in love before—at least a dozen times and sometimes even longer than a month. He had allowed himself to believe that many of his relationships foundered because his familial obligations demanded he travel for long periods of time. But the simple fact was that the relationships had already foundered, and the trips were just a convenient excuse to let things die.

He didn't bear any animosity for the women he'd known. Initial attraction led to discovery, and the dissatisfaction became mutual over time. Everyone is on best behavior when they first meet, then they learn what the other person is truly like. By four months, one knew whether or not a relationship could last.

In six seconds he'd learned that about Nauana, and he knew he could spend the rest of his life with her. He would have hesitated to make that statement, save that he'd opened himself to her, too. She was no longer under the illusion that he was a god-made-man—though she had allowed as how his divinity might be manifesting in the same way a fledgling's molting reveals its true plumage.

He would have rejected that idea, but every Naleni youth had been raised on the tale of Wentiko, the Dragon god, who believed himself an ugly worm until he blossomed into a dragon. Intellectually, Jorim recognized the story as one that taught people to value the person within over the external appearances, but the physical manifestation of the internal also resonated. Everywhere one looked, people grew and changed. In some, the growth was for the better. And in others it was a surrender to the outside world because they did not believe enough in what was inside.

Am I a god within? In the past he would have laughed outright at such a notion, but now he'd been given cause to wonder. Growing up, he and his siblings would joke about how Qiro thought he was a god—and indeed many people treated him with more reverence than they showed the gods. If being skilled at something allowed one to reach the state of *jaedunto,* wasn't it possible that one could manifest as something greater? He would have once rejected that idea because everyone knew there were only nine gods and could be no more, but the whole idea of another god forcing his way into heaven opened up a plethora of possibilities.

Discussions like these occupied the time he spent with Nauana outside training, while his magical education continued unabated—and even accelerated. He could not communicate with her telepathically even as well as he could with his blood kin, but he understood her better. That, coupled with his understanding of essence and how to use it, allowed him to progress quickly. While he still was not as proficient as Nauana, there were indications he had the capacity to handle far more power than she did.

Still, plans had been for him to continue his studies, but then a runner came in from Micyan, a coastal village two days distant. He collapsed from exhaustion, having run all the way with no food, no sleep, and insufficient water. He reported that the Mozoyan had attacked his village.

The prospect of the Mozoyan's return goaded the Amentzutl into action. The city of Nemehyan sat atop a mountain, which was reached by a long, switchback causeway that came up from the plains. Those plains had seen a savage battle against the Mozoyan just over a month before—or "earlier in the week," if one was using the *centenco* calendar. In fact, a tall, pyramidal mountain of Mozoyan skulls marked the Amentzutl victory over their enemy. In that attack the Mozoyan had come in from the northeast, and the prospect of their arrival from the coast meant defenses would have to be shifted.

Captain Anaeda Gryst sent the *Blackshark* north along the coast to look for any signs of the advancing Mozoyan horde. Because the Amentzutl had no maritime tradition to speak of, Micyan had not been built on a harbor. But the ship would be able to land troops at the closest natural harbor for a scouting run and, toward that end, a company each of Sea Dragons and Amentzutl warriors boarded her.

Jorim opted to travel north on the *Blackshark* and Shimik came with him. Nauana stayed behind to work on the defenses with the other *maicana,* and Tzihua came aboard to lead the Amentzutl contingent. Anaeda Gryst remained at Nemehyan and organized the remaining Naleni troops to help defend the city.

Being back on a ship and on the ocean delighted Jorim as Nauana had clearly known it would, which was why she'd not asked him to stay behind. Jorim stood near the prow, laughing as spray wet his face. The wind cooled him, and though he could have worked an invocation that would have warmed him again, he did not. He simply relished the scent of the sea, the vision of the sky, the taste of brine, and the sounds of the ship and the people working it.

This is the essence of life itself. Traveling, exploring, going into danger, all of these were things that he loved. They made him feel alive. *If I have to spend the rest of my life imprisoned in Anturasikun, I will die.*

He glanced down at Shimik, who stood beside him, legs spread, paws on hips. Shimik looked up at him and grinned with a mouthful of peg teeth.

"I know, Shimik, this is wonderful."

The journey up the coast took most of the afternoon, but with a steady wind they made good time and put into the harbor with no difficulty. But though they had traveled close to the shore on the way up, and the sharpest-eyed watchmen had been on duty, they'd seen no sign of the Mozoyan.

The ship's commander, Lieutenant Myrasi Wueltan, lowered the ship's boats and landed the troops quickly. Two trips for each boat got all the troops ashore, and despite the disparate array of weapons and armor between the two contingents, they all moved quickly to secure the white sandy beach.

Shimik clung to Jorim's back as the cartographer joined Tzihua near the head of the column moving inland. The scouts had seen nothing so far, but they had only penetrated the thick rain forest a hundred yards or so. The undergrowth made it hard to see and even harder to travel. Soldiers using steel swords or obsidian-edged war clubs hacked a path through the jungle.

Despite the noise of their passage, the animals did not seem the least bit concerned. A troop of tiger-striped monkeys happily derided their efforts and even pelted some of them with the green rinds from *ichoitz* fruit. Shimik mimicked their calls accurately enough that one bull dropped through the canopy to a branch twenty feet up, started shaking it and hooting loudly.

The Fenn leaped from Jorim's back, scrambled along another branch, and headed straight for the bull. They hollered at each other, shaking branches and posturing. Jorim feared there would be a fight, but then Shimik flashed his claws at the monkey and the monkey fled in terror.

Shimik dropped to the ground and accepted the exaggerated bows offered by all of the warriors.

The column carved a track for another hundred yards before the scouts reported back again. They'd reached the road the boy had used to make his run south. They saw no sign of his passing, nor any of the Mozoyan. As nearly as they could tell, nothing was out of the ordinary.

Jorim frowned. "Twelve hours ago, the Mozoyan raided Micyan, and have not headed south. I can't imagine they expected we would be warned."

Tzihua shook his head. "You have seen them in combat. They do not think."

"Then why the raid?"

"The most simple reason of all. They were hungry."

"You think these were stragglers? Would there have been enough to overwhelm a village?"

The Amentzutl giant shrugged. "We tracked the survivors as far north as possible. Most died; a few disappeared. They were not made for life on land. Those that lived returned to the sea."

Jorim nodded. While they'd located the place where the Mozoyan had gathered for their attack on Nemehyan, they'd found no ships, boats, or any other indication of how the Mozoyan had reached land. They concluded the enemy had swum to shore, and the idea of a sea filled with man-sized demon-frogs with mouths full of shark's teeth was enough to fuel Jorim's nightmares.

"Sending troops along the road to Micyan is the best plan." Jorim thought for a moment. "We probably should have the *Blackshark* head up the coast and see if there is any sign of the Mozoyan. I don't think they could have cut a path as we did, but they might have come ashore anywhere, and it would be useful to know where."

"I agree."

"Good. I'll run back and let Lieutenant Wueltan know what we want, then I'll come and join you for the march."

Tzihua smiled. "It will be good to have Tetcomchoa leading us."

"I'll tell him you said that if I see him." Jorim cut back through the troops and Shimik raced above him through the trees. The Naleni troops were bringing up the column's rear, so Jorim briefed their leader on the plan. He refused the offer of bodyguards for his trip to the shore and sent them on their way.

As he reached the beach, he realized something was wrong. Neither birds nor monkeys had harassed him. He'd just assumed Shimik had scared them off, and kept assuming that until he reached the beach and Shimik cowered behind him, peeking out between his legs.

More than the *Blackshark* inhabited the cove. At first he couldn't tell what it was, because it was as long as the ship, and somehow that didn't seem possible. The front part of it stood open—again something not possible for a ship—and all sorts of creatures were crawling out of the opening. They'd already swarmed over the *Blackshark*—and sailors who dove overboard and began swimming to shore were dragged under by unseen assailants.

Though he was not terribly close to the ship, Jorim knew these Mozoyan were different. The first he'd seen had been fishlike. Those which attacked Nemehyan were truly demon-frogs, but still slender. These Mozoyan had a thicker silhouette, more apelike than simple toad. The way they swung from the ship's ratlines and dropped from crosspieces emphasized this impression.

Beyond that, two things became immediately apparent. The first was that the ship was likely lost. Second, the Mozoyan were coming ashore and that as valiant as the warriors were, sheer numbers alone would overwhelm them. They had no chance to prepare defenses, as hulking Mozoyan had already begun to bob and swim toward shore. The slaughter would be complete and the Mozoyan would feast on men as men had feasted on the Mozoyan dead on the plains before Nemehyan.

Then another of the things containing the Mozoyan

surfaced. It opened its mouth and more Mozoyan began to emerge.

Shimik's terrified mewing brought Jorim out of his fugue. "Shimik, find Tzihua. Tell him to run fast fast. Go fast now, Shimik. Go. I have to do something."

"Jrima stay?"

"Yes, I'm staying, but you have to go, quickly. Now. Very important. Go."

The Fenn darted off down the jungle path. He stopped, looked back at Jorim, waved, then leaped into the trees and disappeared.

Jorim turned back to the harbor and narrowed his eyes. "It's all about balance and essence." He tore off his overshirt and robe, baring his chest. Facing the harbor and the dying sun, he stepped forward until he was knee deep in water. He ignored the Mozoyan and closed his eyes.

He focused on the warmth of the sun as it touched his flesh and hair. He felt the water lapping around his legs—very warm this close to shore, but leaving a chill as it drained away from him with each gentle swell. He let himself feel their essence. The water, fluid; the sun, hot. He sought the warmth in the water, the fluidity in the way the sunlight undulated over the water.

Then he reached out and touched the *mai*.

It was all about balance, and now he sought to shift the balance radically. He had no idea if he could do it or if the effort would kill him. Still, it was the only chance to save his friends. So he reached within himself as well, binding his essence to the *mai*, then channeling the *mai* into the water.

The balance he sought to shift was simple, but the scale on which he wanted to do it was incredibly vast. *I want to make the sea boil.* Transforming the cove from fluid to vapor was possible, though he'd heard no tales of such a titanic task being accomplished before.

Chances are, anyone foolish enough to attempt it died before the first wisp of steam rose.

He opened his eyes and all he saw were Mozoyan drawing nearer. One of them was a stone's throw away. It opened its mouth, revealing the shark's teeth he'd seen before. Its black eyes locked on his and Jorim found himself looking at his doom.

Then it hit him. *Right idea, wrong application.*

He ignored the water and concentrated on the sun. He visualized Wentiko in the solar disk. The Dragon had always stood for courage, and Jorim welcomed that as well as the heat and light. He touched the god's essence and a pulse came through the *mai* that shook him. Every muscle in his body contracted, bowing his back.

He expected to fall helpless on the beach, but instead he began to rise. His feet emerged dripping from the sea. The Mozoyan that had been closest to him looked up, the hungry expression on its face evaporating into surprise.

Jorim wanted to turn water from fluid to vapor. Converting a sea would be impossible, for the water in the cove was linked to the ocean, which was linked to all oceans. To convert all that into vapor might be beyond even the power of a god.

But making a small amount of water do that was not. He'd done it before, countless times. It had become an effortless task.

So he began the conversion with the water in the nearest Mozoyan's eyes.

They exploded, and the creature burbled in pain. It sank beneath the surface, but Jorim still tracked it by essence. He boiled its brain in its skull. Bone cracked and skin parted, releasing a bubble of hot gas to mark the thing's passing.

He turned his attention to another, and another. Mozoyan died writhing. They thrashed in the water, and only as they grew small did he realize he was flying higher, out over the cove. He no longer had to focus himself on any individual. It was enough that they looked up at him and that they felt the touch of the radiance he was projecting. As his rays caressed them, flesh melted and bones blackened.

Soaring slowly, with no more direction or intent than a kite on a light breeze, Jorim approached the *Blackshark*. He glanced down at himself and wondered how he was not blinded. His skin glowed with noontime intensity. The water reflected his golden corona and tiny wisps of steam curled up from around dead Mozoyan.

Jorim looked at the *Blackshark*. He could not see into it, but as his gaze swept over it, he found Mozoyan cowering on deck and hiding in the ship's depths. One by one he touched them and they died.

The enormous fish that had released the Mozoyan closed their mouths. They slowly began to sink, but the harbor's shallow bottom hindered them. But it scarcely would have mattered, for his rays pierced the water easily, and the lumbering creatures could never have dived fast enough to elude him.

With the wave of a hand he burned them from end to end. Their thick tails twitched, stirring up mud, then they sank into the muck. He waited and watched for any

Mozoyan to escape, and boiled those that did inside their own flesh.

Pulling his radiance back in, Jorim floated down to the *Blackshark*'s deck. His bare feet touched the wood. It sizzled and smoked. He stepped back and looked down, gaping at the footprints burned into the deck.

They were the footprints of a dragon.

Chapter Twenty-six

14th day, Month of the Dragon, Year of the Rat
10th Year of Imperial Prince Cyron's Court
163rd Year of the Komyr Dynasty
737th year since the Cataclysm
Disat Forest, West of Moriande
Nalenyr

Prince Cyron smiled. Though early in the year, the day had dawned bright and warm. He'd had ample sleep the night before and rose early to prepare for the day's outing. He'd initially resisted the idea of joining Prince Eiran and Count Turcol, but going along was the expedient course. Turcol had the potential for being a very nasty thorn in his side, so whatever he could do to take care of the problem immediately was best.

Besides, the Disat Forest had always been a favorite haunt of his. In it, on a small hill, his grandfather had accepted the surrender and abdication of the previous dynasty's last prince. This began the Komyr Dynasty and, contrary to rumors, he did not have the man slain on the spot. His rise to power had been tempered by mercy. To remind himself of his grandfather's wisdom, Cyron liked to travel to the hill and meditate, especially on the anniversary of his rise.

His father had made the forests a royal reserve. Poachers knew they could suffer severe punishments if they were caught taking game, but some risked it because they believed that if they could elude the warders and make it to Memorial Hill, the Prince would grant them mercy. Cyron always did, *once.* If a man were caught more than once, he gave him exactly what his grandfather had given his predecessor.

The forest itself had a beauty and serenity that even a trailing troop of attendants could not spoil. Pines predominated in their eternal coats of green. Where other trees—oaks, elms, maples, and birches—peeked through, their bare branches already showed green buds. Spring would be coming early, and with it the birds would be winging their way north again.

Cyron longed for spring and hoped the Virine invasion would not stop the birds. He banished the thought that it might and lightened his expression for the benefit of his host. He tugged back on his reins, slowing his horse enough that Count Turcol and Prince Eiran could catch up with him.

Count Turcol had been inordinately gracious throughout the day. In celebration of his troops' posting to the Helosunde border, he'd accepted a Helosundian title and informed his troops they were now the Helosundian Dragons. He proclaimed Prince Eiran to be his cocommander, gratefully distributed Helosundian pennants, and left his troops repainting their breastplates with dogs and dragons intertwined.

Turcol had even been quite pleasant to Prince

Cyron—though it clearly took an effort. As they rode through the forest to Memorial Hill, the westron count repeatedly complimented the Prince and begged forgiveness for any past misunderstandings.

"I assure you, Count Turcol, I took no umbrage at anything you have said in my presence." Cyron nodded toward him and Eiran beyond. "You are both strong men, and the future will demand strong men. I would hope, someday, that I will have an heir who can learn from the two of you. The courage you show in speaking frankly to me is to be lauded. As well you know, many courtiers only tell me what they believe I wish to hear, and a prince cannot rule if this is the case."

Turcol smiled. "Your Highness is too kind. I know that you cannot rest easily with so many things on your mind. I had hoped this day of riding, hawking, and simple relaxation would provide you comfort—though I am certain you have many comforts."

Cyron followed Turcol's glance and smiled. The Lady of Jet and Jade had ridden out with them. Her horse had gotten forward of theirs, and the dark green of her robe nearly hid her against the pines. As if she had heard the remark, she looked back and smiled—but her smile was for Cyron alone.

He resisted the urge to turn quickly and catch Turcol's reaction. He'd seen it a couple of times already. It clearly galled Turcol that this woman, the famed concubine, would not allow him to buy from her what other women so willingly gave him freely.

Cyron turned his head slowly, giving the westron ample time to control his expression. "Have you ever considered, my lord, what you would do were you in my place, on the throne?"

"Me, on the throne? Please, Highness, I do not think of such things."

Cyron smiled. "Be honest with me, Count Turcol. Your family occupied the Dragon Throne well before mine did, and you come from Imperial nobility. You must have entertained the idea. I certainly hope you have, for, if not, you are not the man I imagined—and certainly not suited to what I have in mind for you."

Turcol lifted a branch and ducked his head beneath it. "Perhaps I have thought of it, Highness. Never with avarice, but just as an intellectual exercise."

"Good, this pleases me." Cyron reined his horse in closer to Turcol, then looked back to see if the four Jomiri attendants were trailing at a respectful distance. He lowered his voice. "As you know, my lord, I have no heir. Until I can procure one, I have to plan for the future of our nation. May I speak frankly with you?"

Turcol answered quietly. "Of course, Highness."

"I have looked at those who might be able to replace me, were Pyrust to send assassins after me. I believe you are the man with the most potential. But I would ask you a question first."

"Please."

"Were you in my place, and you learned of an invasion of a southern neighbor—say Erumvirine—which threatened to destroy that nation, what would you do?"

Turcol sat up straight and his horse slowed, allowing Prince Eiran to ride forward. "I'd find out how much of a threat it was. I would want to know who the invaders were. Is it a fight for the Virine throne, or is it something larger that threatens Nalenyr?"

"That is a good place to start, Count Turcol." Cyron frowned. "Suppose all you know is that the defenders have been forced back, and that very few refugees have fled—not because they are content with the invaders, but because they've all been slain. Moreover, assume the Virine Prince is too slow in answering the challenge, and that even the professional spies are not reporting back. What would you do?"

"In that case, the indications are obvious. I'd shift my best troops south to guard against an invasion, and I would shore up my northern defenses by calling..." Turcol's head came up as his eyes grew wide. "Is this why you demanded troops from the west, Highness? Is there a threat from Erumvirine?"

"It would be dreadful if that rumor were spread about. It might cause a panic, don't you think? Better to start a rumor that troops have become weak and need to be rotated away for training and discipline. And best to start calling up troops who will be needed if the invasion is more than the Keru can handle."

Turcol reached out and caught his arm with a hand. "Is that possible?"

"That is the problem with being a prince, my lord. A prince hasn't the luxury of asking if something is possible. He must just plan for what he will do when it happens." Cyron smiled and pointed ahead. "There it is, Memorial Hill. Let's not have any more dour talk, shall we?"

Turcol looked up, then nodded. "No, Highness. You honor me with your thoughts and your confidence. I wish to assure that if I were to replace you, I should keep our nation safe."

"It pleases me to hear that." Cyron nodded. "Now I can die reassured."

They rode on. Eiran and the Lady of Jet and Jade

reached the hill first. They dismounted and hitched their horses to some bushes. Cyron joined them, and the three walked up to the hilltop together. Cyron strode to the center, where a trio of stones had been placed. Two smaller ones held up a large grey granite slab, forming a rough lean-to.

Resting a hand on one of the support stones, he turned to the other two. "I had these stones raised thus. The slab is my grandfather, the two supports are my father and brother. Perhaps when I am gone my successor will dig up another stone from the hill and place it here for me. The hill once was an old Imperial fort, Tsatol Disat. It had wonderful command of the countryside."

The Lady of Jet and Jade smiled as she slowly spun in a circle, taking in the view. Though not the highest point in the forest, it provided an unobstructed view to the north and east. In the distance Moriande was visible. Forest claimed the hill's western side and the dark trees contrasted beautifully with the stones.

"I understand why you come here, Highness. It is very beautiful and peaceful."

The Helosundian Prince nodded. "I shall find such a spot in Helosunde. It gives you perspective."

"Perspective, yes, but do not underestimate the value of peace." Cyron looked back down the hill to where Turcol, still mounted, was speaking with the attendants. He waved to him, and shouted, "Come join us, Count Turcol."

The count waved back, but fell into conversation again.

The Lady of Jet and Jade came to Cyron's side. "I think it is my fault, Highness. I do not think he likes me."

Cyron laughed. "I think he doesn't like the fact that you don't like him. You've seen how he watches you."

"Does he? I care not for how anyone watches me."

The sincerity of her remark surprised Cyron. "You're quite serious about that."

"Completely, Highness." She laughed lightly and faced both men. "I am a concubine, and a Mystic. As with other Mystics, I have seen more years than you would suppose. One of the things I have learned over the years is that it matters not at all how people look at me. It is how I look at them, and how I reach them, that matters. The external will fade unless one is blessed, but how you present yourself, and how you engage others, is what attracts them to you or not."

She waved a hand toward Prince Cyron. "My saying what follows will not matter to you at all, but the good count would find it cause to react. You see, I could tell you that on this very spot, I made love with your grandfather after he was made Prince. With you, no reaction, no desire to do what your grandfather had done, no sense of competition with the past. You, Prince Cyron, require other things to excite you. If the count heard me say that . . ."

"Say what, my lady?" Turcol reined his horse back and looked down at her. "Do continue."

The Lady of Jet and Jade's eyes sharpened. "If I told you that I made love with Prince Jarus Turcol on this spot, and was willing to have him because he was a prince, you would be driven to take the throne and have me here and many other places. You are not satisfied with your life, so you seek victories that are foolish and petty."

The westron raised an eyebrow. "Am I that transparent, my lady?"

"Prince Jarus Turcol was. It's in your blood."

Turcol's expression hardened. "And would I have to be a prince to enjoy your company?"

"It would be a step."

Cyron laughed and stepped forward. "My lord, you don't see her joking often, do you?"

"She was serious, Highness. And she was right." Turcol planted two fingers in his mouth and whistled aloud. A dozen men and women emerged from the forest depths. Half of them carried bows with arrows fitted to them already. The others had clubs, save for two with swords. They spread out in a semicircle, with two of the archers mounting the stone slab.

Cyron stared hard at Turcol. "You will explain this, please."

"Only because you have been so gracious in explaining your confidence in me, Highness." Turcol rested his hands on his saddle-horn and leaned forward. "You've ruined our nation and left it open to threats from both north and south. You have beggared and humiliated the western counties. We now face a military crisis, and you are ill suited to deal with it. Were you any sort of warrior at all, you'd be out here with more than just a dagger."

The Prince nodded. "And so you hired these bandits. You will explain how you fought them valiantly and while you were able to drive them off, it was not before we were slain, all three of us."

"Not three; two." He looked down at the Lady of Jet and Jade. "I will have you here and wherever else I desire. Unless, of course, you *want* to die."

She shook her head and stepped away from Cyron. "Not for a long time. Forgive me, Highness."

Cyron shook his head. "Nothing to forgive, my lady." He looked up at Turcol. "You know it will have to be a convincing act. You can't come away from it unscathed. Perhaps there, in your right shoulder, an arrow. Not life-threatening, but serious enough to convince many of your effort. My doctor, Geselkir, will take care of it."

Turcol snorted. "Perhaps you're right, Highness, but that's a detail I can work out later."

"Another thing a prince cannot do, Turcol, *procrastinate.*" Cyron pointed up at the westron. "His right shoulder. Shoot him now."

The archer above the Prince drew and loosed in one easy motion. The black barbed arrow pierced Turcol's shoulder and darkness began to seep into his midnight-blue robe. He looked from his shoulder to the archer and back again.

Turcol bit back any cry of pain, clenched his teeth, then looked up at the archers. "You idiots! *I* give the orders. Shoot *him*!"

Bows twanged in unison. Down the hill, the quartet of attendants fell, each stuck through the chest with an arrow.

Turcol blinked and slumped in his saddle. "This is not happening. This is not how it was planned."

"Not how *you* planned it, Turcol." Cyron shook his head. "Had you not made your approaches to Grand Minister Vniel quite so obvious, my Lord of Shadows would not have discovered what you were up to. Hiring assassins in Moriande was a second mistake. That is *my* realm, and loyalties to me run high."

"Loyalties to you?" Turcol shook his head with disbelief. "They are assassins."

"So they are. And I pay well each year to make certain they do not act against me. Surely you did not believe you were the first noble to think of killing me?"

The count started to answer, then closed his mouth. Moving slowly, he dismounted, then sank to his knees. "In the spirit of the day, the spirit of this place and tradition, I ask for mercy."

Prince Eiran laughed aloud. "Are you insane? You've committed treason and you want mercy?"

Cyron held up a hand. "Just a moment, Prince Eiran. I am not deaf to your appeal, Count Turcol. In the spirit of this place, you wish what my grandfather gave his predecessor? Is this it? Nothing less will satisfy you?"

"That's what I want, my lord."

"I can grant you that." Cyron folded his arms over his chest. "The legend is true. My grandfather spared his predecessor's life; but his predecessor was much like you. Bold, brash, ambitious. He was a man who did not know when he was beaten. He planned, even as you do now, of returning to power and returning his dynasty to the throne.

"And he was like you in one other regard. He had no children."

Turcol nodded, puzzled.

"My grandfather didn't kill him, he *gelded* him. Then he sent him to live in a monastery on the coast of the Dark Sea. So, I'll give you what you say you desire."

Turcol's shoulders sagged with resignation, then he launched himself at the Prince. He reached his feet in a heartbeat and drew his dagger in the next. As he raised it, two arrows narrowly missed him. Fury burning in his grey eyes, he rushed forward.

And might have reached Cyron, save for the Lady of Jet and Jade, who stuck a foot out and tripped him. Turcol went down heavily, the arrow's shaft breaking. Eiran delivered a sharp kick to the man's head, and he remained down.

Cyron bowed deeply to the concubine, then to the Helosundian Prince. "You are both yet more dear to me for saving my life."

They returned the bows, but said nothing.

Cyron turned to the nearest swordsman and gave him the slightest shake of his head. In commanding his master assassin to supplant those Turcol had hired, he also asked that Eiran and the Lady of Jet and Jade be left free to act. He'd informed neither of them of what would happen, and in the unlikely event either proved a coconspirator, they would have died as Turcol had.

The Prince pulled back the left sleeve of his robe. "We will tell everyone what Turcol intended to say. Bandits found us out here and sought to rob us, not realizing who we were. Turcol and his men fought them valiantly, driving them off, but not before the count and his men died of their wounds.

"Eiran, because the count so graciously made you his cocommander, you will lead the Helosundian Dragons north and watch over them. Tell them we think the bandits were truly Desei assassins who intended to kill Turcol, so much does Pyrust fear him and his men on the border. That will put steel in their spines."

Eiran bowed his head. "As you will it, Highness."

The Lady of Jet and Jade regarded him openly. "Orders for me, Highness?"

"Yes. Please avert your eyes." Cyron waited until she had turned away, then nodded to his Lord of Shadows and lifted his bared arm. The assassin drew a dagger and held it high.

Cyron sighed and nodded. "It has to be believable, our story, and so it shall be."

The blade fell.

Chapter Twenty-seven

14th day, Month of the Dragon, Year of the Rat
10th Year of Imperial Prince Cyron's Court
163rd Year of the Komyr Dynasty
737th year since the Cataclysm
Quunkun, Kelewan (The Illustrated City)
Erumvirine

Though our number was pared severely in that first encounter with what we came to call the *kwajiin*—their blue skin having made that name inescapable—we reached Kelewan without much further incident. Probes did still arrive, and we fought them back, but the invasion moved at a steadier pace. And as we traveled west, more refugees joined us and the breadth of the invasion became clear.

Ranai had seen it begin at Derros—or, rather, had seen *one* of the beginnings. Towns and villages along the Green River had been hit, as well as locations as far north as the Central Mountains. All the reports talked of total slaughter, which was what Dunos had seen. The general lack of refugees on the roads confirmed that few had escaped the invaders.

Many of those fleeing suggested the invasion was divine retribution for the secret things Prince Jekusmirwyn was doing in his palace. But Moraven had traveled extensively through Erumvirine, and the most annoying thing Jekusmirwyn had done was continue the Virine tradition of long names for rulers. Because Erumvirine had been the Imperial capital province, the local rulers picked names of specific import when they ascended to the throne. Jekusmirwyn actually translated as "the last Prince," which was taken as an omen of immortality, or his role as the Prince who would reestablish the Empire.

The invaders, it appeared, had a different take on it.

The idea of divine retribution was the product of feeble minds rendered even less stable by fatigue and fear. Were the gods desirous of punishing him, they'd show up in Quunkun, deal with him alone, and depart. That was the orderly way of doing things, and the Lords of Heaven were ever about doing things in an orderly way.

As we drew closer to the capital, the roads clogged, and small encampments of refugees set themselves up in open spaces. Some of them had lost the will to live and so lay down to die. Others had taken heart in seeing columns of soldiers heading east to deal with the threat. We'd seen them, too, which is why we were heading west. While few of the refugees chose to follow me, a number of *xidantzu* did. By the time we reached Kelewan, I had a cadre of a dozen warriors, half of whom were Mystics or well on their way to becoming such.

I remembered Kelewan, both as Moraven Tolo and from further past, though those memories still lay shrouded. It had once been known as the "Illustrated City" because of the local customs determining what colors would be used on various buildings and how they would be otherwise decorated. Quunkun, the Bear's Tower, lay at the city's hub. White marble faced it, and colorful pennants hung from towers. Around it, split into twelve divisions that subdivided into yet smaller cantons and wards, each part of the city adopted different colors to identify it. Gold marked the trading divisions, with buildings having secondary and accent colors that identified very specifically what they did. River traders, for example, would paint with gold and green—the latter for the river.

Even the slums were brightly painted. White, of course, was to match the palace, but in reality the slum dwellers could only afford whitewash. In other places, as divisions were divided and subdivided, buildings could end up with a mélange of colors that made the eyes bleed on a sunny day.

I could only hope the *kwajiin* were not color-blind.

Most refugees sought entry through Whitegate, but I refused to go into the capital as a beggar. We recovered Urardsa and Dunos from their fellows and headed for Bloodgate. As would be expected, soldiers warded the entrance to their section of town. A variety of mercenaries and *xidantzu* loitered outside that gate, but I decided they were beneath my notice. The sort of people I needed would not have been intimidated by some princeling's foot soldier.

Those I dismissed likewise dismissed me, confirming my conclusions about their worthlessness.

Before we made to enter the city, I'd commanded all of my companions to wash up and put on their best robes. Despite days on the road and hard fighting, they cleaned up well and looked presentable. From the glances they exchanged, their appearance was a surprise, and I might have even seen growing signs of attraction between a few of them.

That suited me fine. It was good they should enjoy what little life they likely had left.

I, on the other hand, did not clean up. My robe, which had once been white, now had a grey cast to it, save where blood stained it deeply. I'd done nothing to induce the pattern, but I did enjoy the striping effect. Given my crest was that of a tiger hunting, it seemed appropriate.

And, like a tiger, I kept my whiskers, which had grown in very dark. Being charitable, I looked as if I'd been dragged all the way from Derros behind a dung cart. The only thing anomalous about me was my wearing two swords. Of course, that could have been taken as braggadocio, and I did not mind that either.

Being underestimated in some situations is an asset.

A guardsman bearing a spear moved to block my way. "You'll wait here like the others." He moved with a swagger and sneered as he spoke. Some of the loiterers laughed, but the smarter among them just watched.

Deshiel intervened. "This is our master, Moraven Tolo."

The guardsman stared blankly at him. "It would not matter if he was Prince Cyron arrived with all the Naleni troops he could field. Until the Prince issues a call for *xidantzu* and others of their ilk, you wait here. Or, you go to Whitegate, surrender your weapons, and get fed."

Deshiel's hand dropped to his sword's hilt, but I restrained him with my left hand.

The guardsman laughed.

My backhanded slap snapped his head around, then dumped him on his ample buttocks. The other guards at the gate came instantly alert. They lowered their spears and prepared to advance and drive us off. Luric Dosh stepped forward and began to whirl his spear slowly, which gave the guardsmen pause.

With the same hand I'd used to slap him, I pointed the fallen man to the stone circle just outside Bloodgate. Circles such as this could be found throughout the Nine, most commonly outside the larger cities or towns. This one was large, as befitted a capital, easily thirty feet in diameter. Many duels had been fought in it, and the signs of the aftermath were easily seen.

Mystics had left their mark, for when Mystics dueled, the circle contained the wild magic that their actions released. Outside that circle, the world was just beginning to awaken in spring. Inside, the flowers were already in bloom. I especially liked the goldenrod for how it glittered, and I imagined the metal blossoms might ring prettily were I to slice through them. The Iron-bells, on the other hand, might dull a blade.

The guardsman scuttled back from me. "I don't care who you are, you don't come in."

Again I pointed to the circle.

"I know my duty."

Deshiel bowed toward him. "Indeed you do. Are you willing to die in its performance?"

I gave him no chance to reply. I strode forward as if I were the Prince. The recumbent guard said nothing more and his fellows parted before me. My people followed and a couple of the loiterers made to follow us.

I pointed to one and Ranai drew her sword. He continued to follow. She did the guardsman's duty for him, and we walked deeper into the city with no one else in our wake.

I could feel Moraven's distaste for the city, but I liked it. The tall buildings reduced the sky to slender ribbons of blue. The crowds had not yet filtered into the red division and likely would stay out, as it would be the first point of attack. The warriors who lived here kept it clean, and even the yapping dogs slinking through the streets looked as if they'd recently been washed.

What I found most fascinating in the Illustrated City were the small murals painted on the homes. Most had no wording, and were often painted in a stripe no more than a foot high. One warrior's house, for example, showed him in Virine livery, cutting down a Viruk. By this alone he would be known. Little symbols showed his current rank and affiliation and, at this house, his mural was the fourth in a sequence, showing military service going back generations. While each was bright with new paint, the styling of the figures remained appropriate to their era, so each building became a living history of those who resided there.

By contrast, Quunkun remained naked stone. Its smooth walls had no decoration, but it needed none. Everyone was expected to know the history and deeds of the Telanyn Dynasty—and the emperors who had reigned there before them. The Telanyn had assumed control of Erumvirine when Prince Nelesquin died in Ixyll. Though they had been overthrown twice since the Cataclysm, they found their way back to the throne after a generation or two. Once by acclaim, once by marriage and murder—both equally effective.

The palace's tall towers thrust like spears into the sky, but drew no blood. They remained as ineffective as Virine spears often were, and that boded ill for Kelewan. We strode across the wide circle of white marble and mounted the steps, only to be stopped by smartly dressed warriors whose spear blades flashed silver in the sunlight.

A captain held up a hand to stop me. "You go no further without authority."

I reached into my robe and tossed a piece of filthy fabric at him. He recoiled and let it fall to the steps. There it unfurled itself in all its tattered, bloodstained glory. Though it had been pierced and clawed, no one could mistake the insignia of the Iron Bears.

The captain knelt, touched the cloth, then picked it up. "Come with me."

I followed him through the doors and waited for my people to join me. I moved slowly enough for them to take in the palace's heart, which had struck men dumb with awe since before the Empire fell. We entered beneath a massive dome a hundred feet high. Before us and to both sides, stairways started up, then split three ways, crisscrossing in a dizzying webwork of catwalks. A dozen thick pillars supported the dome, and into each one had been carved the image of a god, emperor, or prince. Only one lacked decoration, having only an empty alcove. A statue of Nelesquin had been there, but had been pulled down and smashed in the Cataclysm's wake.

The captain started up the western staircase and I followed him around to the north. When he continued on further, I cut up the northern stairs and ignored his calls to return. The others followed, becoming more alert than before, but they let him pass when I waved him forward.

He reached my side by the time I was halfway down the corridor to the Prince's audience chamber. "You can't go in there. We need to talk to the generals about the Iron Bears."

I gave him a hard stare that drained the blood from his face. He kept pace with me nonetheless, and a certain resolution entered his step. The guards at the audience chamber door came to alert, but he waved them aside. When they hesitated, he snapped, "Leave here. Now."

They withdrew reluctantly.

I made to step forward, but he restrained me with a hand. In an instant, he had Ranai's sword at his throat and Dunos' dagger poised somewhat lower. His eyes hardened as he looked at me. "If you are going to kill the Prince, kill me first, now."

I shook my head.

He relaxed.

I reached up and guided Ranai's blade away from his throat. "What is your name, Captain?"

"Ianin Lumel, first company, Jade Bears."

I took the Iron Bears' standard from him. "Remember that alive and smart is preferable to dead and stupid."

"Thank you, Master."

I nodded toward the doors and he opened them with Deshiel.

I strode through them and mounted the red carpet edged with purple. I knew well how jealously princes regarded their traditions, but I needed to make an impression. For someone who was not a noble to step on the carpet without invitation could be a death sentence.

The Prince, who had been lounging somewhat indolently across the arms of the Bear Throne, instantly swung his legs down. I think he would have stood, save that the heavy robes of state wrapped around his legs and would have spilled him to the floor. His ministers, who knelt to either side of the carpet, shot me venomous glances, but not a one rose in challenge. They were as the ministers ever had been: willing to serve whoever sat in the throne until it served them to unseat him.

I stopped ten feet from the throne and bowed deeply. I held it a respectful amount of time, certainly appropriate for his and his dynasty's years. I came back up but did not wait for him to bow, even if he were inclined to do so. I tossed the standard at him and he caught it awkwardly against his chest. He held it out and began to tremble.

I looked at him through the largest hole. "Your Iron Bears are dead, to a man. Your city will be forfeit. If you want to save your nation, you will abandon Kelewan now and head north to the mountains in the county of Faeut. Send your people to Nalenyr."

He lowered the standard. "No, this isn't possible."

"It is very possible. I watched the Iron Bears die myself. Do you want to know how it happened? The enemy arrayed themselves in a strong line on a rise above the Bears. Your generals sent the Bears uphill against them, which was pure foolishness, bred from the tale about Morythian Tigers eons ago. The Bears did not face Morythians. These *kwajiin* are smarter, and their troops are fearless."

I looked at the ministers, who stared back wide-eyed. "Even before the Bears engaged the enemy *vhangxi,* a black cloud of winged frogs swarmed over them. They are not powerful, but they have teeth and venom, and when several get to gnawing on a man, he stops.

"And that's when the *vhangxi* countercharged. They ripped into the Bears—*literally* ripped into them. Men fell in pieces—*many* pieces, all of them small—then their killers fell to eating them. What's left of your Bears are steaming piles of dung twenty miles east of here."

The Prince narrowed his eyes and tried to appear hardened, but the sweat on his bald pate betrayed him. "If this is true, how did you come to have this standard?"

I rested a hand on the hilt of each sword. "I called to the *kwajiin* leader and challenged him to a duel. He drew a circle, and I killed him." I pulled back the sleeve on my right arm and revealed a serpentine scar all livid and crossed with black thread. "He was not without skill."

"But if their general is dead, then their threat is ended."

I glanced at the minister who had spoken. "It is without generals that they got this far. The man I slew—they appear to be men, but are not—was not their greatest leader. They will come, they will take Kelewan, and they will kill everyone in the city."

The Prince shook his head. "No, no, that is not possible."

"Your denial does nothing to change the reality of what is coming." I pointed back east. "The invaders have devoured the eastern half of your nation. Your troops are insufficiently trained to deal with the invaders. Pull back, give them time, and you might be able to stop them. If you do not, your nation is lost."

Jekusmirwyn stood and pointed a trembling finger at me. "You have killed one of their leaders. I appoint you my warlord. Arrange the defenses of the city as you see fit."

I laughed aloud, offending the ministers and the Prince alike.

"Do not mock me!"

I shook my head. "Silly man, if I could think of a way to save your city, would I come here and tell you to abandon it? It cannot be saved. Do what I tell you, and their victory will be the first step in their defeat."

The Prince raised his chin defiantly. "And if I do not?"

I pointed at the blank wall behind his throne. "Paint yourself a pretty epitaph. It will be the only chance you'll be remembered after the jaws of Grija snap you up."

Chapter Twenty-eight

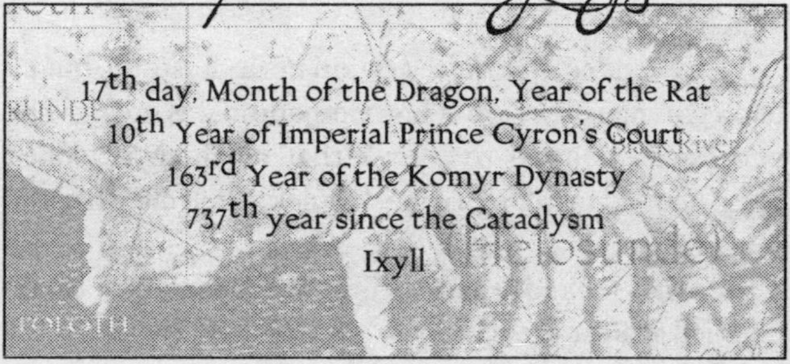

17th day, Month of the Dragon, Year of the Rat
10th Year of Imperial Prince Cyron's Court
163rd Year of the Komyr Dynasty
737th year since the Cataclysm
Ixyll

To Ciras and Borosan the evidence seemed clear: their journey into the heart of Ixyll had brought them very close to the point where the great battle between the Empress' forces and the Turasynd must have taken place. How they knew neither could say exactly, but they both agreed with their conclusion.

And their agreement, while satisfying on one level, left neither of them entirely happy.

Ciras felt a sense of dislocation. He turned to Borosan as they rode up a track along one of the foothills of a jagged line of mountains. "It feels as if everything is just a little bit off. I look at it and it seems to shift."

The inventor nodded. "It's akin to looking through a pane of glass. It's refraction; everything shifts a bit."

"But we aren't looking through glass."

"You're right." Borosan frowned and, despite his fatigue and the reddish dust on his face, he looked almost childlike as he concentrated. "I think the magic here is ingrained so deeply that it bleeds up, like heat from the rocks. We've seen heat mirages of water, and I think the magic here affects our senses the same way. It doesn't stop us from seeing things, just from seeing them immediately."

Ciras nodded, not quite certain he understood, but he had a glimmering of what his companion was saying. The swordsman pointed to a rock that he thought looked like a hooded monk in a robe. "Quickly, tell me what you see."

Borosan looked, then shrugged. "A man in a cloak, huddled against the wind."

"Close enough." Ciras glanced again at the stone and a shiver ran down his spine. It had changed shape, twisting slightly, hunching its shoulders more. It did not move as he watched it, and he tried to convince himself he had not studied it closely enough the first time. But he knew that was wrong—his training had made him a keen observer, and his time with Borosan had only enhanced those skills.

Borosan smiled. "Of course, if magic is working here that way, I could have said it looked like the Lady of Jet and Jade, and you would have heard that it looked like whatever you thought it was. Or you might have thought it looked like something else, and my telling you what it looked like to me might have changed what you thought it looked like."

Ciras held a hand up. "Enough. My head is on fire."

He hunched his shoulders for a moment, hoping just saying that would not make it come true.

Borosan smiled, but did not laugh. "I do have one worry here, and it's not that our perceptions are being changed constantly. With so much magic here, I don't wonder that it should be easy to use. I wonder if it becomes unconsciously simple to use."

"I'm not sure I understand."

Borosan sighed, then turned and pulled one of the round mousers from a saddlebag. He held it out to Ciras. "Please, I know you don't like my *gyanrigot,* but hold it."

Frowning, the Tirati warrior accepted the skull-sized ball. "Now what?"

"Stroke it. Pretend it has fur."

Ciras raised an eyebrow. "Is it time for us to get out of the sun? We can find shade."

"Just stroke it."

Ciras pulled a glove off with his teeth, then stroked the bare metal shell with his fingertips. He stared, then did it again. "It feels like fur."

"I know."

Then the mouser purred.

Ciras tossed it back to Borosan and wiped both of his hands on his thighs. "What did you do to it?"

"I didn't do anything to it." Borosan returned it to the saddlebag. "I *have* been thinking about it, however, even dreaming about it. I think of it as a mouser since that's what I built it to do. Out here, I think just thinking about something may manipulate the wild magic and make things come true."

Ciras frowned. "That makes no sense."

"Doesn't it?" Borosan shrugged. "If you are a Mystic, you access magic and use it to make yourself a better warrior. What you are able to do is governed by your discipline and skills, but you can't control all the magic, so some of it bleeds into the surroundings. The reason you can't control it, however, is because you've been trained to be a swordsman, not a magician."

Ciras said nothing for a moment, then nodded. "And you would say that magic can be controlled because you, with *gyanri,* are able to construct devices that channel captured magic into specific ends."

"Exactly. And we know that magic can be controlled because we have someone like Kaerinus who can use it to heal."

"And we have stories of the *vanyesh* who did other things with it."

"Not just them, Ciras. We know the Viruk can use magic. Even Rekarafi could use it. He helped heal Tyressa."

"But they are not human. You look around us and see what the *vanyesh* helped cause."

The inventor frowned. "Do we know that they did?"

"The stories make it all clear."

"Sure, but who wrote those stories?" Borosan reined back at the top of the hill. "The history says that aside from Kaerinus, *no one* returned from the battle. Given the nature of the Cataclysm, that's no surprise. And yet, we have stories of the Sleeping Empress."

"So you're saying we don't know the truth because the only folks who could have told the truth died here?"

"True—and look at the only evidence we have about the *vanyesh.* Kaerinus has let himself be imprisoned for ages, but he heals people. He's hardly the monster the *vanyesh* were made out to be. Sure, the stories say he returned feebleminded, but how feebleminded can he be if he's able to use magic to heal?"

Ciras sighed heavily. "You make me think troubling things, Master Gryst." He really didn't want to have to think about the *vanyesh* being anything other than monsters. He still had the vision of one striking his master from behind, and that fit his idea of a villain. But by the same token, he'd also had visions of the same *vanyesh* killing a lot of very skilled Turasynd.

He gave his horse a touch of the spur and Borosan rode up beside him. "Master Gryst, what you say about the people who wrote the stories is true, but I would counter that the stories are based on the actions of Prince Nelesquin and his *vanyesh* before the Cataclysm. They would have required some basis in fact if they were not to be dismissed when they were first related."

"I agree." Borosan smiled. "Perhaps, however, Nelesquin's *vanyesh* were not the *only vanyesh*. Maybe others came out, fearing the Cataclysm, and tried to contain it."

Ciras snorted. "They didn't do a very good job."

Borosan laughed. "Then again, they might have contained enough of it that all life was not destroyed."

"I don't like arguing with you. You riposte too well."

The inventor smiled broadly, then bowed his head. "I shall take that as you meant it, not as it sounded."

Ciras screwed his eyes shut as that comment ricocheted through his mind and would have said something in return, but when he opened his eyes again he spotted a dark opening at the base of a sheer mountain cliff. He would have sworn that it had not been there moments before, but the trail down the hill had also seemed not quite so straight, and another hill seemed to have shrunk enough to reveal the opening.

"Do you see that?"

Borosan nodded slowly. "We shouldn't go anywhere near it."

"It might be another grave complex." Ciras settled his hand on the hilt of the *vanyesh* blade. "Every part of me screams that we should not go there."

"And for some reason that's not enough to make you ride away?"

The swordsman glanced at his companion. "Given the nature of how this opening was revealed to us, do you think we could get away if we wanted to?"

Borosan nodded slowly. "Anything powerful enough to hide or reveal that hole probably could have opened this hill and swallowed us alive."

"I think we were meant to come here." Ciras pointed down the hill. "In there, I believe we'll learn what killed the giant and resealed the tomb."

"And why they left you that sword?"

"Probably." Ciras shivered. *And if they intend I use it to finish the killing of my master, they will learn they have made a very bad choice.*

It took them less time to reach the opening than Ciras had calculated, and it appeared to have grown during their journey. Somewhat narrow, the arched opening soared to a height of thirty feet. Just inside it, far enough to be hidden in shadows, stood two guardian figures, but any attempt to identify them failed.

The figures each stood twenty feet tall and, while quite humanoid in shape, lacked any definition. They had been shaped of mud that had hardened, and as Ciras rode past it was easy to pick out places where cracks had been patched. Artistically, they were not much more sophisticated than a child's snowman, and they lacked any discernible features.

Riding between them, Ciras kept his hand on the *vanyesh* sword's hilt. Borosan kept pace with him, his expression fluctuating between wonder and suspicion.

"What is it, Borosan?"

"Those statues were made of *thaumston* mud. Just one would be worth a fortune in Moriande."

"Comforting to know."

They rode forward another twenty yards, having gotten halfway into the tunnel. The reflected light pouring in through the opening revealed another opening further on, but they got little chance to study it as the light from outside began to shrink. In the moments before they were plunged into utter darkness, Ciras turned to watch the entrance iris shut.

"What now, Master Dejote?"

"We keep riding. Don't look back."

"Why not?"

"Because I believe the guardians are following us."

Sitting as tall as he could in the saddle, Ciras gently spurred his mount forward. They rode for another dozen yards, the clopping of horse's hooves echoing through the tunnel. Ciras strained to hear any sound of the guardian statues behind them, but he discerned nothing. *So huge, and so silent.* In an instant he knew what had killed the giant, why the monk-stone had shifted, and why he felt they'd been watched.

Up ahead, a series of torches ignited with a blue flame—the blue of the *gyanrigot* lamps he'd seen in

Opaslynoti. Figures shambled forward, bearing the torches high in one hand, knuckling the ground with the other every four or five steps. As they grew closer and Ciras got a good look at them, he resisted the urge to order them out of his way.

The creatures had once been men—wildmen, the human stock that the Viruk had used as slaves. Shorter than True Men, with narrow chests and foreshortened limbs, they had almost enough body hair to be considered a pelt. These wore loincloths of leather and their bodies were covered, it appeared, in dust of the same stone used to shape the guardians.

More remarkably, however, was the fact that their heads were encased entirely in clay helmets, which clearly had been worked to an elaborate degree that seemingly defied their apparent skill levels. The helmets included a full face mask, and while the faces lacked much expression, they clearly had been created to resemble specific individuals. The dozen wildmen wore three different faces among them and though the torches' blue light did little to reveal color, Ciras detected some differences.

As the circle of light grew, the wildmen stopped and dropped to their knees. Half the number, those not bearing the torches, shuffled forward, then bowed deeply. They muttered something repeatedly, but Ciras could not catch it.

He looked at Borosan, but the inventor just shrugged. "It sounds akin to what you said the night you exercised with that sword."

That sent a shiver down Ciras' spine. Despite his unease, he did hazard a glance behind and got another shock.

The guardians had indeed followed. Each had sunk to one knee and pressed one arm to the ground, while their free hands touched their left breasts. They even bowed their heads, but so tall were they that Ciras could see that the faces had taken on crude definition.

One of the wildmen stood and approached. "Masters our beg you guests our."

The travelers exchanged glances. Ciras nodded. "Tell your masters we would be delighted."

The wildman cocked his head like a dog.

"Let me try." Borosan smiled. "Tell masters your happy guests us."

The wildman bowed sharply, then froze, as did the other three wearing that same face. The quartet then bowed, and the other eight followed a heartbeat later. They rose to their feet and turned as one. The wildman who had been the spokesman waved them forward.

Ciras looked at Borosan. "Did you have to tell them we were happy?"

"Do you want them to think we are not?"

"Good point." Ciras followed the wildmen slowly, and tried to see through the opening at the tunnel's far end. Even as they grew closer, the images remained obscured, and it was not until they moved through something as heavy as a curtain, but invisible, that he got a look at their goal.

As nearly as Ciras could tell, the entire mountain had been hollowed out. Against the walls and working out to the center of the opening, mud dwellings had been constructed in a pattern that, at best, was haphazard. Some clung to walls like birds' nests and others leaned heavily against their neighbors. Some even rose to three and four stories, with crude ladders leading from one level to another. All around the city, wildmen—men, women, and feral children—swarmed like lice over the buildings.

The building at the center, however, mocked the dwellings around it. There was no mistaking it for anything less than an Imperial citadel, with its thick walls and tall towers ending in pyramidal roofs. The roofs had even been tiled as Ciras recalled from murals, and representations of the gods lurked at each corner.

What surprised him about the fortress was that neither mud nor stone had been used to create it. It appeared to have been shaped of swords and spears, shields and armor. There was no mistaking the forms, which fit flawlessly together. *All the things we have been hunting—most all of them anyway—are here.* He saw weapons of Imperial and Turasynd manufacture. Here and there, motes of light played along sharp edges or over some detailed embossing, then trailed up over a web of filaments that rose to connect the citadel to the mountain surrounding it.

"Where are we, Borosan?"

"I don't know."

"Masters welcome bid." The wildman spread his arms. "Name Tolwreen."

Ciras shot Borosan a sharp glance. "That's the name of Grija's Eighth Hell, the one saved for magicians."

Borosan nodded slowly. "The one, according to the stories, from which there is no escape."

Chapter Twenty-nine

19th day, Month of the Dragon, Year of the Rat
10th Year of Imperial Prince Cyron's Court
163rd Year of the Komyr Dynasty
737th year since the Cataclysm
Thyrenkun, Felarati
Deseirion

"Excuse me, did you say something?" Keles looked up from the table. A large sheet of rice paper was weighted with candleholders at the corners and on it Keles had been drafting a map of the new Felarati. He included sketches on separate sheets for other developments that could be overlaid to expand the city.

The woman to whom he had spoken laid her five-stringed *necyl* and its bow across her lap and cast her eyes down. She wore a robe of crimson with silver edging. Her crest, embroidered in silver and black on the sleeves and breasts, featured two doves nesting. A silver tie gathered her long black hair.

"I asked if there was another selection that would please you."

"My lady, forgive me, but I get drawn into the things I am doing. In preparing a map, I can see the way things will be, and I become anxious." He pointed beyond the table toward the balcony. "You've lived all your life here; you see the changes. Imagine this city transformed."

She nodded, then smiled slowly. "It shall forever remind me of you."

"You're very kind." Keles capped his bottle of ink and dried the brush on an ink-stained cloth. Much as Princess Jasai had predicted, Lady Inyr Vnonol had been introduced into his circle of acquaintances just over a week and a half ago and had quickly made demands on his time. She was clearly his to use in any capacity he desired.

He might have, too, were it not for two things. The first was his conversation with the Princess. It put him on his guard, and when Inyr moved into his circle, she'd been simple to spot as a spy.

The other thing that made him wary was really a tribute to the Desei Mother of Shadows. Save for her age and maturity, Inyr might as well have been Majiata Phoesel, his ex-fiancée. Inyr's eyes were a slightly lighter shade of blue, but her hair, height, and form were identical to the woman he'd left behind in Moriande. In choosing her, the Desei thought they had found him the perfect mate. Somehow they had missed the way his relationship with Majiata had ended.

Or maybe they hadn't. Inyr Vnonol did have a maturity that Majiata had lacked. Inyr, from the beginning, had been devoted to Keles. She seemed to want nothing more than to bask in his presence, and she evidenced no interest at all in his work. By contrast, Majiata would have been very interested—at least up to the point where she realized that anything he was willing to show her would be of no value to her family.

Keles turned from his table and smiled at her. "You play beautifully. Whenever I hear the *necyl* played, I shall be reminded of you."

Her head came up and she smiled more fully. "But I understood the *necyl* is not often played in Nalenyr. Did not one of your princes outlaw it?"

And with good cause. "He thought it sounded like a cat being gutted. That's not what he would have thought had he heard you playing it." *He would have thought it sounded like a cat being gutted slowly.*

"Now you flatter me, Master Anturasi." She shot him a gaze that did send a flutter through his stomach. "Toward what end, I wonder?"

Keles widened his eyes. "Oh, my lady, you do not think I mean to seduce you and despoil your honor? I could never do that. What sort of guest would I be to Prince Pyrust were I to use one of his citizens so?"

"I do not take offense, Master Anturasi."

"Oh, but you should, my lady." Keles turned his head so he could not see her. "You come here as a friend, knowing I am lonely and far from home. You play for me, seeking to make me feel better and . . . The truth is, my lady, that a part of me may indeed have been trying to seduce you. A dark, dishonorable part. I'm sorry. You are kind when you say you take no offense, but I know you must be shocked."

"Truly, Master Anturasi, I understand." She set her instrument aside and rose from her knees. "I can see the pain you are in. The longing: for home, for friends, for confidants, for a kind touch . . ."

He held a hand up to stop her. "No, Lady Inyr, you

mustn't. It's all true what you say. You have defined my weakness perfectly. And you, a true friend, would help me."

"I wish to be more than your friend, Master Anturasi." The warmth and underlying *hunger* in her voice would have made him succumb, were he not well aware she was a spy in his household. "I, too, feel loneliness, the need for the touch of a friend . . ."

"No, my lady. No." Keles shook his head, still refusing to look at her. "You are a sympathetic soul. You empathize with me, but at your peril. Your Prince has told me I will be sent home at the end of six months, perhaps sooner. I would be weak and use you, but you deserve more, so much more."

She said nothing, letting the rustle of her silk robe speak for her. She reached out and touched his hand. "Perhaps, Master Anturasi, I would be permitted to leave with you."

A Desei spy in Anturasikun? Even if I were madly in love with her, that would not be possible.

Keles jerked his hand back. "Don't say that, my lady."

"Would it be so horrible?"

"For you, yes. To be ripped from your home and settled in an alien city where you would be viewed with suspicion or pity or both? To have no life save for existing in Anturasikun? I remember the day I met you, in the gardens here. I could never see you captive in my family's tower. Though I might desire it, it would kill you.

"No, you best go now. Hurry, my lady, before my resolve evaporates. Go now, quickly, I beg of you."

"As you wish, Master Anturasi." She walked swiftly to the door, slid it open, and stepped through, but paused a moment to look back before closing it. The moment it closed again, he glanced to the corner where she had been sitting and saw her *necyl* and bow still there.

And now she has a reason to return.

He devoutly wished she would not. He'd not slept well, having had another dream about his sister in some faraway paradise. She seemed happy enough, but spoke only nonsense about the Sleeping Empress. Something about the dream made it feel more like a nightmare, and he feared his sister was in some sort of danger.

A light rap came at the door, and that surprised him, for while he'd expected her to come back, he'd not expected her return so quickly. He turned toward the door, but before he could offer permission to enter, the door slid back. Princess Jasai entered and shut it behind her.

Keles slipped from his chair to his knees and bowed. "Greetings, Princess Jasai."

"And you, Master Anturasi. I have come to see the plans you have prepared." The Princess kept her voice loud for the benefit of the ears on the other side of the room's thin walls. "Has there been much progress?"

Keles answered in kind. "I'm delighted to show you what I have done."

Jasai rose and crossed to his table. She shot a glance at the *necyl,* then shook her head.

Keles smiled and returned to his chair. Jasai joined him at the table. She smelled of roses, for she had a *bhotcai* whose skill was sufficient to grow the flowers year-round—even through the fierce Desei winter. Keles had never really cared one way or the other for roses, but the scent suited her perfectly—beautiful, but thorny.

"As you can see, Highness, the new residences are fairly far along. All that delays them is the need for building stones, which are slow to come from the quarries."

"Ah, yes, of course." Jasai lowered her voice. "It is as you guessed. The strongest among the people are being culled from the work gangs. I don't know yet where they are going."

"He won't hint?"

She shook her head. "I've not seen him for three days." She raised her voice again. "I meant to compliment you on how the building debris has been used to create berms for separating fields."

"It preserves rich earth, Highness, and allows us to segregate fields for flooding in years of drought." He glanced at her, again softening his voice. "If he has departed, vigilance will slacken."

"Save for that woman. She gave me a very satisfied smile as she passed me. Did you enjoy her?"

Keles shook his head. "Nor do I have any intention of it."

Jasai smiled and laid a hand on his shoulder. "Good."

"Let me show you these new sketches, Highness." Keles shifted paper about, knowing his papers would be examined while he was out of the room to see if the two of them communicated in some manner that had been undetected. He'd already examined the paper closely and found one set of tiny marks on it. He was certain all the paper stock was inventoried, and if any of it was found missing, the Desei would grow suspicious.

Jasai did not move her hand and Keles didn't mind at all. In fact, he liked it. He and Jasai had much in common. They were prisoners both of Prince Pyrust and of their bloodlines. They wanted to escape and knew it would be difficult. They also had nations they loved that were the focus of her husband's plans, and anything they could do to forestall those plans would be wonderful.

Keles had also become aware that Jasai would willingly accept him into her bed to forge their alliance more tightly. The differences between what she was willing to do and what Inyr wanted were vast, however. Jasai would be acting of her own free will and clearly doing what was in her best interest. Since her interest was tied so closely with his, it would be to his benefit as well. Inyr, on the other hand, was an agent of the state, and what she did would only be of benefit to the state. There his interests and hers diverged sharply, which was more than sufficient reason for him to stay away from her.

But though the Princess would have made herself available to him, Keles did not avail himself of her charms. Her pregnancy didn't concern him—his mother had explained the mysteries of pregnancy to all of her children in sufficient detail that they knew what was safe and what was not. As a skilled botanist, she also concocted many potions and tinctures to prevent or enhance fertility, or even to rid someone of its consequences.

He'd found one of Jasai's thorns when he'd commented that it would be easy enough for her to lose Pyrust's child if she hated him so. She'd turned on him, icy blue eyes ablaze, and fought to keep her voice down. "This child is not just his, it is *mine* as well. He wants an heir with a claim to the Dog Throne, and now *I* have an heir with a claim to the Hawk Throne. Just because I hate him, it does not mean I hate my child. If love and hate are but faces on the same coin, then the hate goes to him, and the love to my child. You will not speak of this again, Master Anturasi."

He had apologized and she had accepted it, but things had remained icy for a couple of days. She never apologized for her reaction, and he knew she never would. She had, however, realized his comment had not been a malicious one, just something innocently helpful. He did take care after that, however, to hold his tongue until he had worked through the various ramifications of what he was going to say.

"If you look here, Highness, I have laid out a new pattern for the garden. While I am a cartographer, my mother worked with flowers and plants, so I appreciate her art. Each bed would represent one of the nine, and the flowers would blossom in the national colors."

"Yes, but it would be a bad omen were one nation or another to become overgrown with weeds, would it not?" She squeezed his shoulder, then whispered to him, "I believe the Desei are going to attack Helosunde, and there is nothing I can do to prevent it. Even if the Council of Ministers knew it was coming, I doubt there is anything they *could* or even *would* do to stop it."

"The ministers?" Keles frowned. "They are functionaries, nothing more."

She laughed lightly. "You are lucky if you can believe that, Keles. Because of your grandfather and the power he wielded, the bureaucracy could do very little to interfere with your life.

"In my nation, however, the ministers were able to take power. While they have done things like elect my brother as the Prince, they chose him because he was weak. When the last prince died, the nation passed to their stewardship, and they had grown tired of being the power behind the throne. Instead of hiding behind a prince, they cloak themselves in patriotic pieties and claim what they do is for the benefit of Helosunde. And, yet, nothing they have done has won back a single inch of Helosunde."

"They would have done better to elect you, Princess."

She nodded, her blonde hair a shower of gold over her shoulders. "They dared not, for I would have been too strong for them."

Keles looked up at her and smiled. He had no doubt she was right about the ministers. *She's strong-willed enough to be a match for my grandfather!*

"You know, if we try to escape and fail, they will kill us."

She nodded. "There is no guarantee they won't kill us at any time my husband desires, or his Mother of Shadows decides we have outlived our usefulness." Jasai ran a hand over her stomach. "My child will be born in the month of the Rat. After that, my life is worthless."

Keles grinned ruefully. "I don't think I've got even that long."

"And our chances to escape end even sooner. Once I begin to show, my ability to escape dwindles."

"I know, but I've been thinking." He tapped his plans of the city. "The Black River will flood sometime in the next six weeks. We make it out of here by then, or we're never getting away."

Chapter Thirty

21st day, Month of the Dragon, Year of the Rat
10th Year of Imperial Prince Cyron's Court
163rd Year of the Komyr Dynasty
737th year since the Cataclysm
The Plains before Moryne
(Helosunde) Deseirion

Clad in black armor, with a golden hawk emblazoned on his breastplate, standing on a hill and flanked by two banners that proclaimed his presence, Prince Pyrust watched the battle unfold on the plains below. To the southwest, far in the distance, he could see the grey smudge that marked Moryne—the city that had once been Helosunde's capital. The cream of Helosundian martial glory—save those troops in service to the Naleni throne—had arrayed themselves in a formation across his line of march and advanced.

Their intent, it seemed, was to drive his line's center backward until they could overrun his hill, taking him, his banners, and freeing themselves from the Desei yoke forever. He had no doubt many of them dreamed of pushing further, taking Felarati and making Deseirion their plaything. If he lost this battle, he would die. His country would die and his people would suffer.

And that cannot be allowed to happen.

A casual glance at the battlefield, however, would have suggested that that was exactly what would happen. Until four days previous, his Fire Hawk battalion had been the garrison in Moryne. Following his orders, they gathered up all the grain they could find transport for and began a retreat toward Meleswin. Helosundian rebels, having long since learned of the horrible harvest in Deseirion, accepted the rumors that food riots were the reason for recalling the troops and bringing their rice north. They decided they could strike a fierce blow against their conqueror by attacking the Fire Hawks and preventing the rice from leaving Helosunde.

Pyrust had expected a lot of opposition, but the number of troops arrayed against him had surprised him. He'd been able to move two entire regiments southwest from Meleswin—including the Fire Hawks, though he kept the Iron Hawks and Silver Hawks in reserve behind the hill. For all intents and purposes it looked as if he had just under a thousand troops at his command.

The rebels had amassed a force roughly three times that size. Pyrust recognized a number of banners in the rabble—primarily because the originals were displayed in Felarati. The reconstituted units might have laid claim to Helosundian tradition, but many of the soldiers had clearly come to battle with little training and weaponry more suited to agriculture than warfare. One whole battalion held in reserve appeared to be unarmed, but by the time they came to the fight, there would be ample arms to be recovered from the battlefield.

He had no idea who commanded the enemy force, and the absence of a clear command post buoyed his spirits. It appeared as if the Helosundians had been roughly divided into three parts—right, left, and center—each under its own commander. The center, which was set to engage his best troops, had more of the seasoned warriors. Despite their inexperience, the wings could easily encircle his force and, once it had done that, turn his flanks and win the day.

He shook his head. He hoped it was one of the Council of Ministers that sought to fight the battle against him. Bureaucrats repeatedly governed their actions in accord with Urmyr's Books of Wisdom, but they seemed to have forgotten he'd once been a general for Emperor Taichun. He'd written another treatise based on his experiences on the battlefield, titled *The Dance of War,* and Pyrust found his teachings of great comfort.

A battle is won before the first arrow flies or the first sword cuts.

The Helosundians had come northeast expecting to ambush one battalion, so when morning dawned and they discovered that the Desei were not moving on, but had drawn up in a battle line and had been reinforced, they scrambled to prepare for battle. In their hasty pursuit, they had not brought much with them by way of provisions, thinking they would soon liberate the rice and feast. The Fire Hawks had always pushed on faster than the Helosundians, forcing them to march longer than they had any desire to do. As a result, they came to the battle tired and hungry.

His troops, on the other hand, were for the most part rested, well fed, and well trained. He did not doubt that each of them felt fear when they looked at the mob surging toward them. There would be jokes, about how each only had to kill three of the dogs and he could retire for the day, but each knew these Helosundian Dogs would take a fair amount of killing.

He'd arrayed his troops with the Golden Hawks to the fore. The Mountain Hawks and Fire Hawks were positioned to the right and left respectively drawn back, with their flanks overlapping the Golden Hawk rear. The Shadow Hawks were right behind the Golden Hawks.

Pyrust snapped open a black fan with a large red ball emblazoned on it. He raised it above his head, flashing the symbol, then turned it edge on to the troops, and brought his hand straight down.

Commanders in the Shadow Hawks shouted orders. The Golden Hawks spread their rear ranks and the Shadow Hawks ran forward. They nocked arrows, drew, and loosed, rank after rank, into the Helosunde center. Each arrow found a mark, and while a few stuck in shields or skipped off armor, most sank to the fletching into flesh, and men fell screaming.

The Helosundian archers replied, but it was a whisper to what had been a shout. Some of his Hawks did fall when arrows found gaps in armor, but many of the Helosundian bows lacked the power they needed to penetrate armor. *My men are not peahens to be stuck so easily.*

The Shadow Hawks loosed another four volleys, thinning the ranks of the Helosundian center, then stopped and retreated. He didn't know if the leaders on the other side understood the significance of five volleys, but five months hence it would be the month of the Dog, Helosunde's month, and he had chosen to honor them that way.

Honor them before he slaughtered them.

Pyrust waited as his wounded and dead were evacuated. The other side closed ranks, squeezing the center. This he had expected, for what general would not do that? The Helosundian center had been its strength, but now it had become its weakness. The trained troops moved forward to fill in the front line, while the back ranks on the wings flowed toward the middle to take up the empty space.

Which moves them further from the battle than they want to be if they are to be effective.

He raised his fan again, displaying the red ball. He flipped it front and back, showing both sides, then brought it down to wave at the Helosundian lines. Orders were shouted below and the Shadow Hawks, in disarray, shifted behind the Fire Hawks on the right. The Golden Hawks moved forward, opening a gap between them and their supporting units. Their advance slowed as the Golden Hawks realized they had no support, then they began to retreat.

The Helosundians charged.

Barely fifty yards separated the two forces, but the Golden Hawk retreat stretched that distance. The Fire Hawks and Mountain Hawks started to pull back, too, shortening the Desei lines. Both Helosundian wings charged faster, trying to make sure they would all engage the Desei at the same time, but their flank companies never could quite catch up.

When the Golden Hawk flanks again touched the other units, orders were snapped and the retreat stopped. His soldiers tightened their ranks and set their spears. The Helosundians came on, slowing not out of fear but out of exhaustion. Batting aside spears, men smashed into the Desei line. Swords battered shields, clubs smashed limbs, swords stabbed deep, and screaming men rose into the air impaled on spears.

Pyrust lofted his fan into the air, letting it spin end over end. It slowed, then began to fall again, whirling down like a maple seed. The Helosundians, mistaking this gesture for one of surrender, shouted with great hope.

False hope.

Black arrows arced out from the Shadow Hawks, cutting down the ranks pressing the Desei center. The archers shot again and again, as fast as they could draw and release. Their arrows reached deep into the Helosundian formation and the standard-bearers for the Emerald Dog battalion repeatedly died as they fought to keep their unit's standard from touching the ground.

From behind Pyrust came the rumble of thunder—though he was certain no one in the battle heard it. To the right and left of his hill came the Silver and Iron Hawks. Quartets of horses pulled massive war chariots, with two archers on risers behind the drivers. Sword blades four feet in length had been welded to each axle. They spun and glittered in the morning sunlight as the chariots came around the hill and into the battle.

Arrows ate into the Helosundian flanks, then the chariots grazed past. The blades cut men down horribly and their screams sparked panic in their fellows. Each man on the flank knew he was next, and few willingly faced death. Many fought to get deeper into the formation, which destroyed any pretense of discipline or order. Others just broke and ran—and this tactic was rewarded by an arrow in the back.

Chaos reigned among the Helosundians. Their back ranks turned and ran. The flanks buckled, which allowed his wings to push forward, inverting the battle line. While there were valiant and fierce warriors among the Dogs, they were rebels and did not merit honorable treatment. If they managed to kill his warriors in even combat, squads of Shadow Hawks would order the others back and shoot them.

And, curiously enough, he found no valiant warriors among the Helosundian leaders.

Pyrust watched the rebel force disintegrate, then retrieved his fan, raised it, and snapped it closed. His order slowly filtered through the troops, and they returned to camp, save those set out as pickets, those designated to dispatch the grievously wounded, and those sent to look for prisoners who might have information or be good for ransom.

He studied the field, then shook his head. ***As Urmyr has said in*** The Dance of War, ***with an understanding of weakness and strength, an army can strike like a millstone cast at an egg.*** The Helosundian force had been smashed and its yolk lay red and writhing on what once had been a green field.

"Yours is a great victory, Highness."

Pyrust tucked his fan into his left gauntlet. "So it would seem, Mother of Shadows. Then again, a millstone should crush an egg, should it not? We shall see how things go when we meet another millstone."

The crone pointed south toward Nalenyr. "The millstone waiting you there is small and brittle. Prince Eiran commands a Naleni force made up of westron troops. They will not stop you."

"Do they know we are coming?"

"Not yet. Your Black Hawks and Stone Hawks have

cut the road south, so refugees will flee toward Vallitsi. They will have things to tell the Council of Ministers."

Pyrust nodded. "News from home?"

"All is well, though work slows because of those being drawn into the military. No alarm has gone out. The Hyreothi ambassador thought to send a message, but his courier died." The assassin's eyes narrowed. "I do have more news from the south, Highness."

"Yes?"

"The reason the westrons are under Helosundian command is because Count Turcol of Jomir is dead. He was riding with Prince Cyron when bandits ambushed the royal party. All of the westrons died and Cyron was grievously wounded."

"Wounded? How badly?"

"Rumor has it he may lose his left hand."

Pyrust looked down at his own left hand, his half hand. "That could be dangerous. Losing half my hand made me twice as smart as I'd been before."

"Four times an idiot is still an idiot, Highness."

"As is twice an idiot, Delasonsa."

She bowed her head to him. "I did not mean it as an insult, Highness."

"I know, but I also know you are too intelligent to dismiss Cyron so lightly. Those were not bandits. Was it Turcol who wanted him dead, or were the assassins sponsored by someone else?" Pyrust's expression tightened. "They were not *ours,* were they?"

"No, Highness, else they would be dead now. So would the Prince have been. The agent I have in position believes Turcol hatched the plan on his own. But this does not preclude others choosing the same tactic, Highness—even yourself."

The Desei Prince firmly shook his head. "No. It shall not be an assassin of mine who kills Cyron at this time. I reserve that option for one of my troops, or myself." He smiled, imagining the look of surprise on Cyron's face when he pinned him to the throne with his sword.

"I shall let that be known, Highness."

"Very good." Pyrust pointed back toward the battlefield. "There will be survivors. See what they know. Save nine of the most hearty. Blind three, cut the ears off three, and cut the tongues out of three. Send one of each on to Moryne, Vallitsi, and Solie. Let them show their brothers what the fate shall be of all who resist us. Worse will come to their families."

"Your will shall be done, Master."

"And, Delasonsa, let them know that those who choose to fight for the honor of Princess Jasai shall be welcomed as brothers, feted as champions, and showered with glory as heroes."

The crone raised an eyebrow. "Linking their fate with hers, Highness, might not be the most wise course. You will make them think they are men."

"You're doubtlessly right, but they shall be the millstone I cast south, and south again. Better I learn how to fight whatever I face over their bodies than those of my Hawks."

The Mother of Shadows remained still for a moment, then nodded. "There will be war enough to consume them all."

"And dead enough to choke Grija." Pyrust raised his head. "And with a proper knowledge of weakness and strength, we shall not be among them."

Chapter Thirty-one

21st day, Month of the Dragon, Year of the Rat
10th Year of Imperial Prince Cyron's Court
163rd Year of the Komyr Dynasty
737th year since the Cataclysm
Nemehyan, Caxyan

"Jorim Anturasi, you cannot stay in the dark forever."

Jorim turned toward the sound of the voice. "I can, Captain Gryst, and I fully intend to do so." He kept his voice low enough that it barely echoed within the subterranean chamber. Water no longer dripped from the ceiling, and he'd been left alone save for food, which was slid in on a gold plate once a day. He didn't know how many days he'd been there, and he did not care. *When you are never leaving, time is unimportant.*

Up on the catwalk above him, Anaeda Gryst opened the shutter on a lantern. Blue-white light filtered into the room, and she gasped audibly. "You're sick. You have to get out of here now."

Jorim raised his hands to protect his eyes. "No,

Captain, you don't understand." He knew what she'd seen: his skin was coming off in chunks, peeling off the way it would after a savage sunburn. His hair had been bleached white as bones. His eyes remained blue, but when he looked at them in a bowl of water, they had a corona undulating around them in gold and red. Worse yet, his pupils had taken on a lozenge shape, more like a serpent or a dragon. And while she might see him peeling normally, he saw his skin coming off in scales.

"I've heard the stories, Jorim, I know what happened at the *Blackshark.*"

"No, you don't, Captain."

"I thought we had an agreement, Master Anturasi. You don't defy my orders."

"With all due respect, Captain, and I mean that sincerely, I don't think I'm part of your command anymore. I'm a god, remember? I use magic. I am a danger to anyone I come near."

"That last is nonsense."

"Is it?" He looked up at her through narrowed eyes. "Why aren't you as smart as the Fennych? Shimik saw. Shimik knows. He is terrified of me. The rest of you should be, too."

"How can I or anyone else be terrified of you when you saved a ship and part of the crew? You destroyed enemies that had overrun a village and killed everyone in it. You saved the warriors who were with you in the jungle and surely would have died had you not acted."

"Because, Captain, no one knows how I did it, and no one knows what else I am capable of doing."

Anaeda shook her head. "You know, Jorim."

He pounded his balled fists on the stone where he sat. "That's just it. I don't know!"

She laughed. "That's what has you bothered?"

"How can you laugh?" He pointed toward the harbor. "Didn't you see the footprints I left on the deck? Those were dragon's feet."

"And counted as a good omen! You had a skeleton crew to sail her back here and yet everyone says the *Blackshark* never sailed so sweet."

Jorim stood and held his hands up. "No, you just don't understand."

"Jorim!" The commanding tone in her voice brought his head up. "You have gone places no civilized man has ever gone, and you have explained mysteries no one else could. Either this is something truly beyond you, in which case you better figure it out and fast, or it's something you don't *want* to look at. And if it's the latter case, be warned. If you don't understand it or come to control it, it will be worse than you can imagine."

"Fine, you want to know what happened? I'll tell you." Jorim pointed at the lantern. "Put that out first."

Anaeda folded her arms across her chest. "Do it yourself. You know how."

"Oh, so you accept I can work magic? Do you think this is just a collection of conjurer's tricks to terrify children? I can do things that would have made the *vanyesh* envious. All the stories of them *never* approached what I did."

He spun on his little stone island and pointed off north. "The Mozoyan, the new ones, were already swarming over the *Blackshark*. They were coming in toward the beach. I didn't know what to do. Magic is about balance and states of being. I wanted to shift the balance to make the ocean boil, but I couldn't. Then I saw the sun as Wentiko—it *is* the month when the sun rises in his constellation after all. I linked myself to him and drew on the sun's nature."

He balled his fists and held his arms out as he had when flying. "At first, I just looked at the Mozoyan and made their eyes boil. I made their brains boil. I remember doing that consciously. Then suddenly I was flying. I didn't do things to them, my *presence* did it. I could see them melting, and with a casual gesture, I burned their transport black."

"And in doing so you saved many lives."

"Yes, but I wasn't thinking about that. I wasn't thinking at all." He shook his head. "The crew was hiding. If they had looked at me, they would have died, too. You can't tell me that is not true. Tzihua told me of the birds and monkeys from the forest who looked upon me and died."

"Perhaps, Jorim, you were killing things that were not human."

"But I didn't kill the plants." He laughed lightly, then scratched a patch of flesh from his nose. "Some of them blossomed and bore fruit that afternoon."

She frowned at him. "I've yet to hear anything that should make me fear you."

Jorim looked up. "How much different from a bird or a monkey do you think you are? I killed them without even thinking about it. What if the next time I am seeking to kill everything that isn't male, or isn't tall, and you or Nauana get caught?"

"Then the issue is not about what you can do, but how much control you have over it. You can learn control."

"Are you certain? The *vanyesh* played with magic and almost destroyed the world. I could be better at it than they were."

"They're all dead."

Jorim looked down. "Maybe I will be, too."

Anaeda cocked her head. "Is that it?"

"Look at me, Anaeda. I had the radiance of the sun pouring out through me. My flesh is coming off. My eyes have changed. My hair is white. I've aged a generation or two."

"Jorim, you have two issues you are dealing with here, and somehow you've decided there's one solution that will handle both. But it's not the best solution."

"I'm not certain I understand you."

She sighed. "Let's look at the first one. You fear you're dying, or that magic might kill you. Your skin is peeling, but let me ask you, does it hurt?"

"What?"

"Does your skin hurt the way a bad sunburn does?"

He shook his head. "No."

"No bloody lesions?"

"No."

"And the skin is healthy beneath?"

Jorim shrugged and rubbed a patch bare on his left wrist. "It seems to be."

"You said your eyes have changed. Perhaps the rest of you has, too." She smiled. "You know the tales of gods taking the form of men to walk among us. Who knows what the transformation is like?"

"That's not reassuring." Jorim frowned. "But I'll accept, for the moment, that I might not be dying."

"Well, also accept that if you were, your use of magic might reverse your slide."

"Yes, and drinking will cure a hangover—until it kills you."

"This brings us to your second problem." Anaeda

picked at a fingernail. "You're afraid of using magic because you know you can do serious harm. But as I said before, that is just a matter of control."

"What if I can't control it?"

"You can. You just have to learn how."

"What if I fail?"

"No, Jorim, I'm not giving you that out. You're an Anturasi. You've never been given a challenge you did not meet. Your grandfather may not have handed you this one, but you will meet it. It is not in your nature to fail."

He arched an eyebrow. "You hook me with my vanity. Very good, Captain. But maybe this is a challenge I will let pass."

"Why?"

Jorim opened his hands and looked down at the lanternlight dancing over the water surrounding his island. "Would you want to be a god?"

She thought for a moment, then shook her head. "No, it's not a mantle I would accept."

"Then why should I?"

"Because, Jorim, you may be like the Empress Cyrsa. You may be late come to your true talent."

Jorim waved that idea away. "I've had my talent since I was born. I'm an Anturasi and am a cartographer and explorer. It's all I've ever been and all I ever wanted to be."

"And that has nothing to do with your talent." Anaeda smiled. "Don't I remember you telling me that your mother is a *bhotcai*? Her talent is for dealing with plants."

"Yes."

"Then why would the Anturasi talent run any more

strongly in your veins than her talent? Could it be that you just chose to develop your cartography skills, but the other talent is there, too? Remember, the plants thrived when you shone on them."

"And animals died."

"And how many of those same sorts of animals have you killed in your explorations so you would have samples to study? Perhaps your emerging talent, your god-talent, amplifies what you already have."

Jorim closed his eyes. The things she was saying made sense, but he didn't want them to. If she was right, then he *was* a god, or was becoming a god, which meant the power he had handled before was a fraction of what he might handle in the future. The results could be a disaster.

Especially if you do not learn to control that power.

"Captain, this is not idle speculation, and not something borne of this incident."

"No, it's not. You'll recall that I told you that Borosan Gryst is my cousin. He's skilled at tinkering with things. It's the Gryst talent. My mother, on the other hand, comes from a family of mariners. While I am a ship's captain and work hard at it, I also know how things work and how to fix them. This is why, during your time in the dark here, I have been able to maintain the chronometer, which allowed you to calculate longitude."

"I had forgotten about that."

"And your negligence has been noted in my log. There will be consequences for that, Master Anturasi."

Jorim shook his head. "You're rejecting my argument that I'm no longer under your command?"

"God or no god, I *am* responsible for you, Jorim. Not

only are you a valuable asset for my fleet and mission, but you are a friend."

"So, being a ship's captain is like being a god?"

"Not at all." She smiled. "Gods are limited by their aspects."

"Yes, I guess they are. Their aspects, or their fears."

"I've been checking. Tetcomchoa knows no fear."

Jorim scratched at his forehead and more dead skin fell away. Before he could comment, Nauana came through the doorway, holding Shimik. The Fennych's fur had gone completely white.

Anaeda looked at the Amentzutl sorceress. "He may be at a point to listen to reason."

"Thank you, Captain." Nauana set the Fenn down and Shimik sat, clutching his legs to his chest. "Has she convinced you to emerge, Tetcomchoa?"

"More like she's convinced me there is no purpose in hiding anymore. I . . ." He raised his arms toward her, then slowly let them drop away. "If Tetcomchoa knows no fear, then I am not Tetcomchoa."

Nauana smiled quickly, then shook her head. "The translation was not clear. It is not that Tetcomchoa knows no fear, it is that he does not show it."

Jorim snorted. "Well, hiding down here for . . . however long it's been, that's a pretty good show of fear."

"It has not been seen as such, my lord." Nauana smiled. "You are the snake, and you have been shedding your skin. All have heard; all rejoice."

"All except Shimik."

At the sound of his name, the Fenn's head came up. "Jrima smart again?"

Anaeda looked down at the Fenn. "The best we're going to get for a while."

"And it will get better." Jorim brushed his arms off and watched a blizzard of dried flesh fall away.

Nauana nodded. "It must. You are to begin a series of purification rituals."

"Why?"

"News of your transformation has reached the highest circles." She pressed her hands together at her breastbone. "When you are ready, you will meet the Witch-King, and through him you will receive the remainder of that which you left behind when you last walked among us."

Chapter Thirty-two

23rd day, Month of the Dragon, Year of the Rat
10th Year of Imperial Prince Cyron's Court
163rd Year of the Komyr Dynasty
737th year since the Cataclysm
Kunjiqui, Anturasixan

Nirati was certain she'd never seen her grandfather so happy before, and this scared her. She'd seen him pleased in the past—by a new discovery or, more usually, someone else's misfortune. Often enough, Qiro had even been the cause of that misfortune. She'd even seen him tenderly pleased, as when she had brought him a picture or a sweetcake—things she had done as a child.

But no matter the cause of his pleasure, it had always been an adult pleasure—self-satisfied and controlled. Now, however, he exhibited a boyish glee that bordered on madness. In fact, she was fairly certain that he had become unhinged. This realization, which had been growing in her mind as Nelesquin had given Qiro more and more work, shook her to the core. Qiro had always been constant and strong. While he could be impulsive—especially when meting out punishment—decorum had established some boundaries beyond which he did not stray.

She looked at him, sitting there on a muddy flat at low tide, mud caking him and streaking his hair and beard. He reached down with a filthy hand, scooped up mud, spat in it, mixed it up, and shaped it into strange little creatures. He added new mudmen to the crews on the little boats he'd shaped from reeds.

He has *utterly lost his mind.*

From where she stood, his little armada looked nothing like Nelesquin's fleet. The Durrani had marched onto their ships in good order, whereas her grandfather's troops sagged and slumped against each other. The Durrani had all been tall and strong, clean of limb and keen of eye, whereas these creatures had little definition at all.

And when the tide comes in, they will be washed away forever.

Qiro looked up from his place in the mud, then struggled to his feet. "Oh, Nirati, you've come. Good, excellent. If it weren't for you, I could not have done this. Tell me you approve."

She blinked back her surprise and felt Takwee cling to her back a bit more tightly. *Grandfather asking for approval?* "I think it's wonderful, Grandfather. But I have to ask. What is it?"

The old man laughed warmly—an alien sound from his throat. "This is your brother's salvation, silly girl." He nodded toward the west and the area from which Nelesquin's Durrani kept launching more ships. "I would not bother Prince Nelesquin with such a trifling matter. I can handle it myself. Smaller task, smaller fleet, but nonetheless effective."

He waved her forward and began walking at the water's edge, as if a general reviewing his troops. He pointed to several boats jammed with globs of mud that looked like little more than lumps to her. "These are my Neshta. They're small, but quick, with claws and fangs. Hundreds of them, thousands perhaps—they are the first wave. They are like your Takwee there, but her darker, bellicose cousins, bred for war."

She nodded. "Ah, very good."

"And here, these larger ones—hence the larger boats—are my Provocs. They're as big as Viruk, but have *four* arms, not just two. When they begin to fight, there will be no standing against them. Oh, the havoc they will wreak!"

Nirati forced herself to smile. "And these here, Grandfather, the ones with golden sand sprinkled on their heads?"

"Clever girl, I knew you would notice." He clapped grimy hands, his fingernails black. "They are the Dernai. Half-handed, all of them, but with fierce claws, strong bodies, and a conqueror's will. They know no fear."

"It is an impressive army, Grandfather." Nirati pointed to one last boat, a boat that had a lone figure in it. Unlike the others, this one had been shaped of clay and worked with care. Obviously female, she'd been armored and provided with a seashell shield and a quill from a spinefish for a spear. "Who is that?"

Qiro knelt beside that last figure. "This is Lystai. She is my general and will lead my army. But there I need your help again."

"What do you need, Grandfather?"

He beckoned her to kneel beside him, then reached up and caressed her brown hair. "This will hurt for a heartbeat, but I must . . ." With a quick yank he plucked a single hair from her head, then daubed the root with mud and affixed it to Lystai's head.

"There, now she can find your brother and bring him to me."

Nirati frowned. "I'm not sure I understand."

"You probably think I don't remember, but I do. You said you dreamed of him, of Keles, and that he was in Deseirion. We can't have him there, trapped in Pyrust's court. My army will attack Felarati and free him."

"Oh, yes, Grandfather, very good." Nirati kept the smile on her face and looked down at the army baking in the sunlight. Her grandfather had absolutely lost his mind. Prince Cyron's grandfather had been said to learn how to fight battles based on games played with toy soldiers. Her grandfather, in retreating to his childhood, imagined he, too, could wage wars with toys.

She reached over and took her grandfather's hands in hers. "I know Keles will welcome his freedom and praise you for freeing him."

Qiro closed his eyes for a moment, then slowly nodded. "You know, I have not forgotten the past. I know that I have been a horrible taskmaster for your brothers, my brother, your father. I knew the potential in all of them. I had to drive them and drive them hard or they would have squandered it."

He opened his eyes again and looked out at his army. "Toys. Now I squander my talent."

"Hush, Grandfather. You've done great things. You've . . ." She looked around the landscape. "You've shaped all this. It is a miracle."

"No, Nirati, it is not." He smiled at her softly, freed a hand, and caressed a cheek. "Out of love, I shaped a place where I could defy the gods. In doing so I released forces that I cannot control."

"You make it sound as dire as if you've triggered another Cataclysm."

"Sweet child, in some ways it is." He slowly got to his feet and helped her up. They walked up the beach to warm golden sand, then sat again and watched the tide slowly roll in and float his tiny ships away.

"It's not a Cataclysm, Nirati, but could trigger another." He shook his head. "But the world needs purging of its evils, and there is more work to be done before the purge is complete."

Chapter Thirty-three

25th day, Month of the Dragon, Year of the Rat
10th Year of Imperial Prince Cyron's Court
163rd Year of the Komyr Dynasty
737th year since the Cataclysm
Ministry of Harmony, Moriande
Nalenyr

Pelut Vniel tugged back the sleeves of his blue robe and poured Viruk Tears tea for Koir Yoram, Helosunde's Minister of Foreign Relations. He really didn't want to be so hospitable, for the man had been difficult in the past. He promised to be so again, but Pelut had chosen to follow one of Urmyr's dicta and grant mercy and grace to the doomed.

Yoram already looked as if he'd ridden halfway through the Hells, and the fact that he had come immediately to the ministry without bathing or changing his soiled robe marked his sense of urgency. While Pelut was certain Koir meant to use his condition to emphasize the message he bore, he'd not taken the necessary steps to make Pelut feel obligated to him. Yes, his robe had been torn and he'd been mud-splashed; bits of leaves remained in his black hair; but nowhere did he bear a scratch of a thorn, nor did he have any broken bones.

You endured no pain for your cause, so I shall cause you pain. Even before Koir spoke a single word, Pelut knew what he would be asked, and also knew he would deny the request. Their ranks within the bureaucracy demanded the meeting happen, and Koir likely suspected the outcome already. Still, the game had to be played, and if Koir could present an advantage for Pelut, the foregone outcome might change.

Pelut smiled. "You've ridden far and fast. Have you come all the way from Vallitsi?"

"No, I came from Moryne directly and I bear dire news. Four days ago, the Desei attacked and defeated one of our armies, scattering it. Now they advance on Vallitsi." The man's blue eyes were sunken in dark pits in his face. "There are reports of thousands of Desei pouring south. Solie is under siege. Pyrust is pushing for the complete conquest of Helosunde, and Nalenyr must stop him."

Pelut marshaled all his strength and kept his reaction from his face. When Koir had arrived in such a state, he expected that the Desei had pushed into Helosunde again. For them to have already secured Moryne, which had only ever been nominally in their control, meant the Desei had secure lines of supply into the heart of Helosunde and, therefore, could stage for movement south. That they were pressing on to Vallitsi indicated that Pyrust was further stabilizing his power in the region.

And all this just at a time when our own best troops have gone south.

"Drink your tea, please, and eat something." Pelut waved a hand at the bowl of rice and fish on the low table before his guest. "I would not wish to be seen as inhospitable to a man bearing such grave news."

Koir, never one for the civilities, fixed him with a hard stare. "Which means you are not going to help."

"I think, Minister, you misspeak. Fill your mouth with food instead of inanity." Pelut poured himself some tea and sipped it, ignoring his guest for a moment. He savored the rich, dark tea. It was from the island of Dreonath and said to be flavored with the tears of the Viruk.

After his visitor had surrendered and sipped some tea, Pelut lowered his own cup and folded his hands in his lap. "Though you are well aware of it, Minister, you will recall that my Prince recommended against the ill-fated attack on Meleswin. Pyrust retaliated in the New Year's Festival and retook his city."

"*Our* city."

"*His* city, and you know it." Pelut shook his head. "You lost a city, you lost a general, you lost valiant troops, and you lost a princess."

"She was a duchess."

"And he made her a princess when he married her. He was wise enough to leave you a prince. Had he not, your Council of Ministers would have garnered more power by playing nobles off against nobles."

Koir's head came up. "And you do not do this?"

The Naleni minister's expression hardened. "What do you mean to suggest, Minister?"

"It would not be possible for Count Turcol to conceive of or execute a plan to assassinate Prince Cyron without your complicity."

Pelut slowly smiled. "I have no idea what you are talking about. Count Turcol died defending his Prince against bandits. The Prince himself was wounded, and the wound is not healing well."

The Helosundian laughed. "You play the game very well, but there are things you do not know. For example, in searching for assassins, Turcol first approached some of my people. He was clumsy in his attempts, and we deemed the effort doomed to failure, so we rejected it. He did not care. He simply found others to do what needed to be done—and he was not even smart enough to kill those of my people he'd approached. Curious about how things would turn out, and determined Prince Eiran would not die at the same time, my people saw everything."

Not possible. The Prince told me the Lord of Shadows had uncovered the plot. I confirmed Turcol had spoken with me but not about the depths of his treachery, just how to extend the invitation.

"Fascinating information, Minister. I shall tell the Prince about it immediately."

Koir shook his head. "No, you will not. I, on the other hand, will convey that information to Count Vroan, and couple it with an accusation that *you* betrayed his son-in-law to the Prince. You will have to admit that it plays well, since it allowed you to do the Prince a favor—and to rid yourself of the most-difficult-to-control of the westron lords."

Pelut allowed himself a little chuckle. "Well played, but you miss the point, Minister. You, in fact, don't know if I betrayed Count Turcol or not. I may well have, for reasons well beyond your ken or care. Of greater interest to you might be the fact that I have enough information to destroy the westron rebels whenever I desire."

Koir bowed his head for a moment, then smiled as he looked up. "But you have not, because you need them to unsettle Cyron. You wanted him to die because you knew Turcol would be unable to administer the nation without you. Cyron, prince that he is, could do your job and do it well. He's exceeded you in his program of exploration, in fact. And were I to tell Prince Eiran of your complicity in the assassination attempt, he would tell Cyron, and you would be dead."

Fear trickled into Pelut's stomach. He drank more tea, but it had turned sour. He could easily deny what Koir told Prince Eiran and claim that the Helosundians were trying to blackmail him into betraying Prince Cyron because Pyrust was pressing them. Doing that, however, would force Cyron to acknowledge Pyrust's progress south. He might pull troops back from the Virine border, which would leave his nation open to invasion, or call up more troops from the interior to stop the Naleni. That option would increase westron anger, further ripping the nation apart, and would leave Nalenyr open to conquest from the north.

The horror of Desei conquest shook Pelut, but only for a moment. He looked past it because of one of Koir's other comments. He'd been correct: Cyron could administer the nation without Pelut. While that did make him an impediment, it also made one other thing perfectly clear: Cyron was no general. Pyrust was, and the threat from the south was an invasion. The Desei Prince could defeat it.

Cyron could not.

If Cyron continues to rule, all *is lost.*

Just for a heartbeat Pelut pitied Prince Cyron. Time and circumstance, the gods and fate had put on the Dragon Throne the leader most capable of completing the healing of the world. Cyron had sent grain north to Pyrust to buy the Desei leader off, but also because he didn't want the Desei people to starve. Such compassion, while laudable in a time of peace, was weakness in a time of war.

Pelut set his cup down. "What is it you desire, Minister?"

Koir smiled graciously. "We want our mercenaries returned north so they may march against the Desei. We want all grain shipments to Deseirion to stop. We want a Naleni fleet to set sail for Felarati and burn it in punishment for what Pyrust has done."

Pelut bowed his head. "Ambitious and impossible. You know that. There will be no fleet. Grain shipments will slacken, though the Desei likely liberated a great deal of rice from Moryne. We will move troops north again."

"And attack immediately."

Pelut shook his head. "Pyrust is overextended. Cyron cannot allow him to have Moryne, and Moryne cannot be held without supplies. We will cut it off and strangle it. This is the best I can offer."

"It's more than I expected." Koir nodded slowly. "Your position is safe."

"Thank you." Pelut poured him more tea. "I hope you like this."

"It is excellent, especially after such a hard ride."

"It does fortify one." *It shall also be the last tea you ever drink, so I am glad you are pleased.*

Though Koir tried to be gracious, he planned to betray Pelut—not because he had to, but because he *could.* Koir had never accepted that Helosunde had ceased being a true nation and that he would never be treated as an equal in court. He would destroy Pelut and hope that the next Naleni Grand Minister, by some miracle, would not see him in exactly the same light.

Pelut read all that in the expression that passed over the man's face, and knew he had to prevent Koir's plan from succeeding. He could do it easily by having the man assassinated and the blame put on a known Desei agent. Pelut would then tell the Prince that the Desei had killed him to keep the news from the north silent. And Pelut would delay that news long enough that the only reaction Cyron possibly could have would be to call up more troops, then Pelut would deal with Count Vroan personally.

And perhaps it is time to deal with Junel again. While it was too soon to introduce the Desei into the Vroan household, using him as a liaison would work to position the man for later use.

In Helosunde, Pyrust would be victorious. Vroan would rebel, either seeking Desei support or rising to oppose the Desei. Either way it did not matter, since both would weaken the nation enough for it to be taken. Pelut himself would be able to negotiate a peace that would not ruin Nalenyr, and Pyrust would head south to stop the invasion.

And Pelut, having shown a genius for coordination, would rise to be Grand Minister of all three nations. *Four. Doubtless Pyrust will take Erumvirine, too.*

Imperial Grand Minister. Pelut liked that.

He raised his cup to Koir Yoram. "To your health, Minister, and that of our nations."

Chapter Thirty-four

26th day, Month of the Dragon, Year of the Rat
10th Year of Imperial Prince Cyron's Court
163rd Year of the Komyr Dynasty
737th year since the Cataclysm
Kelewan, Erumvirine

I heard Captain Lumel enter the armory behind me, but I did not turn to face him. Instead I tightened the cords binding my armor on. There were only two things he could say to me. One, and I would have to kill him; the other and he would be the man I thought he was.

"So, you *are* abandoning us."

"A statement, not a question; good." I smiled, but didn't let him see it. I concentrated on knotting the orange cords with a tiger's-head knot. Despite my crest's being a tiger hunting, I'd not used that knot in a long time—since before I became Moraven Tolo apparently, because my fingers fumbled at it. Still, I managed, working black cord in for the stripes and eyes. The knots made nice targets for archers with cord-cutting heads on their arrows, but so far the *kwajiin* had not employed them.

I turned, and he covered his surprise well. The armor I'd chosen had been last worn by a Morythian general who died at Bakken Rift, when the Bears had charged uphill and routed their enemies. The Tiger crest on the breastplate did not match mine, but the alternating black and orange cords, as well as the background stripes, suited me.

"You know I'm not abandoning the city. I told Prince Jekusmirwyn at the first that his city was lost. I never intended to stay."

Captain Lumel wore the Jade Bears green-and-black armor well. He cut an imposing figure, and even a few cuts through the paint had not lessened his image. He'd defended against the enemy's first forays, and had already become something of a legend within the city by challenging a *kwajiin* and defeating him in single combat. I'd watched the duel and felt the tingle of *jaedun.* If he survived the siege, Lumel would be a Mystic.

"It was assumed that you would stay because you did not flee with others as the *kwajiin* surrounded the city."

"But that wasn't an assumption *you* made."

He smiled slightly, then shook his head. "I knew you wouldn't stay. Your first analysis was correct. The city is indefensible. Those who got out early are likely to be the only ones who survive. Why did you stay?"

"To see how they fight. I've engaged them in small bands, and the *kwajiin* have changed things. I wanted to see how they would handle a city."

He slowly nodded. "It has been an education."

"For both sides."

The *kwajiin* methodology of warfare promised many

new things, but some I found hauntingly familiar. The invaders came in from the southeast and did make one run at Bloodgate. The *vhangxi* attacked in strength, but it still felt like a probe to me. The grey-skinned horde poured onto the plain and came at the gate. Archers rained arrows down from the walls while the *vhangxi* leaped nearly to the parapets to attack them. They had no equipment to hammer the gates down, so the attack really had no chance of success.

The Jade Bears had been on the walls repulsing them, and Captain Lumel's troops fought hard. Had they been less disciplined, it would have been possible for *vhangxi* to get into the city, though I doubt they had the presence of mind to open the gates to their fellows. In case that was their plan, my companions and I were poised to interfere, but our aid was not called for.

When Captain Lumel issued his challenge to one of the *kwajiin,* I don't think either knew what they were getting into. The *vhangxi* attack had faltered, and the *kwajiin* had come forward to call them back. He slew two of the *vhangxi* when they sought to rebel, and a third drove at his back. It might have gotten to him, but it did not because Captain Lumel ordered archers to bring the beast down.

The *kwajiin* raised his sword in a salute and, in words no one but I seemed to understand, said his life was Lumel's. Lumel then pointed to the circle with his own sword, and the two of them agreed to meet. I translated, because I wanted Lumel to know what was happening. He didn't have to challenge the *kwajiin,* but once events started to unfold, the Virine warrior did not shrink from them.

The two warriors entered the circle—Lumel having

emerged through a sally port at Bloodgate. They saluted each other, then began to fight. The *kwajiin* preferred Eagle, Tiger, and Wolf as fighting styles. They let him be on the attack at all times, and he pressed it. While I sensed no *jaedun* radiating from him, he possessed a native talent that exceeded that of many warriors—even those of superior training.

Virine to the core, Lumel remained patient. Mantis, Crane, and Dragon withstood the invader's attacks. Lumel was skilled, and *jaedun* flashed as he avoided some cuts and parried others. Still, he benefited from the fact that he was a more recent student of the sword, and refinements in techniques made it easier for him to defend against the *kwajiin*'s more archaic forms.

But the *kwajiin* died because Lumel broke form. The invader had lunged while Lumel waited in Crane form three. The blade slid along the Virine's breastplate, but scored nothing more than paint. Lumel kicked out with his right foot, aiming for the *kwajiin*'s right knee. The enemy warrior twisted so the kick missed to the left, but Lumel then hooked his foot back and drove his spur through the *kwajiin*'s right knee.

As the enemy went down, he tried to slash at Lumel, but the Virine grabbed his wrist. Lumel followed him down, then drove his knee into the *kwajiin*'s right biceps, shattering his arm with a sharp crack. He brought his sword's hilt down into the blue-skinned warrior's face, smashing teeth. Two more punches left the enemy dazed and bleeding, then Lumel stood and harvested his head with a single stroke.

He still wore the sword he'd taken from the *kwajiin,* but he had strapped it to his back, where it served as a challenge to others to take it from him.

Thus ended the only noble part of the siege. After that the *kwajiin* commanders brought more troops up and encircled the city. They even placed troops on the other side of the Green River in case any of the city's residents decided to swim for freedom. Their encirclement complete, they sent parties to the nearby forests to gather wood for the creation of siege machinery.

While waiting for their towers to be completed, they launched other attacks. In the depths of the night they released their winged toads. Ranai had seen them before, and many people died that first night. Those who didn't die actually created more of a problem, for the deep bite wounds festered. Moreover, the creatures' vile saliva loosened bowels and soon the city was awash in night soil.

The winged toads came again the next night, but we were prepared for them. Fishing nets had been taken from the docks and strung through alleys and between towers. People armed themselves with broomsticks, candlesticks, short knives and long. They pounded and hacked at anything that flew. While there were injuries visited upon each other in the frenzy, the attacks devastated the winged toads and showed how ineffective they were against a prepared populace.

The second assault proved more dangerous. As with any city, Kelewan had a sewer system. Gates and grates guarded against any enemy soldiers infiltrating that way, but the *kwajiin* employed a different weapon. They released creatures with the sharp teeth and voracious appetites of the *vhangxi,* but most closely resembled small otters or large weasels. They swam into the sewers and up through pipes, crawling into cesspits beneath toilets. They were possessed of singular jumping capabilities.

They attacked when people—many suffering from the winged toad venom—were least on guard. To hear the commotion described could almost make it seem comical—a man runs screaming from a toilet, sporting a furred tail. The fact that the tail shrank as the creature gnawed its way up through his bowels, on the other hand, painted the horror in stark terms that converted buckets into toilets, and the Illustrated City suddenly found itself with brown splashes trailing from every window.

The dung-otters proved almost as easy to deal with as the winged toads, once we learned they preferred live prey to carrion. Their weakness was fire, so dumping oil in a puddle in a sewer formed the basis of a trap. We'd throw a hapless cur down there to whine in the darkness. When it started barking, then yelped in terror, we tossed a torch down and ignited the oil. While we didn't study the results all that closely, we got a fair number of dung-otters for each dog, and the *kwajiin* ran out of dung-otters well before our supply of dogs evaporated.

The Illustrated City endured the siege for a week before the *kwajiin* began to tighten the circle. They decided to attack at Bloodgate. I had no doubt it was a matter of honor, which made them remarkably predictable. According to Urmyr, that should have made them easy for us to defeat. But defeating them would have required an army capable of lifting the siege, and unless Prince Cyron was a day away with the whole of the Naleni military, the siege would not be broken.

In that week, the Illustrated City *had* broken. Aside from the brown stains and the inhuman stink, the bodies decomposing in the streets and the infirm wailing in pain, a more fundamental change had taken place. The

Virine had always prided themselves on having been the Empire's capital. I'm sure they believed that when the Empress returned, it would be to Kelewan and to the sealed throne room where the Celestial Throne waited in darkness. With every day, citizens looked to the northwest for some sign of her coming, then looked to the southeast to know that she would not arrive in time.

This crushed their spirit and, with few exceptions, they resigned themselves to dying with their city. They had lived for it. Their lives had been inscribed on its walls. It was their history, and it was about to be destroyed. Some people even took their own lives, choosing a peaceful passing over to what would befall Kelewan.

I slid my swords through the sash girding my armor. "You know I am leaving with my people. You'll not try to stop me."

He shook his head. "The Jade Bears and I are coming with you. We're only a battalion, but the archers of the Sun Bears are coming as well."

I raised an eyebrow. "What about your duty to the Prince?"

"This is part of it." He glanced back toward the door of the armory. "Crown Prince Iekariwynal and your boy, Dunos, are being fitted with identical armor. We are tasked with getting the Crown Prince away."

"It's better the boy die here, you know." I nodded toward Whitegate. "What he will see there will haunt him forever."

"The same will be true of Dunos."

"No, Dunos has lived through his nightmare." I nodded to him. "Bring the Crown Prince. You know our plan. You hate it, of course."

"Only the necessity of it. Midnight, Whitegate." He bowed to me. "Kelewan will die, but Erumvirine will live."

"Forget Erumvirine. Look to living yourself."

Deshiel had the foresight to line up several wagons near Whitegate. They were actually corpse wagons, but as no traffic could get through Whitegate to the cemeteries beyond, no one had bothered to collect bodies for burial. It occurred to me that one benefit of this situation was that the *kwajiin* army would have its noses full of the stink of death.

My company had swelled to nearly eighty-one, which would have been a welcome omen save that this heavily taxed our supply of horses. In combination with the Bears, we had a substantial cavalry force, and had seen nothing in the enemy to rival it. Especially not in the forces opposite Whitegate, which seemed the least disciplined and weakest of the enemy troops.

Of course, one has to expect discipline to break down when one stations carrion eaters in graveyards.

The wagons had been fitted with barrels of oil and were drawn by four-horse teams. We'd even found people desperate or insane enough to drive them. Everyone knew we would set the wagons on fire and hope to cut a flaming path through the enemy line. It would be the only way out of the city, and countless people gathered amid the rendering houses, tanneries, butchers, and mortuaries of Whitetown to join us on this mad dash for survival.

I gave the signal and the portcullis was drawn up. The bar on the gates slid back, then the gates themselves slowly opened. The moment the gap proved sufficient for a wagon to make it through, Deshiel applied a torch and the driver cracked a whip. I was not certain whether the horses feared the whip, the fire, or the crowd of hungry people milling about, but they shot through the gate. Two more flaming wagons followed, then our cavalry went.

Whitegate pointed west-northwest toward a pair of hills covered with graves and mausoleums dating back to the Imperial period. The road curved north, then broke directly for the hills. The cavalry poured through the gate, then immediately south, to get off the road. We assembled in good order and trotted parallel to the road, onto which spilled a screaming mass of terrified humanity.

People had been reduced to nothing more than herd beasts. We'd started many rumors among them. To some we said that being in front was best, to get through the lines before the enemy reacted. To most others we recommended staying tight with the pack, as they would be but one among many and the enemy wouldn't get them. A few contrarians hung back, assuming their best chance lay in seeing where the enemy went, then going elsewhere. We saw no reason to contradict their thinking.

The enemy reacted, and their *kwajiin* leaders could not control them. The *vhangxi* charged forward from their trenches and fortresses, abandoning barbicans and leaving their commanders screaming orders at them. They raced in at the refugees, saliva slicking their flesh, tongues lolling from their mouths.

Ranai, riding between me and Dunos, spoke sharply. "Don't watch, Dunos."

"He's seen it before."

She turned on me. "He doesn't need to see it again. He's only ten years old, Master."

"And he will be eleven because of those people."

Her eyes narrowed. "You gave them false hope."

"They were dead anyway." I shrugged. "Maybe some will escape."

There was an outside chance that I would be correct, or there was until the *vhangxi* drew close to the first fire wagon. The horses shied and the wagon tipped, launching the burning barrels. They burst when they hit the ground, leaving the road awash in burning oil. A second wagon rode into the fire and its cargo exploded, lighting the night. The third left the road toward our side and flipped, sowing fire in a crescent from the road toward the south.

The people, confronting this vast arc of flames, stopped. The front ranks did anyway, then people slammed into them from behind. The forward ranks got pitched into the fire and the *vhangxi,* undaunted, leaped over it to fall on the milling masses.

By that time we'd ridden far enough forward that the fire hid the worst of the carnage. Three hundred yards from the enemy line, we lowered our spears and formed up in a double column eighteen wide. I aimed us for a point just south of the breastwork they'd raised across the road. As we closed to a hundred yards, we moved into a fast trot, then, at fifty, a full gallop.

The Sun Bears arced arrows above us that peppered the *kwajiin* and *vhangxi* remaining to defend their line. Half the enemy fell to that attack, and most of the surviving *vhangxi* fled. The *kwajiin* drew their swords and though I could not hear them over the thunder of hoofbeats, I knew they were announcing their histories and inviting us to join the company of all those their ancestors had slain.

A woman stepped into my path, facing me straight on, with both hands wrapped around the hilt of her sword. She braced to bat my spearpoint aside, then cut the legs out from under my horse. I knew the tactic. I'd done it before.

I'd seen others killed trying it.

I rose in my stirrups, spun the spear to reverse my grip, then hurled with all my strength. It flew straight, coming in faster than she had expected, and at a sharper angle. Though she did get her sword on it, it still pierced her hip. She spun down and away and I was past her.

Past her, past the enemy line, free.

Still high in the stirrups, I turned to look back at the city. The writhing shadows from the slaughter danced over the city's walls. To the southeast, the first of what would be many flaming projectiles arced up from the *kwajiin* line to spread fire through the Illustrated City. People scurried about on the walls, and some arrows arced back, but the defenders clearly would not survive long.

Our cavalry made it through with few casualties. Had I given the order, we could have wheeled right and hit another part of the enemy line. We could have wrought havoc, and might even have been able then to turn back toward the city, kill the *vhangxi* around the fire, and usher some of the refugees away.

For a moment I considered giving that order. I knew I would be obeyed without question. My people would actually welcome the chance to do more, to avenge their city's death.

The words waited on the tip of my tongue, but I did not speak them.

Had we turned, we would have done damage. We would have given those watching some hope.

False hope.

Kelewan would be avenged. That I knew. But not this night, not this place.

Turning northwest, we rode as if the whole *kwajiin* army pursued us.

Chapter Thirty-five

28th day, Month of the Dragon, Year of the Rat
10th Year of Imperial Prince Cyron's Court
163rd Year of the Komyr Dynasty
737th year since the Cataclysm
Tolwreen, Ixyll

Stripped to the waist and already beginning to sweat, Ciras Dejote entered the circle in the heart of the metal tower. The sword he bore was the one that had come from the Ixyll grave. Over the time he'd been in Tolwreen, between being subjected to a variety of tests or feasts offered in his honor, he'd learned the blade had once belonged to Jogot Yirxan, a Morythian member of the *vanyesh* who had been a swordsman without equal.

Across from him, a hulking silver behemoth stalked into the circle. He bore a resemblance to a man because he had begun as one. All of his bones had been wrapped in silver, and the metal had been etched with very fine dragons coiling and cavorting along the polished surface. Over the years, as the work was continued, the bones had been split and extended, so now the thing known as Pravak Helos stood eight feet tall and boasted a second set of arms. They linked into the body right at the lower edge of the ribs, and were silvery whiplike appendages that ended in short, sharp dagger blades.

In his upper two hands, Pravak bore swords, each the equal of the blade Ciras carried. His opponent hardly needed the swords since his hands ended in long, very sharp claws and the outer edge of his lower forearm bone had been serrated. When he was fully alive, Pravak had enjoyed stalking and killing Viruk. In reshaping himself, he'd become more than their match.

His skull had likewise been coated in inscribed silver, but he wore a mask that resembled what he'd looked like in life. The fullness of his face, as well as the wild tangle of filaments that danced from a warrior knot at the back of his head, let Ciras imagine what he must have been when mortal. The fact that he had hunted Viruk did layer muscle into those bones, painting a picture of a fighter who relied on power more than speed.

And he has the advantage here again. Ciras bowed deeply and held it for a respectful time. His foe did the same, then set himself. He adopted the first Scorpion form, with both swords up and back, but the two tentacles darted forward, promising punishment for a rash attack.

Ciras drew the sword and scabbard from his sash and bared the blade. He kept the scabbard in his left hand. His foe's stance offered him two easy choices for offense, and one for defense, but he really found himself facing two foes. Granted, they were joined at the hip and would coordinate their attacks, but he had to watch out for twice as much as he would with one opponent.

Then again, there is one set of legs, so there is a weakness.

Ciras smiled, though he was truly unable to tell if that insight had come from his own mind, or through his connection with the *vanyesh* blade. He had a sense of having faced Pravak Helos before and having beaten him. That meant Pravak would be looking for revenge. *He'll be dwelling on the last time we fought.*

Pravak took a step forward and Ciras noticed another weakness. His foe had a high center of gravity, so any lunges would overextend him. He would have to recover, but just how fast he could remained to be seen.

That is knowledge I require.

Ciras took one deep breath, then puffed it out quickly. He dropped into Dragon fourth and advanced quickly, his scabbard high and blade low. He twisted away from a slash by the left whip, then parried a sword cut high. He darted past on the left, then leaped back. Pravak's right sword whistled down on a diagonal cut that struck sparks from the marble floor.

Ciras took one step forward, then whirled. He presented his back to his enemy for a heartbeat, then snapped the scabbard up and smashed Pravak in the face. The right tentacle whipped in, seeking to entangle Ciras, but the Tirati ducked. The tentacle wrapped itself around Pravak's spine and, as Ciras spun away to the right, he brought his sword up and severed the slender cable.

The tentacle uncoiled and slithered down through Pravak's pelvis to the ground. The lumbering behemoth turned to the right, but Ciras had already stepped back out of range of the return slash. He continued to move to his own left, keeping the second whip well away from him. He parried when pressed, slipped away when he could, and kept his enemy moving.

With a flesh-and-blood foe—especially one who would have been bleeding from having lost the tentacle—the strategy of avoidance would have proven very effective. But the creature he faced was not flesh and blood, and was drawing sustenance from the world around him. Ciras, on the other hand, was already slick with sweat. He wiped his brow and splashed the ground with a flick of his wrist.

A battle of endurance would only end one way.

Then Pravak did the unexpected. He kicked the tentacle at Ciras. It slithered across the ground and Ciras easily leaped above it. In doing so, however, he froze himself in place. Without a foot on the ground, he could not dodge, and that was the moment Pravak charged. Blades held wide, and the single tentacle extended like a spear, the *vanyesh* drove forward.

Three attacks. He could parry any two, but the last would get him. Panic shot through him, but Ciras fought it down. Then his right foot touched the ground and without thinking, he acted.

And felt himself awash in the tingling of *jaedun.*

Ciras dove forward, face-first, feeling a sting as the tentacle's blade scored the flesh over his right shoulder and buttock. He landed on his chest and slid forward, then stabbed both arms out. The sword and scabbard each sank between the large and small shinbones. Drawing his legs in and then shooting them out forward, he slid between Pravak's legs and past them.

Ciras' weight twisted the behemoth's legs, bringing Pravak's knees together. The scabbard snapped in half, which sent Ciras off to the right. Then the silver filaments binding the shinbone at the ankle parted and Ciras spun away on his rump, sword still in hand.

He slammed up against the foot-high rim of the circle and almost made it to his feet before Pravak crashed down at its heart. Swords bounced free of hands and Ciras batted one out of the circle as he darted back in. Raising his sword over his fallen foe, he stroked the blade downward and slashed through the warrior's knot.

With it went the strength in Pravak's limbs.

Ciras stepped back and bowed to his enemy. He then turned and bowed to the others seated in the small amphitheater where they had battled. Though most of them remained shrouded in shadow, he saw a few shapes he recognized either as hosts at meals, or opponents he'd already defeated.

A low laughter ran from Pravak's throat. "Have I not said he is Yirxan reborn? A brother has returned. It is an omen of the future."

One of Tolwreen's ruling council—a diminutive shape hidden in deep folds of a thick brown robe—bowed toward the combatants. "Ciras Dejote, you have passed through the Nine Trials. You have proven yourself worthy. Tonight you shall be initiated in the final mysteries of Tolwreen."

Ciras bowed and started toward the edge of the circle, but the counselor called out. "Wait."

The Tirati did as bidden and froze in place. The counselor raised his arms and though the robe's sleeve slipped back, Ciras could see no hands or forearms. Still, a green nimbus gathered around where hands should have been. It formed into a green ball, which expanded as it drifted toward the circle. When it reached man height it bounced along on the ground like a bubble. He wondered if it would make it over the circle lip, but it did so without any difficulty. The moment it touched down in the circle, it expanded and fused with it, becoming a huge hemisphere that would have towered over Pravak had the creature been able to stand.

The air thickened within the bowl, and Ciras felt as if the entire weight of the mountain were pressing in on him. He couldn't breathe, which ignited fire in his lungs. That fiery sensation flooded into his back, along the line of his cut. He could feel it mending, then the fire died. In its place came the itch of *jaedun,* like the familiar itch of a healing cut. The faster he recognized it, the easier he could invoke it.

In this fight he'd not consciously done that, but his panic had opened the way to *jaedun.* He'd known from Moraven Tolo that discipline would lead him to that path, but the utter lack of it had truly opened the new doorway. What he had done stood outside discipline, and yet magic had served him.

He would have allowed himself to keep thinking that, save for running over that last series of moves in his mind. While what he had done was of no single discipline, it was in keeping with *all* of them. The Nine Forms had been shaped to pit advantage against weakness. They demanded control of his body, a sense of balance, of speed and power, all mixed to avoid the enemies' cuts while delivering maximum damage. He had recognized his own weakness, and had acted to avoid the enemy while exploiting *his* weakness.

I doubt what I did will ever enter a form, but it did work; just as refusing to show the bandit a form he recognized served to defeat him. Perhaps the route to *jaedun* lay in recognition of the principles underlying all the disciplines.

The green globe evaporated and Pravak, with his warrior knot mended, sat up. He snapped his left ankle back together and wrapped the severed tentacle around it to hold it in place. He then stood and limped over to Ciras. The metal mask creaked as the grim visage shifted to one more friendly, then solidified that way.

"I almost wish I could feel pain again so I could remember this duel more precisely." He laughed lightly, then reached a hand back and tugged on his knot. "You needn't have severed it. I would have surrendered once I was on my back."

Ciras shook his head. "I would not dishonor you by letting you surrender."

"You truly are Yirxan reborn. They were wise who let you keep his sword."

"And I am in their debt." Ciras bowed. "If you will permit me to leave, I shall clean this blade and then myself."

"Of course. You and your servant will be summoned in three hours." Pravak nodded. "Your coming is a good omen."

Ciras smiled, bowed, then exited the circle. He walked to a small corridor and stopped before a circular opening. From a small square hole in the wall he drew a slender rectangle of a white metal that Borosan had identified as a silver-*thaumston* alloy, which, to the best of his knowledge, could not be created by anything short of sorcery. As he handled the metal slip, sigils incised themselves on its surface. He recognized them as the designation for his suite, smiled, stepped into a small spherical chamber paneled entirely with silver. He slid the metal key into a narrow slot and thought of the living quarters he had been assigned high in one of the towers. Behind him, a curved metal panel slid down, sealing the sphere, and his flesh tingled as magic washed over him.

Then the panel slid up again, admitting Ciras to the chambers he shared with Borosan. Because he bore a *vanyesh* sword, the citizens of Tolwreen had accepted him as something special—though exactly what neither he nor Borosan could determine. Every test he'd worked through, which ran the gamut from endurance and intelligence to combat, had ended with promises that he was one step closer to having mysteries revealed to him. And he certainly had been trained, for each opponent he'd faced and defeated became his mentor in preparation for the next test.

Borosan looked up from the table in the middle of the central living chamber and stretched. "You were victorious?"

Ciras nodded. "I wish my master were here. I believe I have found the way to *jaedun*."

The inventor smiled. "Very good. It is, isn't it? I would have expected you to seem happier about it."

The swordsman nodded, crossing the room to a nook where he stored oil and cleaning cloths. "I have dreamed of this since I first began my training, but it almost seems like an afterthought. The path proves so simple that I think I would have grasped it from the start if someone explained it to me."

"It could be none of them understand it as you do." Borosan's mismatched eyes narrowed. "But that's not the whole of your discomfort, is it?"

"No." He sat and began to polish the blade. "I wonder if the instructions and the tests were not meant to push me to *jaedun*. Your speculation that the filaments leading up to the mountain must be bringing the wild magic down has to be correct. I don't think any of the *vanyesh* can survive outside this atmosphere unless they venture out wrapped in *thaumston* mud."

"Then it's good they don't go far." Borosan held up one of the keys. Light reflected from its surface, revealing etched letters. "These keys pick up impressions of us, and when we think of a place to go, the magic knows if we are allowed or not. I still don't know if the balls move, or if we are sent to an identical ball in the location we wish to reach, but that is how we get around. With the special keys, however, the location and permission are etched on them."

Ciras nodded. "It's the only way we can get to places we can't recall in our minds."

"Right, but here's the trick." He let the card in his hand waver back and forth. "Each of my *thanatons* has a difference engine that I give a simple set of instructions. On this blank, I've inscribed far more instructions than a difference engine can deal with. If I replace the engine with a dozen of these cards, even writing big, I can create a creature hundreds of times smarter than they already are."

The swordsman frowned. "If the *vanyesh* knew this, they could create *thanatons,* which could replace the wildmen and might even be capable of complex work."

"Like building more *thanatons.*" Borosan set the key down. "Luckily, since I am your servant, I escape notice."

"Not tonight you won't." Ciras wiped the sword clean and rested the blade on the rack. "Tonight all will be revealed to us. Just a couple of hours from now."

"Is that good or bad?"

Ciras shook his head. "I don't know. I'm not sure I want to find out."

* * *

An hour before the appointed time, wildmen appeared and helped them dress. They'd brought formal robes of golden silk, trimmed with wide red hems and sashes. Ciras' had the crest of a sleeping tiger embroidered in red because that had been Jogot Yirxan's crest, but it was surrounded by a flaming circle in honor of his being from Tirat. Borosan's robe had the Naleni dragon for decoration, but very small since he was only a servant.

Borosan shook his head, for the sleeves of his robe were easily two feet too long, and the hem was long enough that it had a three-foot train. "No one has worn robes of this style since the Empire fell."

"They are designed so you must move slowly in them. It makes formal affairs stately, and prevents anyone from rushing forward to kill the Emperor."

The wildmen also brought with them special keys, etched with sigils neither man could decipher. The two visitors shuffled their way into the sphere, pulled their robes in after them, then inserted their keys into the wall slots. Though neither felt any motion, they exchanged glances. Normally journeys were over in the blink of an eye, but this one took almost a minute.

When the door slid open again, they found themselves in a wide tunnel with a ceiling hidden in darkness. At the far end, they saw another opening glowing a soft gold. They began to walk toward it, and Ciras relished the fact that his robe prevented him from moving too swiftly. His sense of dread grew as he approached their goal.

As they walked along, golden light illuminated alcoves sunk into the walls. Tall statues carved in exquisite detail filled each niche. Each figure's name burned brightly at the base. They had no idea who these were until one lit up bearing the name Pravak Helos.

"So the mask was him." Ciras looked up, studying the person he'd defeated. In life Pravak had been big, but had a softness to his features the metal had not conveyed. Ciras could tell he'd always been large, even as a child, and while this stood him in good stead in combat, his size probably also embarrassed him. Ciras had known countless individuals who suffered from the same mindset and he wondered if Pravak thought he'd lost his battle because he was too big, or moved too awkwardly.

Borosan kept pace with Ciras. "So these were the *vanyesh.*"

"What they were once. Now the gods alone know what they are."

"They don't look evil."

"I doubt evil was part of what the sculptor wished to reflect."

"Good point."

They continued on until near the end, when the alcove with Jogot Yirxan's statue in it appeared. The man wore his hair long—nearly as long as Ciras' master had—and he had a smile that Ciras returned. While they looked nothing alike through the face, their bodies and limbs were proportioned similarly. *Not a surprise, then, that his blade comes so easily to my hand.*

Borosan pointed toward the statue. "Look at his sword. The sigils on it. Can you read them?"

"I don't think I can make it out."

"It seems to read 'shadow-twin.' "

Ciras shook his head. "It means nothing to me."

"Nor me."

They continued on in silence, then reached the doorway and stopped. Pravak, likewise shrouded in a robe of gold, stood just inside the doorway. He ushered them in with a nod, then a sheet of gold flowed down behind them. Silently it solidified. Serpentine sigils writhed onto its surface, and it sealed the room.

Ciras' skin began to crawl, and it was more than the itch of magic. The hall into which they had entered was long and narrow. Seating rose in tiers on either side, and the *vanyesh* had all assembled there. Each wore a formal robe of gold, embroidered as was appropriate. And Ciras found himself thankful for the oversized robes because he wanted to see as little as he might of these creatures.

Fewer than a hundred filled the available seating, and each of them had lived in Ixyll since the Cataclysm. He'd known that Mystics could live beyond the natural span of a man's years, but these people had lived beyond even a supernatural span. Those who most closely resembled humans had shrunk and shriveled until flesh clung to them like sun-dried leather. Some were long and lean, as if they were constructs of deadwood, while others had become misshapen, their bodies infantile and their heads huge.

And then there were the inhuman ones. At least Pravak had some pride of workmanship in his form. He'd maintained bilateral symmetry and only used two elements—silver and bone—to create a new body for himself. Ciras had seen *gyanrigot* in Opaslynoti that had been cobbled together haphazardly and were still works of art compared to some of the *vanyesh*.

It is a blessing for the world they cannot leave this place.

Before them, at the far end of the hall, towering gold curtains hid that end of the room. At the midway point stood two tables, one large, one small, and Pravak pointed toward them. Ciras advanced to the larger and Borosan, as befitted a servant, took the smaller. Plates laden with fruit and cheese sat at each place, and goblets had been filled with a dark wine that steamed.

Pravak advanced behind them, and when he raised his arms, the gathered *vanyesh* rose as one. "We have assembled as you have commanded, oh lord. We have with us a brother born again and come home. It is the omen that tells us you have defeated Death, and will be reunited with your faithful servants once again."

As he lowered his arms, the curtains parted to reveal a blocky throne of immense proportion. The back of it was shaped in a disk with nine stars excised around the edge. Each one had been inscribed with the mark of a god.

Borosan shot him a glance. "It matches the Celestial Throne."

Ciras nodded. "So then, who is that?"

A golden skeleton had been seated in the throne. A robe embroidered in purple with the Virine bear had been draped over it. The skeleton, unlike some of the skeletal *vanyesh,* had no life to it. Ciras wondered if that was because it also had no skull.

The *vanyesh* all bowed deeply, and Pravak's heavy hands forced Ciras and Borosan to bow as well.

"Give him praise and honor," the *vanyesh* intoned. "He is our lord, Prince Nelesquin. His arrival is nigh. The world shall tremble and he shall return all things to right again."

AT YOUR LSA BX/PX
SERVING THE BEST
CUSTOMERS IN THE
WORLD.

ADVANCER V12 71576723000
84.95
BK FANT CARTOMANCY 9780553586640
6.29

TOTAL $91.24
CASHBACK $20.00
DEBIT CARD $111.24
CHANGE $20.00
************6527
EXPIRY: 12/07 UNITED BAN

15 days for computers and
unopened software/periphera

If a sales receipt is not available,
the refund amount will be loaded
on an AAFES Gift Card.

Chapter Thirty-six

32nd day, Month of the Dragon, Year of the Rat
10th Year of Imperial Prince Cyron's Court
163rd Year of the Komyr Dynasty
737th year since the Cataclysm
Ministry of National Unity, Felarati
Deseirion

Keles sipped the tea he'd been offered, then nodded. Somewhere between a black tea and a green, it had floral hints and no acidic bite. That meant it had been harvested recently, probably in the Five Princes, and shipped north. *Smuggled north, most likely. I think it's Tiger-eyes.* For the Desei Grand Minister to be offering it to him bestowed an honor.

And made him very suspicious.

At least it's a nice break from moon-blossom tea.

Keles had been given a black robe trimmed in gold, with his family's crest embroidered in all the right places. He'd not been allowed to wear a sword, but instead had tucked a baton into his gold sash. It marked him as being someone of rank, though he hardly needed it. Most of the people remaining in Felarati had been involved in his building project and knew him by sight.

He'd arrived at the Ministry of National Unity and been surprised to see swordsmen guarding the entrance. Aside from a few old men and women armed with knives, he'd thought anyone with enough training to hold a sword had left the city. Other than the embassies where the visiting nation provided security, Felarati had been left all but undefended. While Keles did not doubt that the Desei had plenty of shadows and secret police lurking, the fact was that very few people inclined to cause trouble remained.

The guards had conducted him to a small room with cedar paneling. Blond reed mats covered part of the floor, but had been edged in red cloth that married them to the redwood floors. On one wall hung a rice-paper painting in black ink with red commentary. The simple representation of a cedar provided a quiet dignity and made the room seem even more of an intimate place.

Then the paper-paneled door had slid back to admit Grand Minister Rislet Peyt and a tea-master. The Grand Minister bowed in greeting, then he and Keles bowed to the tea-master. Keles would have towered over Rislet, and certainly weighed about a third more, yet the young man's presence filled the room. He'd shaved his head so it glowed a soft gold that contrasted well with his deep blue eyes. His robe, decorated with the Desei Hawk, was likewise blue and secured with a white sash.

The only sound in the room came from the preparation of the tea, which the tea-master poured for each of them. He then bowed and withdrew. The Grand Minister offered Keles his cup, then they both drank and sat in quiet contemplation of the tea.

After a respectful silence, the Grand Minister put his cup down. "I take great pleasure in your visit, Master Anturasi. Your work has transformed Felarati. The people are pleased, as is my master."

"Thank you, Grand Minister." Keles took another sip of his tea, then set his cup down. "You have had word from the Prince?"

"Not recently, but tragic news travels more swiftly than good. Had ill befallen him, we would know."

"So then, things are going well?"

The Grand Minister nodded solemnly. "Just over a week ago, our exalted leader met and defeated a Helosundian host nine times the size of his army. He is advancing on Vallitsi and will crush the Helosundian rebels once and for all."

"Very good news for the Prince." Keles smiled slightly to hide his sinking heart. If Helosunde truly were pacified, it would make escaping Deseirion much more difficult. Instead of just heading south, he might have to head out west, then sail on the Dark Sea to the Gold River and down to Moriande. It would lengthen the journey intolerably, and force him to reconsider the supplies they would need to get away.

The Grand Minister smiled. "I shall see to it that your congratulations are conveyed to his Highness."

"You are too kind."

"I fear you have not thought so, Master Anturasi, which is why I invited you here." Rislet smoothed his robe over his thighs. "I have heard that you have voiced dismay over the fact that you are not getting all of the stone and brick you require."

"It's true." Keles kept his voice even. "I know that not as much stone is coming from the quarries because there are too few wagons to transport it, but I was once getting ten an hour. Now I get seven, and yet ten pass through Westgate. I'm told the other three have been diverted to a project I know nothing about."

The cartographer watched the minister's reaction to his lie. When he'd been invited to visit, Jasai had coached him on how to deal with Rislet. "You can tell him what you know, but you cannot accuse him of lying. He is a minister, so lying is taken as given. You must approach everything as if it is a misunderstanding, and allow him to clarify. If the clarification does not satisfy you, ask for further clarification."

"Ah, I see where a misunderstanding has occurred, Master Anturasi." The Grand Minister smiled. "It is entirely my fault. Though I have done well in the ministries, and have risen far further than I ever imagined I would, I fail to communicate as well as I should. You see, I meant to ask for your help with my project, and while my subordinates swung into action, I had not yet scheduled this meeting. Please, forgive my lack of manners."

"It is forgiven. You will appreciate my alarm because I had intended the stone and brick you have taken to build a small stronghold on the river. It would secure the new houses until the walls can be extended."

"We appreciated this, Master Anturasi, but it seems that our Prince's successes make the likelihood of an attack on Felarati very small." He opened his hands. "His successes are creating another demand. We have diverted the stone and brick to begin construction of a new ministry building. There we will house those who will help oversee both the conquered territories and the vast new holdings your work has opened up for us."

Keles nodded. "And you would like my help with this?"

"So kind of you to offer, Master Anturasi." The man gave him a simple smile. "We hoped we could ask you to integrate our building into your plans. I was especially certain you would undertake a construction of this nature if you realized how events were progressing. We wish for our building to fit seamlessly with what you have already created."

Keles picked up his cup and sipped more tea. He might not have been sophisticated in the ways of ministers and bureaucracy, but Jasai had been correct. The Anturasi family had moved beyond the point where ministers could manage them. This attempt to hide the ministry building within his plans, however, was not so much sophisticated as childish. If Pyrust returned and objected, the ministers would place the blame on Keles. They would say they could not countermand Keles since the Prince had given him a free hand. If Pyrust approved, then Keles would gain praise for foresight, and the ministers would get their new building. Control of Pyrust's burgeoning empire would be maintained in Felarati, which would make Rislet Peyt more powerful.

What made it seem more childish was the ministry flexing its muscles in the absence of the Prince. Rislet was far younger than any Grand Minister Keles had heard of. He might well have been brilliant, but Keles guessed he'd been offered the position because the other ministers felt he was expendable. If Pyrust did not approve of his actions, Rislet would end up dead, but would have insulated those who began the policies that angered the Prince. Rislet, by creating the new building, would position himself to advance over those who had been using him.

It was a ploy that both fascinated and disgusted Keles. But, as Jasai had taken pains to make clear to him, it was part and parcel of how the world worked. Rislet had to make his move at this time because if Pyrust died on his campaign, he would be without an heir. The nobles who sought to replace him would have to deal with Rislet, and there was every possibility that Helosunde's Council of Ministers formed a model for how Deseirion might be governed in the future, making Rislet prince in all but title.

Ministries manipulated to get what they wanted and, therefore, could be manipulated themselves. This, too, Jasai had assured him would be part of his discussion with Rislet. Between the two of them, they came up with a few things he could ask for.

"I believe, Grand Minister, I can accommodate your request." Keles set his cup back down. "And your news is interesting in that it plays along with a dream I had recently. A prophetic dream, akin to those which guide Prince Pyrust."

The Grand Minister smiled, but clearly it took a bit of an effort. "Please, relate to me your dream."

Keles nodded, and for a moment was tempted to tell him of the one where he had found himself walking with his sister in her paradise. *That would confound him.* Instead, he stuck with the script he'd created with Jasai.

"Deseirion has a rich Imperial history. I've studied maps and, west of here, there are several ruined Imperial fortresses. I would like to travel there and select stones to incorporate into the new buildings. It would create a linkage between old and new. You see the importance of that."

"I shall have people fetch you stones, Master Anturasi."

"No, I am afraid that will not do." *I need to get out there to scout the landscape.* "Truth be told, I do have an ulterior motive."

"It would not matter, Master Anturasi, because the Prince's orders were clear. You are not to leave the precincts of the city."

"I know what his orders were, Grand Minister." Keles flashed a smile. "You know that Lady Inyr Vnonol has been my companion. I hoped to take her with me on these trips, so I could spend time with her away from Felarati. You can understand that."

The Grand Minister nodded. "I do, but again there is the matter of the Prince's orders."

"Yes, I have thought of that as well. I suggest, Grand Minister, that, in the Prince's absence, you simply annex those sites and make them part of the city. You can even be credited with the foresight of seeing growth in that direction, too. When Felarati is the Imperial capital, you know it will continue to grow."

The small man's eyes narrowed. "Your plan has merit, Master Anturasi. I shall consider it."

And approve it once you have bought up the best tracts of land in that area.

"As I shall consider the best design for your new building." Keles looked around the cedar room. "I can see a room like this becoming your sanctuary in its most heavenly precincts."

The Grand Minister raised his cup. "And, if you do travel west, you will agree not to escape?"

Keles gave the man a surprised look. "I have promised the Prince I should not leave Felarati. I will maintain my word until released of it by him." *Or by necessity.*

Rislet Peyt bowed his head. "Then let us drink to the growth of Felarati and Deseirion. The world will look here to see where miracles were wrought."

"So they shall, Grand Minister." Keles likewise raised his cup. *The first among them being the escape of Princess Jasai and the free birth of Deseirion's next ruler.*

Chapter Thirty-seven

33rd day, Month of the Dragon, Year of the Rat
10th Year of Imperial Prince Cyron's Court
163rd Year of the Komyr Dynasty
737th year since the Cataclysm
Vroankun, Ixun
Nalenyr

Though he detested the pious mouthings of sympathy to Jarana Vroan, the widow of Donlit Turcol, Junel Aerynnor was happy to be out of Moriande. As a result of Turcol's death, he had been summoned again to the opium den and given an assignment. He traveled to Jomir for the funeral, and from there, he'd accompanied the widow's party back toward Ixun. It had been far too soon for him to do anything but express his deep regrets to Jarana, but she seemed to welcome his offer of looking in on her again, at a happier time.

Junel could hardly imagine a happier time, for things were progressing perfectly. He didn't know, nor did he care, who had betrayed Turcol's plan to Cyron. He did allow that it might not have been betrayal at all, since

Cyron's Lord of Shadows was hardly stupid, whereas Turcol had all but wandered the streets of the capital throwing gold at anyone he could imagine was an assassin. Regardless of how Cyron had learned of the plan, it had ended badly for Turcol and worked out better for both his patrons.

One thing he had not accounted for was Jarana Vroan and her influence over her father. Jarana had actually loved her philandering husband and had desperately wanted to bear his child. Junel suspected her dead mother had groomed her as the link that might bind both counties together. Count Vroan seemed to dote on his daughter, and her distress became his.

More important, her desire to avenge her husband's death likewise became his.

Junel had been accepted into the Vroan household because of his rank—at least, that was how it appeared initially. Someone spoke to someone else, and word filtered through to the count that Junel might be of especial use. The count summoned him to a private meeting in chambers that were paved with stone and sparsely decorated.

The count still wore a white mourning robe, but comported himself as anything but serene and contemplative. The tall, slender man poured Junel a generous goblet of wine and the Desei agent sipped politely, despite detesting the local vintage for its lack of subtlety.

Count Vroan slapped a hand against the tower's stone wall. "I know most lords in Moriande have paneled their private chamber with wood, and enclosed it with delicate paper panels. They serve tea and quietly lie to each other. You've seen it as well, I'm sure."

"Yes, my lord."

"You know, I've visited Felarati. I did so as part of a delegation negotiating a bit of peace. I liked Felarati." Again the white-haired man slapped a hand against stone. "The Dark City, but one that is strong. I know you have your differences with the Prince, but I wanted you to know that I think the place of your upbringing breeds men, not the vermin that thrive in cities like Moriande."

"I appreciate that, my lord." Junel set his cup of wine down. "Your opinion is shared in a variety of places—even in Moriande. If I may have leave to speak frankly, my lord . . ."

"Please, tell me what goes on in the capital."

"You don't want to know the whole of it, my lord." Junel clasped his hands behind his back, much as he'd bound the hands of his last victim. He'd taken her outside the opium den while she wandered in a stupor. The drugs dulled her sense of pain, but as he dissected her, realization of her death blossomed in her eyes. Had she not been gagged, her screams would have been delicious, but he had to be satisfied with the terror in her eyes. She died well—though not as well as Nirati Anturasi—and his need for death had been assuaged for another period.

"I've told you already, my lord, how much your loss pains me. There is no doubt that this tale of banditry is pretense to hide murder. Prince Cyron brought Prince Eiran and his courtesan out with him to watch Count Turcol die. He then dishonors your troops by putting Eiran in charge of them. Eiran, having seen the murder, is terrified of saying what truly went on, but one has to ask a simple question. If it were bandits who attacked, why were none displayed? Why are none awaiting trial?"

Vroan finished his wine at a gulp and poured himself

more. "This I know, Count Aerynnor. Turcol was murdered most coldly." He lowered his voice slightly. "I have no doubt he had planned things himself and got caught in his schemes. There are times he trusted charisma more than he did his intellect, which is a problem for one so vain. I was actually happy to send him off in command of our troops because it sent him east and, quite frankly, prevented me from having him killed."

"Really, my lord?"

"I'd have done it. I'd have hated to do so since it makes Jarana so sad, but better she's mourning him than mourning me."

"I agree." Junel nodded solemnly. "I believe, since Nerot Scior is also resident here, that you know I have been involved as an agent for investments his mother had made in Moriande."

The count laughed. "I knew she had someone in Moriande. That idiot Melcirvon couldn't find the ground if you threw him from this tower. She has consulted me about events in Moriande, feeling me out about my reaction to her plopping her ample bottom on the Dragon Throne. I remained noncommittal."

"The idea has been advanced, my lord, by people in Moriande, that you, she, and the late Count Turcol might have formed a triumvirate. You, of course, have the advantage, being a Naleni hero and having a child with ties to Helosunde. I believe events in Helosunde will swing things more in your favor, and that the duchess can be convinced to support you in return for promises you will never have to keep."

The westron lord's head came up. "What events?"

Junel looked down at the ground. His ministry patron had given him one view of the events in Helosunde that downplayed the reality. Based on inquiries for information from the rest of the Desei network in Moriande, Junel was able to figure out what must truly be happening. While Vroan would be alarmed by the news from the ministry, he wouldn't be alarmed enough for Junel's purpose. Vroan had to move quickly and boldly to effect the ends that would most benefit Deseirion.

"The news has not circulated far at all, but a week and a half ago Prince Pyrust crushed a Helosundian army. He's cut off all communication to the south and has advanced on Vallitsi. He is laying siege to it, and will take it by the end of the month. He then intends to move south and, in the month of the Hawk, he will attack Nalenyr."

Count Vroan stared at him for a moment, then set his cup of wine down. "How reliable is this information?"

"I would stake my life on it. You know my relations with the Desei court are less than cordial. Had I not come here, I would have been tying up my business in Moriande and heading south to Erumvirine."

Vroan pursed his lips and nodded ever so slightly. "And Prince Cyron is not a war leader."

"No, my lord, he is not. I would expect he will call up more troops, *westron* troops, and ask you to lead them against the Desei. The mountain passes can be held, but the fighting will be bloody. It's your people who will preserve his realm. The Komyr have relied on you to deal with Pyrust in the past, and they shall do so now."

"No. No, that cannot be allowed to happen. If Komyr blood is so weak it cannot hold its realm, it must give up the Dragon Throne."

"I would agree, my lord. The question is, how does one craft the most favorable approach?"

Vroan watched him carefully. "I'm not certain I follow."

"It is simple, my lord. An assassin is the best solution to the problem of Prince Cyron. He has no heir. With his death you can step forward and accept the mantle of the Prince to save your nation." Junel raised a finger. "However, if the plot were to be discovered, you would be tainted and likely face a revolt in the east."

"There is wisdom in what you say, but this still leaves Cyron on the throne."

Junel nodded. "True, but Nerot Scior is the sort of schemer who likely could be convinced to press for an assassin. Regardless, he is the sort who could be positioned to accept the blame. Once the Prince is gone, you expose him, kill him, and step into that vacuum yourself. Until then, given your ties to Helosunde and your concern for Nalenyr, you can raise a force and be prepared to intervene in the coming war. Even if Cyron does not die, he comes to rely on you and you supplant him later with the blessing of a grateful nation.

"And then, my lord, if you have occasion to push north into Helosunde, you are simply doing so for your daughter. If you retake Helosunde, I can assure you, Deseirion will fall soon after."

Vroan folded his arms over his chest. "How much of this do you think is truly possible?"

"Uniting three realms? I believe it will be done in my lifetime." Junel shrugged. "Killing Cyron and getting Nerot to take blame for it will be simple. With proper coaching he could even stand up and proclaim his complicity, believing he has rid the nation of a tyrant."

"True. He could be made to see how that would work

to his advantage." The westron lord smiled. "And you, Count Aerynnor, what would be to your benefit if events were to unfold as you describe them?"

"My lord, I am a modest man and not one given to ambition. I have learned to be thankful that I am alive. I should very much like to see the Desei Hawk with its wings broken, but that is the extent of my desire."

"But you believe I would be grateful for your aid."

"Your lordship has already showed me the hospitality of his house, the bounty of his cellars. My reward would be to be of continued help to you. You will rise to heights I can only dream of."

Vroan snorted, then recovered his cup and drank. He wiped his mouth on his sleeve. "I don't believe you are modest or that you lack ambition. I think you do want more than you say, and I know you'll end up with it."

"My lord is kind to say so."

"I do, and I would be willing to guarantee it, provided we agree on one thing."

"And that is, my lord?"

"That your advance is not at *my* expense."

Junel lifted his cup. "Done and done, my lord."

"Good." Vroan refilled his cup and drank. "Now, let us plan how Nerot will murder Prince Cyron and pave the way for our ascent."

Chapter Thirty-eight

34th day, Month of the Dragon, Year of the Rat
10th Year of Imperial Prince Cyron's Court
163rd Year of the Komyr Dynasty
737th year since the Cataclysm
Maicana-netlyan (Lair of the Witch-King), Caxyan

Visiting the Amentzutl Witch-King was not as simple as visiting even the Naleni Prince. Jorim underwent a full week of purification rituals paralleling those he performed before beginning to learn magic. During that time he could converse with others, but was strictly forbidden to touch or be touched—which put Shimik and Nauana off-limits.

In those nine days, he did manage to scrub off all traces of dead skin and found that what lay beneath was healthy. In fact, it seemed healthier than he remembered. Though still quite young, the time he'd spent out under the sun, exploring the world, had begun to take its toll. He'd had dragon talons at the corners of his eyes, but now they'd vanished. Moreover, a number of the scars he'd picked up on his travels disappeared, as did an Ummummorari tribal tattoo on his right hip.

His hair and beard remained white, but did not have the brittle quality of an old man's hair. Most unsettling were his eyes—and, try as he might, he could not get used to them. It was more the lozenge shape of his pupil than the fiery corona that bothered him. It reminded him too much of dragons and snakes, which reminded him he was supposed to be a god reborn.

He still fought that idea, because he'd seen the sort of naked power that might be at his command. If he was a god, he could do anything with it, provided he could control it. If he was just a deluded man, then control would be an illusion, and the probable result of his actions would be evil. Certainly, his first true use of such overwhelming power had been to destroy an enemy, but what would happen if people displeased him? *I've been accused of being quick-tempered in the past. That's not a good trait in a god.*

He was still wrestling with the problem of who he was and how much he wanted to accept when he was packed up for the trip to Maicana-netlyan. The Witch-King lived in a mountain two days away to the southeast. Once the party arrived, Jorim would have one day to get cleaned up, then he, alone, would enter the Witch-King's lair.

Anaeda Gryst had to restrain Shimik at Jorim's leave-taking. The Fenn had gotten over any fear he had, and Jorim envied him being able to forget so quickly. He would have loved to take Shimik with him, but his only companions would be two of the eldest *maicana* sorcerers.

Anaeda nodded. "We'll care for him and make certain he does not follow you."

Jorim nodded. "Shimik, stay here. Guard *Stormwolf*. You."

The Fenn stopped struggling in Anaeda's arms. "Jrima, Shimik mourna sad."

"Don't be sad. Jrima return soon." He winked at the creature. "I'll teach you a magic trick when I get back."

Shimik's eyes widened. "Shimik guard good-good."

"What I expect." Jorim looked at Anaeda. "I hope he won't be too much trouble."

"Not likely, until you teach him how to make fire."

Shimik nodded happily at that suggestion.

"I'll think of something else. I don't know how long this will take."

"As long as it takes." She glanced north out over the plains before Nemehyan and beyond the skull pyramid. "I have troops out scouting for the Mozoyan. It will give us warning and we'll be able to hold them off. At least, that's the plan."

"I'm sure it will work." Jorim bowed to her, then turned to Nauana. "Will you walk with me a short way?"

"As my Lord Tetcomchoa desires." The slender woman fell in beside him and they started off on the road toward Maicana-netlyan. The two *maicana* who would join him on the trip had two *cunya* laden with supplies in tow and followed discreetly.

Jorim frowned and looked down at his hands. "I want to apologize for how I've acted."

"Gods need not apologize."

He shot her a quick glance. "Maybe not, but they should. You opened a wonderful world to me, but one that scared me. Where I come from, magic such as the *maicana* wield is a frightening thing. You showed me, in little bits and pieces, that it was not evil. I accepted that, but when I acted out there, I . . ."

". . . you became yourself."

Jorim shook his head. "Part of me is afraid you're right."

"Why afraid, Lord Tetcomchoa?" Nauana reached out for him, then held back. "You should rejoice in discovering who you are. When you were first with us, you were wise enough to know we would have to show you the whole of your glory. We have been faithful to you for cycles of years. You honor us by learning."

"And shame you by retreating?"

"I have done my best to teach you." She glanced down, tears glistening in her eyes.

Jorim wanted nothing so much as to brush those tears away, but he was forbidden from touching her. Then, without thinking, he touched the *mai* and floated the tears away, merging them with the air. *If I can give comfort through* magic, *it cannot be all I have feared. I just have to be more than I fear I might be.*

Nauana brushed a hand over her cheek. "Thank you for that kindness, my lord."

"Understand something, Nauana. You taught me as I needed to be taught, and *all* I needed to learn. Had you not done that job well, the Mozoyan would have killed everyone on the *Blackshark*. Our victory, that day, was *your* victory."

"Thank you."

"And know something else." Jorim lowered his voice. "Your opening yourself to me is what reminds me of who I am, who I have been, and why I am here. Your openness shall be my shield against fears. I don't know what I am: man, god, or some mix; but the being I am is better for your efforts."

He smiled at her and she returned the smile. "I think, my lord, you believe this."

"I do. I shall remember it, no matter what." He sighed. "Now, you best depart before I touch you and need another week of cleansing."

"As you desire, my lord. I shall be waiting for your return."

"It will not come soon enough."

The trip to the mountain of the Witch-King passed uneventfully. His companions said barely a word outside of prayers and commands to the pack beasts. At a time when he would have relished distraction, they were determined not to disturb his thoughts.

So, Jorim did what he always did when not wanting to think about things that were too serious: he studied the flora and fauna, mentally cataloguing them for his journals when he got back to Nemehyan. His companions did take notice of his preoccupation and he feared that this would be translated by some as Lord Tetcomchoa's taking note of every living thing, its condition, and determining if it would survive the time of *centenco*.

Maybe I am. Thoughts like that were about as far as he was willing to go in analyzing his situation. He told himself it was because he wanted to consult with the Witch-King and get the benefit of his wisdom. It was as good an excuse as any, and so he used it.

After a final day of rest and ritual cleansing, Jorim donned his robes from the *Stormwolf.* Purple silk edged with gold, the robe bore the Naleni dragon on breasts, sleeves, and back. He carried no weapon with him, and aside from having braided his side locks, he was otherwise undecorated. Bowing a farewell to his guides, he walked a serpentine trail through the rain forest to a cavern at the foot of the mountain and began the long journey up. While the first part of the cavern appeared to be natural, it quickly gave way to carved steps that twisted forward and back, up, down, and around in a circuitous route that seemed designed only to exhaust anyone following it.

Then he came to a break in the path. The mountain had split at some time, and by the look of the sharp edges on the broken stone, it had done so recently. A good twelve feet of the pathway had fallen onto a pile of debris three hundred feet below. He recalled seeing it in one of the lower chambers, but hadn't thought about its significance.

Jorim shrugged, backed up a dozen steps and ran. He reached the gap and effortlessly cleared it. He crouched upon landing, then looked back at the gap and smiled. Doing that simple thing, and again observing life on the journey, had reminded him about the simple pleasures of nature. *There are just times we make things far too complex.*

He rose and walked forward and, as the stair climbed away to the left, he kept walking forward. His feet stepped through the stone, then he pushed on through what had been a wall. He felt a tingle as he passed through, but no fear, no ill effects. Entering a short, dark passage, he turned around and could see the stairs and gap clearly. *It was an illusion. I wonder how that was done?*

He continued on and passed into a huge domed chamber, which opened onto an even larger chamber to the north. They both had been shaped by the hand of man and decorated with paintings after the Amentzutl fashion. He looked up at the dome and found the stars arrayed in the Amentzutl Zodiac, with the sun poised to be moving out of the sign of Tetcomchoa.

As he entered the chamber, a man wearing nothing more than a loincloth smiled down at him from the larger chamber. Jorim couldn't even guess at his age, because his body seemed young and slender and his brown hair hadn't even a hint of grey. Still, his hazel eyes held years beyond numbering. There was something else odd about the man, but exactly what it was eluded him for a moment.

The Witch-King smiled. "I have been expecting you, Tetcomchoa, and am honored by your visit." He paused for a moment and his smiled broadened. "Shall we converse in the Amentzutl tongue, or will you indulge me in my desire to hear the Imperial language again?"

"What?" Jorim's jaw dropped. "You speak Imperial?"

"I do, and I'm certain I would have forgotten it save that time here seems to flow in odd currents." His right hand came around and a gorgeous butterfly with wings of emerald outlined in black rested on a finger. "And I should have been more prepared to greet you, but I was distracted. I thought you'd use magic to bridge the gap and I would have warning of your arrival."

"I just leaped it, then walked through your illusion."

"My illusion? Fascinating." The man lifted his hand and the butterfly fluttered off. "Perhaps you *are* Tetcomchoa after all."

Jorim held a hand out, but the butterfly ignored him. "Beautiful specimen. I've not seen one like it before."

"And likely won't again." The Witch-King executed a

formal and respectful bow. "I welcome you to my humble dwelling. I am known as Cencopitzul here. I already know you are Tetcomchoa."

"Jorim Anturasi. I came with a Naleni exploration fleet." Jorim mounted the steps to the central chamber. "How is it that you are here?"

Cencopitzul waved him to a pair of rough-hewn wooden chairs. "That's not really what you want to know, but it's a good place to start. I found myself here during the last time of *centenco.* I was able to help them survive the years of no summer. The *maicana-netl* then decided I was not Tetcomchoa, but his envoy, and he chose me to be his heir. Here I have dwelt since that time."

"How were you able to help them?"

The Witch-King smiled. "You know the answer to that question, and that answer raises many more. I was schooled in the use of magic. You thus suppose I was one of the *vanyesh,* and you would be correct. You would therefore assume I must be insane, and I would counter that I am no more insane than a Naleni cartographer who thinks he might be a god born again."

"But if you were one of the *vanyesh* . . ."

Cencopitzul raised a hand, then slid into the chair across from Jorim. "I did not summon you here to discuss me and my fate, but to address yours. You know Tetcomchoa's history: he arrived, he taught the Amentzutl magic so they could defeat the Ansatl, then he sailed west with his most trusted warriors. Taichun arrived from the east and carved the Empire out of the warring states that had been the domain of Men after they destroyed the remnants of the Viruk Empire."

Jorim nodded. "That's what I have been told."

"Then you should have two questions. The first is whether or not Tetcomchoa was a god-made-man, and the second is if you are Tetcomchoa-reborn." The Witch-King sat back. "I've given this much thought. We have ample tales of gods visiting the world as all sorts of creatures, including men and women. There is no reason to suppose Tetcomchoa was not a god—one of ours, one of theirs, a new god, it doesn't really matter which is true. There also seems no dispute that he taught the Amentzutl magic."

The cartographer leaned forward, resting his elbows on his knees. "I can accept that."

"Further accept this: there is no historical record in the Empire indicating that anyone save the Viruk employed magic in the sense of invocations. While *jaedun* always appears to have been possible, during the Viruk Empire the only training humans got was limited to useful tasks, and any Mystic slave was valued. Humans were not put under arms, so they did not develop the skills needed to become Mystical warriors."

"I can see the sense in that."

"Good." Cencopitzul smiled easily. "The next is my speculation. The *centenco* prior to Taichun's arrival heralded the invasion of True Men. They overthrew what was left of the Viruk Empire, freeing the slaves. They may have come down from the Turasynd Wastes, or in through the Spice Route. Again, we have no record of their using magic beyond *jaedun;* and the Viruk, for reasons known only to themselves, do not seem to have used magic to oppose them. At the next *centenco* Taichun arrives from the sea, and is able to establish an empire. That would seem to be difficult, wouldn't it?"

Jorim nodded. "Yes, though with all the warring states, he just had to play one off against another to win."

"Easier said than done, my boy. The Nine are still nine despite the same dynamic prevailing. My point is that as nearly as can be determined, Taichun also brought magic to the Empire, and the magic I learned well enough to join the *vanyesh* was magic instantly recognized by the *maicana-netl* as being in the tradition of Tetcomchoa."

The Witch-King's recital of facts held together well enough to make Jorim recast history in its light. "If all this is true, then my question would be, why would Tetcomchoa choose this time to be reborn?"

"That's simple—the invasion of the new god."

Jorim frowned. "He foresaw that and arranged to be reborn in Moriande as a precaution?"

"I don't know. Did *you*?"

Jorim stopped, his mouth hanging open. "I don't know."

"I hope you figure it out." Cencopitzul stood and pulled his chair back, then pointed to the center of the large chamber floor. A silvery-white stone slab had been set in the floor. It measured roughly six feet long and three across. As Jorim looked at it, what had appeared to be scratches on the surface resolved themselves into writing of some form, which shifted and writhed as if it were alive.

The Witch-King waved him toward the block. "Before he left, Tetcomchoa sealed something in this stone. I have no idea what it is. Legend has it that only his reincarnation can unlock the stone and fully claim his heritage."

Jorim folded his arms over his chest. "And if I fail, I die?"

"Nothing so dramatic. Trying hasn't killed me yet." The Witch-King shrugged. "Then again, in seven hundred years of trying, I'm no closer to a solution than I was at the start."

Chapter Thirty-nine

35th day, Month of the Dragon, Year of the Rat
10th Year of Imperial Prince Cyron's Court
163rd Year of the Komyr Dynasty
737th year since the Cataclysm
Vallitsi, Helosunde

Prince Pyrust allowed himself to take pleasure in the misery of the Helosundian Council of Ministers. For years they had denied him control of Helosunde. While he acknowledged that they could never have done what they did without Naleni support, they were the ones who procured that support and employed it.

Laying siege to Vallitsi was something Pyrust had neither the time nor the inclination to do. He was not concerned about taking the city, since it would definitely fall. Spring crops had not yet been harvested and winter stores were low, so the ability of the people to resist would be limited. Still, they might be able to hold out for the better part of a month, and in that time Cyron would be able to send troops north to lift the siege or otherwise harass his forces.

After arranging his forces around the city such that the only avenue of escape was to the northwest, Pyrust had his troops dig in and raise a circular berm. In the northwest, his engineers began digging a deep trench that slowly filled with seep water. They brought the trench to within fifty feet of the Kuidze River, which ran past the city's western walls on its way north to the Black River.

And further downriver, another of his units began to build a dam. The river level rose, then the engineers breached the wall between the river and their trench, flooding the land inside the berm. The water level rose quickly and by the second morning two feet of water had flooded through the city.

The ministers had figured out his intention and had sent envoys to him. Pyrust had made it very clear he wanted the entire Council to come to him, and would accept no conditions. The next envoy came with a list of conditions, so Pyrust had the list nailed to the man's forehead and sent him back.

So the ministers came, each wearing his finest robes, which were wet to the knees. Some had found robes from a time when Helosunde and Deseirion had been friendlier, but a few still wore robes where Helosundian dogs were devouring hawks and licking up the residue of broken eggs. These ministers, he made certain, would kneel closest to him.

The day had dawned grey and cold, full of the promise of rain. Pyrust had a pavilion set up on the dry side of his berm, with the side flaps raised so his entire army could see the ministers, and they could see the troops. He'd also located it close enough to the berm so that the ministers, on their knees, could not see the city. He, on the other hand, dry and enthroned in armor, could see it easily.

The ministers filed into the open-air pavilion and knelt on either side of a rich red carpet that had been rolled out over the ground. They all shifted uncomfortably and the scent of sweat mingled with that of wet silk. They kept their heads lowered and then, as one, bowed deeply toward him.

Pyrust stood and returned that bow solemnly, which seemed to surprise many of them. *Good. Surprise means they are not thinking well.*

"I would thank you for joining me here. I would have come into Vallitsi and treated with you in your council chamber, but I did not bring a boat."

The ministers looked stricken for a moment. They exchanged glances, but said nothing.

"That was meant to be funny."

One or two ministers laughed.

"And serious as well."

The strained laughter stopped immediately.

"It was meant to be serious because we all are in the same boat, on a storm-wracked sea. The survival of the world is in doubt. We must work together, and I believe you know that. If you did not, you would not have come here to negotiate."

Pyrust stalked the carpet as he spoke, turned at the far end, and started back again. "One of you is missing."

"Koir Yoram, Highness." A young minister bowed deeply. "He was slain a week ago in Moriande."

"Your name?"

"Karis Shir, Highness. I was chosen to replace him."

"Very good, Minister Shir. You are Foreign Relations, but that situation may have to change. No, not that you need to resign, but that you need not think of me as a foreigner."

"As you desire, my lord."

Let us hope the rest of your fellows are as quick as you are, Shir. Pyrust raised his left hand and removed his glove. He openly displayed his half hand, making certain each of the Helosundians got a good look at it. Most shied from it, a few paled, and fewer smiled.

"You know I lost half my hand in your nation. Desei blood has been spilled here for years. I have had no love for your nation, for you have been an annoyance since before I took the throne. I could easily have you slain and would be happy to turn Vallitsi into another Dark Sea. In fact, were it not for the spirit your warriors have shown me down through the years, that is exactly what I would do."

He casually tossed his mailed gauntlet onto his chair, where it landed with a heavy thump. "Your warriors are your salvation, or can be. It is not because I feel threatened by them. Moryne should be ample proof I do not. The threat I feel comes from the south—the *distant* south."

He mounted the steps to the small dais where his chair sat and plucked the gauntlet up again. "Prince Cyron will not be coming to your salvation because the threat I speak of threatens him as well. Erumvirine is being invaded by forces that have conquered as much as a third of the nation. They may have taken Kelewan even now. This is the reason Cyron pulled his troops from your border and sent them south."

Pyrust sat and studied the ministers as they mulled

over what he had said. Their surprise seemed genuine, and a few of the oldest of the ministers wore expressions of panic. *They will likely have to die so more dynamic men may replace them.* The others waited for him to continue, realizing the gravity of the situation but interested to hear what he had planned.

Minister Shir raised his head. "Highness, how certain are you of this information?"

"So certain that every Desei citizen capable of holding a pitchfork or paring knife is moving into Helosunde. Things are urgent enough that I have sent them here without sufficient training, weaponry, armor, or provisions. I know many will die, but I will not have Deseirion conquered."

Pyrust held out both hands, one maimed, one mailed. "You will have to make a choice. You will surrender Helosunde to me entirely and issue calls upon your citizenry to support me. Your troops will move south with mine, through Nalenyr, to face the invaders. You will reap much glory and I shall be generous in my rewards."

His mailed hand closed into a fist, then he extended his half hand. "If you do not surrender, I cannot move into Nalenyr or beyond. I will still face the invaders, but I will fight them here, in Helosunde. I shall lay waste to your nation, consuming every kernel of grain, burning every stick of wood, flooding the lowlands, flattening villages, slaughtering livestock, and salting the fields where I do not sow bracken and thorns. I will make Helosunde an inhospitable wall warding Deseirion. What happens to you and your people will not concern me, because if you do not join me, you are allied with the enemy and therefore must die."

Shir sat back on his heels while the other ministers

kept their heads down. "Even if we accept what you tell us as true—and you have us at a disadvantage, so there is no reason you should lie—getting our people to join with the Desei will be very difficult. Generations of hatred cannot evaporate overnight, no matter the importance of the cause that unites us."

Pyrust smiled carefully. "Your observation is wise, and has not been lost upon me. I have a solution. You know I took Duchess Jasai to be my wife. You know she is with child. You will elect her child as your next prince, and I shall make Helosunde autonomous beneath his rule. His mother shall serve as princess-regent until he is of age to assume the throne himself. I had sent you a message about this before, but apparently you did not believe it. The circumstances are real. The offer is real."

Shir's brown eyes tightened as he considered. Both men knew that Pyrust's firstborn would also be heir to the Hawk Throne, so in his person both realms would be united. *Then again, my son is not yet born, and many treacheries will live and die before he reaches his majority.*

For a moment Pyrust realized how awkward a liaison between Jasai and Keles Anturasi would be. Materially it would mean nothing, for the Prince would claim the children and that would be that. He could and might well take other wives and have more heirs to play off against each other. *Many treacheries.* He slowly shook his head.

Shir nodded. "There is only one difficulty with your suggestion, Highness."

"The matter of Prince Eiran."

"Yes, Highness."

Pyrust tugged his gauntlet on again. "It was this

Council of Ministers which made him a prince. *Unmake* him."

One of the older ministers sat upright. "That cannot be done."

"No? I can think of a dozen ways." Pyrust rose slowly and drew a knife from over his right hip. "In fact, I believe you were hoping I would terminate his reign at Meleswin. I did not simply to vex you. Now his existence vexes me. You do not want me vexed."

Pyrust raised his right hand and brought it down. Soldiers stationed at the walls loosened ties so the pavilion's walls flapped down. "I shall allow you to deliberate, but do not take too long. I can be patient when sufficiently motivated, but there has been little motivation so far."

He strode from the pavilion and let the last flap slide into place. He motioned to the captain of the Fire Hawks. "Ten minutes, then go in and slay the old, fat minister in blue. Cut his throat, but try to keep the blood off the carpet."

"Understood, Highness." The man bowed.

Pyrust returned the bow, then walked up to the top of the berm. He studied Vallitsi, with its stout wooden buildings and low stone walls. He actually didn't like it very much, and would be happy to see it washed down the river like so much debris. The only thing useful in it were the people—people with spirit, who had spent a generation learning how to fight against an organized host.

They are the treasure of Helosunde.

He felt the first patter of rain and watched the lake his men had created dance as drops struck it. Vallitsi's reflection shattered on the water. Then the rain increased, and the lake reflected only chaos and the wrath of the gods.

He turned and found the Mother of Shadows there, huddled beneath a cloak. "Did you know of Koir Yoram's death?"

"We had nothing to do with it. Koir overstepped himself and Vniel had him killed."

"Not the question I asked."

A low chuckle came from within the cloak's hood. "I learned of it two hours before you did, but had no verification. We believed Koir to be in Vallitsi, so I had to wait and see if he would emerge."

"Any other news from the south?"

"From Erumvirine, no. Those who do manage to cross the border are segregated. No news travels north, if there is any. Kelewan must be under siege by now."

"And a long siege that will be." Pyrust stroked his jaw with his half hand. "It would take nine regiments to seal it off, and nine times that many to be assured of victory without unacceptable losses. And then all you would have is a city, not a nation."

"Perhaps the city is what is desired, Highness."

"What do you mean by that?"

The assassin shrugged. "I mean that not every general considers the greatest gain when he begins a campaign."

Pyrust laughed aloud, then wiped rain from his face. "Would you apply that axiom to me, Delasonsa?"

"Not on this campaign." She nodded toward the pavilion. "Neither Cyron nor his nobles will come to you like dogs. You will succeed here, but only because you have Jasai and can offer the dogs hope with her child. Cyron will have nothing."

Pyrust nodded. In *The Dance of War,* Urmyr counseled that one should always allow an enemy a route to escape. But circumstances conspired to deny that route to Cyron. He couldn't flee south. North would be denied to him, and the west of his own nation had little love for him.

"Perhaps he will sail down the Gold River and follow his *Stormwolf* wherever it went."

"Or perhaps the Empress Cyrsa will arrive and save him." The Mother of Shadows slowly shook her head. "Both are equally improbable. Cyron will fight and many of his citizens will stand with him. Moriande may fall, but chances are just as good of its falling to the invaders as you."

"If the invaders come north, you mean." Perhaps the invaders only wanted Erumvirine, but the sense of that defied him. The forces they'd expended to take Erumvirine could easily have eaten up the eastern half of Nalenyr and could be surrounding Moriande even now. Nalenyr was far more rich a prize.

He looked at the assassin. "Why Erumvirine?"

"Not having met the enemy, my lord, I cannot guess his mind."

"An invasion requires a great deal of planning. I would have expected probing attacks over several years before an invasion could be mounted, but these people came prepared. Either they had superior intelligence about Erumvirine, or something is chasing them, giving them no choice but to find a new home."

"Given how swiftly they've eaten into Erumvirine, *that* may be the most dire idea of all. If they are fleeing, whatever chases them will swallow the Nine whole."

"Let us hope this is not the case." Pyrust nodded slowly. "Yes, Captain, you have news?"

The Fire Hawk captain bowed as the rain washed blood from his armor. "The ministers asked to speak with you, Highness."

"Thank you."

"Highness, I was unable to spare the carpet."

Pyrust shrugged. "Fear not. Soon many of the ministers will be without employment. I will have them clean it."

Chapter Forty

1st day, Planting Season, Year of the Rat
10th Year of Imperial Prince Cyron's Court
163rd Year of the Komyr Dynasty
737th year since the Cataclysm
Uronek Hills, County of Faeut
Erumvirine

There are generals who look at war as a game. They study maps, not battlefields, and think of their warriors as toy soldiers. They think of casualties in terms of "acceptable losses" or "inevitable costs." While they may be wise, they have their troops fight to shift colors on a map and, in their minds, all is reduced to dipping a brush in ink and painting.

I would give my opponent the grace of judging me and my troops based on the Virine troops he'd faced during the invasion. Doing that, however, would inevitably lead to the conclusion that he was stupid, precisely because he assumed I was stupid and that my men were incapable of fighting. He chose to underestimate us, which is as sure a sign of intellectual weakness as a military leader can display.

The first axiom in war is to assume the enemy is as clever as you are, if not more so. This forces you to look at all his actions and to ask yourself why you would be doing the same thing. If you can find no advantage to his action, then you may have discovered a mistake. If you can see a gain to exploiting that mistake, then you exploit it.

My difficulty lay in choosing *which* of his mistakes I would exploit.

Our withdrawal from Kelewan resulted in no serious pursuit. Once we had eluded the battalion he'd sent after us, we moved northwest through the central Virine plains toward the County of Faeut. We followed the Imperial Road, but I did send riders out to villages and towns advising them to evacuate north. My people found many of the villages already deserted, and these we put to the torch after hauling off anything of use.

We did leave one village intact, after a fashion. We put livestock into pens, then arranged every manner of trap we could think of in the houses. We poisoned the wells and prepared everything to burn. I left a squad there to observe what happened when the enemy reached it.

The refugees who preceded us raised the alarm, so local nobles met us on the road with whatever household warriors they could muster. They thought initially to oppose us, but when Captain Lumel introduced them to Prince Iekariwynal, they decided to join us. This swelled our number to over seven hundred, which was a decidedly useful force in the rugged hill country of County Faeut. Moreover it gave us guides and scouts who had an intimate knowledge of the battlefields we might use to engage the enemy.

Here was another mistake my enemy made. Because his army lived off the land, including the people, he had no locals to advise him. While the invaders advanced in good order, even the best maps could not account for places where spring runoff had collapsed part of the road, or where seasonal flooding turned a plain into an impassable marsh. The terrain forced his troops to stop where they needed to keep moving, and to take paths they knew nothing about.

Our campaign was not without surprises either, and the Prince turned out to be one of the pleasant variety. Though quite young, he did not lack for intelligence. He trusted Captain Lumel and struck up a friendship with Dunos. Dunos' unwavering confidence in me became transferred to the Prince, and among our company, my word became law.

I divided my force into three battalions. Captain Lumel had his Jade Bears and had we ever arrayed ourselves for open battle, they would have held our center. Deshiel commanded the Steel Bear archers and two companies of local troops. Ranai commanded our heroes and whatever other locals came to fight.

Not all of my heroes led companies or even squads, for heroes do not always make good leaders. If they expect of others what they can do because of years of training, they willingly thrust their troops into situations where survival is impossible. I made it clear to all of my officers that our intent was to hurt the enemy as much as we could, and to allow them to do as little as possible in return. We would not duel with them, we would not engage them in any honorable pursuit. We would strike when they thought we could not, we would escape when they thought they had us trapped, and when they attacked from their right, we would strike from their left.

Urardsa attended all the briefings and watched the proceedings carefully. Many of the fighters found having a Gloon among them rather unnerving, but the fact that he never predicted doom was heartening. Even without suggestion, he would spend time peering off south toward the enemy host, then shake his head and turn away. My warriors' confidence that he had seen doom for the enemy was worth ten warriors for every one I already had.

One night, when I woke in my tent, deep in a forest, I found him crouched in a corner, a ghostly presence that sent a chill through me. "What is it, Urardsa?"

The quartet of small eyes closed. "Your life is a tangled skein. I cannot find a clean line."

"Should I be disturbed by this, or is it enough that you are?"

The Gloon smiled, then crawled closer. "Strands tangle, but yours are merging. Your future mirrors your past."

"Those who forget their journeys are forever doomed to tread the same path." I threw my blanket off and came up into a sitting position. "I know I have fought battles like this before. Perhaps even here, in Faeut."

"You have been here before, many times."

"Not just as Moraven Tolo. I have his memories, and they have been useful." I wiped sleep sand from my eyes. "I am tempted to ask you if what you see is strong."

The Gloon shook his head. "You will not ask. I will not tell."

I smiled. "Battle is a place where possibilities shift too quickly for me to believe your predictions regardless."

The Gloon laughed, not an altogether happy sound. "But you have told your people that a battle is won before the first arrow flies."

"And it is. So it shall be tomorrow."

What I had learned from the village helped greatly in planning the first significant fight. The *vhangxi* had been under slightly better control than at the graveyard, and the *kwajiin* made up more of the force pursuing us. Even so, the *vhangxi* tore the village apart. Many fell prey to our traps, and the *kwajiin* dispatched the most seriously wounded. The blue-skins did get ill from the water, though not as grievously as a man would have. Even when the village began to burn, they were not prone to panic and withdrew in good order.

In the troops themselves, we only noticed one flaw. The units seemed made up of clan groups, which did not mix and even seemed hostile to each other. The commander of the troops coming after us fought under a banner of a bloody skull, and all other troops chafed under being subordinate to his kinsmen.

We set our trap carefully to utilize all we had learned. We picked a point where a wooden bridge on the Imperial Road had been washed away and, in two days, cleared enough trees from a hillside track to make it appear as if woodsmen had created a road paralleling the gorge. It went east up and over two small hills, then through a ravine that angled back to the southeast. At the far end, the land dropped away into a deep cut that led down into the gorge roughly a thousand yards east of where the bridge had stood.

The thick forest, save where some discreet clearing had been done, allowed for a hundred feet of visibility. A sodden carpet of leaves and needles hid the ground, and the troops entering that southeast ravine might as well have been boxed up in a large coffin.

The *kwajiin* vanguard advanced under the bloody skull banner, and when they reached the gap in the road, they had no problem in deciding to head up the hill onto our track. They had already outstripped the rest of their force and posted two men on the road to inform the others. Ten minutes separated the vanguard from its main body—though when they twisted back into that ravine, the only thing that separated them from the bulk of their force was a steep wooded ridgeline paralleling the gorge.

The sun had reached its zenith by the time the vanguard started off on the detour. Once the last of them passed over the first hill, two archers killed the men they'd left behind, then we dragged the bodies into the gorge and let them float down among bridge debris. When the main body reached the bridge, the direction the vanguard had taken seemed obvious and, after some deliberation, they set off in pursuit.

The head of the vanguard stopped when the trail ended, and four blue-skins headed down into the ravine. Halfway down they fell into tiger traps, impaling themselves on sharpened sticks in six-foot-deep holes. To their credit they did not scream in pain, but they did implore others to help them. Those who did advance found themselves under attack by a handful of archers.

Then, from atop the ridgeline behind them, a full volley of arrows struck the vanguard. The *kwajiin* bolted up the sides of the ravine and a number of them encountered staked pits. Most of these were simply post holes with a single stake in the bottom and several pointing downward. The single stake punched through even the thickest boot, and the others prevented the warrior from pulling his foot free.

Kwajiin archers shot back in both directions, but had no real targets. They advanced as best they could, squeezing through on a serpentine path that took them up the ridge. They crested it and started down the other side. Suddenly arrows shot up at them from below. They shot back and charged downhill.

Their own rear guard, who had likewise been shot at by Deshiel's men on the ridge, fought fiercely. The *kwajiin* archers shot at each other and while they did not kill many of their own, the fight left the vanguard among their own rear guard, exhausted and without an enemy in sight.

And by that time Deshiel's men had withdrawn further southeast, then north, crossing the gorge over a narrow, makeshift bridge created by two felled trees.

The hardest work we had done in preparing lay not in creating the road but in creating the surprises along it. The *kwajiin* walked four abreast, and on my signal, ropes were pulled that released stake-studded logs. They swung down out of the trees and swept the road at waist height. The luckiest men were knocked from the road to tumble down into the gorge. Others were impaled, while the least lucky got stuck on the log and pulped against trees.

The wounded did scream now, and the blue-skins' composure broke. Two of my best archers—one who might one day become a Mystic—shot the *kwajiin* leader. Their arrows might have killed him, save he moved so swiftly—preternaturally so—that he took them in his right arm and flank instead of breastbone and stomach. His wounding made the others cautious, and the only people we shot after that were those seeking to help wounded comrades.

Well before darkness fell, my entire force had melted away and was miles ahead of the *kwajiin*.

That evening I assembled my leaders, this time including the Virine nobles who had brought troops but who I had not allowed to lead them. I praised the leaders for their troops' performance—citing cases of bravery which had been communicated to me. I singled Deshiel out for special praise, since he had deployed his people between two enemy forces and had withdrawn them with no more harm than a sprained ankle.

Lord Pathan Golti—a small, sallow man who, though a good archer, hadn't the temperament needed to be in Deshiel's force—stood up to protest what had happened. "You have let them get away. We could have feathered the lot and avenged Kelewan."

I watched him for a moment, and I'm certain many thought my hand would stray to one of my swords. "Would that have gotten Kelewan back? Would that raise your Prince or your nation again? Would that raise all the dead?"

"Of course not, but it is a matter of national pride."

I spat at his feet. "National pride is the province of those who have a nation, my lord. You do not."

The man looked stricken. "You have no right to speak to me thus."

"If you wish to resolve this as a matter of honor, Lord Golti, *draw a circle.*" I pointed outside the circle of firelight and back in the direction of the battle. "The troops we faced today are but a fraction of those the *kwajiin* have in Erumvirine. For all we know, they've likewise invaded Nalenyr and the Five Princes. We do not fight for what is lost because we are not strong enough to regain it. We fight to prevent more from being lost—and this we might well be able to do."

I stared at him hard enough that he took a step back. "Every time one of them thinks of leaving the road, he will remember the screams of the men who had their legs trapped. He will remember their flesh rent and bloody, and he will hesitate. Every time one of them sees the stump of a fresh-felled tree, or wood chips or leaves which are wet where others are dry, they will imagine a trap. If we knock down another bridge, they will fear another slaughter."

Golti met my stare. "But they will not be dead."

"We don't have to kill them; we just have to guarantee they will not fight. Every day they must eat and sleep and drink, but if they have no food, no water, and no rest, they cannot fight. And all that they seek to threaten will be free. And we shall be alive to enjoy it."

I gave him a cold smile. "But rest assured, Lord Golti, there will come a day when we will meet them in combat. If that is the day you desire, I will keep you alive until then, and place you in the front line so you can kill to your heart's content."

The man stood straighter. "I won't shrink from that assignment. I am not a coward."

"None of you are. Nor are any of them." I folded my arms over my chest. "But by the time we face them in open combat, they will know hunger, thirst, fatigue, and fear. They will come to the battle knowing they will lose. *That* will be our victory."

Chapter Forty-one

3rd day, Planting Season, Year of the Rat
10th Year of Imperial Prince Cyron's Court
163rd Year of the Komyr Dynasty
737th year since the Cataclysm
Tolwreen, Ixyll

Ciras Dejote had to keep reminding himself that the *vanyesh* were evil, because once they had honored him in the Prince's Hall, they all turned out to be terribly *nice*. Intellectually he knew they were malignant creatures who had clung to life awaiting the return of Prince Nelesquin. Nelesquin would again raise them to glory, restoring them bodily, and would lead them back to Erumvirine, where they would remake the Empire and rule over a *jaedunki*.

Besides, they made a very good case for the need for an empire run by sorcerers. They traced their history back to Taichun and said he'd intended the mages to rule over the Empire. Not only was it in keeping with the social system of the Viruk, but it made sense. Since mages could work miracles, they needed to be supported by the people and feel an obligation to them. Taichun had created the bureaucracy to administer things so mages would not be bothered by the trivial. They could spend their time refining their art so they would be ready when they were to be called upon to act.

Pravak took great pains to explain this history when he invited Ciras to visit him. The *vanyesh*'s chambers were, as to be expected, oversized and generously appointed. Though Pravak was nothing more than a gilded skeleton, he had thick carpets in his rooms, plush and heavily upholstered furniture and tapestries that, while having no images Ciras could discern, displayed an interesting weave of colors.

The giant wore thick leather bracers to protect his furnishing from the edges of his forearms. Lounging back on a daybed, he held his right hand up and watched, bemused, as the tiny *gyanrigot* Borosan had fashioned for him as a gift leaped from finger to finger and back again.

"It *is* rather like a kitten, despite looking very much like a spider." Pravak's metal mask twisted into a smile. "I had forgotten the simple pleasure of watching such creatures cavort. We brought no cats with us on the campaign, and those that somehow made it into the city ended up in some wildman's belly."

Ciras sat in a large chair, feeling as if he were five years old and listening to his mother's brother explain about trade with the mainland. "Here you've fed us both mutton and beef, yet I see no creatures ranging about."

Pravak lifted a finger to point up at the mountain, and the little mouser promptly pounced on the tip. "There are mountain meadows. We have your horses there as well. Some of us are good at *bhotri,* so keeping the grasses growing year-round is not difficult. The sheep produce a lot of wool—again a by-product of magic—and the wildmen have become adept at spinning and weaving. They are not much for pictures, but they love color."

"So Tolwreen is self-sufficient."

"Largely. We do get some things in trade, but for a long time we were isolated." The *vanyesh* let the mouser climb up along his arm and begin to play with his knotted-filament hair. "Likely about the time your father was born we had a visit from the east and were finally able to put into place the beginnings of our master's plan. A Naleni explorer became our agent. Kero Anturasi, I believe."

"Qiro?"

"That was it. Do you know him?"

Ciras heard no guile in the question, so smiled. "Just *of* him. He is famous the world over for exploring. I have heard no mention of Tolwreen, however."

"Our master would not have permitted it. Knowing the correct order of the universe, our master has been very careful in his plans. You may not realize it, but you are a part of things. We expect more like you to come to Tolwreen in the next months or years. Many will be trained, as will you, and when all is ready, we will be summoned."

"But I have been trained."

"Indeed, you have, but you need more." Pravak's hands came together with the muffled clash of cymbals. "People come to the *vanyesh* in two ways. You and I were warriors first, who have touched *jaedun*. Others have recognized our value. They will show you what Emperor Taichun taught his most trusted companions: how to wield magic. *Jaedun* of the sword is a portal to working *jaedun* in life."

Ciras managed to suppress a shiver. "And the others?"

"Oh, they were apprenticed to masters of magic and have learned to manipulate *jaedun* directly. We try to train them in more practical ways, like *jaedunserr,* but they resist it. Their magics can be powerful, and will help us once we take control again, but it will be warrior-sorcerers such as you and me that will make our Master's dream possible. He needs heroes, and we are they."

Ciras smiled, masking his true thoughts. The *vanyesh* seemed to define heroes as those who used magic in service to Nelesquin. Ciras saw heroes as those who served the common good, shielding the unfortunate from evil and ambition, not keeping them down so the ambitious might soar. *They make heroes a part of their evil.*

Ciras let his expression become wistful. "I wonder if I will be worthy to return to Tirat as its lord."

The *vanyesh* giant laughed. "If that is all your ambition wishes, I can guarantee it. You, my friend, are capable of so much, I should think that anything you desire will be yours."

"You are too kind."

"No, just aware of how generous our master is." Pravak nodded solemnly. "And soon you shall see that for yourself."

From the moment they had been told that the *vanyesh* still considered Nelesquin their master, both Ciras and Borosan knew they had to escape. Their mission had been to find the Empress Cyrsa and awaken her to conditions in the Empire. That her enemy still lived and was plotting to destroy what she had left behind made their mission all the more urgent. Moreover, the *vanyesh* and their mastery of magic would be something the Nine would be hard-pressed to defeat.

So, they set about gathering food and water against any opportunity to escape. Ciras learned which tunnels led up to the meadows, and while he hated being predictable, he knew they would need their horses. Ciras even located and set about repairing their tack, noting to any of the *vanyesh* who asked that to neglect even the most simple thing was to abandon the discipline that made him worthy of the honor they had bestowed upon him.

The most difficult part of escaping had been finding an opportunity. When they explored, either together or singly, wildmen watched them constantly. They didn't think the wildmen were spying on them, but just found them a curiosity. And when wildmen were not dogging their footsteps, one of the *vanyesh* would find them and offer his hospitality. Some still took food and drink, though none seemed to enjoy it, and the two of them were offered enough food that they concluded the *vanyesh* were living vicariously through them.

Finally, as planting season began, they received a visit from one of the *vanyesh*, who told them that they must remain in their chambers until summoned forth again. While there was no punishment noted or even implied, their acquiescence seemed assumed. Their visitor did assure them that all would be explained shortly, but that for the moment they needed to remain hidden.

As the *vanyesh* departed, having taken with him the gift of a tiny mouser, Borosan swept spare parts into a leather satchel with his arm. "I think we go now."

Ciras nodded. As much as he wanted to know why they were being restricted, he figured there would be no better chance to get away. "If we are caught, we say we decided the best way to be unseen was to go outside the city and tend our horses."

Borosan looped the satchel over his shoulder, then pulled another device from a similar leather bag. A foot long, not quite so wide, and edged with wood, the flat tablet had a surface made of the silver-white metal. Odd characters etched themselves into the surface, then the inventor nodded.

"I've given out a dozen of the mousers. A number of them are converging in a subterranean room. The Prince's Hall, I would bet."

"Welcoming another of the *vanyesh*?"

"Better than Nelesquin."

Ciras gathered up his swords and two satchels laden with dried meat and waterskins. He followed Borosan and his large *thanaton* into the silver ball. His companion selected a blank key and used a *thaumston* stylus to etch a word on it. He slid it into the slot as the door closed and then the door opened again. They emerged in the northwestern quadrant, near the tunnel leading up to the horse meadow.

Ciras looked around. "No wildmen."

"Fewer chances of our passing being revealed." Borosan settled the satchels over the large *thanaton*'s broad back, then took Ciras' burdens from him. "Just in case you need to deal with something."

The swordsman nodded and led the way. He moved quietly and soon got used to the ticking of the *thanaton*'s metal feet on the stone. The tunnel meandered somewhat, but had been carved wide and tall enough that, had they wanted to, they could have easily ridden their horses two abreast through it. Though quite steep, it leveled out as it reached the meadow.

Ciras held a hand up and Borosan sank back into the shadows of the chamber that served as a tack room. Two silhouettes lounged in the shade near the tunnel's mouth. Men, obviously, and they both wore swords. Even though they were in silhouette, Ciras could see enough of their clothing to know they weren't from the Nine.

They're Turasynd.

The idea that the *vanyesh* were talking with the Turasynd reminded him of a tale Borosan said the Gloon had related. Prince Nelesquin had betrayed Empress Cyrsa by entering into negotiations with a Turasynd god-priest. Fury pulsed through him as he realized the *vanyesh* were compounding their earlier treason.

"What are we going to do, Ciras?"

The swordsman slipped into the tack room. "Gather two saddles, six bridles, and be ready to move. I'm going to deal with these two. Quickly. If we're discovered, we will be pursued."

Ciras moved back into the tunnel, stepping to the center. He kept his gait easy—eager yet casual. He let his hands dangle open at his sides.

He was a dozen steps away from them before they noticed him. They came instantly alert, and his stomach tightened. Their hands went to the hilts of their swords, then they relaxed. They exchanged glances and laughed. He forced himself to laugh, too, then reached inside and, for the first time, invoked *jaedun*.

His vision changed. Though he saw no more color or less, he somehow saw more clearly. Each man seemed to glow—the one on the right more so than his companion. *He is more dangerous.* As Ciras closed, he raised his left hand in greeting, broadening his smile, and they aped his expression.

His right foot touched down and he began to pivot toward the dangerous man. Ciras drew the *vanyesh* blade in a smooth motion. Even before his foe's right hand had touched the hilt of his own sword, the draw-cut opened his throat to the spine. Blood gushed and the man gurgled as he fell back.

Ciras continued his spin and brought his blade down and around in a parry. He batted the other Turasynd's lunge wide, then snapped his sword up high. It fell in a slash that clove the Turasynd from crown to jaw, and dropped him like a bag of rocks.

Ciras completed his turn as the second swordsman's blade clattered to the ground. He crouched and waited, listening for anything in the echo of the sword's fall. He heard nothing. Finally, without sheathing his sword, he made his way to the second man's side and yanked open his leather jerkin.

Black feathers covered the man's chest. Taken from black eagles, they'd been inserted into the man's skin, and then he'd willfully entered a place of wild magic. There he'd undergone rituals that Ciras could only imagine, which fused the feathers to his flesh and completed his initiation into the Black Eagle Society.

He quickly checked the other man and found he'd been similarly fletched. This was not the first time he'd seen a Black Eagle. His master had dueled one to entertain Prince Cyron during the last Harvest Festival in Moriande. The Turasynd had been good, and had borne a blade of similar antiquity to the *vanyesh* blade.

Ciras thought for a moment. He could not directly connect these two with the man in Moriande, but their presence certainly indicated the Black Eagle Society was flourishing. He couldn't recall if the Turasynd god-priest had been a Black Eagle or not, but it really didn't matter. He didn't even know if the Turasynd had another god-priest to lead them, but that didn't matter either.

I have to assume there is a new one and he is a Black Eagle or allied with them. He sighed. *And he or his envoys are in the Prince's Hall, negotiating an alliance with the* vanyesh.

Borosan came up with the *thanaton* laden with tack. "That was quick work."

"It had to be. The same must be true of our escape." Ciras grabbed a bridle and headed out toward the horses. "Ancient enemies are renewing alliances. It won't be good for us, or the Nine. Let's hope, my friend, that the Sleeping Empress has spent her time dreaming up a way to deal with them."

Chapter Forty-two

5th day, Planting Season, Year of the Rat
10th Year of Imperial Prince Cyron's Court
163rd Year of the Komyr Dynasty
737th year since the Cataclysm
Thyrenkun, Felarati
Deseirion

Keles knew he was dreaming. He looked from the window of his room and down toward the Black River. There, slowly drifting up the river in the darkness, a fleet of small ships grew to enormous proportions. They began to disgorge warriors and other creatures that slipped into the shadowed city.

Fires and screams followed in their wake.

More important than the havoc was the image on the largest ship's mainsail. It bore his grandfather's face. As he watched, Qiro's eyes came alive and turned to look at him. His mouth moved and in his voice the words "I'm coming for you, Keles" echoed in his head.

"Grandfather, how can you be here? It's impossible."

"Nothing is impossible for me, Keles. You must know

that by now." A look of anger passed over his face, then the sail fell as if torn loose in a gale. It hit the deck and burst into flames.

Keles sat bolt-upright in bed, bathed in sweat. He tossed back the blanket, pulled on trousers, and stepped into his boots. He reached for a robe and slipped it on, fastening the sash as he opened the door to his chambers. He ran to the library where he worked, and shivered when he found that the warriors who had stood guard throughout the palace—grizzled veterans as long on scars as they were short on hair—had all abandoned their posts.

He bolted inside and crossed to the balcony. Throwing open the doors, he stepped out and looked south toward the river. There, lit by fires rising in factories and the dwellings on the river's north bank, lurked a fleet of black ships. The flagship appeared as it did in his dream, save that the mainsail did not bear his grandfather's image. It had been marked with a white line-image that very few in Felarati would have recognized.

Very few outside Anturasikun would know it. The sail bore the outline of the world as his grandfather had painted it on the wall of his sanctum. *Only there is a new continent off the southeast coast.*

This confirmed that the fleet had come from his grandfather and he certainly didn't view it as his salvation. His grandfather had sent him off to survey Ixyll on a mission that would most surely have killed him. That Qiro had found him in Felarati would compound his grandfather's anger. His absence from Ixyll meant Keles had defied his grandfather, and Keles had no desire to face the old man's wrath in person or by proxy.

The cartographer watched, transfixed, as the black

ships grounded themselves on the riverbanks and troops poured forth. Each ship disgorged an improbable number. Huge and tiny creatures leaped out. The smallest swarmed over buildings, while the largest stalked through streets.

The invaders kept coming, and the defenders had no chance to oppose them. Even if crack troops had been available to defend the capital, the onslaught would have been overwhelming. Already refugees began streaming from their homes, fleeing west from the invaders.

Now is the time we can escape! He dashed back into the library, opened a chest, and dug down through carefully stacked paper and rolled maps. He uncovered the two leather satchels he'd hidden there and had slowly filled with supplies. The waterskins were flaccid, but he could fill them later. The other two bags contained dried meat and cheese, tea and uncooked rice, as well as a small pot. He'd meant to get some rope, but hadn't managed it yet. *This will have to do.*

The smallest of the invaders leaped the palace walls and bounced into the library. Two of them, looking like harmless monkeys until each flashed a mouthful of sharp teeth, leaped for him and grabbed his arms. They started screeching so sharply their cries rose to silence, then bit him when he fought being dragged toward the balcony.

"Ouch!" Keles grabbed the wrists of the one on his right arm and whipped the creature around. He smashed its head against the stone wall, then flung its limp body away. The other's screeching shifted to hooting and its fangs snapped shut, just missing his hand. Keles cracked it over the head with a bronze candlestick, crushing its skull.

Brandishing the candlestick, he ran from the library

and took the stairs up two at a time. Two levels up the corridor remained deserted, but the door to the Princess' apartments stood open. He ran in, and then toward her balcony. He saw Jasai with her back against the railing, her hair platinum in the moonlight, and fear etched on her face.

With a dagger in hand Lady Inyr approached Jasai. She held the blade low, poised for a gutting thrust. She moved easily enough to make clear she knew her business well.

Keles hurled the candlestick. Inyr twisted far more quickly than he would have thought possible. The candlestick passed between her and the Princess, striking sparks from the balustrade before falling to the garden below. Inyr swept forward in its wake, grabbed Jasai's hair, and yanked her head back as she pressed the dagger to the Princess' throat.

Keles held his hands up. "Don't do it, Inyr. The Prince would not be pleased."

The woman sneered at him contemptuously. "Idiot, I do this with the Prince's approval. If you two were to take the chance to flee, I was to kill her. You are to remain his captive, as you are too valuable to lose."

"But she's carrying his child."

"He can find another broodmare; an Anturasi is far too rare." Inyr smiled at Jasai. "You played a good game and kept me from him. I'll be punished for my failure, but praised for my attention to duty now."

"Don't, Inyr." Keles let his shoulder bags slip to the floor as he stepped onto the balcony. He knew he couldn't reach her fast enough to stop her from slitting Jasai's throat, but he had to try something. "Let her live,

I'll remain here forever. You'll just have to get us to safety—which means away from here."

"So you can escape later?" The assassin slowly shook her head. "I'm not a fool."

"Then you should realize that if we don't go immediately, we're all going to die."

She stared at him and laughed. "I'm not going to die."

Her defiant expression never had a chance to fade. Long dark fingers shot over her forehead and clamped down over her face. Her head twisted sharply to the right and her neck cracked audibly. The clang of her dagger hitting the balcony floor covered the soft thump of her body falling beside it.

Jasai sank to her knees and scrambled for the dagger with both hands as the Viruk grabbed the balustrade and vaulted over it. He landed in a crouch, his talons clicking against the stone. His left hand closed over Jasai's hands, engulfing them and the dagger.

The Viruk smiled, his ivory teeth a ghostly presence in the moonlight. "If she is yours, Keles Anturasi, I will bring her, but we have to travel fast."

"Rekarafi?" Keles' mouth hung open. "How did you . . . ?"

"I followed you from Moriande to Solaeth. Tracking you here was nothing."

Jasai, still shaken, tried to pull her hands free. "Who is this?"

"A Viruk friend of mine who's earning a pile of white stones." Keles gathered up his gear. "This is Princess Jasai, Pyrust's wife. She's coming. We'll take the stairs inside."

Rekarafi released Jasai's hands, then pointed down to the garden. "Meet me. Be quick."

"Outside the library, right." As the Viruk slid over the railing and disappeared again, Keles grabbed Jasai's hand and pulled her back into her chambers. "We have to go, fast. Felarati is under attack."

"Who?"

"It doesn't matter. With the defenses the way they are, two beggars with three good legs and a crutch between them could have kicked the city to pieces." Keles hurried her down the stairs and batted one of the black-furred monkey creatures out of the way. The two of them ran to the library, then out and down steps leading to the garden below.

Keles stopped short and gaped. Jasai tore her hand from his and ran forward. They both shouted, "Tyressa!" but their tones differed as much as their reactions did. The cartographer remained frozen in place, while Jasai flew to the tall Keru and embraced her.

Keles watched the two of them hug. His mouth gaped in joy and disbelief. It *was* Tyressa, she'd survived. *Survived and come all this way.*

He shook his head to clear it. "You're alive?"

Tyressa released the younger woman, hurried to Keles. She stared at him for a heartbeat or two, then grabbed him and hugged him tightly. He hugged her back, reassured by her warmth and scent that she truly was alive.

"How is it possible?"

She released him and laughed. "What, Keles? That I'm alive, or I know Jasai?"

"Alive; both."

Rekarafi growled and sniffed the air. "They're of the same blood, Keles. And now we have to move or we shall die."

"Right, right."

They ran to the garden's west wall. The Viruk boosted Keles to the top and he leaped down easily. Tyressa came next and tossed him her spear before she leaped to the ground. Lastly, Rekarafi reached the top of the wall with Jasai in his arms.

"Careful, she's pregnant."

The Viruk sniffed again. "I know." He leaped down effortlessly, then they all started running west. Quickly, they merged with a throng of terrified citizens. Mothers clasped wailing infants to their breasts, while toddlers screamed for lost parents. Tired old men and women ushered along grandchildren and great-grandchildren. Keles and his group passed through them quickly, more by dint of the fact that they were in their prime than that they had the Princess or a Viruk with them—though neither fact went without notice.

The crowd's progress slowed, then stopped, but Keles forced his way through to the front. The road had been blocked with two overturned wagons, and men with spears and swords kept the crowd at bay. Across the road lay the walled compound of the Ministry of National Unity. Guards patrolled the walls, and a couple of bleeding corpses provided stark evidence of how serious they were about not giving anyone sanctuary.

Keles pointed at one of the guards. "I'm Keles Anturasi. I want to talk to Grand Minister Rislet Peyt immediately."

The man sneered at him. "You're the fifth Anturasi we've had here tonight. Go away."

Jasai stepped up beside Keles. She pointed to the man standing in the first guard's shadow. "I am Princess Jasai. Slay him."

A sword cleared scabbard, but the first man dropped to his knees and bowed low. "Forgive me, Princess, I did not see you."

"You should have opened your eyes." She nodded to the man with the drawn sword. "Bring me Rislet Peyt, or his head, whichever is most convenient." She stepped forward, resting her foot on the bowing man's head. "Hurry."

Keles looked from her to a smiling Tyressa. "Sister?"

"Niece, but I taught her a great deal."

"I see."

Rislet Peyt appeared on a balcony overlooking the intersection. "I regret I cannot receive you, Princess. The omens are inauspicious."

"I understand that, Grand Minister." Jasai raised her voice and chin at the same time. "I just wanted to thank you for the lend of your personal troops. If you survive the invasion, I shall return them to you, and praise their efforts to my husband."

"You can't take them."

"You'll have to come down here and stop me." She shifted her foot, hooked it beneath the bowing man's shoulder, and toed him back onto his heels. "Right these wagons, load those who can't walk, and get your people out here. We're going west and getting out of the city. Now!"

"Yes, Highness."

"No! Do not move," Rislet countermanded.

Jasai pointed back toward the fires in the east. "I guarantee you will die here if you don't move. By the invaders or my hand, your choice. The Grand Minister cannot save himself, and he certainly can't harm anyone who joins me."

"Yes, Highness." The man stood and issued orders. Guards left their posts and could not be lured back no matter the curses or rewards Peyt offered. They opened the gates and once the wagons were on their wheels again, they hitched teams of horses to them. A bunch of the guards drifted off into the darkness, but quickly returned with their own families.

Once the way had been cleared, most of the people continued on toward Westgate. A few did enter the ministry compound, but quickly abandoned it again when Peyt and his senior officials hustled out and joined the throng.

Tyressa grabbed Jasai by the wrist. "We have to go."

"I know, just a minute more." Her voice dropped. "They're taking heart from my presence. I have to give them that, because if I don't, they won't make it."

A low rumbling thunder came from the east. It took Keles a minute to identify it as the tramping of booted feet. He ran quickly to the ministry compound and mounted the wall to give himself more perspective. He stared, barely believing what he saw.

Warriors were walking nine abreast, in ranks nine deep. They came down the road, working west, always west. At any crossroads, the first squad turned north, the second south. Odd and even they split and walked to the next intersection. There they turned back west, and at the next toward the middle again. Once they returned to that original intersection, then crossed it and the process began again.

Throughout the city, squads moved that way, searching, ever searching. Behind them, moving through the city in much the same way, other squads put the city to the torch. Block by block, Felarati burned.

And they're searching for me. He had no doubt that his grandfather had sent the fleet, both to find him *and* to punish Felarati. *To punish anyone who ever defied him.*

Across the intersection, one of the monkey-things crouched like a furred gargoyle. It pointed a slender arm in his direction, then began hooting, punctuated with a screech. And back along the street, a company stopped. The squads that had already turned away spun about and rejoined the formation marching west. As one the soldiers drew their swords.

The stragglers screamed and began ducking into alleys and buildings. The invaders ignored them, but when the monkey's hooting grew louder and faster, the soldiers began trotting. *And when they charge, they will slaughter everyone in their way.*

One of the ministry guards silenced the monkey with an arrow. For a moment the invaders faltered and then they started to run. Swords rose and fell. Peasants screamed and reeled away, clutching severed limbs or split faces. The invaders slew everyone in their path as if merely clearing foliage.

The press of refugees slowed them slightly, then the ministry guards countercharged. Their archers shot true and well, dropping the short, thick invaders. The spearmen ran them through and kept pushing, knocking front ranks into back. They looked as if they might succeed in forcing the invaders to retreat, but other companies came at a run, some directly and others fanning out to flank the defenders.

Rekarafi waved Keles down from the wall. "We have to go."

The cartographer fled the compound and raced along the street, with the ministry warriors forming a rear guard for the column. He caught up with Tyressa and grabbed her arm.

"They're looking for me. If I give up, they'll let everyone else go."

Tyressa shook her head. "Rekarafi and I did not cross half the world to give you up. Besides that, you're wrong." She pointed to the lurid flames spreading in the east. "If all they wanted was you, they would have made demands before they started burning things. They *may* want you, but whoever sent them also issued orders that Felarati must die."

Keles nodded. *My grandfather would do that. If he sent them to rescue me, he would send them to punish Pyrust for being arrogant enough to take me prisoner.*

Keles looked back and watched his work burn. "My grandfather did this."

Tyressa looked at him with half-lidded eyes. "How is that possible? I don't recognize the warriors or their insignia."

"I don't know. I don't understand it." Keles shook his head. "And unless we can figure it out, I don't know how we can stop them."

Chapter Forty-three

7th day, Planting Season, Year of the Rat
10th Year of Imperial Prince Cyron's Court
163rd Year of the Komyr Dynasty
737th year since the Cataclysm
Wentokikun, Moriande
Nalenyr

Prince Cyron paused in front of the enclosure housing the clouded linsang. With the owl-moon just rising, the slender tan creature with black stripes and spots should have emerged. He caught a quick flash of tan at the hole, then saw two dark eyes peering out at him.

The Prince smiled and slowly raised the basket he held in his left hand. He plucked a small blue egg from it and extended it toward the linsang. The creature's face appeared at the hole. His nose twitched, then he hid his face again.

Cyron, shaking his head, returned the egg to the basket and set it on the ground. The sanctuary staff would come by later and feed the creature.

The Prince turned to his companion. "Perhaps I should let you try to feed him."

The Lady of Jet and Jade politely refused with a shake of her head. "Perhaps he is not hungry, Highness."

"He's hungry. My gamekeeper believes the linsangs have mated, and Jorim Anturasi's notes indicated the male would be hunting more. He tucks the eggs into his cheeks and brings them back to the den." Cyron sighed and glanced at his left arm. "Linsangs have sensitive noses. He smells the rot."

"I would counsel against your taking this as an omen."

"And you are doubtlessly right, but the fact of rot cannot be denied. My arm, everything else."

The Prince's wound had not healed well. The Lord of Shadows had stabbed all the way through his forearm, as the Prince had directed. Such was his skill that he avoided nerves, tendons, and blood vessels. It had hurt, but the Prince's physician, Geselkir, had been confident it would not suppurate.

It did, however. The Prince had tried to ignore the pain, and had not summoned his physician to look at it in a timely manner. Then, in the middle of the night, the pain had been such that Cyron, hot with fever, had risen from bed to get water and to summon help. He fainted and fell on the arm, reopening the wound.

Geselkir had done what he could, cleaning the wound and packing it in poultices. The Viruk ambassador had even come in and offered to work magic to help. Others had suggested that the Prince send a message to Kaerinus to get him to effect a healing, but a half-dozen messages to the *vanyesh* survivor had gone unanswered.

Which is an answer in and of itself.

The Lord of Shadows had offered to kill himself for

what he had done, but the Prince had refused him. Geselkir worked very hard and was confident he had the infection under control. The Viruk had suggested sewing maggots into the wound to let them devour the dead flesh, but Cyron had refused that idea. *I already feel dead inside. How would they know when to stop eating?*

The Prince gestured gingerly with his left arm. "I don't know which hurts more: the wound in my arm or the wound in my heart."

She nodded solemnly. "Both are grievous, Highness. Do not feel you would burden me if you chose to speak your mind. You know that though your words will reach my ears, they will never reach my tongue."

"I know."

He reached down and gently grasped his left wrist. Earlier in the day he'd learned that Prince Eiran had gone missing from the Helosundian border. While neither the messenger, his Lord of Shadows, nor the Grand Minister could tell him if Eiran had been assassinated, there seemed little question. The Helosundian Minister of Foreign Relations—a man Cyron had no liking for at all—had been killed in Moriande. It seemed as if the Helosundians had not yet tired of killing each other.

"Here, in my sanctuary, barely three months ago, I shamed Eiran and challenged him. I thought he would break, but he rose to that challenge. He proved himself a loyal and valuable ally. Had I gotten to know him better, we would have become great friends."

The courtesan smiled and slipped her hand through his good arm, leading him deeper into the sanctuary. "He stopped Count Turcol from reaching you, Highness."

Cyron laughed lightly. "It was your foot that stopped Turcol."

"And his that made certain the man did not rise again." She gave his arm a slight squeeze. "Eiran was devoted to you. Had he lived, he would have been a strong ally."

"And it was that possibility that killed him." Cyron ducked beneath a tree branch laden with green buds. "As he grew stronger, his legitimacy as the Prince of Helosunde likewise increased. This made him a rival for the Council of Ministers. His sister's marriage to Pyrust means that Eiran's legitimacy would transfer to her children if he died without heir. It would seem someone killed him to cut her children off and bar Pyrust from any legitimate claim to Helosunde."

He glanced at her. "My ministers say they hear nothing of Pyrust and his planning, but they're lying. They dare not say what they're hearing because they know I'll have to act. They're concealing bits of news from me, hoping clarifications will undercut their fears. The problem is that their very worst fear is that I will act."

The Lady of Jet and Jade looked up at him. "You are certain Pyrust is ready to attack Helosunde again?"

"He already has. I can feel it." Cyron hesitated, afraid to say anything more. Then the absurdity of it all struck him, and he laughed aloud.

"What amuses my lord?"

Cyron stopped and turned to face her. "Your beauty is ageless, which makes it easy for me to forget you have lived many lifetimes. I know you are *jaecailyss.* The times we have spent together in communion likely have not extended my lifetime, but have enriched it immeasurably. Your mastery of the art of love is, I am certain, unparalleled."

"You are quite kind, Highness, but how does this bear on the point you were making?"

"You are also a remarkable judge of human nature. You knew how to read Turcol and acted so you could draw close enough to him to strike. Don't deny it. I would not presume on your affections enough to assume you would have struck *for* me, but certainly *against* him."

She glanced down. "You underestimate your charms, Highness."

"And that comment eases some of my pain." Cyron smiled. "The fact is that Pyrust has always been a wolf. I called him as much when we met here. I offered him grain to hold his forces at bay, but I knew that would be intolerable. He surprised me when he took Jasai to wife. I had expected him to marry a Virine princess, thereby creating a link between nations that would get him whatever he needed—including an ally with little love for Nalenyr."

"Prince Pyrust is most dangerous, Highness, because he is capable of planning ahead *and* acting swiftly to seize an opportunity."

"And I fear moving troops south may have seemed such an opportunity." Cyron shook his head. "More so if he knows what is happening in Erumvirine."

She nodded, her voice becoming a soft whisper. "And you have to assume that he does."

"I have other choices, but each is more stupid than the preceding. If I assume he has remained north of the Black River, I won't be able to stop him when he moves south. So, I have issued a call to the westron lords for troops, and I've gathered all those I can in the east. The latter I have sent south because I can trust them. The westrons, I can't."

Cyron sighed and sat on one of the sanctuary's stone benches. The Lady of Jet and Jade, wearing a white silk gown trimmed in emerald and embroidered with black dragons, looked a vision of loveliness that eased his heart somewhat. She reached up and plucked a blue blossom from a tree branch and tucked it behind an ear. Her silver eyes flashed playfully and his heart leaped.

"Were my brother still alive, he would have a solution to this problem. He'd pull troops back from the passes in the Helos Mountains, luring Pyrust down."

"What are the chances that Pyrust would accept the challenge and invade Nalenyr?"

"Knowing my brother, none." Cyron smiled. "My brother would have our troops in the south and would quickly smash the invaders, then move an army north to punish Pyrust. Aralias would have been able to get Count Vroan to lead the army of the south and keep the invaders occupied. That was his strength, inspiring troops. He was a leader."

"You inspire as well, Highness."

"Yes, but what I inspire does not seem to bear on this situation."

"Do you see no solution at all, Highness?"

The Prince leaned forward, wincing as he rested his left forearm on his thigh. "This is the one problem the Empress Cyrsa did not anticipate. She assumed that by splitting the Empire into the principalities she would guarantee no one was powerful enough to reunite it in her absence. Setting aside the effects of the Time of Black Ice, her plan has proven sensible. No one predominates, so no one launches a large-scale war. The masses avoid the hardships and the chances of triggering another Cataclysm are minimized.

"The difficulty right now is this: outsiders who may be strong enough to take principalities have attacked. We've no news from Erumvirine, and none from the Five Princes. If the enemy has overwhelmed all of them, taking the northern principalities is not a matter of *if* but *when*."

The courtesan slipped her hands into the opposite sleeves of her robe. "Were the Empire intact, there would have been a solid response that could have crushed the invasion."

"I think so."

"Then why don't you make Prince Pyrust an offer of unity? Certainly Nalenyr, Helosunde, and Deseirion united could oppose the invaders."

"That would be my hope, but it is not something I can agree to in good conscience. The war against the invaders would likely be fought here, in Nalenyr. It would lay waste to my nation."

"But that is likely to happen anyway, isn't it?"

"True, but I have to hope we can hold them in the mountains. Pyrust and his troops would be of great value there, or even pushing into Erumvirine. I do not doubt his skills as a general—I respect them enough to fear them." He sighed with exhaustion. "To put him on my southern border, however, requires him to pass through Nalenyr. It is inviting the wolf into your house to help rid it of vermin. The wolf may not choose to leave again. If he were to drive into Erumvirine and liberate it, he would not put the Telanyn family back on the throne. Nalenyr and Helosunde would be trapped. Helosunde would fall because of his wife. Nalenyr would be next, and the Five Princes after that."

She smiled bravely. "Perhaps that is just your take on things. He may see things differently."

"No, he's read things the same way. Likely he read them before I did. He's coming, and I have to act to save my nation or save my people. It's a difficult choice, because I cannot save both."

"Is there no other possible solution?"

He smiled indulgently. "The *Stormwolf* could return from the other side of the world with a fleet bristling with warriors."

"Is that so impossible?"

"Perhaps not." He nodded, then levered himself off the bench with his good hand. "It is a dream that is worth having, I suppose."

"You don't think it likely?"

He shook his head. "Most likely is that the invaders learned of us because of the expedition. The *Stormwolf* found the new continent, which Qiro Anturasi named after himself. I've seen the map. He even may have tried to warn us. In his own blood he wrote, 'Here there be monsters.' "

The Lady of Jet and Jade came to him and caressed his temple. "Be careful, Highness, that you let no monsters dwell here. What you face are men. If they were utterly wise or invincible, they would have long since reunited the Empire. That they have not, that Nalenyr yet exists, means there is hope for a solution."

"Do you truly believe that?"

"Have I any choice?" She took his hand in hers and kissed it. "Your true enemy is despair. Surrender to it, and the gods themselves could not save you or your nation."

Chapter Forty-four

7th day, Planting Season, Year of the Rat
10th Year of Imperial Prince Cyron's Court
163rd Year of the Komyr Dynasty
737th year since the Cataclysm
Kunjiqui, Anturasixan

"Yes, my lord, it is magnificent." Nirati's eyes shone brightly as she hung on Nelesquin's arm and stared up at the huge ship. In design, it reminded her very much of the *Stormwolf,* yet this ship was bigger in every dimension. The figurehead was a bear rampant, clawing the air as if, by the strength of his massive arms alone, he could drag the ship through the waves. "What will you call it?"

Nelesquin chuckled warmly. "This is the *Crown Bear*. I'm having my smiths create a crown of gold for the figurehead."

She looked up, surprised. "What if it falls off?"

He turned to her and took her face in his large hands. "What if it does? Anturasixan could produce a crown for every person in the Empire—nine times over. The riches in this land know no equal—and the greatest treasure here is you, my love."

She smiled and stood on tiptoes to kiss him. "You are too kind, my lord."

"Only to you, Nirati."

She smiled and looked back at the ship, secretly acknowledging the truth of his comment. Nelesquin had moved heaven and earth for his building projects. He'd required Qiro to find a slice of his continent where vast forests could be raised, then another where creatures suited to harvesting them could be created. Once that work had been done, mountains rose to create the valleys through which rivers would flow to carry the wood to the coast, and there the shipwrights could begin their work. Back in the mountains, yet other creatures burrowed, and fires burned within the mountains as smiths worked day and night—both of which passed swiftly there—fulfilling the demands of Nelesquin's army.

Nelesquin drove everyone hard, and while he did grant them rewards for their successes, his punishments were often cruel and final. He tolerated no revolt, accepted few excuses, and seemed more content to have her grandfather create a new race that would bend to his will than retraining those who had already failed him.

Only once had she seen his darker side directed at her. Her fondness for Takwee had inspired her to set aside a portion of Anturasixan where surviving members of the races he'd destroyed could live in peace. Ever practical, Nelesquin would not destroy one group until another was ready to take their place, which gave her time to spirit a small population away.

When he discovered what she'd done, his fury had been monumental. She'd quailed and Takwee had bristled, baring her teeth. This show of defiance seemed to amuse him and broke his mood. From that point forward, he allowed Nirati her sanctuary. He referred to it as the Land of Lost Toys, and seemed further amused by what these creatures did when left to their own devices.

Fortunately, he did not have much time to observe them. "The *Crown Bear* will be magnificent, and I cannot wait to be on the ocean again. I used to love it so. Wind in the face, spray washing the deck. I was quite the mariner in my youth, but then other interests and politics drew me home to Erumvirine."

He smiled, but his eyes focused differently. "Before the Turasynd ever threatened the Empire, the Dark Sea pirates bedeviled us. A great deal of trade came through Ixyll to Dolosan ports and across the Dark Sea to the Empire. The pirates preyed on all of it. The Emperor tasked me, among others, to crush the pirates. Fight them we did, and ended their scourge. I was part of the conquest of Dreonath."

Nirati shook her head. "I know nothing of that, my lord."

"No?" Nelesquin drew her down with him to sit on the grasses in the *Crown Bear*'s shadow. "I can barely believe subsequent events have eclipsed what was the greatest naval campaign ever waged. The pirates had gathered under one leader, a Viruk named Dosaarch. Outlaws all, and renegades against Imperial authority, they fought us tooth, claw, and blade.

"We chased them from the sea to Dreonath. The Viruk claimed a ruined fortress, saying it had once been a family holding. I don't know the truth of that or not, but it was an evil place—a fell warren full of traps and sorceries that killed many a valiant man and hero alike."

His face tightened as he spoke. "In that campaign, your Cataclysm was born—and had I known what would have resulted in years hence, I would have counseled my father to show mercy to the pirates. Whatever they could take in raids would be a small price to pay for the preservation of his Empire."

Nirati caressed his cheek. "You could not have known the future, beloved."

"Perhaps not, for men's hearts can be as black as Gol'dun and we have no way of knowing." He glanced down and snorted a laugh, rocking back slightly. "Back then, I was young and had many a companion I counted as good friends—men I would trust with my life; and not just men. As we went into Dreonath, a Viruk named Rekarafi was at my right hand, and Virisken Soshir was at my left. A few of those who would join me in the *vanyesh* were there as well. Some meant to win glory, but for many others the glory was in serving."

She smiled despite recognizing the name of the Viruk who had attacked her brother, and kissed Nelesquin's shoulder. "Serving with you should have been glory enough for any."

"You're right, of course, but many could not see the wisdom in that." He frowned for a moment. "Back then, the provinces you now call the Nine were just provinces. You didn't think of yourself as Naleni or Morythian; you were just of the Empire. You might owe your allegiance to a Naleni noble, but that was just a geographical descriptor, not any sense of nationality. In fact, generals and administrators often bore a title from one place, but served in another, which made it difficult for anyone to gather enough power to rival the Emperor."

He smiled at remembering. "My father had two types

of wives—just like the Emperors before him. Wives of blood were the daughters of nobles whom he married in formal ceremonies. Their children would be princes and princesses, and he could designate any of them to be his heirs. I was third from the throne when I went to fight pirates, and I shall admit I had hopes of moving up were we successful.

"His other wives were wives of pleasure. They, too, might be the daughters of nobles, but more often were highly trained courtesans who were gifted to the Emperor to curry favor. Their children, if there were any, were bastards who drew titles from their mothers, or earned them through merit. Despite their illegitimacy, however, they were treated equally at court with the rest of us, and many were the schools that vied to have them join up for training."

Nelesquin's smile split his black beard. "We had adventures in the Empire, but facing the pirates, that was to be the grandest of all. And so off we went, getting our feet wet with water and blood. While our fleet landed an army in the north, I took three companies in from the east. Rekarafi knew a way into the pirate stronghold and while their eyes were on the roads from the north, we attacked. We chased them down through that warren and I harvested Dosaarch's head myself. I presented it to my father and he made me Crown Prince."

"A position you certainly deserved, Highness."

Nelesquin took her right hand in his and kissed her palm. "You flatter me, for you do not know how much I've lied in this recital."

"I think you were far too modest." She smiled. "If you were Crown Prince, why did your father not send you out to deal with the Turasynd threat?"

"There were many reasons, complicated reasons." Nelesquin sighed. "My father was very good at paying attention to details—more suited to the bureaucracy than leading the country. The pirates threatened how smoothly his Empire ran; they did not threaten the Empire. The Turasynd did both, and while my father scrambled to keep the Empire running, he didn't have enough perspective to see how to deal with the threat.

"And then there was politics to contend with." His voice shrank. "I shall not deceive you, Nirati; I played at politics. My position was not assured, so I took steps to solidify it. My friend Virisken Soshir was rewarded with the leadership of my father's bodyguard. I courted other factions and became initiated in the ways of the *vanyesh*. This frightened some nobles, and they conspired to turn my father against me. When he most needed my counsel, I was not permitted to see him. He made no decision when one was sorely needed. He dithered and Cyrsa, one of his pleasure wives, murdered him and usurped his throne."

"Then she sundered the Empire and headed off into the wilderness to face the Turasynd."

"Exactly." Nelesquin's lips pressed tightly together, then he looked away. A tear glistened on his left cheek. "I joined her, bringing all those who felt loyalty to me. She'd humored me by making me Prince of Erumvirine. She mocked me. She gave me and the *vanyesh* an impossible task, then betrayed us, and we were defeated. And we had to be, since her usurpation would never have withstood my return."

"You sought the best for the Empire, my love." Nirati reached up and brushed the tear away with a finger. She brought that finger to her mouth and tasted the tear. "I know that you do what is best now as well."

"There are wrongs that must be made right. I have waited a long time for that."

She listened to him, but only distantly. While he spoke sweetly, she tasted bitterness in his tear and knew he had not told her everything. She did not imagine he was lying to her. While she had no doubt he was capable of deception, she also knew he would not willingly deceive her.

By the same token, what he had told her did not easily reconcile with the stories she'd grown up hearing. The *vanyesh* were evil and, therefore, their leader must have been evil. Empress Cyrsa was a heroine for saving the Empire. While she was willing to accept that there might be more than one point of view, and that those who survived the Cataclysm had a vested interest in casting the status quo as legitimate, it seemed that truth lay closer to what she had learned as a child.

She had no difficulty in imagining a prince choosing to patronize those bards who sang tales that vilified Nelesquin. If Nelesquin were correct, had he returned, their claim to power would have evaporated. Just as what her grandfather drew on maps determined how the world was seen, couldn't history likewise be shaped?

Her brothers had enjoyed the tales of Amenis Dukao, one of the soldiers who had ventured to the west with the Empress. The stories of his adventures had been labeled as fiction, though many of the observations in them, especially about the Wastes, were deemed accurate by those who had traveled to such places. *What if the stories were* true, *and just deemed fiction to render them impotent?*

And what if I choose not to remember dying so I can rob death of its potency? A shiver shook her. Kunjiqui had always been her paradise, a perfect place conjured of dreams that had been a sanctuary when she was a girl. Her grandfather had somehow made it real to provide her a retreat from something horrible in life. *And after my death have I accepted this place as a heaven to which I am entitled?*

Nelesquin reached out and gently took her chin in his hand. "What is it, beloved? You shivered."

"It's nothing."

"Tell me."

She looked up into his eyes and saw them brimming with compassion. "I have died, and I cannot remember why or how."

He nodded slowly. "I have died as well, and I *do* recall the circumstances. Be comforted that you do not."

"Yes, my lord."

He lifted her chin. "I have been remiss. There is a task I've meant to perform, but I have neglected it. I beg of you forgiveness and permission to act."

Nirati frowned, puzzled. "To do what, my lord?"

"To do for you what I have been doing for myself." He gestured with his left hand, closed it, then opened his fist. A beautiful green butterfly with wings edged in black flapped peacefully there.

Nirati smiled. "Oh, my lord, it's lovely."

"And it shall serve you well." He raised it to his mouth, whispered something she could not hear, then launched it skyward. The insect fluttered about for a moment, then began a lazy, meandering flight toward the north.

"What is it doing?"

"I have been devoting myself to righting the wrong that destroyed the Empire. Now I've just set about righting the wrong of your death." He bent his head and kissed her. With his lips brushing hers, he added, "The person who killed you will soon find himself dead."

Nirati kissed him back, softly and fleetingly. The idea of violence being done in her name bothered her, but slaying the person who killed her did seem just. "It will be quick?"

"From one perspective, yes." Nelesquin pulled back and smiled. "From his, probably not."

She considered for a moment, then nodded. "Thank you, my lord."

"It is my pleasure." He stood and pulled her to her feet. "Come, my love, I shall show you the grand cabin we shall share as we sail north. This ship shall take us home and allow me to reclaim the throne that has long been meant to be mine."

Chapter Forty-five

7th day, Planting Season, Year of the Rat
10th Year of Imperial Prince Cyron's Court
163rd Year of the Komyr Dynasty
737th year since the Cataclysm
Maicana-netlyan, Caxyan

Had it not been for his facility with languages, Jorim would have spent the rest of his life on the floor of the Witch-King's home, staring at the silver-white slab. As that thought came to him, he smiled, because what he had learned might guarantee he did. *I'll be here eternally if this does not work.*

Cencopitzul helped as he could. While sympathetic to Jorim's plight, he did not enjoy languages. He politely listened to Jorim's discoveries—and having to explain his conclusions helped Jorim immeasurably. He would have been angry that he was not getting *more* help from Cencopitzul, but one discovery provided a reason why that might have been impossible.

Jorim had looked up from the slab and its shifting

scripts. "You made a comment about time not always flowing in one direction here."

The Witch-King had nodded. "I relive days—the boring ones, alas. When something interesting happens, I enjoy it, but then I fall back into a cycle of tedious days. It *has* occurred to me that when I focus, I am able to counteract the effects of timeshifting, and when I am bored I surrender to it."

Jorim nodded, then pointed at the slab. "I think this is the source of the timeshifting."

"What do you mean?"

The Naleni cartographer pointed to a pile of skins on which he had written words in charcoal. "We've been watching the sigils change over the face of the slab, and we have assumed that the characters are shifting their shape. I think there is another solution. We've identified five different scripts, and there are two others we can't identify."

Cencopitzul nodded. "The Viruk variant and the Writhings."

"Right. Now, the same message appears to be written in each language, and covers the slab entirely. While the words appear randomly in time, they always show in the same spot on the slab."

"Exactly. The same phrase is repeated endlessly and the phrases revealed themselves at different times."

"I've figured something else out." Jorim stretched. "The slab has eight surface layers: one for each language and a blank one. We see portions of each surface at different times—a Viruk word, then Imperial, then a blank. We see all the layers at the same time, but only little pieces of them."

The *vanyesh* had stopped to consider that. "It's

conceivable that could happen, but the power and control it would have required is almost unbelievable. It's certainly beyond the ability of a man to do it."

"But not a god, right?"

"I would not presume to define a god's power." The Witch-King shrugged. "I think your analysis is sound, however. The magic would also explain the timeshifting problems."

Jorim had painstakingly written down and checked the messages. They'd managed to identify five scripts: Imperial, Viruk, Soth, Amentzutl, and an Imperial variant that the *vanyesh* said had been used by the sorcerers for recording magic formulae. Jorim could only translate the Imperial and Amentzutl, and Cencopitzul agreed that the *vanyesh* message matched.

In Imperial, the phrase consisted of two lines and six words: Open in out/Closed out in. The formulation marked it as an old Imperial puzzle and the format had survived to Jorim's childhood. In fact, every child over the age of five knew the answer was *door*.

That realization left Jorim little better off than before. "It could mean the obvious, or have many meanings."

The Witch-King had sliced a green fruit in half, revealing a large seed and a fragrant orange flesh that dripped with sweet juice. "Assuming for a moment that you are Tetcomchoa and you decided to leave something here for yourself, would you want to make the solution simple, or complex and incredibly idiosyncratic?"

"Both, probably." Jorim had taken a bite of the fruit, then licked juice from his hand. "We both know this was a riddle because we've seen that style of thing in the

Nine. Do the Amentzutl have that same riddling tradition?"

"Not in that format. Their riddles are usually six lines or twelve, and they usually have two answers."

"So, Tetcomchoa leaves this message here, knowing he's going to found an empire and someday he will return to the world through the person of someone born in the Nine, who will come here and discover he's left a riddle."

Jorim winced. "That's assuming an awful lot."

"What if a god only knows that things *will* work, but not how or when or even why?"

"You mean just trust that *door* is the key and not worry about anything else?"

Cencopitzul lifted his chin and sucked juice off his lower lip. "Is that what you meant yourself to think?"

"You're not much help."

"Forgive me. I think *door* is the portal to the solution. It's simple enough to reach, but unlocking the truth of it is going to be more difficult. *That* might be something that only Tetcomchoa's reincarnation can manage."

Jorim had almost dismissed that comment as glib persiflage, but something in it started resonating. Perhaps only *he* could work the solution to the problem the slab presented. Not knowing exactly how to define that problem made things more difficult, but Jorim did know that hidden within or beneath the slab lay something he was meant to have. *I have to get in there.*

This realization took him back to the puzzle again. He analyzed it, then watched the slab, and finally saw something he'd not seen before. He caught it in the Amentzutl script, and in the Soth. Both languages dealt with pictograms that remained very graphic and recognizable. The Imperial script, like the Viruk, also dealt with pictograms, but they had become highly stylized and no longer looked like the words they represented.

Both the Soth and Amentzutl scripts could be read from right to left, or left to right. Scribes usually recorded things from left to right, but architects and those decorating buildings would swap the facing of letters so they could have inscriptions that were symmetrical. The meaning would not change, and could easily be deciphered if you read toward the mouths of the people and animals represented. *The conversation is face-to-face, yours and theirs.*

The Soth and Amentzutl scripts changed directions, but the phrases remained in their places on the slab. This meant there had not been eight faces, with one blank, but ten. The repetition of the phrases in those two languages had to be significant, so Jorim played the riddle forward and backward in his mind, and hit upon a solution.

Cencopitzul looked down at him. "I think what you're going to attempt is possible, but only if you are correct in your thinking. If you are not, it will kill you."

"Better be correct, then." Jorim stretched himself out on the slab. He'd removed all of his clothing. The stone chilled him, but he couldn't feel the writing change against his back. That was just as well, as his flesh was crawling anyway.

The Witch-King gave him a formal bow. "I hope you know your own mind. Or both of them." He straightened up, then smiled. "I shall leave you to this."

"Thank you. You'll know if it works."

Jorim closed his eyes, shifted his shoulders, and got comfortable. He reached with his mind and sought the slab. He had tried to identify it through the *mai* before, but it had eluded definition. Until he had considered the puzzle more deeply, his problem with the slab made no sense because it was as difficult to define as a living creature.

And that's not because it's living, but because it is matched to someone who is living.

In running the riddle forward and backward, he turned it into a circle. The door was closed to the outside, which meant only something within could open it. Once opened, the door would admit something from the outside. That thing then would become the key inside and able to open the door. This meant that the key within and without were identical, and their merging would be what unlocked the puzzle.

Setting himself, he touched the *mai,* then, as he had done with Nauana, he projected his own essence into the slab.

Agony wracked him, spasming every muscle tight. His back bowed and his body convulsed. Sparks exploded in front of his eyes and blood flowed in his mouth from where he'd bitten his tongue. He wanted to panic, he wanted to flee, but he hung on. He pushed his essence harder, armoring it with the *mai,* and punched it past the initial resistance.

His sense of self pushed in quickly, then hit another barrier. This time his blood turned to acid in his veins. His brain felt as if it were boiling and his eyes were set to burst. Images of what he'd done to the Mozoyan tortured him. He felt as if he were burning and freezing at the same time; as if only arcs of pain bound his body together.

He pushed himself past that, then almost lost control. What had been himself, what he had seen as one solid shaft of white light piercing the slab, fractured into a rainbow of *selves*. Each ray shot off and hit something else, then each of those rays thickened and brightened. They plunged back at all angles, converging at one point, and when they collided, they exploded in a blinding burst of light.

Jorim felt himself drifting and he struggled to surface. He did not so much feel he was drowning as buried. He felt no distress at that fact, just a desire to orient himself.

Colors flashed past and he reached out for them. He couldn't see a hand, but he could feel something. Sometimes it was a hand, other times a claw. He tried again and again to pull in one of the lights, but they eluded him.

Then he caught one and found himself in the world again, standing atop a building he recognized as Imperial, but ancient. He stood there, looking up at the sky. He recognized Chado the tiger and Quun the bear, each of whom had sunk his claws into the spray of stars they shared as prey.

Someone spoke behind him. He turned and smiled at the armored man standing there. Though he wore the sort of armor that was common in the Empire, and his coloration and features were Imperial, the design painted on his breastplate and the way he wore his hair were purely Amentzutl.

"Yes, Urmyr, we have done well in pacifying the Three Kingdoms. From here we can take the five to the south, and northern wastes. It will be a bulwark against the return."

The warrior bowed. "I will do all you ask, Master, but I will not understand some of your pronouncements."

Jorim felt himself laugh. "Content yourself that you

will not. Some of these things are not meant for the mind of man."

That vision shattered and flew away in a million sparks. Another flash came and he caught it. A vision of war washed over him, with eight-foot-tall reptiles raising obsidian-edged war clubs and charging at Amentzutl lines. The bipeds wore no armor over their leathery green skin, though they painted themselves with lurid colors in chaotic patterns. He knew these had to be the Ansatl, and that the patterns somehow bound magic to the creatures.

He raised his hands and concentrated. The balance shifted, and what had been cool became molten, flaring and searing. An Ansatl screamed and fell. His fellows came on, swords rising and falling . . .

Another image slammed into the first and exploded it. He found himself on another battlefield, this one in the Empire. He saw more armies and recognized the banners as current, though he did not know the place. What struck him as odd was that Virine and Desei troops were arrayed on one side, and other troops—alien troops—attacked them. Giant metal creatures, like *gyanrigot* but so much bigger, waded forth into the lines, casting broken soldiers about like a child scattering toy soldiers.

Image after image came to him. Memories and experiences and visions mixed and merged. At times, he heard nothing and was seared by stark visions. At others, everything seemed invisible, but he heard voices and sounds. Sometimes he was a man, and at least once he was a beast. Some things he experienced intimately, and others remained so distant that only by straining could he observe what was happening.

Everything came faster and faster. He tried to study it all, but it overwhelmed him. Colors swirled around him—a cyclone of experiences. Pain and peace, the shock of death and the comfort of release, the agony of life and the joy of having lived all pulsed through him. He felt lost and alone, and at the same time in the company of the most stalwart companions he could imagine, and they were all him.

At some point, when it all closed in, blackness overwhelmed him. He felt certain he did not pass out, but when he opened his eyes again he knew time had passed. How much he couldn't tell, and the Witch-King was nowhere about to help him.

He lay there for a moment in the shallow hole that had once held the slab. *The magic was because the slab was me, all of me, all the incarnations through all time.* Tetcomchoa had divested himself of anything he did not need to be Taichun. That part of him had waited here to be reclaimed.

Jorim sat up and hugged his legs to his chest. *I am a god. I've always been a god.* He slowly shook his head. *So, just what does that make the rest of my family?*

Chapter Forty-six

7th day, Planting Season, Year of the Rat
10th Year of Imperial Prince Cyron's Court
163rd Year of the Komyr Dynasty
737th year since the Cataclysm
Moriande, Nalenyr

Grand Minister Pelut Vniel peered at Junel Aerynnor through the screened hole. The young man did not seem nervous at all, but then he never had. He projected a calmness that spoke well of his usefulness.

Vniel spoke through a thick woolen scarf to disguise his voice. "You positioned yourself well within the Vroan household. This pleases us."

"It is only what you wished."

"But pursued on your own initiative. Now, tell me, what have you heard of Prince Eiran?"

"Everyone knows he has gone missing. He is presumed dead—assassinated." The slender man pointed off in the direction of the temple district. "Prince Cyron appeared at the Dragon Temple to burn incense. He clearly believes Eiran is dead. More important, there is no reason the Helosundians would just kidnap him. That serves no purpose. They slew him."

Vniel wiped away tears with a handkerchief. The opium smoke stung his eyes, but the opium den was the most convenient place he knew of to keep the meeting completely confidential.

"You are certain Count Vroan did not order the Prince's death?"

"He would have been happy to do so, but he saw no point to it. He was content to assume control of those troops himself, and would have been happy to have had the Prince turn them over to him. Vroan knows the value of leading armed men, and his return to prominence will remind people of past glory."

"And positions him to take command in the event of an emergency."

"That is his belief."

Vniel watched the Desei carefully. "But the count is not averse to employing assassins?"

Aerynnor smiled. "Do you refer to him or me?"

"Both."

"The answer is the same. He and I did speak of it, and he liked the idea of letting Nerot Scior assume responsibility for any assassin attacking Prince Cyron."

"Whether he truly is involved or not?"

The man in the center of the room nodded.

Vniel closed his eyes for a moment and considered. He'd already met with the highest ministers in the Naleni bureaucracy, and all of them lamented the position the nation found itself in. He had been quite frank in describing the threat from the south, the agreement Pyrust had negotiated with the Helosundians, and his assessment of Prince Cyron's inability to deal with either threat—much less two of them at once. To a man, the ministers agreed that if Cyron were to leave office so someone more capable could handle the crisis, it would be a blessing.

Which meant they all tacitly agreed to the use of an assassin. Prince Cyron, and even his father before him, had taken an unhealthy interest in the mechanisms of how the state functioned on a day-to-day basis. They established their exploration program outside the bureaucracy, minimized its interaction with the bureaucracy, and, as a result, yielded far too little to the ministries in the way of power or wealth. The ministers resented Cyron for that, so they were more than willing to see him dead.

Especially if their hands would remain clean.

He did, however, find their lack of foresight rather shocking. Removing Cyron would not solve the problem of the threats from north and south. While Vroan might be able to keep the Desei in Helosunde, the fact was that their total control of Helosunde would not be overturned and Deseirion would become a serious power lurking on the border. Without constant vigilance, Pyrust would push south and Nalenyr would fall.

But the need for constant vigilance in the north meant that Vroan would be hard-pressed to fight against the invaders from the south. The Helosundian troops Cyron had moved down there did have a personal allegiance to Cyron. While Vroan had a Helosundian wife and child, Pyrust's seizure of Helosunde and the call for all true Helosundians to return to their homeland would weigh heavily on the minds of those troops. Would they stay in the south and protect Nalenyr, or retreat to the

Helos Mountains and protect their own homeland from invasion?

This Vniel didn't know and couldn't tell. But if Vroan were removed from the picture and Prince Pyrust assumed power in Nalenyr, all the resources from three nations could be directed toward fighting the invaders—even adding Erumvirine to the fold. Pyrust, while no friend of the ministries, would find himself very much dependent upon them to administer an empire.

And he is no more immortal than any princes before him.

Vniel opened his eyes again. "How difficult will it be to get Scior to purchase an assassin?"

"It would be simple."

Vniel considered. Pyrust was likely only five days away with his army. "I would like it done soon."

Aerynnor smiled. "A Scior agent deposited some money with a person of questionable repute here in Moriande. That money could be used to buy the services of an assassin who could strike very quickly indeed."

"He would have to be very good. This is the Prince. Failure would be punished swiftly."

"It will be expensive, since the chances of a successful escape are minimal. A *vrilcai* might accept the job to enhance his reputation." Aerynnor raised an eyebrow. "How will that sit with you?"

"Anyone that good will be in the employ of the Desei and I prefer to distance them from the attempt." Vniel's eyes narrowed. "Find a disaffected Helosundian. Tell him there is proof that Cyron had both Koir Yoram and Prince Eiran killed. If you think documentary proof would be useful, it can be provided."

"Rumors to that effect are already circulating."

"I know. I had them started."

The Desei exile laughed. "Then you understand that conspiracies are the favorite fodder of the gossips down here, especially in the exile community. Most believe it is the truth and finding someone to avenge the honor of Helosunde should not be too difficult. We can claim that both men wanted more support for Helosunde and desired Cyron to stop sending grain north until Jasai was returned to her people. Avenging her honor will also provide motivation. In fact, a Helosundian is a good choice, for enough of them work in Wentokikun that slipping into the palace will not be difficult."

"Good."

Aerynnor sat forward. "And shall Nerot Scior still be blamed?"

"Unless you have a better candidate in mind."

"No, he will do nicely."

And when it comes time to repudiate Vroan's efforts, documents will surface exposing the Scior-Vroan-Turcol cabal.

"I only have one concern, Minister." Aerynnor smiled when Vniel did not reply. "You will forgive my presumption, but you are in a ministry. If you were not, you could not—and would not—be discussing these matters with me. And you would not have the information you do to make such judgments. I have to assume, therefore, that you also have information to which I am not privy. It seems obvious to me, however, that the Vroan Dynasty may be extremely short in duration."

"You may assume whatever you will."

"You previously enticed me by dangling the chance of my assuming the throne after Count Vroan died. While I accept that circumstances may preclude this course of events, I do intend to be rewarded for my action. I shall assume, therefore, that what befalls the count need not befall his daughter. I could find myself very comfortable in Ixun."

"And you would find yourself positioned to move to Moriande should the need arise?"

The Desei noble opened his arms. "Have I not acted well as your agent so far? It is obvious that you will need someone in a position to move against the sitting prince if other plans do not work. We already know the west is a breeding ground for rebellion, and the loss of Vroan will not sap its strength."

Vniel considered for a moment, then nodded. "I believe Jarana can be insulated. Perhaps her husband was even assassinated by her father, since he opposed usurping Prince Cyron."

"I think that highly likely, Minister."

Vniel smiled in spite of himself. Aerynnor was proving to be a very smart and valuable agent. He knew how to reassure people that he had their best interest at heart. He'd clearly been manipulating the Scior agent, and now Count Vroan. Vniel could even feel the man's fingers trying to bend Vniel to his will.

This means he is too *smart.* Vniel let his smile spread. He would use him, then discard him, but he would do so carefully. As long as it would benefit Vniel and himself, Aerynnor would continue to play the intelligent servant. Once he thought Vniel could no longer be of use, he would find a way to betray.

I should just kill him now. It would end all risk.

"My friend, please arrange for the Helosundian intervention we discussed. A day or two, three at the most. This is very important."

"Do I let Count Vroan know this operation is in progress?"

"You've heard rumors and want to know if you should act to stop it."

Aerynnor's eyes widened for a moment. "Very good, Minister. Deniability for all."

"It is good to know many things, including those you choose not to remember."

"I shall remember that." The Desei noble nodded. "And Nerot Scior?"

"Were he any sort of a man, he would have slain the Prince himself, not hired it done."

"My thoughts exactly. He is here in the city, so I shall arrange incriminating evidence to be found, if needed."

"Very good." Vniel smiled. "And please know your suit for the hand of Jarana Vroan will meet with approval at very high levels."

"Thank you."

If Aerynnor said anything more than that, Pelut Vniel did not hear. He'd slipped through the false panel in the wall and into a tight corridor. He felt his way along, pushed on a broken brick, and another doorway opened. He wormed his way into it, then closed and barred the door behind him. He stepped away from that door, then rested against the wall, forcing himself to breathe slowly.

He smiled as his heart slowed and stopped pounding in his ears. Negotiating with exiles to commit treason was something to sour the stomach. He hunched over, feeling as if he wanted to vomit, but nothing came up.

He steadied himself against the corridor's narrow walls. He would have preferred any other choice but the one he'd been given. Killing a prince and fixing the blame on others was not an easy thing, but it had to be done.

Not for the good of the nation, or even for his own good.

For the good of the ministry.

For order.

No higher cause could be served.

Chapter Forty-seven

8th day, Planting Season, Year of the Rat
10th Year of Imperial Prince Cyron's Court
163rd Year of the Komyr Dynasty
737th year since the Cataclysm
Tsatol Deraelkun, County of Faeut
Erumvirine

Scouts from the Derael family had been watching us for several days, but we took no action against them. Tsatol Deraelkun had a special place in Virine history because it had held the pass in the Central Virine mountains since before the Empire had been sundered. During the Time of Black Ice and the oddities that wild magic had spawned, it had been heavily damaged by monstrous armies and all but razed several times. Regardless, the Derael family had not let the enemies get into the Virine heartland, and had made their home stronger every time they rebuilt it.

And as I had known since we left Kelewan, it would be at Tsatol Deraelkun that we would make a stand.

While many passes through the mountains existed,

most could handle little more than wandering shepherds, their flocks, and smugglers. Emperor Dailon IV, who got seasick at hearing the cry of a gull, went to great expense to establish the Imperial Road running from Felarati to Kelewan. Cutting a road through the Virine range had not been easy, but it was done, and the first Deraelkun had been built astride the road as an Imperial way station.

Down through the eons it had changed a great deal, and by the time of the sundering, it had become a massive fortress with three circles of walls, and secondary fortresses linked by tunnels and redoubts carved so artfully from the native stone that they remained undetected until one was right on top of them. Moraven had passed through the area a number of times and occasionally been a guest of the Derael family.

I recognized the colors and arms of the soldiers blocking the Imperial Road, and assumed that for every dozen I saw before me, five times that number lurked in the woods and ravines. Their armor had been tied with alternating cords of black, red, and yellow, making one mindful of poisonous snakes. The family crest featured a bear rampant and still fighting, though stuck with two spears and four arrows. Each wound indicated a time they'd rebuilt Deraelkun, and the bear seemed eager for the next assault.

Two riders left the center of their formation and approached me. I left my lines alone and rode toward them. I still wore the Morythian armor, but had set aside my mask. Having them recognize me would not hurt, nor would letting them mistake me for the Moraven of their acquaintance.

The woman held up a hand and her son reined back.

She came forward another couple of feet, then stopped her horse. Both of them were tall, and she quite uncharacteristically. Strands of white worked through her long black hair. She could have hidden them as many women would, but many women her age wouldn't have donned armor and come out to meet an armed force. She wore a sword, but I knew she'd never use it. The bow and quiver on her saddle, and the jade thumb ring on her right hand, reminded me of her skill.

I bowed my head to her. "Countess Derael, it is a pleasure."

Her hazel eyes studied me closely. "You look like someone I know, but he's never showed an inclination toward displays of nationality."

"Change is necessary." I looked back toward the south. "You've seen enough refugees come through to know what is happening."

She shook her head. "Those who get this far are traveling on rumor. I hope you have solid information."

I turned back and nodded. "We do. We also have Prince Iekariwynal with us."

Her son, Pasuram, nodded grimly. "Kelewan has fallen?"

"If not, it's only by a miracle." I looked at both of them openly. "Are you going to allow us to join you in Deraelkun, or shall we die here contesting the road?"

"Fighting us or those chasing you?"

I smiled at her question. "Them, preferably."

She nodded. "Come. The count will welcome you and will listen eagerly to what you have to say."

"How is he?"

"Better." The countess allowed herself a small smile. "News of the disaster in the south has enlivened him."

* * *

Moraven had first met Count Jarys Derael when the count was just a young boy. I'd seen him in the years since grow up, grow older and, in the last few years, watched a wasting disease slowly destroy his life. Luckily for him, he had married very well, and his children had inherited the strength of their parents, as well as a deep pride in the family tradition.

We reached Deraelkun after only two hours' ride. My troops were given billets in the lower circle, while I rode on to the main keep with the Prince and a handful of Derael vassals. The nobles were sent to clean up, while the countess took me directly to the count's chambers. The warning look in her eyes prepared me for what I would see, although keeping my reaction from my face was not an easy matter.

Jarys Derael had always been quite vital. Very tall and slender, he favored the spear to the sword, and had learned from some of the best *naicai* in the Nine. He'd used his reach and speed to great advantage and had he not been called to duty after his father's premature death, he might well have become *jaecainai.*

Not that his being a Mystic would have necessarily saved him from disease. I had no idea what it was, but his body had begun to atrophy and he had lost control of his large muscles. I found him still quite quick of mind, but for someone so strong to fall victim to such weakness was a curse that can devour the spirit. In recent years, he had become a recluse within the family tower, and I was the first person who was not blood kin or a close friend of long standing to be admitted to his presence.

He clearly had been positioned for our interview, as

the high-backed chair in which he sat had behind it a south-facing window. The sunlight glowing through it backlit him enough that I could not get a good look at his face. Even so, it wasn't hard to see that his once-thick shock of red hair had thinned and turned grey. A blanket hid him from the waist down, and I could not tell if he'd been belted into place or not. He held a stick in his left hand, and it pointed at a map of the countryside, but I didn't expect him to move it.

And his voice had a watery sound, as if he were half-drowning.

"Please, *Decaiserr* Tolo, be seated."

I accepted his invitation and slipped into the chair facing him. "I appreciate the time you are able to give me, my lord."

"And I appreciate the information you will give me. Did you see Kelewan fall?"

"No, but it could not have taken long." I outlined the situation as I'd seen it, then gave him a report on the nature of the enemy—starting with my arrival in Erumvirine, but declining to mention how I got there. I even showed him the scar on my right forearm and upon seeing that, he fell silent for a moment.

Even with the backlight, I could see the intelligence burning in his eyes. "The *kwajiin* were not present in the first battles your people reported?"

"You may ask them if you wish, but until I fought the first one on the road to the capital, none of us had seen them. Still, it is possible they were directing things behind the scenes."

"But they did not show up in the ranks until the battle with the Iron Bears?"

"Again, not to my knowledge—but they could have been traveling along the river and I just never saw them."

With great effort, he shook his head. "It would make no sense to divide a force that way. Having your troops under discipline is the best way to win. And the way they sent bestial creatures against Kelewan suggests the *kwajiin* are not averse to sacrificing their unruly comrades."

I nodded. "I see no reason to doubt your analysis. I'm not certain, however, that they want to destroy them foolishly. The *kwajiin* seem anything but foolish."

"To assume they would use them poorly is to assume the enemy is stupid." His voice faltered for a moment and he swallowed hard. "If you are correct, however, we have to wonder why they are coming here to Deraelkun."

"Three possible answers come to mind, my lord." I smiled easily. "The first is to clear the way to invade north. The second is to close the avenue for an attack from the north. And the third is to have the honor of destroying Deraelkun."

"I'll believe the first two, but the third is not a consideration—not if I want to believe them a worthy foe."

"To discount it, however, you discount their having a knowledge of Deraelkun, which suggests they will bring insufficient force against your position."

The count's head canted to the right, and I believe it was a deliberate motion. "That is something to consider, certainly. I have had scouts out. The *kwajiin* have slowed their advance since you ambushed them. Given the rate at which new troops have been joining them, and the speed of their advance, I anticipate a siege force of twenty-five thousand within a week."

My stomach tightened. "That would be the siege force from around Kelewan, which means the capital has fallen. It also means they've brought in many more troops to pacify the country they're leaving behind."

"That, or they have killed everyone."

I wasn't certain which prospect sounded worse. The idea that they had murdered everyone in Kelewan revolted me, but made the number of troops in Erumvirine manageable. If, on the other hand, they had brought more troops up, we were looking at fifty thousand invaders at a minimum. If all of those were *kwajiin,* the invasion would not stop at the Virine border.

"Which would you prefer?"

"Neither." The stick in his hand rose slightly, then flopped back down. "I have much thinking to do. Please take your time and review the defenses here. Perhaps, between the two of us, we can come up with a way to stop the invaders."

"Of course, my lord." I stood, bowed, and withdrew.

The countess met me in the corridor outside as servants moved silently past and into his room. "He's not the man you remember, is he?"

"I'm afraid not."

"He's been worse." She led the way down the corridor. "Come, I want to show you something before we look over the defenses. It's something you've not seen before. Few have, who are not of Derael blood."

I kept pace with her. "How many troops are here?"

"Not counting yours, there are roughly five thousand." Consina kept her voice even but quiet. "Three are our house troops, and we may get more as the lords you brought in send for their households. The other two are militia—poorly trained but well led. We pair them with more established units or give them support duties. Harassing the enemy gives them experience without much chance of being overwhelmed."

"There is a value to that. What is the ratio of archers to swordsmen?"

She smiled. "All of our soldiers can do both, Master Tolo. We have a regiment of archers who are our sharpshooters."

We descended a circular stairway that went from new construction to old, then older. It let us into the foundation of the tower. She took a torch from a bracket on the wall and lit it, then conducted me along a dark corridor. We paused before a round door built as a plug into the wall. Taking a key from around her neck, she unlocked it and, surprisingly, the door swung open easily on well-oiled hinges.

"Originally this room served as the Emperor's treasury when he visited, and it is the only room that has survived every siege. The Derael family converted it to their own treasury, then a museum."

She set the torch in a bracket beside the door, then took up a small taper and went before me, lighting small lamps hung on chains from the ceiling. As light filled the room, a chill ran down my spine.

Eons of treasures filled the room. Tapestries depicting great battles and momentous events lined the walls. Banners, some bloodied, burned, cut, torn, and yellowed with age, hung from the ceiling. Broken carriages of siege machines and one whole ballista had been rebuilt in the center of the floor, and marble statues representing heroes surrounded them. In another circle that filled the room to the walls, weapons and armor hung on wooden trees, memorializing Derael warriors and others who had fought at Deraelkun.

Consina paused next to a suit of armor that looked untouched. Behind it, standing tall, a spear almost touched the ceiling. I joined her, admiring the armor.

"This is his, as well you know. It's not like most of the others, with cut strings and dents and even blood-stained holes. By the time Jarys took command, Tsatol Deraelkun's reputation defended this place more than any soldier."

She glanced down. "It was always his dream that he would be able to prove his worthiness as a warrior and have his armor installed here, but no one ever came to test him. And now, when someone *is* coming, he's not able to defend Deraelkun."

I smiled. "The best warrior is one who defeats his enemy without ever having to fight."

"I have told him this many times, and while he acknowledges the right of that wisdom, it eats at him that he can no longer fight."

"It will take more than Jarys' donning his armor and picking up his spear to defend this place." I ran a hand over my unshaven jaw. "You say we have five thousand. By the time they come we might get twenty percent more, but they will still outnumber us five to one. If they use the tactics they did at Kelewan, they will hurt us before we begin a formal battle."

Consina nodded. "We are not without our own plans. We will erect many banners and light many fires, making them think we are ten times our number. That will slow them down."

"That's a good idea, to be certain." I turned and studied the other armor and the tapestries, drinking in the history of the place. "I think, this time, however, it's not the right tactic."

I turned and looked at her, smiling broadly. "I think, in fact, this time we will defeat them by appearing weaker than they could ever hope we are."

Chapter Forty-eight

8th day, Planting Season, Year of the Rat
10th Year of Imperial Prince Cyron's Court
163rd Year of the Komyr Dynasty
737th year since the Cataclysm
Voraxan, Ixyll

Ciras Dejote and Borosan Gryst resumed their trek northwest once they quitted Tolwreen. Even though that had been the direction they'd been traveling when they found the *vanyesh* stronghold and, therefore, would seem a logical course for the *vanyesh* to take in pursuing them, it still seemed the best possible choice. Northeast, which would have taken them toward the Turasynd Wastes, seemed a bad idea, and retreating along their previous passage would have been worse. They also still had their mission to find the Empress, and the alliance between the *vanyesh* and the Turasynd—as well as the *vanyesh* claim that Nelesquin was soon to return—made their mission's successful completion vital.

Ciras scratched at the back of his neck. "What if the story of the Sleeping Empress is just that, a story?"

"It can't be." Borosan spurred his horse along a narrow trail that snaked up a cliff side. "If she'd been destroyed—if the place where she's been waiting had been destroyed—the *vanyesh* would have mentioned it."

"That's if they did it." Ciras looked back to make sure the packhorses and *thanatons* were following. "Besides, she might never have survived."

"I'm sure she did."

"How can you be so sure?"

Borosan shifted his shoulders uneasily. "Rekarafi told us where we would be going and what we would be doing. He travels through Ixyll without any protective clothing, and can absorb the wild magic and use it. I think he knows she's out here."

Ciras frowned, not liking the fact that he'd missed that clue. "But if that's true, why didn't he tell us exactly where to go?"

The inventor laughed. "In this land? The chaotic magic constantly switches everything around, so no landmarks stay the same."

"Still, that is no guarantee we will find the place."

"True, but I think there might be something else."

"What?"

Borosan sighed loudly. "I think you can find her sanctuary if you want to find it."

"I'm not certain I follow you."

"We found Tolwreen because the *vanyesh* saw you fight grave robbers. They left you the *vanyesh* sword and watched. I think that if they'd decided we were not meant to be at Tolwreen, we'd never have gotten there.

Similarly, our path may lead to Cyrsa, but those who are her enemies can never find her."

"You mean to say that the *vanyesh* and the Empress could exist very close to each other and not even know about each other?"

Borosan shrugged. "I think the fact that one has not destroyed the other bears this out."

Ciras was about to protest that having hidden the Empress' sanctuary so completely would take a lot of magic, but he stopped, given where he was. "So if what you are saying is true, couldn't we have found a more direct route?"

"Perhaps the journey is not just about direction, Ciras." Borosan turned in the saddle. "If you look back at your life's journey, is it a direct line?"

The swordsman thought for a moment, then smiled. "Any path looks direct in hindsight, but there are many choices made along the way."

"Exactly. I think maybe we can't really *want* to find the Empress until we know we *need* to find her. Before we saw the *vanyesh* and knew they were allied with the Turasynd, our mission was to find her and ask her to help prevent a war within the Nine. There have been plenty of battles between principalities before, so how would this one be different?"

"You're saying she could not have been found until the need was urgent?"

"Yes."

"But urgency is in the mind of the seeker. What is urgent to us might not seem so to another, and what is trivial to us might seem earth-shattering to someone else."

Ciras frowned. "Do you think others have found her in the past?"

"It could be. Probably so."

"But she did not return."

"Rekarafi did say we'd have to be convincing."

The swordsman nodded. "I wonder what has happened to those who found her and could not convince her to return?"

"I don't know, my friend." Borosan stood in his stirrups and shaded his eyes with a hand. "I think, however, we're going to get our chance to find out very soon."

They rode hard to the northwest, moving down into a desert valley and along it. Ciras felt confident they'd found a portion of the old Spice Route and, from the look of it, the site of the battle that triggered the Cataclysm. His flesh began to itch as they descended to the valley floor and the land itself changed minute to minute, from hard-edged stone to a fluid putty that shifted up and down before it solidified again. At times, Ciras was certain that he saw the forms of men moving beneath the red rock surface, like children beneath a blanket, reliving bits and pieces of the battle fought there.

Fortunately for them, their path skirted the actual battlefield, for Ciras' impression had been correct. Stone armies rose and fell, shrouded by magic and the passage of years. Chariots wheeled in unison, carving swaths from infantry formations. Turasynd cavalry charged and Imperial infantry lowered spears to fend them off. Warriors stepped from the lines on either side to challenge each other, exchanging blows until one or both melted away.

At first, Ciras found the battle thrilling. Though muffled in stone, the warriors fought hard. He could not hear the sounds of steel ringing on steel, or the thunder of hoofbeats, but the fluidity of action could not be mistaken. In the duels, swordsmen matched skill with speed that defied the stone's ability to keep up. Any number of times he wished the red rock veil would part so he could admire the swordsmanship displayed.

For a moment or two he thought it might have been simply marvelous to go through eternity fighting, but the endless repetition mocked both heroism and glory. There, moving through the rock, was a living testament to the futility of battle. This had been the greatest battle of history, fought to save the world from destruction, but all it had done was to destroy the world. Even war lived past it, and still threatened mankind.

Even the evil that spawned this battle survived it.

He had spent his life learning the way of the sword. He sought skill and knowledge because he wanted to be a guardian against the evil that spawned war. Even so, his actions could set into motion events that would cascade beyond control and might result in another war. And that war would lead to more wars.

Try as he might, he could see no end to the cycle.

They rode on in silence. The roadway remained stable, but the land to the south rose and fell disturbingly. Having been raised on an island, Ciras had spent a certain amount of time on a ship. The heaving landscape reminded him of mountainous waves in a storm, which he found curiously comforting.

Borosan, on the other hand, averted his face and went visibly pale. As the road rose, the land became more solid and Borosan haltingly reiterated his thoughts that magic had to flow like water and collect in the low places.

Ciras smiled. "And that battlefield got a very good soaking."

They topped the rise and both men reined back, because the image before them could not possibly be there. Borosan had seen the hint of a flash in the distance, then the roiling land. Ciras thought it might be a piece of metal or a mirror. *Yet, at the same time, I knew it was our goal.* Had he thought about it for a moment, he would have dismissed what he *felt* for what he *knew,* but his feelings had won out.

He looked at Borosan. "The reason the *vanyesh* have not found this place is because they can think and know, but they've left behind *feeling.* They *know* what is possible, and what is impossible, and refuse to believe in the impossible."

Borosan nodded. "And they believe that finding this place is *impossible,* so they will never find it."

The two men slowly started their horses forward again, moving them into green grasses that grew up beside a silver river flowing with sweet water. Little bugs skittered over the mirrored surface, and fat fish rose after them, apparently unmindful of the fact that the river flowed into nothingness a few yards further downstream.

Upstream, however, the river broadened and flowed through a massive gate made of crystal. Both the gate and the crenellated wall surrounding the entire city were a deep, pure amethyst. At the gate, onyx cobblestones paved the way through a collection of buildings, twisting off through countless paths. Sometimes the roadway split for a small building, and at other times ran through tunnels piercing larger buildings. At points it even rose to an elevated roadway that linked two buildings before sloping back to the ground.

Though their course seemed without direction, and neither man steered their horses, both knew they drew closer to their destination with each passing moment.

Borosan, clearly awed, gaped at his surroundings. Even the *thanatons* appeared to be dazed. They sped up and slowed, slipping side to side, then darting forward or back. Whatever information they'd be collecting to map the city would be worthless, and it occurred to Ciras that one of the city's greatest strengths might be that it *was* unknowable.

And those who come here and do not have sufficient cause to win the Empress' support are doomed to wander forever.

Though that prospect would have been enough to daunt him, another aspect of the city overwhelmed him. The buildings had been shaped of crystal. Some were ruby and others emerald, citrine, topaz, or diamond. While other, more colorful stones—like opal—decorated many buildings, those that were shaped out of a single stone all had one thing in common. They resembled mausoleums—sometimes with just one occupant, often with more. Men and women—clad in armor and clutching their weapons, lay on biers as if sleeping, preserved forever in their crystalline graves.

Ciras caught himself, because he knew, somehow, that these warriors were not dead, but *sleeping.* They would rise to the challenge the Empress set before them. Just as they had set out with her to keep the world safe, they would return to the Empire to save it once again.

Regret flashed through him. For that moment, it seemed better that they wait forever than have to leave peaceful sleep and endure warfare again. There might be some who gloried in it, but he suspected far more of them had seen quite enough of war. Even so, they would answer the call because they were *heroes.*

How odd it is that we are willing to fight for peace, and yet we know that the greatest of warriors never has to fight. That paradox surprised him, because he had never been overly philosophical. He had concentrated on perfecting his skills with the sword so one day he could become a Mystic. And now, having reached that threshold, he looked beyond the skill to the consequences and *responsibilities* of *jaedunto.*

Which is exactly the sort of thing Master Tolo had tried to make me realize throughout our journey together. The swordsman smiled and bowed his head back to the southeast, toward the cave where his master lay. *Your wisdom has made itself manifest. I trust it is not too late.*

The horses took them around a hematite building and into an onyx courtyard. A diamond fountain in the shape of a dragon dominated the center. The water flowed from nine wounds pierced in the dragon's side, though the dragon appeared to be in no distress.

Beyond it, dominating the far end of the rectangular courtyard, rose a small ruby tower. Though built on a modest scale, it matched the images of the Imperial Palace in Kelewan. It rose four stories, and though the stone was dark enough to deny clear sight of the inside, Ciras was fairly certain he detected an interior room with a throne and something, perhaps golden, glinting from within.

Further speculation on what that was became moot as a man turned from the fountain. Water dripped from his hand and mouth. He wore armor marked with a dragon, and appeared to be only a dozen years older than Ciras' master. White had crept into his dark hair, but only as a forelock. His pale eyes, though flanked by dragon's feet at the corners, remained quick and intelligent. He wore two swords, but made no movement toward either.

He drew himself up and bowed respectfully, holding it longer than Ciras would have expected.

The swordsman slipped from the saddle and bowed lower and longer. He reached out to steady Borosan, then they both straightened up. "I am Ciras Dejote of Tirat, and this is Borosan Gryst of Nalenyr. We have traveled all this way to speak with the Empress."

The man nodded solemnly. "Welcome, travelers. I bow in respect for all you have done to get here. You are the first visitors we have had in a long time."

Ciras looked about. "You seem quite alone."

The man laughed. "I am the one who has sentry duty." He opened his arms wide. "I have many comrades, but this is why you are here, isn't it?"

"That will be for the Empress to decide." Ciras nodded toward the ruby tower. "May we speak with her?"

"It is possible. Eventually." The man shrugged. "I am but one soldier. I will awaken those who can make such a decision, then it will be made. Until then, avail yourselves of the peace Voraxan offers. If you prove worthy, it could be yours forever."

Borosan's eyes widened. "And if we do not?"

"It *will* be yours forever."

Chapter Forty-nine

1st day, Month of the Hawk, Year of the Rat
10th Year of Imperial Prince Cyron's Court
163rd Year of the Komyr Dynasty
737th year since the Cataclysm
Tsatol Pelyn, Deseirion

Dawn brought the first group of refugees to the ruins of Tsatol Pelyn, west of Felarati. The sun came up slowly, shrouded by the black smoke that rose from the city. The smoke began to settle, covering the landscape, but it could not hide the thin line of survivors escaping to the west. Throughout the next several days the survivors continued to swell the population at the ancient Imperial outpost.

Keles found it rather ironic that their flight took them to Tsatol Pelyn, as it had been his first planned way station on the escape route from Felarati. He'd chosen it because of the tributary of the Black River that provided water. Shepherds regularly grazed flocks in the area, and those flocks had suddenly been converted into food for the hungry refugees.

Had he just been with the Princess, and if they'd had horses, he would have struck further west, then turned south. The refugees destroyed any plans for escape, however. They looked to the Princess and Grand Minister and Keles for salvation and leadership. Part of Keles would have been willing to abandon them because they were from the nation whose leader intended his permanent imprisonment, but he knew that wasn't their fault.

They are every bit as much prisoners of their birth as I am.

Princess Jasai would not have left no matter the inducement. Despite her feelings about her husband, she accepted the responsibility the people had thrust upon her. She offered comfort and encouragement where she could. More important, she put pressure on the Grand Minister, forcing him to follow her example and get his hands dirty.

Because of his dream, Keles knew the invaders had come for him. His grandfather had sent them to find him in Felarati and that meant Keles really *had* spoken to his sister in that dream. He'd never before been able to reach her that way and could only get glimmers of his grandfather and brother—letting him know they existed and little more. He couldn't understand this new and strong contact with his sister, and it unsettled him.

The new refugees did bring information from Felarati and it gave the others a bit of hope. The soldiers who had been doing the searching had repeatedly been referred to as "the Eyeless Ones," which quickly got shortened to *blinds*. The half-handed blinds were searching the city, and it seemed the smoke confused them. Keles suggested they were tracking him by scent.

They tested the theory by collecting his urine and clothes and depositing them at various points on the plains between Tsatol Pelyn and Felarati. Scouts reported that the blinds functioned very much like ants. They continued their scouting patterns until they hit something with his scent. Then they headed straight back to the city. In their wake came more soldiers, and a new search pattern spread out from that point.

The inevitability of his discovery escaped no one. Keles had offered to head away and draw the invaders off, but since there was no guarantee that the others would be able to escape, that plan foundered. It mattered little because the refugees had other plans.

Keles didn't see what they were doing at first, but when he did, it made a curious sort of sense. People came up to him, begged his pardon, and asked if he thought moving stones from one part of a midden to another would strengthen their position. Others would ask if clearing debris from what once had been a moat would be a good idea. Still others asked if digging a canal to flood that moat would work.

Keles stood at the fortress' highest point and watched the people work. They had been terrified the night of the attack, and exhausted by their flight. Yet despite their exhaustion or age, they began to work, shifting rocks, digging, making mud for mortar, fetching water for workers.

Jasai joined him and stroked his back with a hand. "They had been reshaping Felarati for you, and now they will rebuild Tsatol Pelyn."

"They're working for you, Princess." He took one of her hands in his and turned it over. Her palms had cracked and dirt lay caked beneath her nails. "They follow your example, and that's forced the ministry clerks to do the same. Some take to it, and some are plotting revenge."

Jasai shook her head as she looked east. Fifteen miles separated them from Felarati, but already the inky stain of invader search parties spread over the dusty landscape. "Any idea how many?"

"Tyressa could tell you; I can't." Keles sighed. "You and she should get away from here. The people would understand, and we'd sell ourselves dearly to make certain you did survive."

"The people would lose heart if I left."

"No, they'd love you even more for the chance to make sure you and your child live."

She turned and faced him. "What about you, Keles? What would your motivation be? Would it be that you, too, love me? Or is it that you love my aunt and want to see her safe?"

Keles' mouth dropped open. "Highness, I don't think the answers to those questions really pertain."

"Of course they do, Keles." She laughed lightly. "I grew up learning that men are easy to control. Flatter them, stroke their egos—stroke other parts of them—and they can become yours. There *are* exceptions. My husband is one. I am not certain what he loves, but it is not me. You are another, but not for the same reasons. You *are* capable of love.

"I will admit, Keles, that I did try to make you fall in love with me. I needed your help to escape. Making you love me was the fastest way. Please don't think harshly of me for this, but it's the truth."

Keles shook his head. "You needed me to escape, and I needed you."

"But don't let yourself think I don't have feelings for you, because I do. In the months I have known you, I have come to admire and trust you—both of which are things I do not do lightly." She smiled. "And, I will also admit, that I found your resistance to my charms rather frustrating. I knew we were partners in escape, but I did wonder why you did not accept the invitations I offered."

He started to speak, but she pressed a finger to his lips.

"And then I saw your reaction when Tyressa appeared. I've seen men infatuated with the Keru before, but there we were, in a city under invasion—flames flaring, smoke swirling—and you looked as surprised and happy as it was possible to be. And I remember thinking, 'Someday a man will look at me that way.' "

Keles nodded and looked down toward where Tyressa was levering a large stone block into place in a makeshift wall. "She was assigned to ensure that I didn't get killed in Ixyll and there was, at first, some of the Keru thing there. I couldn't help it, being raised in Moriande."

Jasai nodded. "You know the Keru find it amusing, don't you, all the little boys looking at them all moon-eyed with fantasies?"

"I'm glad, because if they found it annoying, there would be a lot of dead little boys." Keles grinned. "On the trip, she took care of me. She spoke with me, she nursed me to health when I was sick. And, at the end, when one of your husband's agents shot her and I thought she was dead..."

A tightness rising in his throat strangled his words.

Jasai stroked his arm.

He swallowed hard. "Back in Moriande, I'd been engaged to someone who saw me as a means to an end. When my grandfather sent me out to Ixyll, I was happy because it took me out of the capital and out of her sphere. I wasn't even looking for anything, then Tyressa was there."

"And you couldn't let yourself imagine you had feelings for her because you knew the Keru never married, never had children?"

"Why open yourself to being hurt?"

"Because you don't always get hurt." Jasai smiled. "Being chosen to join the Keru is an honor for a Helosundian woman. She sacrifices a great deal to accept that honor. But she does *not* sacrifice everything, Keles. She does not remove her heart."

He glanced down at Tyressa again. "She doesn't have feelings for me."

"Can you imagine duty alone being sufficient motivation to travel with a Viruk across a continent, to enter an enemy nation, penetrate the capital, and enter the Prince's palace to steal a prisoner away from him?"

He smiled. "You know your aunt. She'd do that for sport."

"True, but she didn't. Not in this case." Jasai nodded toward her. "She watches you while you sleep. People ask her if they can approach you. She may not know exactly what she's feeling, but the others see it. I see it."

"So you're saying that she wouldn't leave here either, even if it was the only hope you had for a future?"

"I'm afraid you're stuck with us." Jasai looked back east. "Of course, 'future' is a relative term. How long until they arrive?"

"At their rate of advance, a couple of days. Rekarafi

thinks he can sneak through their lines with more urine and make them think I've gotten behind them. That might slow them up for a while. And by the time they get here, we'll have makeshift fortifications. But unless a lot of the folks down there are Mystics in disguise, the battle isn't going to last very long."

"They will do all they can."

"I know. They might win if Tsatol Pelyn were again what it once was." He pointed toward the east, then around along the dim line of the moat. "This was a classic Imperial outpost. The garrison would have been a battalion, perhaps two, but it could have easily housed all the people we have. Down beneath us would be storerooms full of arms and supplies. The moat . . . Well, folks are pulling rocks out of it now, but are barely down a couple of feet. It would have been nine feet deep, eighteen across, and every bit of stone in there would have been part of the walls. The walls themselves would have been eighteen feet tall, with a tower rising to twice that. Main gate to the east, and there, to the northwest, a second, smaller sally port for cavalry. It was a beautiful thing, all gone to waste."

She shook her head. "It's not gone to waste, Keles. It may not protect people the way it once did, but it is giving them hope and purpose. How many people ever have that in life?"

"Too few, I imagine."

She nodded, then kissed him on the cheek. "I think you should go talk to Tyressa."

"What am I going to say to her?"

"By your own estimation we've got two days to live. I think she might like to know she's more than a spear-carrier. Being Keru, doing your duty, these things are important, but they're not the only important things in life. Given that we've got little time left, focusing on the important things should come first."

Keles descended from the tower ruins and found Tyressa helping to dig another large stone from the moat. "Tyressa, do you have a moment?"

She looked up, swiped her forearm over her forehead, smearing dirt, then nodded. She straightened up, her spine cracking. Smiling, she began to walk with him, but the moment they got out of earshot of the work crew she'd been with, she rested a hand on his shoulder.

"My niece has been talking to you, hasn't she?"

He nodded.

"I take it you told her this sort of thing just isn't going to happen?"

"I, ah." Keles frowned. "I think maybe I'm confused."

Tyressa turned him to face her, resting both hands on his shoulders. "She wants us to get away. She knows I won't leave her, but I have my duty to you, so I'd be forced to go. She wants me out of here because I'm her blood kin, and she wants you out of here because of her feelings for you."

"Now I'm really confused."

"Keles, can't you see she cares for you? You were her only hope for escape, and when things started going very badly, you came for her. There's not a woman in the world who wouldn't have fallen for you. You can be a rock in the midst of disaster, and you don't even see it. The people here are taking heart just because you're confident in their efforts. It's just like you were at the pool in Dolosan. You didn't hesitate to act."

"Yes, but you know that was just me being naïve and foolish."

"No, that was you being you, Keles. I've learned that." She squeezed his shoulders. "She loves you and, from what I've seen, you love her. I'm pleased."

"But she said . . ."

"She was lying to save you."

Keles' head began to spin. Jasai had him convinced that she didn't love him and that Tyressa did. Tyressa was being just as convincing in the opposite direction. The possibilities inherent in who was lying to whom—including themselves—began to unfold in a legion of permutations that threatened to overwhelm him.

He reached up and grabbed Tyressa's wrists. "Stop, please. I have to say something."

The Keru nodded.

"I don't know what Jasai feels. I know what she said. I don't know what you feel. I know what she said you feel. I can't do anything about her perceptions or yours. The only thing I know is what *I* feel, and given that I'm probably going to stop all feeling pretty soon, I need to say something."

He swallowed hard. "I don't know what you thought or felt or hoped all the time you were coming this way with Rekarafi. I can tell you what I was thinking. I thought you were dead. I saw you shot; I saw you fall back into the earth and disappear. My heart followed you right down into that hole."

"Keles, I'm sorry . . ."

"Just wait, I'm not done. You were the only person who didn't see me as a means to an end. You got to know me even though it wasn't part of your job. I was able to share part of myself with you, and you did the same with me." He closed his eyes for a second and saw her bloody body slipping away. "When you died—when I thought you were dead—a part of me died inside, too. I was happy when the man who shot you got eaten alive in Ixyll. I was happy to redesign Felarati for Prince Pyrust because I planned many avenues for the Keru and Naleni troops to pour through the city. Unable to express what I felt for you in any positive sense, I channeled it into hatred."

He opened his eyes and looked up into hers. "You can assume that what I feel is just a grown-up version of the infatuation all boys have for the Keru. Or you can see it for love, because that's what it is. And maybe it's not something you want—I can understand that, too. Maybe everything was duty, and maybe you slipped a couple of times. I understand that, and I can live with it. I'll probably die with it, but I want you to know that you're more than just Keru, and I see you as more than that."

Tyressa's hands fell from his shoulders. She hugged her arms around her middle. She looked down for a moment, but when she brought her head up, tears had eroded the dust on her cheeks.

Keles lifted a hand to brush them away, but she shook her head and turned away from him.

He let his hand fall slowly. "I'm sorry I made you cry. I'll get back to work. If I work hard enough, maybe, just maybe, that won't be my last memory of you."

Chapter Fifty

2nd day, Month of the Hawk, Year of the Rat
Last Year of Imperial Prince Cyron's Court
163rd Year of the Komyr Dynasty
737th year since the Cataclysm
Imperial Road North, Nalenyr

It pleased Prince Pyrust that his presence shocked Count Linel Vroan. The Naleni noble had been summoned to the Inn of Gentle Seasons by envoys, promising a Desei representative to negotiate Nalenyr's fate. *To whom else does he imagine I would have entrusted such important talks?*

Pyrust smiled and stepped away from the fire. "Please, my lord, join me."

Vroan bowed respectfully, then doffed his cloak and tossed it to a minor functionary. "You are very kind, Highness."

"Words I do not hear often from the Naleni."

The Inn's common room had been cleared of all patrons and the host had been well compensated for the disruption of his trade. Pyrust's aides had removed the furnishings, leaving only one small round table and two chairs near the fire. A platter with cheese, smoked sausage, and rice balls sat in the middle of the table, along with a pewter wine pitcher and two goblets.

Pyrust waited for his guest to sit, then joined him. He poured wine, but did not raise a toast. He watched the Naleni closely and found things in the man that he could like. He already knew Vroan was a fierce fighter and shrewd leader. He'd recovered from his surprise quickly, and apparently had assessed the situation to the point where he was beginning to feel comfortable.

"Count Vroan, I will not insult you. I know that your accepting what amounts to an invitation to treason is not easy. You have ever been a champion of Nalenyr, and I assume you act out of that motivation."

"Thank you, Highness." Vroan's green eyes flicked warily toward the kitchen, whence a crashing had come. "I act in the best interests of my nation."

"Have you entertained the notion that my rule may be best for it?"

The Naleni noble leaned forward, resting his elbows on the table. "That has never been part of my consideration, Highness. I sought to oppose you, and hoped the invitation to negotiate would be one in which we could avoid hostilities. I had hoped you had stopped north of the Helos Mountains, but I can see this is not the case. May I ask how many troops you have with you?"

Pyrust sat back and took his cup in his half hand. He studied its dark depths. "I have six armies with me. Two are crack troops; two are Helosundian, one militia, the other well trained; and two are Desei militia. They are better trained than you would imagine. I have three more armies in Helosunde, again militia, but well trained."

The numbers staggered Vroan. "And my troops in the mountains?"

"Helosundians have long garrisoned the posts your men were occupying. Because your people did not know I had convinced the Council of Ministers to ally themselves with me, your men were happy to welcome Helosundian warriors who were fleeing my conquest. We outnumbered your men and they were taken with a minimum of deaths. At the successful conclusion of our negotiations, I shall return them to you."

"And my cooperation will be their ransom?"

Pyrust sipped his wine, then set the cup on the table again. "Though I have no obligation to explain my actions to you, I shall. I believe this will prompt you to understand the position you are in. I should state at the outset, however, that if your sole desire is to become the Naleni Prince, your ambition will be thwarted. While I live, that shall not be possible."

"I see." Vroan took up his cup, and only the ripple in the wine betrayed any nervousness.

"Prince Cyron has moved his best Helosundian mercenaries and house troops south toward the Virine border. You've been told this is because those units need time to retrain. I doubt you accepted this rationale, but you have done little to learn what his true motivation was."

The Prince continued, ignoring Vroan's confirming nod. "Erumvirine is under invasion. I know of this because an agent of Prince Jekusmirwyn brought to Felarati a message, which outlined the peril. I have every reason to believe the eastern half of Erumvirine has fallen, and I fear the capital has been taken as well. I further assume that Prince Cyron got a similar message and this is why he sent troops south."

The evident shock on Vroan's face told Pyrust all he needed to know about the man's knowledge of the situation. And blaming the dissemination of information on the Virines hid just how much information Desei spies were providing the Prince. While Vroan doubtless had informants in his county and in the capital, his intelligence network probably did not extend much further.

"You are a military man, Count Vroan. Unlike Prince Cyron, you understand the importance of engaging an enemy well away from your own territory. I know you love your nation, as I love mine, so you will understand that I choose to fight this invasion in Erumvirine."

Vroan nodded. "And Prince Cyron refused requests for your troops to transit through Nalenyr to the south."

"Can you imagine a positive reply to such a request? Your Prince is a proud man, and were he half the warrior his brother was, I would have placed my troops under his command so we could stave off this threat. But since he is not, this is not possible."

Vroan smiled. "You could place them under *my* command, Highness."

"Don't think that was not considered, my lord." Pyrust kept his voice cool and sharp. "It was rejected because Cyron would see it as a rebellion, and that would trigger a civil war. You would spend more time fighting him than the invaders, in which case my troops would be wasted and the invasion would push through to Deseirion. This was deemed unacceptable."

"Yes, of course." Vroan drank a bit more wine, then

brushed a drop from his lower lip with his thumb. "What is it that you expect of me?"

"Do you see the threat to Nalenyr? To all of us?"

"Assuming you've told me the truth, of course."

"And you would agree it must be dealt with?"

"Of course."

"Good." Pyrust stood and gathered his hands behind his back. "I will require you to swear fealty to me when I topple Cyron. I would have you move your troops south to help attack the invaders. I would further expect you to enlist other Naleni nobles, and even the citizenry, to this cause."

Vroan sipped more wine, then looked up. "What do I get in return?"

"Did you not listen? The invaders will crush Nalenyr, and your holdings will go right along with everything else."

"That I understand, Highness. But, as you said at the start, the invitation to treason is not one I accept lightly. Assuming we can stop the invaders if we work together, I should have some reward for my efforts. You *might* be able to accomplish your ends if I work with you, but your chances shrink if I oppose you."

Pyrust smiled grudgingly. "You make an excellent point. As I noted before, you will not be Prince of Nalenyr. I can arrange, however, for you to administer Nalenyr and the international trade the nation conducts. If circumstances dictate that border realignment take place, I could carve a province out of the western halves of Nalenyr and Erumvirine that would be yours."

"But would be part of your Desei Empire?"

"My ambition to be Emperor has been well known, but only necessity has forced me to reach for that prize."

Pyrust leaned forward on the table. "You would be part of my Empire, yes."

"Then in the spirit of empire, I should ask the Emperor a favor—a favor I shall return. "

"What would that be?"

Vroan smiled. "I have a daughter who was recently widowed. You have but one wife. A Naleni wife would help you in so many ways."

Pyrust stood and laughed. "Very well played, my lord. I knew you were quick of wit, and this you must have just thought of, for you could not have anticipated this turn of events. Tell me, had you thought of offering her to Cyron?"

Vroan shook his head. "She loathes him for killing her husband."

"Ah, I see." Pyrust nodded. "Consider it done, if your favor is of equal value."

"It is of greater, my lord." Vroan picked up a small cheese cube. "You won't have to lay siege to Moriande. By the time you reach the capital, Prince Cyron will be dead."

"The injuries he already has?"

"Another, more grievous." Vroan bit the cheese in half. "Fatal."

Pyrust frowned. "He's to be assassinated?"

"Yes. Does this not please you?"

The Prince crossed his arms over his chest. "It does simplify things a great deal."

Vroan set the half-eaten piece of cheese back on the table. "But you are disappointed."

"I am." Pyrust smiled slightly. "I had wanted to kill him myself."

Vroan returned the smile. "I understand the sentiment. I would love to throttle him."

"No, a thrust to the heart. Simple and quick but slow enough for him to look at the sword, then to look up at me." Pyrust closed his eyes for a moment, then opened them again. "That is how I saw it in a dream. That one, I see, was not of the future."

"No, perhaps not." Vroan drank again. "Nerot Scior has hired the assassin. Blame can be fixed to him, and you arrive to avenge the murder of a brother Prince. I side with you, the dissidents are pacified, and we force the invaders from Erumvirine. Once you take Kelewan, I would imagine the Five Princes will join or fall as you desire."

"I hope the gods accept and bless your plan."

"Grija certainly will."

A thrill ran down Pyrust's spine. *Why did he mention Grija?* "I hope so, even though our negotiation here has prevented many from entering his realm."

The Naleni set his empty cup on the table and stood. "Delayed, my lord, not prevented. We all enter his realm eventually."

"A point well taken." Pyrust narrowed his eyes. "It would have been interesting to fight you. I would have met you at Tsaxun with twelve thousand."

"And I would have defended with five. You *might* have prevailed, but there would have been no one left to bury the dead." Vroan bowed deeply and held it, then came up slowly. "It is better to fight at your side."

Pyrust bowed low, matching the depth, but cheating a bit on the duration. "You are quite right, my lord. This choice is an ill omen for the invaders. Please give my best wishes to your daughter."

"I will. Would you have me meet you in Moriande with my house troops?"

"A regiment would be appropriate."

"And if Scior comes to me for sanctuary?"

"Treason is punishable by death." Pyrust nodded. "I'll want his head to display from the gate of Wentokikun."

"As you desire. Moriande, within the week."

The Naleni noble withdrew and Pyrust refilled his own wine goblet. He glanced at the empty kitchen doorway, then drank. When he lowered his cup again, the Mother of Shadows filled the doorway.

She glanced at the Inn's door. "For one come so reluctantly to treason, he seems very comfortable with it."

"You didn't know they were going to assassinate Prince Cyron?"

She shrugged. "There has never been a time when someone or other was not going to kill him. We do not know if they will be effective this time or not. His cabal has failed once already."

"I recall." Pyrust frowned. "He can't be trusted, clearly. If he would plot to kill Cyron, he would certainly do the same to me. Still, he'll be valuable in the field against the invaders. We'll wait to see how successful he is. I want someone in position to kill him in the wake of his greatest glory."

"You could let him liberate Kelewan."

"His glory should not be *that* great. He has committed treason. He'll win a battle, then die."

"Yes, my lord." She bowed her head solemnly, then looked up. "Something else troubles you."

"Yes, the party we have not heard from. Twice the westrons will have hired assassins to kill Cyron. They cannot do that without compliance by a minister."

"The ministers are ever operating against their Princes."

"True, but we need them in the coming war." Pyrust drained his cup. "If they are not with us, the effort will founder and we all shall die. And the difficulty with the ministers is that they won't mind, just as long as it is all done in an orderly manner."

Chapter Fifty-one

2nd day, Month of the Hawk, Year of the Rat
Last Year of Imperial Prince Cyron's Court
163rd Year of the Komyr Dynasty
737th year since the Cataclysm
Nemehyan, Caxyan

Though the Witch-King's continued absence worried Jorim a little, he really didn't mind the solitude. His ordeal had exhausted him to the point where something as simple as wandering into the rain forest to harvest fruit left him staggering back to the chambers. For every two hours awake and active, he required six hours of sleep, and that sleep was far from restful.

Accepting the fact that he was a god took a lot of adjustment—even though Nauana's unwavering conviction had certainly pointed him in the right direction. It struck Jorim as rather ironic that he'd not been at all devout earlier in life. While he had worshipped Wentiko, it was more because the Dragon was the state deity of Nalenyr than due to any true belief.

In fact, his grandfather had been part of the movement away from religion. Qiro had stressed veneration of ancestors—clearly because he wanted that tradition continued after he passed away. *Actually, he saw himself as a god, so none of us had to leave our home to worship.* Perhaps that had been the root of his problem with Qiro: here he was a god incarnate, dealing with a human who believed himself a god.

But, as fascinating an idea as that was, Jorim knew that wasn't the whole of the truth. Qiro brooked no insubordination because he had a need to be dominant. Jorim had no idea what he might have been afraid of, but that need to make all acknowledge him as supreme was one of the consistent notes in the man's life. When his son and grandsons rebelled, he sent them all off on expeditions meant to kill them.

But Keles is not dead. Jorim concentrated and tried to reach his brother. He would have known if Keles had died, and he did get a dim sense of him, but there was no contact. Keles was concentrating on something else, and all Jorim got were fleeting glimpses of nightmare images. He tried to send a calming message to his brother, but had no idea if it got through before the contact faded.

Dreams interrupted Jorim's sleep, and he awoke multiple times, his head bursting with images. Some of them seemed hauntingly familiar, and others had obviously been drawn from stories he'd heard about the Heavens and Hells. He recognized gods and goddesses, but they would shift in his vision. Sisvoc, the beautiful goddess of love, would flow from being a woman wearing a robe with eagle embroidery to an Amentzutl woman in a loincloth and gold pectoral, each of them worked with eagle symbology. And then she would change again and again into other shapes he barely recognized, but could guess at belonging to the Viruk, Ansatl, and Soth.

Most disturbing of all were dreams that paralleled stories about the gods. He'd always listened to them as mythology, but now he was living them, *remembering* them. He would live through bits and pieces of stories that had been lost or—more likely—edited out to tailor the story to whatever moral the teacher wished to emphasize.

In some cases, the omissions reversed the lessons that might have been learned. The omissions also limited the gods, because the gods drew life from the nature of their people's beliefs. If the gods were reduced to one aspect and revered for that aspect only, they would slowly grow into that shape. Tetcomchoa and Wentiko, because they had worshippers from two cultures that revered them for a multitude of aspects and virtues, became more than simple abstracts.

And what must it be like to be Grija, *worshipped and hated because he would sort good from bad, consigning the evil to his Hells and sending the good on to the Heavens?* Jorim shivered. The gods may well have created the mortal races, but they found themselves in the same trap as parents who produce children, then become dependent upon those children for sustenance in their later years. They become powerless to govern their own beings, and are at the mercy of whatever charity their children give them. If a family were to tell its patriarch that he would only be fed if he wore a mask and sang songs before supper, the old man would become a masked singer.

Are the gods in their dotage?

That idea scared him. It seemed unfair that here he had discovered he was a god, then had to contend with the fact that he was already failing. Moreover, he had the inherent sense to know that his mortal body limited his ability to wield divine powers. While he might well have been able to destroy the Mozoyan force, his body had paid a price. He *could* die using the powers that were his, and Jorim had neither the knowledge to be able to catalogue those powers, nor the experience to figure out how much he could use them without perishing.

Jorim spent the next couple of days recovering his strength and enduring the dreams. He gradually grew stronger, and decided that waiting for the Witch-King to come back was an exercise in futility. He decided to return to Nemehyan to complete any training he still needed to do, then head back to Nalenyr to help oppose the rising of the tenth god.

Jorim packed up what little gear he'd brought with him, wrapped some fruit in leaves, and filled a waterskin. At the entrance to Maicana-netlyan he shifted the balance of rock from solid to fluid and let it seal the entrance. He had no doubt the Witch-King would be able to reverse the magic to get back in, and secretly suspected the man had more than one way into his sanctuary anyway.

He set out for the camp where he'd left his *maicana* guides. He reached it without incident but found it deserted. There were ample signs that the men had been there, but the fire's ashes were cold and had been flattened by rain. The rain also erased any footprints that might have given him clues as to what had happened there. It could have been nothing but . . .

He reached inside and viewed the site through the *mai.* The rain and time had almost restored the balance, and had he been six hours later, he never could have detected anything wrong. As it was he just got the barest ripple of trouble—Zoloa, the destructive aspect of the Jaguar god, was slipping away quietly.

There was a fight here. The Mozoyan must have . . .

Before he could complete that thought, something heavy and hard slammed against the back of his skull. Jorim pitched face-first into ashes. His mouth filled with them and his world collapsed to black.

As consciousness returned, pain wracked Jorim, ankles, shoulders, wrists, and head. He had no idea how long he had been unconscious, but his mouth and throat tasted of the bitter narcotic draft he'd been forced to drink. Fingers slid along his temple, ripping away his blindfold, and a wave of nausea hit him as he opened his eyes.

Above him a cloud of skulls reached to the heavens, and the sky had taken on a burned brown color that he'd never seen before. His hands reached to the heavens, but he couldn't move his arms, and his fingers felt bloated and stiff.

Then, from the right, a Mozoyan smacked him across the stomach with a stick. Jorim jerked and began to sway. The Mozoyan warrior somehow defied gravity, because he stood with his feet on the skull cloud. Nothing made sense.

An angry cry from the distance focused his attention. He looked in that direction and saw crowds of people holding a mountain up with their feet. And then, out in the bay, the *Stormwolf* and other ships lay with their hulls in a sea-green slice of sky.

Reality slammed into Jorim more heavily than the

stick. *The Mozoyan caught me, brought me back to Nemehyan, and are attacking the city.*

The cloud of skulls didn't exist. After the last Mozoyan assault on the Amentzutl capital, the people had severed the heads of all the dead Mozoyan. They piled them into a tall pyramid. Jorim hung from a gibbet planted at its apex. His ankles had been bound together and to the crosstree. A sapling eight feet long had been bound to his wrists and he hung there upside down, slowly swaying with the breeze and beatings.

Around him, on the plains before the city, the Mozoyan horde surged forward. In the previous battle, the Mozoyan had been primitive creatures incapable of much thought or planning. This time they had arrayed themselves in formations and marched forward in good order. They maintained discipline until they reached the Amentzutl lines, then concentrated their attacks at one particular point.

The Mozoyan attacked with the same ferocity as their predecessors, but being heavier and stronger, they couldn't be fended off easily with the thrust of a spear. While arrows and spears had killed many before, he now watched Mozoyan bristling with arrows leap across the defensive trench at the mountain's base. Those who fell short impaled themselves on stakes, but more than one wrenched the stakes loose and clawed his way up the breastwork.

The Amentzutl and Naleni troops responded. Flags waved, trumpets blared, and troops shifted from one point to another. Black clouds of Naleni arrows rained down, momentarily breaking a Mozoyan charge. Brave archers mounted the breastwork, picking specific targets, and drove arrows through shallow Mozoyan skulls.

Amentzutl warriors wielded their obsidian-edged war clubs in vast arcs, lopping off limbs and flaying the Mozoyan. The dead reeled back, drawn away by their comrades, and more surged forward.

And then, when the battle was fully engaged at one point in the line, Mozoyan formations would split and drive at another point. More flags would wave, calling reserves forward. The Amentzutl opposed the crush of Mozoyan, but quickly enough the last of the reserves had been called up.

And the edge of the Mozoyan formation has not been dulled.

High atop a pyramid, two Naleni trumpeters blew a retreat. Warriors began to pull back, starting with the edges of their semicircular formation. The warriors in the middle then withdrew through them and the first Mozoyan caught volley after volley of arrows. Yet still they pressed on, and the archers pulled back to the causeway that snaked up the mountain's face to Nemehyan.

The causeway would have been the perfect place to defend against Mozoyan, but their ability to leap forced the Amentzutl and Naleni to pull back. The Mozoyan surged up the causeway, but the warriors stopped them, and only, very slowly, gave up more ground.

Then, from the city itself, a volley of fire arrows rained down. Some struck Mozoyan, but more hit their intended target. They struck the trench the Mozoyan had breached and ignited whatever fluid had been poured into it. The flames licked up, consuming Mozoyan. The rear ranks halted, though those closest were pushed in by their fellows. Those on the other side still thrust forward toward the causeway, but without the crush of numbers, the causeway assault slowed.

Then a drumming began at the skull pyramid's base. A slender Mozoyan, closer to a man than anything he'd seen so far, with grey-scaled skin that flashed with rainbow hues as the sun caught it, appeared at his left side. He held out his right hand, then hooked his fingers, letting Jorim see his talons. He slapped his hand down over Jorim's stomach, right below his navel, then dragged his claws down to Jorim's breastbone. The quartet of furrows bled freely and little rivulets of blood flowed down to drip onto the skulls.

The cuts burned, but Jorim ignored the pain. The bloody-handed Mozoyan priest—Jorim sensed the creature could be nothing else—reached down and grabbed a skull onto which his blood had dripped. Obscene and blasphemous-sounding words slithered from his mouth and the skull began to glow. The priest tossed it down to a waiting warrior at the pyramid's base, then that Mozoyan leaped with all speed through formations to the front lines.

Fear pulsed through Jorim because, as weak as he was, he sensed the play of the *mai* in what the priest was doing. It wasn't magic the way he'd learned it. There was no gentle balancing of elements. This magic *twisted* things, and that should have required far more power than the priest could muster.

But he is drawing the power from my blood, a god's *blood.*

Jorim shifted his senses to the realm of the *mai* and almost vomited. Each of the skulls—for a dozen had already headed toward the lines—burned with destruction. Zoloa stalked the battlefield and raked his claws through the Amentzutl ranks.

The first skull made it to the causeway. A Mozoyan clutched it tightly to his chest, then leaped forward. He soared over the front lines. Arrows flew, piercing him again and again, splashing more blood over the skull. The dark power it contained flared. And when the Mozoyan corpse landed, the skull exploded.

Amentzutl warriors pitched off the causeway and fell into the writhing grey mass that was the Mozoyan army. The lucky had been slain by the blast. The others were rent to pieces by claws and teeth. A defiant roar from the Mozoyan troops muffled any screams and Jorim chose to believe the men went bravely and silently to their deaths.

Destruction gained momentum. More skulls arced upward, some just thrown, others held tightly by suicidal Mozoyan warriors. As each of them exploded, bodies flew and blood splashed. Men retreated quickly. One Mozoyan leaped for the causeway, but an Amentzutl tackled him in midair. Together they fell into the Mozoyan army and the explosion opened a hole in their ranks.

But it quickly closed, and the Mozoyan surge pushed farther up the causeway.

People at the top began to throw stones and burning pots of oil. The projectiles flew into the Mozoyan ranks, but for every warrior killed, nine more took his place. The Amentzutl warriors retreated more quickly, but as they reached the causeway's first switchback, they faced being flanked again. Skulls arced and burst, men screamed and fell, and the retreat quickened.

Jorim's blood flowed and skulls enriched with it streamed away from the pyramid. He hoped that the whole pyramid might collapse, but it wouldn't make any difference. The Mozoyan had momentum. Destruction had momentum. Nothing could stop them.

But perhaps the key is not *to stop them.*

Gritting his teeth, Jorim tried to pull his head up. He tensed his stomach muscles and blood flowed anew. The Mozoyan soldier slapped his stomach again with the stick and the priest raked his talons over Jorim's chest. Fire blossomed anew in his body, his shoulders ached as the sapling dragged at his arms.

Jorim reached inside and touched the destruction within him. The Mozoyan intended that he die and they were using his death to hasten the deaths of all those who believed in him. Jorim had unconsciously been opposing them, but now he stopped. He touched the *mai* and tipped the balance in favor of the twist. More magic poured into the destruction, entering the world through his blood.

He pushed the *mai* out, feeding it into Zoloa's aspect. The shadowy Jaguar god became more voracious. Its snarls encouraged the Mozoyan who had their spirit steeled by the other god's silent calls. Jorim watched the shadow cat's muscles bulge and its fangs grow longer.

Not enough.

He pushed harder, drawing all the *mai* he could into himself, and pulsed it out faster. Zoloa gorged on it and swelled. Swelled like a leech tapping an artery.

Zoloa tried to pull away, but Jorim clamped a hand—*a dragon's taloned claw*—over the god's muzzle. He made it drink, pumping more power into it, taking his own life, twisting and rebalancing it, forcing the Jaguar god to accept it.

Does a god have a limit as to how much magic it can control?

Its brave snarl having been reduced to a puling mew, the obese god of destruction burst. Havoc flooded out in a black cloud of *mai* that washed over the battlefield. Its power gouged the ground, then crested in a dark wave that lifted successive Mozoyan ranks. They curved up the inside of the wave, then dissolved in the foam that curled downward. Where it touched a skull, where it merged with his blood, the skull exploded, vaporizing Mozoyan.

The Mozoyan priest either sensed the magic or knew Jorim had something to do with his army's destruction. He slashed down with his claws, opening Jorim's throat. Blood gushed, splashing over the priest's hand and leg. The blood burned and in a heartbeat turned the priest into a torch.

And then the wave hit the pyramid of skulls.

It snuffed out the priest.

It carried past and spread, killing everything in its wake from the plains below Nemehyan, outward for the next fifty miles. It spread in a cone, leaving nothing alive, not an insect or plant, bird or fish, animal, Mozoyan, or man.

It did not even spare a god.

Chapter Fifty-two

2nd day, Month of the Hawk, Year of the Rat
Last Year of Imperial Prince Cyron's Court
163rd Year of the Komyr Dynasty
737th year since the Cataclysm
Moriande, Nalenyr

Though not having done so would have led to his discovery, Junel Aerynnor sincerely regretted removing the woman's larynx. Not only did it prevent her from screaming, but her breath whistled and gurgled most annoyingly. And the way she screamed with her eyes let him know she would have been a delight to hear. She would have hit notes beyond hearing, and they would have resonated within him for a long time indeed.

Junel had come far, and had decided to take the slender slip of a girl apart in celebration. She'd actually caught his eye days before, as he had come to meet with his shadowy benefactor. She'd really been nothing, just a hollow-eyed wastrel, addicted to opium, willing to do anything to earn the price of a pipe. It was her eagerness that attracted him and, in retrospect, it was that same eagerness that doomed her.

He could have killed her right then and no one would have cared, but she intrigued him. She had survived somehow without having her spirit broken. He'd asked her what her name was, and she could have—almost had—replied that she could be whoever he wanted her to be. After a moment's hesitation, she said she was Karari.

He bid her join him and bought her a bowl of noodles, which she devoured so quickly he expected her to vomit. Though she had told him her name, he wasn't certain the story she told was true. She said her mother had been mistress of a ship's navigator who worked for the Phoesel family on the *Silver Gull.* It had run aground off Miromil and the crew took her father for a jinx. They wrapped him in chains and threw him into the sea. Her mother, taken ill with grief, had died. She, with no one else in the world to help her, had fallen on hard times and taken to the pipe to ease her pain.

Junel knew of the *Silver Gull,* and supposed the story could be true. The girl's descent could have begun five months earlier. She was not so far gone that she could not be saved, and she had enough civilization in her to be grateful.

And enough of the street in her to see him as her benefactor. She would cling to him. She would do as he bid, not questioning. To question would be to turn her fortune from good to ill, and she'd become too hungry on the street to do that thoughtlessly.

Junel had rented rooms and sat with her while she sweated through the battle with opium. He cleaned her up and moved her away from the slums, where she could fall back into her old habits. He even enjoyed buying things for her. Her transparent joy and gratitude was all the more potent in light of her eventual fate.

The only regret he had was that he had not the time to groom her for bigger things. Karari was too frail of body and too kind of spirit to have been brought into the world of shadows that he inhabited. When the Desei Mother of Shadows had found him, Junel had been trapping rats in his family's tower and devising a variety of ways to dispatch them. While he was good at setting up devices that proved quickly lethal, he enjoyed the things that worked more slowly. There was just something about watching a rat struggle against a slowly tightening noose that had warmed the pit of his stomach. As its eyes bulged and blood vessels burst, he became excited.

He learned early on that death can provide pleasure.

The Mother of Shadows had done her work well, building on the foundation he'd already provided himself. His family didn't mind his being taken to Thyrenkun as a page at court. They considered it both an honor and a simple way to rid themselves of a younger son. It meant one less split of the family estate, one less mouth to feed, and a slender chance of royal favor.

Junel had trained very hard, enduring punishments for failure and accepting rewards for success. He learned early on that he would never get all he felt was his due, so he awarded himself little pleasures, then happily reported what he had done to his superiors. He made certain that he followed all of the rules and exceeded expectations so that his self-indulgence would be excused. And, often enough, he included others in his rewards, which made his self-pleasure a stepping-stone to another mission.

After he had betrayed his family's treason to the Desei crown, he watched them all die, then escaped south "to avoid Prince Pyrust's wrath." This won him immediate acceptance among the southerners, and he gladly put it to good use. His mission had been to get to the Anturasi clan. If he could not steal information, he was to find a way to slow Qiro Anturasi's work.

Murdering Nirati had accomplished that rather nicely. His involvement with her had been great fun, for he was able to inflict minor tortures that built her resistance to pain. At the last, she had endured so very much.

And he delighted in giving her that pain.

Since killing her, he had often awakened from dreams reliving the experience. He had taken her apart slowly, and he watched the conflict in her eyes. What he was doing horrified her, and she fought it. But while she did not want to enjoy it, the very act of fighting it took her back into the behavior patterns that told her she *was* enjoying it. Her own body betrayed her, and she slipped away. He'd not noticed it, but she'd slipped into ecstasy, which wrapped her and insulated her from the horrible finality of death.

In some ways, she had ruined him. So intent was he on his work that her final moments had escaped his attention. Now he found himself preoccupied with wondering how others might react when brought so close to death. Count Vroan, he knew, would stare death straight in the eye and defy it until the very last. He could be roasted alive in an iron coffin buried in coals and would never utter a word, save perhaps some family motto that would have little bearing and provide less insight on the situation.

Nerot Scior, on the other hand, would writhe like a

snake stuck on a spike. Junel had often thought impaling would be good for him. He'd use a blunt stake and let the man try to escape his doom by standing for as long as he could. Nerot would fight the tremble in his legs, buying seconds of life with sheer willpower, all the while confident his mother would be coming to his rescue. Even when his legs failed him and he slowly sank onto the stake, he would be looking for his salvation. He would die believing a deal could be struck and his wounds healed.

And Prince Cyron... Had there been the least chance of his escaping death, Junel would have undertaken the mission to kill the Naleni Prince himself. The challenge drew him. Slipping through the remaining Keru would have been all but impossible. While the citizens of Nalenyr might accept him as an ally because Prince Pyrust hated him, the Keru trusted no Desei regardless of pedigree. Their mothers' milk flowed with bitter hatred for the Desei and the Keru did nothing to expand their vision of the world.

Of course, he would have had an advantage. The Prince knew of him. Prince Cyron had been concerned for his welfare after Nirati Anturasi's death. Junel had even been promised that her killer would be found and the evil done to the both of them avenged. Junel had even offered his help, but the Prince's ardor for catching Nirati's killer had long since faded.

How will he accept death?

Junel suspected Cyron would not go easily into Grija's realm. He might have once, but accepting a serious wound to mask the murder of Count Turcol had shown an aspect of him Junel had not believed was there before. *They believe Cyron incapable of fighting because he's never been forced to fight. But he is a son of the Dragon State, and a dragon without fangs or claws is still a dragon.*

He looked down at little Karari. He'd drawn her hair up and away from her head so it would not get matted with blood. He wanted to take her scalp off in one piece so he could use it to form a beard for her. It struck him that that would be interesting, since she already looked so old. It would also mask the hole in her throat.

"How do you think the Prince will die, little one? Will he be as brave as you are?"

Her eyes widened, then her gaze began to flick. He thought for a moment that she might be having an allergic reaction to the tincture he was using to immobilize her voluntary muscles, but then a shadow fell over her face. When it touched her, she smiled.

He turned. The room's thick drapes permitted no sunlight, so he'd lit several lanterns to illuminate his work. A butterfly had lighted on one, slowly beating its wings. Its placidity contrasted with the violence he'd already done to Karari and prompted him to think about her body as a cocoon and the chance for her to blossom into a beautiful creature in the afterlife.

He stared at the butterfly and was fairly certain he'd never seen its like. It was large, which made it unusual—not to mention that it was still very early in the year for butterflies. Moreover, the green-and-black markings were something he was quite certain he'd never seen before.

He swiped at it. The butterfly rose easily, eluding the blow. Being a master of *vrilri,* he could have killed it without much effort, but it pleased him to have a witness to his work. He'd long ago learned that butterflies can be drawn to carrion, and its presence confirmed he was working well.

Picking up one of his knives, Junel leaned forward. He reached out with his left hand to smooth the skin on Karari's brow. He pressed the tip of the blade to her flesh and waited for a red drop to collect. He waited for the surface tension to break and for the blood to inscribe the line he would follow.

It made things so much more artistic.

But his hand jerked as something stung him in the neck. He dropped the knife and turned, clapping his right hand to his neck. He could feel a slight swelling, but knew it was nothing of significance. In fact, he was certain it meant nothing, then it occurred to him that he wasn't stopping his turn.

His legs wrapped around each other and he sat down hard on the floor. His shoulders hit the wall and his head smacked into it hard enough to crack plaster. He felt flakes slip down his collar. He ordered his right hand to brush them away, but it fell to the floor, limp, beside him.

Junel looked up and found a tall, slender man standing beside the chest of drawers. He held the bottle of hooded viper venom and was replacing the stopper with the needle in it. The man had incredibly long fingers and hazel eyes that seemed to shift colors.

Junel tried to speak, but only managed to open his mouth.

The man nodded and his cloak closed—a cloak woven with the emerald-and-black pattern of the butterfly's wings. "You will be wondering if I was the butterfly, or if it merely served to distract you while I entered the room through a locked door, unheard and unseen. My transformation from insect to man, despite being the more improbable of solutions, is the one you will believe. Your vanity will not allow you to accept that someone could be more skilled in the shadow arts than you are, would you, *vrilcai*?"

The man squatted and closed Junel's mouth with a finger. "You'll want to know who I am, and why I am doing this. I am Kaerinus. You know of me, the last *vanyesh,* the magical imbecile who lurks in Xingnakun, save when he emerges once a year to heal those who don't have enough sense to fear him. I *can* heal them, you know. The blind, the lame, the diseased."

Kaerinus glanced at Karari. "Alas, you've done too good a job on her. I can't heal her."

Though the man's voice had a cold edge to it, Junel took pleasure at his words.

"And you have figured out, Junel Aerynnor, that I'm here to kill you. I will. I would even enjoy taking my time at it, but I haven't much to spare. I'm meeting a friend to the south, and the sooner I arrive, the better for everyone."

The *vanyesh* stood, then crouched again in a billowing of his cloak. "Oh, yes, the *why* of it. You killed Nirati Anturasi, and she is most dear to a friend of mine. Next time, don't choose a victim with powerful friends."

Kaerinus stood, then laughed. "Next time. There won't be one. And, yes, I know the hooded viper venom isn't fatal. Your body will recover."

He looked at the girl. "Yes, you've quite broken her. I can't fix her, but I can do *this*..."

Kaerinus gestured and light sizzled before Junel's eyes. It poured over his face and burned into his brain. His world went black for a moment, then vision snapped back. During the time he'd been unconscious, the *vanyesh* had moved him.

Then, as the pain began to gnaw at him, he glanced to the right and saw his body propped up against the wall.

Junel's eyes widened with horror.

Not my *eyes,* her *eyes! I am now in her body, and she in mine!*

"Splendid, you understand." Kaerinus smiled. "You did very good work, *vrilcai.* It will take you hours to die."

It did take him hours to die, many hours. And while pride in his work insulated Junel at the start, despair and horror claimed him at the last.

Chapter Fifty-three

2nd day, Month of the Hawk, Year of the Rat
Last Year of Imperial Prince Cyron's Court
163rd Year of the Komyr Dynasty
737th year since the Cataclysm
Tsatol Deraelkun, County of Faeut
Erumvirine

I could scarcely imagine a finer martial display. Though I had the sense that I'd seen it all before, I could not summon up any memory that matched what I saw from the battlements of Deraelkun. The *kwajiin* had drawn itself up in a broad line running from the Imperial Road to the east, paralleling the fortress' broad front to the west. Bright banners flew, each of them with legends in precise Imperial script, and I imagined this is why I was thinking I'd seen this before. Sunlight glinted from swords and spear blades, and bamboo mantlets protected the front ranks from our archers and ballistae.

The troops defending Deraelkun, though numbering no more than four thousand—roughly a fifth of the force facing us—had raised their own banners to proclaim membership in a military unit, a noble household or, with a few *xidantzu,* the schools where they had gotten their training. I actually thought our display outdid theirs, for each banner marked a hero, while most of the *kwajiin* wallowed in anonymity.

Still, the enemy had to take heart in the fact that they had five for our every one. Deraelkun could fall, and if the *kwajiin* below were half the fighters of those I'd already faced, the fortress would be lost before the day was out.

Taking it would not be a simple matter, however. The road itself curved west and ran along below the first fortress wall, and the two bridges that spanned the gaps had been drawn up. This cut the road and split the front, so that the armies would have to come in three sections. Shifting reinforcements to any one of the sections would necessitate a withdrawal and redeployment—or a deployment from so far back in the line of battle that they wouldn't be able to advance for a critical amount of time.

The ravines that trifurcated the battlefield had been expanded so that a small island existed in the center. From the roadbed heading south, and the battlefield heading north, two narrow bridges connected the island with the fortress. This island made the center utterly impractical for attack and had long been used as a spot where warriors fought duels of honor. The center had been set with a ring of stone, and dotted outside with several small monuments to warriors who had fought and died there.

So, in reality, any advance to take Deraelkun would be heading uphill, would be divided into two parts that could not communicate with or support each other. Siege machinery could be brought up to breach the first wall at the place where the road turned to the west, but archers in the towers overlooking that point would murder the soldiers trying to break the wall.

I listened to the snap of banners in the breeze. The wind blew north, toward the fortress, bringing with it the faint stench of the *vhangxi.* The *kwajiin* had herded them to the center and would release them as a distraction. I did not think they could leap to the top of the battlements, but they might be able to scale the walls. Even though we would slay them all, they would use up arrows and demand attention at a point away from the two main assaults.

And I knew it would be *assaults,* two of them, coming hard and fast. The enemy leader had no other choice. If he concentrated on one wing or the other, we could mass our troops and fend him off. Along either of the two fronts we could match his strength easily. Only by engaging us along the entire front could he tax our supplies and slowly bleed us to death.

And the logic of it was not the only motivating factor he had. He was arrogant and overconfident. He'd already had reports of troops abandoning Deraelkun, heading north into Nalenyr. If we knew the defense of Deraelkun was hopeless, our morale would be low and his troops would be that much more elated. He'd not faced any strong opposition prior to this and Kelewan had fallen easily, so he had no reason to suppose his troops would not function perfectly and take the fortress without much trouble.

But, trouble he would have, and I meant to be much of it.

I descended from the battlements, taking the broad stone steps two at a time. At the base I bowed to

Consina and her son. They returned my bow, then I turned toward the fortress' central tower and bowed again. I held it deeply and long. Without a word I straightened up, turned on my heel, and marched out through the small sally port in the center of the fortress wall.

I quickly crossed the road and mounted the narrow footbridge to the island. Once there I bowed to the enemy, then turned and saluted the fortress and its defenders. A great cheer rose, then a dozen flaming arrows arced down and struck the bridge I'd crossed. It began to burn merrily.

I turned from it and entered the circle. Like many circles where duels had been fought for ages, this one had absorbed a fair amount of wild magic. The grasses in it, long-bladed and supple, were silver, and tinkled as my legs brushed them aside. I moved around toward the east so the rising sun's reflection would not blind me. I took off my helmet and the snarling tiger mask, and set them on the circle's white marble edge.

Looking at the *kwajiin* arrayed to the south, I began speaking a challenge, using the same formula and archaic words I'd heard from the first *kwajiin* I encountered far to the east. I kept my voice even but loud, allowing the barest hint of contempt to enter my words.

"I am Moraven Tolo, *jaecaiserr*. For years beyond your counting I have defended the people of the Nine. I have opposed tyranny. I have slain highborn and low-. In this spot, over a hundred and seventeen years ago, I killed the bandit Ixus Choxi. Before that I slew eighteen disciples of *Chadocai* Syyt, and then I killed him, ending his heresy. In the east I have slain your brethren. I led the escape from Kelewan. I do you a great honor by considering you worthy of dueling with me. I fear nothing you can send against me."

I knew my words would slowly spread back through the *kwajiin* army, though I had meant them for only one pair of ears. Whether or not their leader deigned to meet me in combat was important, but my fighting others would suffice to accomplish my goal. Making his people wait meant they would become hungry and thirsty, hot and tired. Every minute I gained was a minute in which they worsened.

A *kwajiin* commanding the *vhangxi* prodded one with his sword's wooden scabbard, then pointed at me. The beast began to gallop in my direction. Its powerful shoulder and chest muscles heaved as knuckles pounded into the ground. It didn't even head for the bridge, but made to leap the gap and, in another jump, pounce on me.

I exhaled slowly and set myself. As I did so another mask and armor settled over me. *Jaedun* flowed, filling me, strengthening me, and altering the way I saw the battlefield and my enemy. Even before the beast made the first leap to the island, I knew how it would die.

I strode forward quickly, drawing the sword from over my right hip. As the *vhangxi* began his descent, claws raised high, mouth gaping, I reversed my grip on the sword. The blade stabbed back along my forearm, the tip touching triceps. I leaned forward, letting its left hand sweep above my head, then I twisted my wrist.

The blade's tip caressed the *vhangxi*'s armpit. Blood gushed, steaming, splashing silver grass. It pulsed scarlet over the stone, spraying out in a vast arc as the *vhangxi* spun to face me. It took one step, arms raised, letting blood geyser into the air, then it collapsed. It clawed at the green grasses outside the circle. More blood jetted from the severed artery, then it lay still, grunting, as its huge lungs emptied for the last time.

In one fluid flash of silver, I resheathed my sword and turned to face the *kwajiin* again.

"Am I mistaken for a butcher that you send a beast at me? Or have you less courage and less honor than this lifeless lump?"

I had actually hoped that the *kwajiin* in the front rank would send several more *vhangxi* at me, in a group this time, but he saw the consequences of doing that. If I defeated three, he could send five, and if I killed five, he could send nine, but none of that would show his courage or honor. He had only one option.

He stepped forward and bowed. He wore the crest of the bloody skull and raised his voice for all to hear. "I am Xindai Gnosti of Clan Gnosti. I have fought for years beyond my own remembering. I have slain many here, and slew many of my kinsmen to earn the honor of leading troops . . ."

I interrupted him. "You are a beastmaster, not a warrior."

He stared at me, startled, and faltered as faint rumblings of displeasure filtered back from the *kwajiin* line. He began again. "I am Xindai . . ."

Again I interrupted. "Your name, your lineage, and history bore me, herdsman. If you have courage, come, meet me."

He drew his sword and began to run.

I turned my back on him and moved to the center of the circle as I awaited him. His footsteps thundered over the bridge. They thumped more softly as he sprinted toward the circle. They chimed metallically in the grasses, then stopped six feet from me. He leaped into the air, his sword raised high, both hands on the hilt, already bringing the blade down for the blow that would split me from crown to breastbone.

I took a half step back. Raising my arms, I crossed my wrists and caught his wrists firmly. Bending forward, I shortened his leap's arc and smashed him into the ground. He bounced up, grunting, but before he had hit the ground again, I tore the sword from his grip, reversed it, and stabbed it through his throat, pinning him in place.

I turned, not wanting to watch him thrash out his life, and let the din of the grasses describe his final agonies. When the ringing faded, I opened my arms and looked to the south.

"I see now why you let the beasts fight for you." I seated myself on the circle's edge. "Is there no one among you who is a warrior?"

More came, fifteen in all. The young came swiftly and foolishly, and died quickly. Some came cautiously and fought formally, but their fear hobbled them, and their ancient forms served only until they met an attack they had not learned how to counter. The most dangerous came nonchalantly, without a care in the world. His blade cut me beneath my right eye, and he took great delight in watching my blood flow.

So I blinded him, such that the beauty of that vision would never be eclipsed.

Finally, their army split as a wedge of banners moved forward. Tallest among them was one featuring a ram's head; the beast seemed quite angry. Below it flew a number of pennants, each with the crest of another clan subordinated. The front ranks parted and a tall, slender man strode forward. Like me, he wore two swords and had abandoned his helmet and face mask. He came to the far end of the bridge, stepping aside so the blind warrior could stagger past, then gave me a short bow.

I decided to bow in return, deeply and respectfully. The warriors on Deraelkun's battlements cheered.

The *kwajiin* shook his head. "I am Gachin Dost. This is my army."

"I am Moraven Tolo. I do not need an army."

My enemy smiled slowly. "I know what it is that you are trying to do."

"It is what I am *doing.*" I let my eyes half lid. "Stop me if you are able."

"I am more than capable." He drew both of his swords and held them out to the sides, their points raised to heaven. He brought the right sword down in a slash. Drums began to pound to the east and that wing of his army marched forward. The other blade fell, and that half of the *kwajiin* force began its assault.

He crossed the bridge, then paused. Flaming arrows sailed from behind his lines and ignited that bridge. Grey tendrils of smoke swirled forward and around him. He advanced to the circle's edge, then crossed his blades over his chest. "I have dueled with gods and won."

I shrugged. "I've had dreams I thought were real, too."

He shook his head. "Enough of this. If you want to kill me, try. Succeed or fail, it will not change the outcome of the battle."

I opened my hands. "Let your steel talk."

On either side of us, the battle unfolded. Arrows darkened the sky. Men pitched screaming from battlements. Swaths of blue-skinned warriors fell transfixed. The wounded cursed and moaned or just sighed and died, bloodstained fingers trying to staunch rivers of blood. Assault ladders rose, and men with polearms pushed them back. More men fell as ballistae launched clouds of spears.

Above it all, with smoke rising in a dark grey swirl, the wounded bear banner flew high over Deraelkun.

And below the fortress, Gachin Dost and I dueled.

Twin blades flashed and rang as we parried. Swords whistled through empty cuts and grasses pealed as we landed from leaps. The sting of pain, the flow of blood, minor cuts that but for a twist or slip would have cost a limb or opened an artery. A hard parry with two swords trapping a third, which whipped away through the smoke. Another sword plucked from a corpse, slashing, tracing a red line above a knee, and another clipping inches from flowing locks or harvesting an ear.

We closed and passed, more feeling each other than seeing in the smoke; our movements cloaked, the sounds smothered by the din of battle. A quick cut severed lacings so a breastplate hung loose, and another freed it all the way. A bracer stopped a cut, but mail links parted and gnawed at the flesh beneath. A thrust, a grunt, and finger probing a wound to the belly.

We sprang apart, chests heaving, blood flowing from nicks and cuts. Sweat ran into them, igniting pain in places I did not know I'd been wounded. I tore away the ragged armored skirts that had meant to protect my legs. I hunched forward, feeling every year of my age, and eons more, then licked my lips and beckoned him forward.

Gachin, black hair pasted to his face with sweat and blood, smiled easily. "You will not kill me."

"That was never my plan." I nodded toward the south. "I just wanted to kill your army."

Above us, the wounded-bear banner descended on the tower's pinnacle, and a tiger-hunting banner took its place.

"Another desire that will be thwarted."

I shook my head. "It's already been fulfilled."

The troops that had left Deraelkun had gone north, then worked west and back south through smuggler trails to flank the *kwajiin* army. They had met with very good fortune, as a breathless runner had informed Count Derael, because they'd encountered the First Naleni Dragons Regiment and a full battalion of Keru Guards. This added a third to their number and increased the competency of the task force Deshiel and Ranai had led from Deraelkun. The raising of my banner was the signal for them to begin their attack, which would take the *kwajiin* left wing in the flank.

I couldn't hear commotion from where they were supposed to strike, for it had been my right ear that was taken. Gachin must have heard something, however, for his eyes narrowed and his lips peeled back in a snarl. He knew, as I'd known, that the only chance his people had of breaking the flanking attack would be a coordinated withdrawal of the left wing and a counterattack by the reserves from the right.

But with him trapped on a smoke-shrouded island, he couldn't give the orders that would save his forces.

So he tried to kill me before his army died.

We became the stuff of smoke ourselves, save that we bled. Swords did not clang, but hissed. Parries misdirected, not deflected, and a blocking blade twisted up and around in a riposte before the tremor of its hitting the other blade had reached the wielder's shoulder. We spun away from attacks, slid into others, gliding low and striking high, leaping higher and slashing downward. Unseen blades whispered past each other, cold metal seeking warm flesh, hunting a fluid sanctuary where all fighting would cease.

And then he did it. He feinted low with a slash and I leaped over it. Gachin lunged as I came down, then drew his elbow back and thrust again, a heartbeat after my left sword had swept past. His sword pierced my chest on the left side, halfway between my nipple and the other scar I'd long borne there. He slid it home to the hilt, and his face, contorted with hatred and matted with blood, color vivid around his amber eyes, emerged from the smoke and thrust straight at mine.

I know he meant to say something, something I could dwell on as he ripped his blade free, slashing it from between my ribs. He'd have taken my left arm off at the elbow as well, then spun, harvesting my head in one fluid motion. It would have been a thing of beauty, an ending to a duel that would have been sung of for generations, and might have earned me a monument at the foot of Deraelkun.

But such monuments have never been to my taste.

I snapped my head forward, driving my forehead into his face before he could yank his blade free. His nose cracked and blood gushed. His head jerked back and I drove mine forward again, smashing him in the mouth. Teeth broke and slashed my forehead bloody. Ivory chips sprayed over my face, and blood painted my lips and throat.

He started to twist his sword in my side, but my right knee rose and crushed his groin. It occurred to me that *kwajiin* might not be as men are—I'd not checked any of those I'd slain—but my fear was unfounded. I slammed my knee up again, as hard as I could. His breath exploded, spraying me with blood and saliva, then a third blow from my forehead into his face pitched him backward.

He staggered and tried to remain on his feet. He still clutched a sword in his left hand, but stabbed it into the ground in an attempt to stay upright. He caught a heel on a corpse and tumbled back. His sword sprang out of his grasp, and I pounced, stabbing one sword through his belly and deep into the ground.

And then, ruined though it was, I took his head as a trophy. I stood slowly, still transfixed by his sword. I raised his head by the hair, blood still dripping from the neck, and as the smoke parted, I displayed it to one and all.

Strike the head from a snake and the body will die.

By the end of the day, the *kwajiin* army had receded from the walls of Tsatol Deraelkun, and the mountain fortress remained unconquered.

Chapter Fifty-four

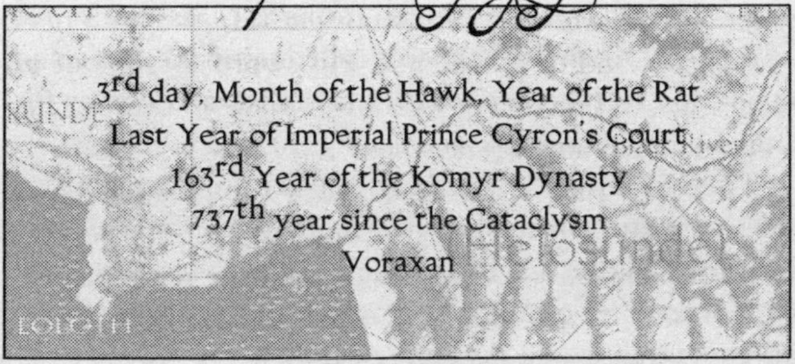

3rd day, Month of the Hawk, Year of the Rat
Last Year of Imperial Prince Cyron's Court
163rd Year of the Komyr Dynasty
737th year since the Cataclysm
Voraxan

Ciras Dejote stood outside the circle between the fountain and the steps to the ruby tower, wearing his best robe. It had seen better days—though he had patched the white silk as best he could. The red embroidery that worked a flame pattern had faded a little, and the intensity of the red sash had been dulled. Still, it was the best he had to wear, and he would not disappoint the Empress by appearing in anything worse.

Tsirin Donitsa, the man they had first met in Voraxan, stood opposite him, at the bottom of the stairs. "Ciras Dejote, you have passed all examinations save this last. You have impressed us with your skills and your diligence. Your tales of adventure through the journey here have also pleased us. Pass this last test and you will surely be suited to joining our number and serving the Sleeping Empress."

Ciras bowed to him, then to the half-dozen men and women standing at the top of the palace steps. They had examined him and Borosan both, though the two men had been segregated so neither knew the nature of the tests the other had endured. For Ciras, it had been endless repetitions of fighting forms. Sometimes he was to move through a progression of forms as called out by his examiner. Other times he was called upon to strike and maintain a form, and once his examiner walked away for a time before returning and calling another.

They examined everything he did, from waking to sleep. Another time, all of that would have driven him utterly mad, but he reached inside and embraced the peace of Voraxan. So close to his goal, he did not want to do anything that would get him rejected.

The only thing that had caused him any trepidation was telling them about the time spent in Tolwreen. While he felt that Borosan was probably right and that only those who sought the Sleeping Empress with the right thoughts in mind could find her, he found it very easy to believe that her guardians might think he was a spy. After all, the *vanyesh* had trusted him and he had betrayed them, so why couldn't he do that to Cyrsa's people?

His examiners listened to his story without much reaction, save for evident pleasure when he described having to kill two Turasynd to effect their escape. Ciras supposed that killing Turasynd was the one thing they had in common, and he hoped that bond would be enough to carry him through the examinations.

Aside from the tests, the stay in Voraxan had been

quite pleasant. He'd been given an emerald home all to himself and found it very restful. If he sat in the center of the largest chamber and closed his eyes, he could hear the surf crashing against the beach at Dejotekun on Tirat. When he breathed in, he caught the tang of salt air and the calls of gulls echoed through his head.

Dreams there became quite vivid, and he found himself home again, walking through the gardens in the morning. From what Borosan had told him about the sun, it would be up in Tirat hours before dawn in Ixyll, so his dreams allowed him to wander with his mother in the garden. She couldn't see him or hear him, of course, but he heard her and shared her delight as his older brother brought his children around for visits.

Most curious of all, no blood nor war entered his dreams. He would have thought he'd relive the exercises or the lessons in which he'd originally learned the forms, but he didn't. Even in recounting how he'd slain the Turasynd, he presented things in a matter-of-fact manner that dulled the impact of the event.

Even the *vanyesh* sword seemed at peace. While the writing on it did shift, it did so slowly and with no urgency. Though he could not read it, he imagined the lines being from a poem about a woman wandering through an orchard, plucking ripe plums. He tried to remember such a poem but couldn't. That didn't surprise him, for most of the poems he'd learned had been of a martial nature—but then he found himself unable to recall any of them.

Tsirin pointed to the circle with an open hand. "Advance, Ciras Dejote."

Ciras bowed and entered the circle.

The slender warrior stepped into it opposite him. He

drew his sword and assumed the first Dragon form. "Your final test is to slay me."

Ciras shook his head. He drew his *vanyesh* sword and scabbard from the red sash and laid it on the ground, then knelt and sat back on his heels. "I will not kill you. I will not fight you."

Tsirin stalked forward to the center of the circle and dropped into third Wolf. "Your final test is to slay me."

"I will not." Ciras bowed deeply to the man and remained low. "When we entered Voraxan, you bid us the peace of the city. Dwelling here, I have only known peace. To strike you down would be to violate the peace of this place—meaning I should never be worthy of it."

Tsirin's feet appeared inches from his head. "Your final test is to slay me."

Ciras came up and let his hands rest in his lap. The man towered over him, his blade raised and ready to fall. Part of Ciras knew that if he were to lean left and flick his right leg out, he could sweep Tsirin's legs from beneath him. By the time the man hit the ground, Ciras could draw his sword and kill him, then resheathe the blade before blood spattered the onyx.

He simply shook his head. "May the peace of Voraxan be yours."

The Imperial warrior retreated three steps and slid his blade home. He bowed deeply, then knelt. The other warriors strode down the steps and into the circle. From behind Ciras, Borosan and his *thanatons* came into the circle. The inventor, smiling, gave him a nod as he knelt.

The eldest of the examiners, Vlay Laedhze, stepped to the fore of his companions and bowed to the two travelers. "It has been a long time since any have come here. Through the years there have been some, though Ixyll has been harsh. Of those who do make it to Voraxan, very few pass this last test. I congratulate you."

Ciras bowed his head. "Thank you, and thank you for the peace we have known. I am loath to shatter it, but I need to speak with the Empress. We must waken her."

Vlay shook his shaved head. "I'm afraid that is quite impossible."

"But we need her. The *vanyesh* and Turasynd are allied. The Nine are fighting, and the *vanyesh* say Nelesquin is returning. They are planning to bring to fruition the plans they made before the Cataclysm, and without the Empress' help, there will be no chance of stopping them."

"We understand this, Ciras Dejote, but complying with your request is impossible."

"But is this not what you wait for?" Ciras opened his arms. "Everyone here, sleeping in Voraxan, dreaming of peace and those they love, of homes they've left and promised to defend, aren't you all sworn to return to the Nine in a time of trouble?"

Tsirin shook his head. "We are sworn to answer the Empress' call to action."

"Yes, exactly." Ciras pointed to the ruby tower. "If we do not waken her and explain the situation to her, how is it that she can issue that call? You must let me waken her so she can decide if the time to call you is now."

Vlay frowned. "We have not made ourselves clear, Master Dejote. We await her call. We would gladly let you waken her so she could issue that call, but we cannot."

"Why not?"

Vlay glanced at the ground. "We cannot because the Empress is no longer here."

"What?" Ciras' mouth hung open. "She's not here? We came all this way, and she's not here?"

"No, she is not." Vlay's grey-eyed gaze flicked up. "She departed many years ago, over five hundred by our reckoning. She said that when the time came, she would send word, and we were to come. So, here we wait."

"I don't . . ." Ciras scrubbed hands over his face. "I don't know what to think." He glanced at Borosan. "She's not here. They're waiting."

"I know." The inventor nodded solemnly, then looked at Vlay. "She said to tell you, 'Unsheathe your claws, spread your wings, and answer the call you have waited so long to hear.' Evil times have come to the Nine, and she bids you march with all haste."

Chapter Fifty-five

3rd day, Month of the Hawk, Year of the Rat
Last Year of Imperial Prince Cyron's Court
163rd Year of the Komyr Dynasty
737th year since the Cataclysm
Tsatol Pelyn, Deseirion

Keles joined Rekarafi at the easternmost point of the moat. The excavation had sunk it to all of five feet, but the canal had not been completed and, as the sun set, the chances of water ever filling the moat again were nonexistent. Keles handed the Viruk a waterskin, then looked further east. There, a half mile off, the Eyeless Ones had drawn up in companies nine wide and deep. He'd counted eighty-one companies, meaning the enemy numbered almost three times the refugees.

And most of us are old or young, and all of us are exhausted.

The Eyeless Ones were not the only troops the invaders arrayed against them. The monkeys skittered around the ranks and another company of large creatures lurked in the center. Hulking beasts with four arms, they reminded Keles of the Viruk, save that they were much bigger and had an extra pair of taloned hands.

He glanced at Rekarafi. "What are they waiting for?"

Water gushed down over his chin and chest as the Viruk lowered the waterskin. "Night. They're blind. We will be at a disadvantage."

Keles shook his head. Though everyone had worked slavishly rebuilding the fortress, they'd barely been able to raise a five-foot wall on the old foundation. The fact that he saw no siege machinery amid the enemy ranks meant the wall would hold for a bit.

"I don't think they need any more of an advantage."

"But they will likely have one." The Viruk pointed east toward a dark line of thunderheads moving toward them. "By midnight the rain will be here. We won't see them until they are two hundred yards off."

"We don't stand a chance, do we?"

The Viruk's lips peeled back in a terrible smile, revealing needle-sharp teeth. "I have seen such situations before."

"And you survived? Then there is hope for us yet."

Rekarafi shook his head and pointed east. "I was in their position."

"Oh." Keles' shoulders slumped, aching with the exertion of the day. "You've never been a defender?"

"I have. I was in the company of heroes." He looked back toward the peasants swarming over the walls. "They have been heroic, but they are not heroes."

"Yeah." Keles shook his head as the Viruk drank again. "I'm sorry I got you into all this."

"Ha!" The Viruk crouched until he was eye to eye with Keles. "I am the one who brought myself here. My impetuous action left me in your debt. And know this, I shall be dead ere they harm a hair on your head."

"I don't know if you meant that to be comforting or not, but I don't take it that way." Keles dug inside his robe and pulled out a small leather pouch. He weighed it in his hand, then extended it toward the Viruk. "I remember what you said when we were out west."

Rekarafi gave him the waterskin, then accepted the pouch. He opened it and poured a dozen white stones into his palm. He studied them for a moment, then poured them back into the pouch and flipped it back to Keles.

"I do not accept them."

Keles caught the pouch against his chest. "But you said that when a Viruk dies, if there are more white stones in his grave than black, he'll be allowed into paradise."

"The white stones are earned, Anturasi, not just collected."

"And I could tell you a good deed you've done for each one. A good deed for me, a good deed for these people. If I told them what the stones were for, you'd have one from each of them, and then some." Keles pointed at the Eyeless Ones. "Just venturing back behind their lines to delay them a day should earn you a mountain of white stones."

"That matters not." The Viruk poked him in the chest with a finger. "I do not accept them because it would mean I agree with you that we are lost. I do not."

"But you said . . ."

"No, you read into my words." Rekarafi's dark eyes became slits. "You gather stones to ease your mind of a burden. You have responsibility for *all* the lives here.

The threat they are under is because of you. If I accept those stones, I am agreeing you have done all you can to save them."

"I have!"

"Have you?" The Viruk cocked his head. "Here is the question for you, Keles Anturasi: have you done all you can to show these people how to *live,* or have you just shown them how to delay *death* a little longer? How you embrace death means nothing. How you live your life is everything."

Keles tossed the waterskin aside, peeled his robe down, and knotted the sleeves around his waist. "You think that's it? You think I'm ready to die?"

"Talk, talk, talk. An epitaph echoing."

"Fine, let's go." Keles bent over and dug at a stone. "You want stones, you want to earn stones, let's go. I'll match you stone for stone."

The Viruk laughed. "This is not a fight you can win."

"But it's the best fight I have, until they come."

Fury and shame raced through Keles, coloring his cheeks. He ripped stones from the earth and staggered to the walls with them. He shrugged off attempts to help him carry them. He placed a stone and twisted it, fitting it to those below tightly, then returned for another, again and again.

Rekarafi matched him, stone for stone, curse for curse, harsh laugh for harsh laugh. They laughed at how silly they looked, caked with dust and streaked with sweat. They laughed at the Eyeless Ones who couldn't see how hard they labored at a futile task. They laughed at their own mortality.

And yet somewhere within the futility and defiance, a thought took root in Keles' heart. *One more stone. One more stone.* Somewhere there was a stone, *the* stone, the stone that would make the defense work. The stone that would hold the enemy back, the stone that would turn a sword or crush a head and break the back of the enemy advance. There would be a stone worth nine men or nine times nine.

All around him the others began to work anew, as if his energy rejuvenated them. Though they had already worked themselves to the point of death, they rallied and worked harder. Those who fell were pulled aside, given water and revived, while others stepped up and accepted their burdens. A few did die, and a few others were too exhausted to continue working, but most returned to the construction with a few minutes' rest.

Someone began to sing. It was a simple song, an old song normally sung by farmers as they plowed their fields and cast aside rocks. The song spoke of their battles against weather and insects. The irony of it all prompted laughter, which people spun into singing even louder. As long as the song kept going, so would they.

After nightfall, as the clouds rolled in to hide the stars and moons, Keles himself collapsed. He wasn't aware of when he'd gone down or how long he had been unconscious. He realized he was dreaming when he heard thunder crack and echo through his skull. He opened his eyes and found himself in the bottom of a pit.

It's a grave.

People passed by him on both sides. Lightning flashes revealed their faces. Some people he recognized from among the refugees even though their skulls had been crushed or faces slashed open. The children were the worst, for the wounds left by spears and sword were so much bigger. As each of them passed by they opened a hand above him and released a stone.

A black stone.

Ghoal nuan. Damnation stones!

He struggled to escape the grave, but he couldn't move. He couldn't breathe. Lightning flashed again and Rekarafi dropped a huge black stone in that smashed his legs. Majiata tossed another black stone. His brother and sister, his mother, uncle, and grandfather also pelted him. Even his father, shrouded in silhouette, gave him a black stone.

Then Tyressa came, and with her Jasai. Worse than the stones they cast were the looks of pity. They mourned not only the loss of their lives and his, but the loss of what their lives could have produced together.

Thunder exploded again and rain began to pelt down. He raised a hand to wipe his face and opened his eyes again. Cold rain hit him. Fat, heavy drops exploded on stones. In the backlight of lightning he saw everyone surrounding him still working, though the song had died and the rain was beginning to erode their strength.

Not yet half-awake, Keles rolled onto his stomach and began to claw at the midden that had once been the fortress' central tower. "One more stone, one more stone, one more stone . . ." He tore at the dirt with his fingers, cast aside rocks and handfuls of mud. The rain splashed a ragged edge clean and he dug his fingers in.

He tore at the rock and his hands slipped. Flesh ripped. "One more stone, one more stone." This was it. It was *the* stone. He was sure of it. Once he had it, they would all be saved.

But it would not come up. More rain revealed that the crack ran several feet, then turned across a clean edge.

The stone he was trying to pull free would have filled the grave he awoke in. He could no more have moved it than he could have felled a moon by throwing a rock.

"But it is *the stone*!"

He pounded his fists against it as he screamed into the storm. Blood and tears and rain stained it, then flowed into the crack. He screwed his eyes shut and clenched his teeth, screaming louder to defy the storm. He hammered the stone harder than the rain and felt the distant pain of bones breaking.

It wasn't right.

It was the *stone!*

In his mind's eye he could see where the stone belonged, where *all* the stones belonged. Tsatol Pelyn *lived,* incarnated again in all its glory. Towers tall, pennants snapping, its promise undiminished as the Empress and her heroes rode past toward Ixyll. The garrison stood tall on stout walls, sunlight reflected from the moat. It would take hours for her army to pass, but no man or woman would waver or turn away. Always alert, always ready, those defending Tsatol Pelyn would never be defeated.

Yes, this is how it must be. If Tsatol Pelyn were once again what it had been in its youth, we would not die!

Thunder crashed again and again, but the quality of it changed, muting and echoing. Wind whistled and shrieked, then something snapped above him. Keles looked up through rain-blinded eyes, then wiped them and stared again.

Pennants snapped on the tower above him. He knelt on a walled parapet. He pressed his hands flat to the stone, ignoring the pain of fractured bones sliding against each other. It seemed solid enough, and the pain meant he wasn't dreaming. He scrambled to his feet and rushed to the parapet's edge, to look out.

Tsatol Pelyn had been born anew. The moat had been hollowed and the rain struggled to fill it. The walls, which had just been rubble middens, again stood tall and strong. Towers had risen at the eastern corners and the west, and he stood in the tallest of them all. The handful of ministry warriors ran up to the top of the eastern wall, and Rekarafi laughed defiantly from atop the northeast tower.

And beyond, the Eyeless Ones came. The uniform tramp of their feet rivaled the thunder. Lightning flashes moved them forward in jerks, closer, ever closer, with their hindmost ranks still hidden by distance.

Keles clutched the stone. *This is not enough! The fortress is worthless without its garrison. We* must *have the garrison.*

A sheet of rain whipped across his face, driving him back and blinding him. He shook his head to clear his vision, then stepped up to the parapet's edge again. He narrowed his eyes against the rain, and though it washed away his vision more often than not, he clearly saw what was happening below.

The adults stood, some frightened, some resigned, staring up at him. As lightning strobed they changed. They shed years as a snake sheds skin. Twenty, thirty, forty, and even fifty years sloughed off, returning them to their prime, when they were hale and hearty, brimming with courage, determination, and confident in their immortality. Hair darkened, bodies thickened and shrank, straightened, and gap-toothed smiles became whole again.

As they held their arms out, mail sheathed them. Gauntlets materialized, and breastplates and helmets.

Fierce battle masks covered their faces, armor covered their legs. Spears and swords filled hands. Bows appeared, as did quivers of arrows.

And then the children rose. They pulled on the years their elders had discarded. As if wearing adult raiment, they looked odd for a moment, then they began to grow into those years. They sprouted up and muscles thickened. Childish softness hardened into angular adulthood. Armor wrapped them and implements of war came to hand.

They followed their elders to the walls, and awaited the Eyeless Ones.

The invaders came undaunted. Perhaps they imagined they were a wave that would wash over a lowly sand castle. No dismay registered as they began their descent into the moat or had to scramble up the other side. Mindless as well as blind, they crawled over each other, rising higher and higher to find the top of the wall.

Arrows slashed down at them, twisting them around with the force of impact. Following commands that Jasai shouted above the wind, the archers drew as one and shot. Whole ranks of dead and dying Eyeless Ones wilted and thrashed.

Still their companions tromped over them, climbing ever higher, only to be met with spear thrusts that toppled them down into the pit.

Yet other Eyeless Ones pressed on and their line wrapped the fortress' perimeter. They came at it from all sides, and here and there they reached the top of the wall. A sword cut would spin a warrior away, making room for another blind and another.

Tyressa whirled into the battle, a blur of black and silver. She spun her spear over her head, slashing down through one blind, then shattering another's skull with the weapon's butt end. That blind arced back over the wall into the darkness. She swept two others from the edge, then stood there defiantly, challenging blinds to attack.

Rekarafi proved no less magnificent. He leaped from his tower and scattered five blinds that had gained the wall below him. His claws flashed, shredding their flesh. Keles winced as sympathetic pain rippled up the scars on his back. Rekarafi grabbed one of the blinds at hip and throat and raised it above his head. He bowed the creature's spine, then touched its shoulders to hips with a sharp crack.

Still, it is not enough. Keles spat down into the courtyard. *Tsatol Pelyn is not yet complete.*

Yet uncertain as to what was happening, Keles stalked around to the western side of the tower and gazed at the dug-out canal. It had once been eighteen feet across and half that deep, but the digging had only produced a shallow, three-foot-wide track. He'd seen deeper wheel ruts on a road.

He closed his eyes, picturing the canal as it must have been. He saw it on the day the workers cleared the last bit of dirt. Water from the river pushed at the thin wall. The earth darkened, then crumbled, dissolving into a thick mud that the rush of water carried into the moat. He watched the water pour into the moat in a torrent, a fast-moving torrent that filled it quickly, washing away the Eyeless Ones, collapsing their pyramids of bodies.

He pictured it in his mind and merged that image with reality. His body tingled as he forced reality to surrender to the image. As the fortress had been made whole, as the people had become the garrison, so the ditch would become the canal and it would be *enough*.

And so it was.

The water roared, leaping and foaming. It pushed a wall of mud with it that swept through the moat. Tumbling rocks shattered legs. Eyeless Ones pitched from the walls and disappeared in the roiling black water. Almost as if they had been made of mud themselves, the Eyeless Ones melted as they bobbed to the surface.

Yet even this did not wholly stop them. One of the four-armed creatures leaped the moat and scrambled to the top of the wall. He scattered warriors with flicks of his hands, then rushed at Rekarafi. He roared furiously, and the Viruk matched his battle cry. People between them leaped to the courtyard below.

As strong as the invader was, he lacked the Viruk's speed. The two upper arms slashed harmlessly above Rekarafi's head. The Viruk caught the creature's lower arms by the wrists, then yanked. Ligaments popped as the arms tore free. The creature, stricken, looked down, then the Viruk battered it to death with its own arms.

The battle for Tsatol Pelyn raged long into the night, and only broke when the storm slackened. The moat had become a swamp of dead blinds. Some human corpses bobbed there, but remarkably few given the ferocity of the fighting. As the clouds parted and the first faint dawn glow painted the eastern horizon gold, the blinds had withdrawn toward Felarati and every defender of Tsatol Pelyn knew they would not return.

Chapter Fifty-six

3rd day, Month of the Hawk, Year of the Rat
Last Year of Imperial Prince Cyron's Court
163rd Year of the Komyr Dynasty
737th year since the Cataclysm
Wentokikun, Moriande
Nalenyr

The gnawing of the maggots in his arm kept Cyron awake. He had never wanted them sewn into his flesh, but the infection had gotten worse. He'd been feverish, and the Viruk ambassador had said that if he did not do something, he could lose the arm. Afraid and weak, delirious, he'd let Geselkir, under the Viruk's watchful eye, plant the squirming white worms in his arm and sew the wound closed.

And now he could hear them chewing and devouring him. He'd taken to naming them. Pyrust, Vniel, Turcol, invaders, Vroan. The last had been voracious and would not stop. Vroan was eating his way through Cyron's system, to his heart, then to his brain. The Prince knew this as certainly as he knew it was night and that both he and his realm would likely be dead in the morning.

He had done all he could, he knew that, but he had been pulled in so many directions. As much as he had expected and feared invasion from the north, the destruction of Erumvirine had just not been something he anticipated. Had the Virine ever cast lustful eyes north, he would have had time to react and to crush their ambitions. He might not have been a military man, but the Virine believed themselves invincible because of their Imperial heritage.

Cold comfort in the grave now, I imagine, Prince Jekusmirwyn. The Telanyn Dynasty surely had to be dead. Even if the Prince had gotten any of his children out of Kelewan, no one who forced the invaders from Erumvirine would ever put a Telanyn back on the throne. *I would not have.*

As he had done many times in his fever, Cyron ran over the events of the past months and years, seeking that point where he went wrong. There *had* to be one, just a simple one, a little mistake that just began to compound in ways he could not have anticipated. But he couldn't see one. He had hoped to rebuild the Empire peacefully through exploration and trade. He hoped others would be persuaded to reunite the Empire without bloodshed. True, he did want it reunited under a Komyr Emperor, but wanted it for the benefit of all.

That ate at him the most. Had he been coldhearted, he could have let the people of Deseirion starve. Had he done that, Pyrust would have been forced to launch an invasion, but his army would have marched on an empty belly. They would have been broken against the Helos Mountains. Naleni forces could have liberated

Helosunde, then taken Deseirion. He would have come with food for all, would have shared the wealth of his nation. He would have made life better for them.

But that was not to be. It was a future that would not be realized because he could not have allowed them to starve.

Unbidden came the thought of the *Stormwolf* expedition. Since Qiro Anturasi's departure, he had learned nothing of what they had accomplished. He feared the fleet had met with disaster—a fitting end since he launched it, and clearly his other efforts had been disasters. Then again, the brave men and women who had undertaken that bold adventure deserved better than to be devoured by sharks.

He wondered for a moment if they *had* found the continent of Anturasixan. *It had been drawn in Qiro's own blood!* The thought of the map dripping blood, and the legend "Here there be monsters," sent a shiver through him. It dawned on him then that Qiro was the author of the troubles in Erumvirine, and somehow this did not wholly surprise him.

The man had ample reasons to be angry with Nalenyr. The Komyr Princes had kept him a prisoner in Anturasikun once he had returned from his unsuccessful journey to Ixyll so long ago. The aggressive exploration urged upon him had cost him his son. A murderer stalking Moriande had butchered his granddaughter. Cyron himself had denied the man the chance to walk free to celebrate his eighty-first birthday, and the needs of the state had demanded both his grandsons be sent into the unknown.

Keles and Jorim. In some ways it would be best if they were both dead. Cyron twisted and flopped in bed, trying to find a comfortable position, but every little jostle jolted pain up his arm. He sat up, cradling the burning limb in his lap and panting as sweat stung his eyes.

What a changed world they would return to. He would no longer be on the throne. Cyron laughed weakly. Who would be on the throne he couldn't tell. He was certain Vroan would wiggle his ass into the Dragon Throne, but it would only be for a little while. The invaders would come north and Vroan couldn't oppose them. He would move to try it, though, and Pyrust would sweep in from the north.

The Hawk will perch on my throne after all. He sighed and licked cracked lips. "Perhaps that will be for the best."

His shoulders slumped and a lump formed in his throat. Staring into the darkness he saw his nation laid waste by war. All that had been golden and green became red and black, awash in blood, smoldering. And Moriande, his white city, gone; towers broken like teeth, walls shattered, and streets echoing with the anguished cries of mourners.

He could see wretched survivors, brokenhearted, wandering listlessly through streets strewn with rubble. Men with bodies tangled with scars. Malnourished women with flat dugs and exposed ribs. Children who were little more than skeletons, so weak they could not lift their own heads. Sores covering everyone and fever, like the fever he had, roasting people from within. All of them would turn red eyes toward what was left of Wentokikun and wonder why he did not save them. He had promised them a better life, and all he had given them was the miseries mankind had known from time before remembering.

They will devour my nation as they do my flesh. Cyron tried to lift his left arm, but could not. Angry pain pulsed through him, warning him to remain still. He accepted the warning, hunkering down against pillows. He cried silently at the pain, for himself, for his nation. His right hand tangled in the sheets and he hung on so he would not scream.

The pain, slowly, incrementally, subsided.

Which allowed him again to feel the maggots feasting on him.

Cyron roared and threw back the bedclothes. He swung his legs out of bed and stood quickly. A wave of blackness washed over him, but he grabbed a handful of sheets and remained upright. He staggered from his bedchamber to the outer room, then barked his shin against a low table. He caught the doorjamb and again avoided falling, then stepped to the corner where his armor and swords rested in their stand.

The door slid open to his left, silhouetting a servant. Cyron raised his left arm, displaying the leather wrapping it and the thongs securing them. "Yes, yes, quickly, come here. Help me get this off. Now, help me."

As the man approached, Cyron reached down for the dagger he would use to cut the maggots from his flesh. As his fingers closed on the hilt, he glanced up and saw the man had drawn a short sword and had raised it above his head.

"Die, tyrant!"

Cyron's left arm rose and intercepted the blow. The sword stroke carried through the leather and snapped the heavier of the bones. Had it not been for the leather, it would have cut cleanly through the limb. The blade, slightly impeded, just lodged in the second bone.

Curiously, the sword harmed none of the maggots.

Screaming in pain, Cyron twisted and drove the dagger into the assassin. He pierced the man's body right below the breastbone, puncturing his heart. So fierce was the Prince's frenzied blow that it lifted the Helosundian from his feet and pitched him over onto the low table. It collapsed beneath him.

Cyron staggered back and broke through the paper-paneled wall. The sword's hilt caught on a stout piece of wood and ripped the blade free. The Prince screamed again, then felt a jagged piece of wood stab into his back as he hit the floor.

He looked down and saw his robe tented over his right breast. He laughed.

An assassin can't kill me. How odd that enemies from without cannot stop me, but my own home will be my death.

Chapter Fifty-seven

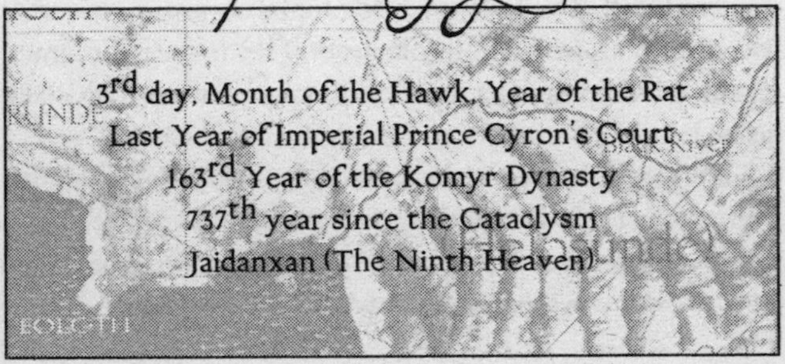

3rd day, Month of the Hawk, Year of the Rat
Last Year of Imperial Prince Cyron's Court
163rd Year of the Komyr Dynasty
737th year since the Cataclysm
Jaidanxan (The Ninth Heaven)

He had the sensation that he was floating, light and ethereal, as if he had no body at all. Then he realized that he really had no physical sensation—the illusion of floating was because he felt nothing. He had no physical self; he was only being.

And this was the correct way of things.

Jorim did not will his eyes to open, but rather willed that which surrounded him into existence. Slowly it came—at first a blur of colors. He heard muted sounds and recognized them before he saw anything. They were the songs of birds he'd heard the world over, all singing in concert—though he was fairly certain the diverse species had never heard each other sing in the real world.

In the mortal world.

He acknowledged himself to be Tetcomchoa and Wentiko, as well as other names in scripts he'd never seen, comprising sounds his throat never could have produced. The moment he made that judgment, he knew it was wrong. He no longer had a throat. He was no longer a man.

He had no reason to cling to the name Jorim, but he did because it labeled his most recent existence. Those memories burned hottest in his mind. He was not through with them and felt he had left some things undone. He needed to finish them, but had a sense of grander things that also demanded his attention.

His surroundings focused loosely as if he were viewing them through a translucent silk veil. He reached out to brush it aside and instead found himself raking it to shreds with a taloned paw. He turned the paw and studied it—golden leather flesh on the inside, black scales over the back, and hard gold talons in which he caught a distorted reflection of himself.

He willed his paw into a hand and recognized it as Jorim's hand. With it he drew aside the tattered veil and stepped through into a magnificent room. Cool white marble stretched out beneath his feet, flowing down in broad steps through a forest of columns. The steps opened onto a balcony and he flew there in an instant. The balcony overlooked a vista more beautiful than anything he had ever seen before.

The whole of the world lay as a distant carpet, green with jungle, gold with desert, and blue with water. Clouds floated above it, casting shadows and playfully shifting shapes. Above them floated small hunks of rock, which he instantly realized were not small at all, but mountains that had been ripped from the earth like teeth torn from a jaw. Jungle still clung to them, snow decorated them, and streaming water poured off to congeal below as clouds. Each one of them was the palace of a god, so there would be nine, and he stood on one of them.

They orbited in a circle much as the Zodiac girded the heavens. Below, as if it were the hub of the circle, lay the Dark Sea and beyond it Ixyll, from which he could feel a trickling thrill of wild magic. Once he had desired to go there and now, were he willing to open his mind, he could know most of its secrets. That wealth of knowledge would have been a treasure trove to him at one time, and now it seemed almost trivial—both because of the ease with which it could be gathered and the sense that whatever was happening there had little or no bearing on his existence.

He caught a light sound from behind and spun. A tiny woman stood there with arms wrapped around herself in a fleshy cloak that became a black silk robe, belted and trimmed in ivory. He did not need the flying bats embroidered on the breasts to recognize her, for he'd seen her sharp features and wide eyes on statues in temples from Helosunde to Ummummorar.

He dropped to a knee and bowed to her.

Her high-pitched, gay laughter reminded him that she was his sister the bat, goddess of Wisdom.

"Have you finally learned to respect your elders, Wentiko?"

"I have always respected you, Tsiwen."

"So you have, little brother, so you have." She smiled at him and he rose. "Jaidanxan has been quiet without you."

He shook his head. "I've not been gone long, have I? Only twenty-three years."

"You have been gone far longer than that." She gestured off to the darkest of the floating palaces. "Grija was always against your decision to incarnate in mortal form. He thought you would be another disaster, so he delayed your return."

Jorim tried to remember anything that might pertain to what she was saying, but couldn't. "Perhaps he thwarts me still."

"You'd not be here if he were." She smiled carefully and came to join him at the balcony's edge. "When you first chose to be born of a mortal, you chose a human—a bold choice. You brought them a gift of magic, and those you call the Amentzutl took to it well. You decided to share magic with others, those to whom you were born this time. You had come to love men and Grija found support among some here to visit you and offer you a bargain."

Jorim arched an eyebrow. "He convinced me to divest myself of much of myself—my divine nature—and leave it in the land of the Amentzutl."

"You remember."

"No, I have just benefited from wisdom."

Tsiwen laughed and Jorim caught fleeting memories of winging his way through the night with her in eons past. "Wisdom had eluded you when you agreed to the bargain because the portion of you that you retained had become overly human. When your body died, your spirit became his to play with, and he did. He often withheld incarnation, or let you be born into a situation where you could never find your essence again."

"I've had more than one incarnation?" Jorim shivered.

"And I have been gone from Jaidanxan since I was Tetcomchoa?"

"Things you will remember as you let slip your grasp on who you have been most recently."

Jorim shook his head. "It's not time for that yet. I have friends and family back there."

"I know." She gestured with a hand toward the center of the balcony and a hole opened in it. It filled with water that roiled, then cleared. "You'll want to know how they fare."

He approached the hole cautiously. Dread coiled in his belly, bringing with it echoes of the pain he'd felt upon death. Though many claimed the transition from life to death is painless, they are mortals who have no knowledge of it. The ripping of the spirit from the physical eclipses the most acute pain, for it is felt in the soul even more sharply than the body.

Preparing himself, he looked down. It was nighttime at Nemehyan. His body had been wrapped in a white mourning robe with the Naleni dragon embroidered on it in black. He lay atop the city's largest pyramid and people hiked up the steps, passed by him, and down again, a long line of them. Members of the *Stormwolf* expedition mixed freely with the Amentzutl.

Anaeda Gryst, Nauana, and Shimik were closest to his body. The two women spoke with those who passed by. Though they wore brave expressions, he could feel their loss. Anaeda would reach out and squeeze Nauana's shoulder or caress her hair from time to time, and that seemed enough to keep his lover from dissolving into tears.

Even so distant, he could feel Nauana's pain. He had touched her essence, and she had touched him. The pain of separation gnawed through her, and joined with the frustration in Jorim. He wanted to reach out and touch her, but his body no longer responded to him.

I am a god. How can this be prevented?

Shimik, by way of contrast, appeared calm and even happy. The Fenn sat near his head but did not seem the least bit disturbed. He just chattered to himself as he often did, and spoke to Jorim as if he were still there. More important, the last time he'd seen Shimik, the Fenn had been white. Now his fur was darkening, and the flesh of his hands and feet was taking on a golden hue.

Shimik looked up to the heavens and smiled. He held his hands up. "Jrima, Jrima, Shimik comma."

Nauana reached down and pulled the Fenn into her arms.

Jorim looked at his sister. "They believe I am dead."

"They saw you die." She smiled easily. "Your death was truly spectacular. You accepted death so they would not know it. Grija was expecting to gorge on the Amentzutl and instead you gave him offal."

"I gave him his own creations."

"No."

"But I saw him there. The Amentzutl Zoloa is Grija."

"Oh, that's true. He was stalking that killing ground, devouring souls."

"And I would have devoured them all had our brother not interfered. I love how desperate people pray to me, begging me not to take them. So piquant." Wearing a grey robe, Grija materialized on the other side of the hole, tall and slender, with short dark hair, black eyes, and sharpened teeth. "You know you would still be my plaything, except that those you saved prayed fervently for you."

Jorim shook his head as Grija's expression soured. "Prayers of thanks were never to your taste, were they?"

"No, but no matter. I would have allowed you to come home this time."

"So gracious. What makes this time different from any other?"

The death god walked to the balcony's edge and pointed down below the circle of palaces. "Look there."

Jorim nodded. "The Dark Sea."

"Deeper."

Jorim moved to the balcony edge and studied its depths. The dark water did not so much clear as his vision just pierced fathoms. There, over a mile deep, a stone glowed with opalescent fury. Energy pulsed within it, at first slowly, then in a frenzy. He sensed it was a heartbeat, one which pounded without rhyme, reason, or purpose, but that this had not always been the case. *Nor shall it be.*

"I see."

Grija snarled. "Let go your humanity, Wentiko; matters here are too critical for you to be trapped with small thinking. That is Nessagafel. He awakens."

"'Nessagafel' is a Viruk word." Jorim shook his head. "I don't know it."

"You once did. Everyone did." Tsiwen hugged arms around herself and seemed to shrink. "The world knew it and trembled."

Grija lifted his head and sniffed. "Nessagafel is the tenth god, or the *first* god, depending on how you wish to reckon things. He incarnated through the Viruk and built their empire. He grew powerful and sought to enslave all of us. We had to destroy him, and we did."

"You killed him?"

Grija nodded. "Chado and Quun tore him apart. That's why, in the human Zodiac, they share prey."

"But if he's dead, how is he coming back? Why did you let him out of your realm?"

"I didn't." Grija's nostrils flared. "Something happened. Someone else defied me and escaped, and Nessagafel slipped out as well. Now he seeks to regain his power and when he does, he will kill all of *us*."

Jorim nodded slowly. "How do we stop him?"

"Nessagafel is yet anchored in my realm, so the one who escaped me is the key. She is dead, but she is not dead. When she is mine again, the portal will close and he will be trapped. However, she is beyond my reach, but not yours."

"Who is it?"

"Your human sister, Nirati." The god of Death smiled coldly. "Kill her again, Wentiko, or everything that is known will perish."

Chapter Fifty-eight

3rd day, Month of the Hawk, Year of the Rat
Last Year of Imperial Prince Cyron's Court
163rd Year of the Komyr Dynasty
737th year since the Cataclysm
Tsatol Deraelkun, County of Faeut
Erumvirine

The door to my chamber slid open. I barely heard the gasp, more because Pasuram Derael kept his voice politely hushed than a problem with the ear that had been sewn back on. I turned slowly toward the door and gave him and his father an abbreviated bow.

The count, whose pale and painfully slender body could have benefited from shadows to cloak it, regarded me carefully. "The physician said you would not be out of bed for days."

Urardsa finished rewrapping a loop of bandage around my chest. "His thread is slender, but still strong."

I glanced at the Gloon. "And still a tangle?"

"In places."

I shook my head, then turned to my host. "You know

what I am. Mystics are blessed or cursed with life beyond our years. We tend to heal more quickly than others." I coughed and winced, but they were polite enough to let that escape notice.

Pasuram guided his father's wheeled chair into my chamber. This task was not easy since the young man had taken an arrow through his thigh and his father had a long, thick, leather-wrapped package lying across his lap. I did not offer to help the son, as I would not have dishonored him in front of his father. All three of us men were locked in mutual denial of our weakness and, truth be told, Pasuram was the strongest of us.

The Gloon just crouched in a corner and watched.

The count waited in the center of the chamber while his son fetched both of us chairs. Pasuram sat beside his father, with his left leg stretched out, and I sat facing the older man. Pasuram had placed the chair close enough that I could hear, and I nodded thanks, since it would be my severed ear and not his father's soft whisper which would make listening difficult.

"*Jaecaiserr* Moraven Tolo, I have known you since I was very young. I anticipated having this talk with you many times, for once I heard the story I will tell you, I knew it was for you that this package was meant. There could be no other, but my instructions were very specific, and until yesterday I could not be faithful to the duty charged me."

I considered his words carefully, nodding slowly, and allowed him to catch his breath.

"What I will tell you now has been handed down through the Derael family for two hundred seventy years, parent to child, husband to wife, in a duty considered as sacred as warding this pass. What I have here in my lap has lain in the museum for that time, save twice when danger threatened and we could not chance it being taken as plunder."

The count's grey eyes flicked toward his son. "I recently told Pasuram what you will hear and he, too, thought immediately of you."

I bowed my head toward the both of them. "What you are telling me is an honor. To be held in such high regard is more than most *xidantzu* can imagine."

"But you are more than most *xidantzu,* Master Tolo." The count smiled and the effort taxed him mightily. "Long ago a man came to Deraelkun. He appeared here, just appeared, without having been admitted, and he bore this package. He called himself Ryn Anturasi and begged of my ancestor a favor which, he promised, would be returned. 'Grant this, and Tsatol Deraelkun will not fall.' I believe the favor has been repaid through your action yesterday."

I shook my head. "You know the *kwajiin* will be back, this time with far more warriors and a far smarter general. Deraelkun may yet fall."

Jarys Derael coughed. "We have ever known it would, *jaecaiserr.* We merely sought to prolong the time until then."

"For your enemies, the time to take it shall seem an eternity."

The count hazarded a nod and I almost thought he would not be able to raise his head again. He did, but needed to rest. We waited and doubtless all benefited from the sweet scent of the healing unguents with which our various wounds had been slathered.

"I wish I had the strength to hand this package to you. We will tell many it is a gift from Deraelkun, from our history, for it has been here in the museum. It has been kept with an ancient suit of armor, one from before the Cataclysm. That armor was left here by an Imperial bastard who humiliated a Crown Prince in a military exercise, much as you did the *kwajiin* yesterday."

Pasuram slid the package from beneath his father's hands and brought it to me. I let it rest on my thighs. I could still feel the warmth of the count's hands, but far too little of it to believe the man would live much longer.

I looked Jarys in the eye. "What was said?"

"We were told that someday a man would come to Deraelkun. He would be young, but very old—the old formulation for designating someone a Mystic. He would be a wise man who could be daringly foolish."

I laughed at that latter bit of description.

The count did not. "And we were told he would laugh when he heard himself described thus."

A chill puckered my flesh. "What else?"

"We were told he would not be of Derael blood and that anyone who claimed this package as being meant for him would not be the man for whom it truly *was* meant." The count lifted a trembling finger. "Open it."

I untied the braided purple cord that secured the package. Even before I began to remove the leather sheet, I knew what the package contained. Of course, being *jaecaiserr,* feeling the presence of swords even within thick leather presented little challenge.

And fine blades these were. From hilt to point they were five feet long. The wooden scabbards were scarlet washed in black, with gold decorations and covered in a clear lacquer. The pattern on them matched the interwoven cords wrapping the hilts—the hilts and scabbards were boldly tiger-striped. Beneath the cords on each hilt, a stalking tiger charm of bronze had been bound, linking the warrior using them to Chado, and marking him a Morythian.

The disk-shaped handguards revealed more about the swords even before I drew one. The Zodiac rimmed each disk, but Chado did not occupy the spot of honor atop the blade. That had been given to a dragon, the *Imperial* dragon. The blades dated from well before the Cataclysm. The handguards and the weaving on the hilt also indicated the swords belonged to a member of the Imperial bodyguard.

I stood slowly and bared a blade with my left hand. The silvered steel came free easily, not just the way a fine weapon would be expected to do, but as something meant for my hand alone. Perfectly balanced, the sword felt like an extension of my arm. With that blade in my left hand and its mate filling my right, I would not know defeat.

Save through treachery.

Thoughts and memories exploded in my head. I remembered the day before, but a day in a different time when I faced a man, tall and dark, wearing a crowned-bear crest. We fought on that same island before Tsatol Deraelkun for hours, trading blows, never drawing blood—but refraining because we had no desire to hurt each other. Even so, we came so close and closer, daring each other to trim a lock here, bare a patch on an arm or leg there. It was a dangerous game we played, but one we had to play.

And then, another time, darkness and the slice of a blade into my chest. It should have felt cold, that steel, but instead it felt molten. It shattered ribs and opened a lung. I could hear my breath hissing from my chest as I fell. I tried to look back over my shoulder to see who had struck me down, but I could not. The only clue to his identity was a softly whispered "I'm sorry," and the hushed rustle of his feet as he made his escape.

I sat down hard in the chair and looked at the blade. I saw my reflection in it, distorted and twisted, but no less recognizable. I had seen it so often before, in that sword, that I could not help but know who it was.

"Count Derael, tell me, to whom did the swords belong?"

"The chief of the last Emperor's bodyguard. He rode past here with Empress Cyrsa and died in Ixyll."

I nodded. "Virisken Soshir."

"The very same."

I looked at the dying man. "You know you have returned to me the swords I bore to Ixyll."

His pale eyes narrowed. "If this is true, there is a message for you."

"What?"

"Your duty to the crown has not been fulfilled."

A jolt ran through me and the last bit of fog cleared from my mind. I knew two things—two things as certain as the sun's rising in the morning and setting at night. "Prince Nelesquin has returned. He covets what he always coveted. She always feared he would come back to claim the Empire." I raised the bare blade. "I am Virisken Soshir. He'll ascend to the throne over my dead body."

"A poor choice of words, Master Soshir." The Gloon stared at me with all seven eyes. "Now you know who you are. Now you are free to die."

Chapter Fifty-nine

4th day, Month of the Hawk, Year of the Rat
Last Year of Imperial Prince Cyron's Court
163rd Year of the Komyr Dynasty
737th year since the Cataclysm
Tsatol Pelyn, Deseirion

It seemed to Keles Anturasi that he could have had a blanket for every survivor in the fortress draped over him and he'd still not stop shivering. He sat on the parapet of the north wall, looking down into the courtyard. The people, still in armor, still in the prime of their lives, moved about, lining up the dead, straightening their limbs, saluting comrades in arms who had fallen.

And it all made no sense to him.

Though he did not know what he had done, he knew he had done it. He hoped that as the sun made it over the horizon the fortress would fade. He hoped it had been an illusion. It just couldn't exist, but he could see the dancing reflections of sunlight from the moat, still hear the pennants snapping in the breeze, and could hear the crisp, strong footsteps of people who, hours before, could have barely managed an exhausted shuffle.

The way they dealt with each other baffled him. They gathered in groups—family groups, he assumed, based on the crests on the armor—but it was no longer a grandparent gathering children or elderly maiden aunts comforting each other. These people had become warriors. Some had regressed to a life they knew, others had become things they had long ago abandoned dreaming they could be. And children . . . the children had grown into the sort of soldiers who inhabited heroic stories of the Imperial period.

Some people had escaped transformation, but it had touched even Rislet Peyt. The diminutive minister had swelled into a warrior with a double-handed great sword. He'd chopped one of the four-armed things in half with it. He'd gotten an arm broken in the process, but he sat there with his arm in a sling, joking with the men who had previously been his bodyguards.

Keles clutched the black blanket around his shoulders more tightly, but his broken hands had swollen to the point where they were all but useless. This had all been his doing, but he couldn't undo it, nor could he do it again. All he could remember was that he knew he had to do something, and he rebelled against the situation that doomed so many people.

Somehow I must have touched magic.

But even that explanation defied logic. He was a cartographer. It was true that he had been working more as an engineer in making the changes in Felarati, but everything he had done had been something he'd learned as a by-product of his main pursuit: cartography. They were all things he could not have helped but learn, and many of them he'd learned without even realizing it.

That could have explained, maybe, what happened with the fortress itself, but not what happened with the people. As much as he tried to figure things out, he couldn't. Even a convoluted scheme by which their desires to avoid death had combined with his desire to save them—letting all of them touch magic and thereby be changed—fell short. That might have worked for the adults, but not the children.

What made what happened to the people even worse was that while the children had become adults, they had no memories or experiences of the years that should have passed. To make things even more confusing, most of the survivors were drunk with victory and, save those who volunteered to stand sentry, were wandering off in pairs to enjoy carnal experiences they'd never known, or had long since forgotten.

A shadow fell over him and he looked up at Rekarafi. "Do you know what happened?"

"I did not know the first time."

"First time?"

The Viruk pointed to the west. "In Ixyll, we escaped a chaos storm by entering a cavern. It proved to be a mausoleum."

"I remember."

"You were certain that there was a chamber beyond an arch. Borosan and I said we had moved. You did not believe that and drew a map to show us what waited on the other side of the arch." The Viruk crouched and scraped the rough map on the stone. "When you did that, Moraven and Ciras reacted. I felt it, too. We moved *again*. The first time the storm moved us. *You* moved us back."

Keles felt the blood drain from his face. "By drawing the map, I moved us?"

Rekarafi nodded.

"Why didn't you tell me? I could have drawn my way out of Felarati if I had known that."

The Viruk laughed. "No, you could not have. You did not know then what you did. You do not know *now* what you did last night. You have touched magic, Keles, very powerful magic, but you do not know how to control it."

"Can I learn? Can you teach me?"

Rekarafi closed his eyes and raised his head, letting the breeze blow through his black mane. "There was a time, Keles Anturasi, when magic was so plentiful in the world that doing what you have done would have been simple. The Viruk mastered this magic, but in our mastering there was a flaw. It destroyed our Empire. What little I know would not serve you well. You've discovered this power on your own. You will have to learn how to control it yourself as well."

"What if I get it wrong?"

The Viruk shrugged. "It will kill you."

"That's reassuring."

"It is an urge to caution."

"Caution, yes." Keles nodded. "That's the other thing about everyone. They look at me and they are wary. Respectful but cautious. Who is more afraid of what happened here last night, them or me?"

Rekarafi growled out a low laugh. "The Eyeless Ones are the most afraid."

"You have a point there."

The Viruk rested a hand on his shoulder. "And you

won our contest. You shifted more stones than I. It has been many years since a human so humbled a Viruk."

"It'll probably be a few more before that happens again, Rekarafi."

"Pity." The Viruk smiled. "Being humbled is an interesting experience if one lives through it."

The Viruk withdrew as Tyressa came up the stone steps toward Keles. She carried a bowl and a pitcher. Bandages had been looped over her shoulder. She knelt beside him and set her burdens on the stone.

"Your hands must be cared for."

"They'll be fine."

"You forget my duty to Prince Cyron. You are my responsibility."

"Are you sure you want to take responsibility for me?"

Tyressa's expression sharpened. "I don't have that choice. Your hands."

Keles frowned, then let the blanket slip. He presented his hands to her, all bloody, torn, swollen, and purple. He stiffened as she took them in her hands, but refused to cry out. She brought them down into the bowl, then poured water into it, which sent another throb of pain through his hands.

Tyressa wetted a cloth, then took his right hand out of the water. She began to gently scrub at it, holding his right wrist. He pulled back at the first touch of the cloth, but she tightened her grip. "Don't struggle; it will only make it worse."

"Sorry. It hurts."

"It should. You've hurt your hands badly."

Keles tried to laugh, but a wave of exhaustion killed it prematurely. "Funny that I can change people the way I did and not heal my own hands."

"Why is it funny that you cannot do things for which you have no gift or training?" She washed his hand, removing dirt and crusted blood, which gave Keles a better look at how much damage he'd done than he'd wanted. "We all are what we are, Keles. Change is not easy."

"But I've changed, and I don't even know how or why."

The Keru glanced back down into the courtyard. "You're looking at why, Keles. You changed so they could live."

"So everyone could live. Them. You. Jasai. Rekarafi."

"I am corrected." She lowered his right hand into the water and began to work on his left. "There are things for which I have no training, no gift."

"You seem pretty gifted to me, Tyressa."

She stopped and looked in his eyes. "What you said to me the other day . . ."

Keles shook his head. "You don't have to say anything. I'm all grown up, but sometimes the dreams of youth remain."

"That's not what you said."

"Ouch." Keles winced. "Maybe that's what I should have said. That's what you heard."

"That's not what I heard. What I heard was something for which I have no gift or training. I've been Keru for years, and dreamed of being one for longer. And you know I've dreamed of my people finding a way to escape the trap of being a captive nation. These are all things that are outside myself. They are things for which I am willing to fight and willing to die."

"I understand that."

"Then understand this: these things have precluded me considering other things. I set other things aside.

Desires. Feelings." She glanced down at his hand. "When you spoke to me, I couldn't . . ."

She sighed heavily and her shoulders slumped a bit. "When you have so long been a warrior, anything you are not prepared to deal with is seen as an attack. I parry. I riposte. I elude and disengage."

"You thought I was attacking you?"

"Not attack, no, but I felt ambushed."

Keles nodded slowly. "I guess that makes sense. So what you said about Jasai having feelings for me, that's not true?"

Tyressa lowered his left hand into the water again. "It *is* true, Keles. She loves you and will do everything she can to hide it, because she believes I love you."

"Do you?"

"It's not something I have a gift or training for."

Keles pulled his hands from the water and gingerly crossed his arms against his chest. "You still see it as an attack, don't you?"

"There are nine hundred ninety-nine reasons you should love her, Keles. She would make you a good wife."

"She's got a husband." Keles laughed. "Right now, he has better hands than I do."

"Loving you is not part of my mission."

His eyes narrowed. "But will it stop you from doing that mission?"

"It already has."

"What?"

Tyressa's chin came up. "If I had done what Prince Cyron ordered me to do, you'd already be dead."

Chapter Sixty

4th day, Month of the Hawk, Year of the Rat
Last Year of Imperial Prince Cyron's Court
163rd Year of the Komyr Dynasty
737th year since the Cataclysm
Kunjiqui, Anturasixan

Anger gathered on Nelesquin's forehead the way thunderclouds hovered on the northwestern horizon. Nirati knew he didn't see her, for his face would brighten when he did. It always did, and that made her happy. She didn't like seeing him angry; it frightened her.

Nelesquin studied his scrying stones. The black and white stones had fallen into a pattern she did not recognize. The black ones had clumped together. A smaller bunch of white stones had also come together, but the significance of these things eluded her.

"What troubles you, beloved?"

The dark man's head came up, and his smile blossomed almost too quickly. "Not so much troubled as confused, my dear. I fear there have been some setbacks, and I am frustrated that I had no real chance to prevent them."

"But you would have if you could?"

"Of course." He pointed to the gathered black stones. "We suffered a reversal in Erumvirine. I believe Gachin Dost exceeded his orders and suffered as a result. He may even be dead."

Nirati remembered the blue-skinned Durrani leader. "I am sorry to hear that."

"It *is* a pity, though it will give Keerana an opportunity. Gachin was a good leader, but Keerana is more adaptable. Supplied with the tokens of appreciation I have aboard ship to thank them, he will find a way to excel in my service."

Nelesquin gathered the stones up and slipped them into the leather pouch. He stood, then extended his right hand to her. She took it and they began to hike over the hill to the harbor where the *Crown Bear* waited. It sat in the harbor like a mother goose, surrounded by countless goslings all ready to sail northwest to Erumvirine.

Nirati hesitated, her breath frozen in her lungs. *So many ships.* Each one brimmed with soldiers and machines of war; nothing could stand before his forces. She realized that it was petty of her that she had not been overly concerned with what he was doing when his focus was Erumvirine, but now that his forces would range north and attack Nalenyr, her stomach began to knot. She could see Moriande crushed.

Mother is there in Anturasikun, and perhaps Keles and Jorim, too. And Uncle Ulan and my cousins. Just as there would be no defeating Nelesquin's Durrani, there would be no stopping this invasion. Even if she were able to deflect him into the Five Princes first, he *would* reestablish the Empire and any who would stand in his way would be destroyed.

It suddenly occurred to her that she would be included in that number.

Nelesquin smiled grandly, posting fists on his hips. "Never has there been such a fleet. Not even the fleet that brought the first True Bloods, nor Taichun's fleet, can rival mine. They knew success with less, and were lesser men. How can we not succeed?"

Nirati smiled. "The question is not worthy of asking, beloved, for there is no answer."

He leaned down and kissed her softly. "You will be my empress, Nirati, my only wife. We will make this empire greater than any that has gone before. Certainly greater than Taichun's. It shall rival the Viruk Empire and even exceed it. Your face shall be on coins coveted from here to Aefret and beyond. Countless throngs will bow to you and worship you."

"Will I be an empress or a goddess?"

"Either or both, and deserving of worship regardless." He laughed aloud and the sound echoed from the hills. "Come, it is time we board the ship."

They walked hand in hand to the shoreline, then out along a wharf next to which the *Crown Bear* was moored. The ship, with its nine tall masts, hid the far headland and seemed to be a world all by itself.

He turned and smiled, grasping her left hand in both of his. "Come, Nirati, we will sail to our new empire and the adoration to which we are due."

She smiled and stepped after him, then stopped abruptly as if she'd slammed into a wall. Her hand slipped from his grasp and she rebounded from the collision. She fell back hard.

She raised her left hand to her face and touched her upper lip. Her hand came away wet and red, but she didn't feel like she'd bumped her nose.

Nelesquin stared for a moment, then knelt by her side. "What's the matter, beloved?"

"I don't know."

He scooped her into his arms and started toward the ship. Her left shoulder hit an invisible barrier and they both bounced back. Nelesquin turned, walking sideways, but her toes jammed into the unseen wall.

He stepped back and set her down again, then passed through the barrier without difficulty. "I don't understand."

Nirati rubbed at her shoulder. "Neither do I."

"Ah, wait." Nelesquin looked beyond her toward the hill they'd descended. "He doesn't want you to go."

Nirati turned. Her grandfather stood at the crest of the hill, holding Takwee's hand. Nirati waved and both of them waved back. "Can he stop me from leaving?"

Nelesquin laughed. "He created Anturasixan, so it operates by rules only he can imagine. He created Kunjiqui as a sanctuary for you, to protect you from the world that hurt you. He may not know it, but he will not let you leave if he believes you can be hurt."

Everything Nelesquin said made sense to Nirati, but she wasn't certain he'd gotten to the core of things. Something else was happening to keep her in Kunjiqui. She didn't want to dwell on it, but just knowing sent fear through her.

Nelesquin's eyes hardened. "I understand his reasoning, for I would not have you hurt either. I will make the world a place that will never harm you."

Nirati turned and looked at him. "You are still going?"

He nodded solemnly. "The events I read in the stones are a bit more dire than I told you. In them, I saw a glimmer of an old enemy returning to oppose me. He was the source of Gachin's problem and, if he is not eliminated, he could be worrisome."

"But you are in no danger?"

His booming laugh reassured her. "No, beloved. I long ago took steps to assure neither he nor anyone else could harm me." He reached a hand through the barrier. "Because I love you, I am called away. I will come back for you, Nirati Anturasi. You are my empress, and I shall go become the emperor who is worthy of your love."

She smiled bravely, took his hand, and drew him to her. "I know you will, beloved. I will be with you in spirit."

"That shall not make me miss you less." His arms enfolded her and pulled her tightly to him. He peered down into her eyes, then kissed her deeply.

Nirati clung to him, not because she wanted to prevent him from leaving, but because she knew she would never hold him again.

Nelesquin broke the kiss and slipped from her embrace.

She stepped forward and rested her hands against the barrier.

Nelesquin smiled, then bowed to her grandfather and her. "I go a prince; I return an emperor."

"Go bravely, then." Nirati smiled softly. *The barrier is death, beloved. Go bravely, but remember, becoming an emperor does not make one immortal.*

She hugged her arms around herself and waited there, watching until the ships had vanished over the horizon, and Takwee came to guide her home.

Chapter Sixty-one

4th day, Month of the Hawk, Year of the Rat
Last Year of Imperial Prince Cyron's Court
163rd Year of the Komyr Dynasty
737th year since the Cataclysm
Wentokikun, Moriande
Nalenyr

Even low grey clouds and rain could not diminish the magnificence of Moriande. Rain pattered against Prince Pyrust's cloak, and his horse splashed through puddles as he rode toward the Dragon Tower. Count Vroan's Ixunite troops had manned Northgate, and the Shadow Hawks had cleared the streets. It had nominally been agreed that Pyrust was entering the capital to pay his respects to Prince Cyron, and the Keru busied themselves with a hunt for Duke Scior.

The appearance of a Desei host on the hills north of the city had rendered the idea of resistance ridiculous, and there were those nobles who allowed that Nalenyr's fall had been the product of Cyron's pride. While he looked overseas for trade to strengthen his nation, he had not paid attention to more dire threats closer to home. Pyrust had no doubt that the perceived wisdom would become Cyron's historical epitaph, and that few would ever look at the true facts surrounding his fall to see how shortsighted a judgment that truly was.

It did not surprise Pyrust to hear that Cyron had survived the assassination attempt, though stories differed about how he had fared. The Mother of Shadows had scoffed at the ineptitude of Helosundian assassins, but Pyrust felt something more was at play. Grija had promised him great glory, and very great would be the glory of ending the Komyr Dynasty. He had wanted to kill Cyron himself. The gods and circumstances had conspired to let him do so.

Pyrust looked up and around at the buildings lining the street and took heart in the flashes of eyes peeking out at him from doorways and behind shutters. Had a conqueror been riding through Felarati and the order had been given that no one was to look upon him, the Desei would have remained hidden within their homes until told they could emerge again. Learning to obey orders had been what preserved life in Deseirion, but here, in the south, spirit and initiative had created a more vibrant society.

He admired their spirit, and for the first time truly realized how difficult administering an empire would be. He did not let that problem overwhelm him because he still needed to fight the invaders. If they defeated him, all problems of empire would be nothing. Moreover, the bureaucracy would continue to function, keeping the Naleni state working as it should. He felt fairly certain that once he made the nature of the southern threat known to the bureaucracy, they would do all they could to facilitate his destroying the invaders.

It did concern him, however, that they had clearly condoned the assassination and usurpation that would have occurred under Duke Scior or Count Vroan. While bureaucrats often embraced their duty first, they could not be divorced from nationalistic sentiments. The ministers of Helosunde had directed their nation for years, and he had no doubts that Grand Minister Pelut Vniel would gladly seize power if Pyrust were to fall in battle.

The bureaucracy here has willingly played politics. He began to draw up a short list of individuals the Mother of Shadows would have to make disappear. Timed correctly, their deaths would not seem overly suspicious, yet would encourage obedience among other ministers. Similarly the deaths of certain Naleni nobles would disorganize any movement against him.

A tiny piece of him wondered if Cyron would have stooped to preemptive murder had he known the extent of the plotting against him. In general, he would not have put any man above it, but Cyron had been odd in that way. Pyrust never would have sent grain to Nalenyr. While he understood Cyron's motivation, he still viewed it as weakness. He'd not shoved the knife in when he had the chance, and that was what allowed him to lose.

Not a mistake I shall make.

The gates to Wentokikun stood open. Pyrust rode through alone, then up the broad steps to the tower's doors. There he dismounted and threw off his cloak. He entered through the open doors in rain-dappled armor of black, with the Desei hawk painted in gold. He wore a single sword and marveled how his footsteps echoed within the vast entryway.

When he had been in the Dragon Tower before, he had come as a visitor, swathed in formal robes that restricted his strides. He'd shuffled his way down the long corridor to the throne room, having to study the murals depicting Naleni dominance over its neighbors, including Deseirion. Now the Desei murals had been covered by tapestries that showed older scenes, when Desei and Naleni heroes had united against the Turasynd or an ambitious Helosundian prince.

The presence of those tapestries told him that though Cyron might be gravely injured, he was far from dead. Pyrust quickened his pace, stalking down the hallway to the Naleni throne room. He passed around the wooden screening wall, then paused in the doorway. His gaze followed the line of the red carpet to the Dragon Throne.

He struggled to control his reaction to the man seated there.

Cyron had been dressed in armor, but wore neither helmet nor face mask. His left arm ended in a bandaged stump, which was still leaking. He sat as straight as he could, his face grey and wet with perspiration. A sheathed sword sat across the arms of his throne and his right hand rested on the hilt.

Pyrust removed his own helmet and face mask, setting them down by the door. He bowed, then approached slowly. He checked himself, for his gait had gone from that of a conqueror to that of someone entering a sickroom. He considered for a moment, then continued forward sedately, stopping nine feet from the foot of the throne.

Cyron swallowed hard, then licked at dry lips. "I was urged to meet you in robes of state. I would have, but as much as I hate wearing them, I do like the colors. Blood would spoil them."

"Your robes are magnificent, much like your city and your nation."

"Hardly mine anymore." Cyron's expression tightened. "I wanted to meet you in armor. You'll kill me, and we needn't have it said I cowered or you murdered me."

"Armor or robes, those things will be said regardless." Pyrust rested his left hand on the hilt of his sword. "How bad are things to the south?"

Cyron smiled weakly. "I tried to keep that from you."

"You were right to. I have stripped my nation of those capable of fighting. I have united the Helosundians. We are heading south to fight the invaders."

"Vroan is with you?"

"For as long as he is useful."

The Naleni Prince nodded. "Destroy the westrons."

"I'll let the invaders do that." Pyrust paused and looked around the room, at the golden wood and simple artistry of the Dragon Throne. "I can understand how you became complacent."

"If that is what you understand, brother, then you understand nothing." Cyron winced, then struggled to sit forward. "You see the Nine as an empire that needs reuniting."

"As you did."

"But I saw it as more. United as a people, in contact with the rest of the world, we could learn and teach. We could make life better." Cyron slowly sagged back into the throne. "War can only destroy, not build."

Pyrust pointed to the south. "We did not choose the war."

"No, but you will use it. Only do not destroy so much that you cannot build again."

Pyrust paused for a moment, allowing Cyron's words to sink in. He would not have expected Cyron to beg for his own life, and was pleased that the Prince did not. It surprised him, on the other hand, that Cyron would offer advice. *He has accepted his own death, but wishes his dream to live on.*

Cyron's dream surprised Pyrust. He'd seen bits and pieces of it and, as recently as the ride to the tower, had dismissed it as weakness. The fact was that Cyron's looking beyond empire mocked Pyrust's shortsightedness. He *had always* looked to empire for the sake of empire.

But what use is it for me to have my name on monuments that will be crushed if the Empire is not sustained? Growth is all that can *sustain it. Soldiers may be able to* guard *and* preserve, *but war cannot advance a culture into a peaceful future.*

The Desei Prince slowly nodded. "I will treat your request with the sincerity and thought it merits."

Cyron nodded slowly. "Thank you." He shifted his right arm, so the sword tipped forward and down. The scabbard half slid off, then he shook it the rest of the way clear. It clattered down the dais steps and lay halfway between them.

Pyrust drew his own sword. "I would keep you alive for the value of your ideas, brother, but you will become a rallying point for opposition. Even after I kill you and mount your head on a spear at the gate, there will be those who say I only killed an impostor. You'll be reported in the east or west, the Helos Mountains; you'll be in the company of Keru who are bearing your children. I'll never be rid of the Komyr curse."

"Shall I lift my chin so you can make the cut clean?"

Cyron laughed. "I trust your blade will be sharper than the assassin's. I'd not want to live through the first stroke."

"It will be quick." Pyrust took a step forward, bringing his blade back, but a rustling at the doorway caused him to turn.

A slender, dark-haired woman in a robe of jade, trimmed with jet, stood on the carpet. "Do not kill him."

Pyrust lowered his sword and glanced at Cyron. "Are these the liberties you allow courtesans? She treads where only nobles may walk, and gives orders to princes?"

"Do *not* kill him."

Pyrust stared at her. "You order me? Who do you think you are?"

The Lady of Jet and Jade looked at him with ageless eyes. "This is my Empire, Prince Pyrust. I am Cyrsa, and when I give you an order, you *will* obey."

About the Author

Michael A. Stackpole is an award-winning author, editor, game and computer game designer. As always, he spends his spare time playing indoor soccer and now has a new hobby, podcasting. Mike is currently at work on *A New World,* the sequel to *Cartomancy,* and ideas for a half-dozen other novels.

To learn more about Mike, please visit www.stormwolf.com (his website) and to learn more about podcasting, please visit www.tsfpn.com (the website of The SciFi Podcast Network).

BE SURE NOT TO MISS

The New World

by

Michael A. Stackpole

the exhilarating conclusion to
the Age of Discovery series

Coming from Bantam in summer 2007

Here's a special preview:

The New World

On sale summer 2007

Ciras Dejote sighed, and wished that the peace of Voraxan might once again infect him. Instead, he wandered the empty onyx streets of the city, passing between buildings carved from ruby and emerald, topaz, lapis, and citrine, and felt nothing. The architecture reminded him of the grand palaces of the Empire—relics of a time when heroes walked and epic tales were born.

He had grown up listening to such stories and had dreamed of someday becoming a hero. He knew the path to immortality would require learning the way of the sword so completely that he would touch *jaedun*—the magic that transformed an ordinary warrior into a Mystic. Through diligent study and practice, he could become a superior swordsman. But as a Mystic, he would be *supernaturally* gifted.

In pursuit of this, he had set out with his Master, Moraven Tolo, on a quest into the Wastes—a place where wild magic still warped the land. There they encountered villainy and adventure, and his mission had changed. In company with Borosan Gryst, he had then journeyed deep into Ixyll, to find Voraxan, the resting place of the Sleeping Empress. They were to awaken her and convince her to reunite the army she had sundered over seven centuries before, and bring it back to save the Empire.

Ciras paused beside a small emerald building. He ran his fingers over the elaborate characters carved into the lintel. *Shan Tsiendao*. Within the building he could see a recumbent form—sleeping, dreaming, waiting to be summoned once again to war. Though he could feel the urgency of their mission, he found himself saddened by the idea that these warriors would be wakened from their idyllic slumbers.

Ciras walked on, wending his way back toward the courtyard in front of the ruby palace that had been the Empress' resting place. In that onyx courtyard, between the palace and a diamond fountain, Borosan Gryst sat tinkering with one of the magical machines he loved creating. Ciras frowned. Despite the hardship of their journey, the man was still sloppily overweight. He wore no sword, and had neither martial skill nor sense. In Ciras' world, this made him an object of contempt.

And yet on their journey Borosan had proved himself to be clever. *Almost too clever.*

Ciras crossed the courtyard, his shadow falling over Borosan, and stared down at him. "I cannot believe you concealed the fact that Empress Cyrsa had left this place! We traveled across the known world, through strange lands and countless perils, and still you kept this hidden from me."

Borosan smiled indulgently. "It was not a matter of trust, Master Dejote. I had been given a mission by the Empress, and that mission was a secret. I did not tell my father, and I would not have told Prince Cyron, had he asked. You should not feel betrayed."

The slender swordsman crouched beside his thickset companion, though he remained outside the reach of the spider-like *thanaton* on which Borosan worked. "I do not feel betrayed on my own account. I understand secrecy. It is just that the message you carried was of vital importance. What would have happened had you died on the mission? The call would not have gone out."

Borosan shrugged. Both arms were elbow-deep in the inner workings of the *thanaton*'s spherical body. "I imagine I am not the only person the Empress dispatched with her message. I'm just the first one to make it. And . . ."

The *gyanridin*'s right hand emerged from the machine's bowels and tossed Ciras a small, yellowed ivory cylinder, with a delicate script carved on it. "Besides, if I died, there was always this."

Ciras caught it. The writing was in the old Imperial script, and was therefore taxing to read. "A poem?"

"By Jaor Dirxi. A meditation on the beauty of a woman who became the Empress." Borosan smiled. "I was told he inscribed ivory himself."

The swordsman twisted the top and slid the end off. A small scroll of rice paper fell into his hand as he upended the cylinder. He unrolled it and found it contained a copy of the message Borosan had delivered. The hand that had wielded the brush had been strong yet delicate. And something else struck him about the note, though he could not immediately identify it. Then he raised the note to his nose and breathed in its subtle scent.

Ciras' head snapped up. "This wasn't written by the Empress. This was written by the Lady of Jet and Jade. My master knows her. I caught the scent on his robes . . ."

Borosan shook his head. "You're too quick to jump to conclusions. Yes, it *was* written by the Lady of Jet and Jade. But why would you assume that she is not also the Empress?"

Ciras rocked back and sat staring at the ruby

palace. The Empress had led an army of Mystics to destroy the Turasynd horde raiding from the north. Their grand battle released untold amounts of magical energy, which swept over the continent, triggering the Time of Black Ice. The Nine Principalities had been devastated, and were only now beginning to regain their former glory and power.

The swordsman frowned. "The Lady of Jet and Jade is a courtesan of incredible skill. She, too, is a Mystic, hence her longevity. But . . ."

"You must have known that Cyrsa became one of the last Emperor's wives as a gift from a courtier. What did you imagine she had been previous to that?"

Ciras shook his head. "I know the people of Nalenyr think those of us from the island of Tirat provincial, but we, too, have our houses of pleasure. I have no difficulty with the Lady of Jet and Jade, but I have met her. She is anything but a warrior, and it was a warrior who led the army. I mean . . . from the stories, I expected someone more like one of the Keru."

Borosan laughed and closed the *thanaton*'s body. "Yes. Tall, strong, able to kill a charging elephant with a single spear. Apparently skill-at-arms was not where the Empress' strength lay—and I don't intend that as a pun. She had the world's greatest warriors to call upon—many of whom are now being wakened from their slumbers."

"And they will answer her call." Ciras

frowned. “I wonder what else she will ask them to do?”

“We will see when we return with them.” Borosan stood and brushed off his hands. He bowed to a slender man with a bald head who was approaching.

Ciras stood immediately and bowed as well. “Greetings, Master Laedhze.”

The warrior returned their bows. “Greetings. I have news to impart and a favor to ask.”

“Of course,” Ciras answered for both of them. “Whatever you need.”

Vlay Laedhze waved a hand back toward the city. Throughout, people could be seen stirring within their jeweled homes. “We are waking our companions, and many are consenting to answer the call.”

Ciras arched an eyebrow. “Many? I would have thought they all would answer.”

The tall man hung his head with resignation. “I have little doubt they all intended to answer when they first lay down. Over the years, a few of them have done their duty when wakened and have departed Voraxan. But others returned to their homes here, and embraced the peace of this city. You too have enjoyed this.”

Ciras nodded. During his time in Voraxan he had slept well, dreaming neither of violence nor warfare. In those dreams, he'd been able to journey instead to far Tirat and visit his family. They knew nothing of his sojourns, but he was able to watch them and see that they were happy. And that warmed his heart in a manner that was beyond value.

Laedhze smiled gently. “The dreams are very seductive, and some will not leave them. And, alas, some of our companions do expire in their sleep. They will rest happily in Kianmang, awaiting the call of another time to fight again.”

“So how many will we have?”

“It is my hope we have a battalion.” Laedhze nodded solemnly. “We may have a few more.”

Ciras' stomach twisted. “Two hundred and forty-three warriors? Granted they are all Mystics, but only three companies? How is that possible?”

Borosan caught Ciras' sleeve. “Ask him how many survived the battle.”

Laedhze's expression became grim. “Just over four hundred.”

“Impossible!” Ciras tore his sleeve from Borosan's grasp. “All the stories . . . Even this place . . . How could only four hundred have created it?”

The warrior from Voraxan clasped his hands at the small of his back. “You have traveled past the battlefield. You have seen how the corpses continue to fight. Such was the violence of that day that even death will not release them. Would you care to see the scars I bear from that day? To say we triumphed is an exaggeration. We barely survived.

“We were the Empress' Bodyguard. There were two thousand of us held in reserve, and we were but a tenth of our army—and a twentieth of the horde we faced. The *vanyesh* had already been broken, though they had destroyed much of the Turasynd horde in the process. By rights, the nomads should have retreated, but they believed the Empress had brought her treasury with her, so on they came. And came and came and came. And we killed and killed and killed."

Ciras nodded, his anger abated by the sober tone of the man's voice. "But this place, four hundred of you . . . How could you?"

"You forget, Master Dejote, that this place was alive with wild magic. We were steeped in it, all of us. There were those who could work magic—not all of the magicians belonged to Prince Nelesquin's *vanyesh*. They and a Viruk companion of ours shaped the magic, and made this place. They made it to be our haven. And if what you tell me of Tolwreen is true, then the *vanyesh* survivors have done the same thing."

"But not as well." Borosan smiled. "This place nourishes you, but Tolwreen is just an elaborate mausoleum."

"I am certain they would call this place a mausoleum, too." Laedhze looked up, his face again a pleasant mask. "But it is not, and we have not all just lain sleeping. It is with this in mind that I need your aid, Borosan Gryst. You may come, too, Master Dejote."

Ciras agreed with a nod, his mind still reeling. The trio set off, Borosan's *thanaton* pacing beside them. Its metal feet ticked loudly on the onyx road, reminding Ciras of the ringing of one blade against another. The peace of Voraxan was something he would know no more, and he felt certain none of those waking would ever return to it, either.

Laedhze led them into a bloodstone building and down a broad set of stairs. They emerged into what might once have been a natural cavern, but had since been shaped and carved into a stable of stone that extended into darkness. The nearest end had been transformed into a smithy and though the fires were out, there was ample evidence that it had been very active throughout the ages.

Borosan gasped and drifted toward the nearest stall. "I don't believe it. I have dreamed, of course, but . . ." He raised a hand and stroked a sleek metal muzzle.

The *thanaton* had wandered forward, and there was a clear kinship between it and the tall mechanical horse Borosan stood admiring. The *thanaton* had an insect's simplicity, but the steed revealed gearing and springs, support pieces and joints, which Ciras could not really explain, yet which clearly went together perfectly. Each mechanical beast had been fitted with armored plating, more as decoration than anything, making them as beautiful as they were sturdy.

Laedhze pointed off into the darkness. "When we awakened to rotate through sentinel duty, we each constructed at least one of these creatures. We were given plans for how they were to be constructed, and examples of the pieces. The plans have long since been lost, though each of us has memorized them. We know they are meant to be ridden, yet each is immobile, and we know no magic to make them work. Yet we are certain some must exist."

Borosan moved into the stable and slowly made a circuit of the steed. He ran his hand over the flanks and along the neck, then reemerged at the head. He stared closely at it.

Cautiously, Ciras drifted over—though he almost retreated again when he saw himself reflected in the steed's dead, ruby eyes. "What have you found?"

"Up here, by the ear, is a spring-loaded catch." Borosan pressed down on it. Something clicked.

Ciras jumped, one hand dropping to the hilt of the sword at his waist. With his other hand, he reached out and tugged Borosan back.

But his companion just smiled. "No. It won't hurt us."

With a hiss, the faceplate tipped up near the ears and extended straight out, coming down near the muzzle. At the same time the steed's head dipped, bringing the cavity behind the faceplate into clear view. The fact that the ruby eyes still stared at Ciras did not make him feel any better.

Borosan stepped forward and poked at five narrow slots in the flat plate. "Of course. Brilliant."

The Voraxan warrior came forward. "What is it, Master Borosan?"

"The most useful thing that I discovered in Tolwreen was an alloy of *thaumston* which could store both wild magic and the directions for the operation of a *gyanrigot*. Properly inscribed, they should power and direct one of these mounts. They work in the *thanaton*, so there is no reason they won't work here."

Ciras folded his arms over his chest. "I will not ride one of those things."

Borosan smiled. "On our horses, we can go maybe thirty miles in a day. What if these will take us sixty, and in half the time? In a quarter of it?"

Laedhze nodded solemnly. "And think of these mounts in tactical combat. Just their weight alone will shatter an enemy formation in a charge."

Ciras frowned. "And where is the heroism in that? It takes no skill, and wins no honor."

The ancient warrior pressed his hands together. "In our final battle, there was no question of skill. There was no honor to be won. It was a war of survival, and we did what was required. We won *because* we survived."

Ciras bowed. "I meant to suggest no dishonor . . ."

"And I did not think you had." Laedhze smiled cautiously. "But the Empress has summoned us, and it is not to display skill or win glory. She would only have summoned us if the world's survival was at stake. Believing this is the case, I will not hesitate to use whatever means are at my disposal to reach her as fast as possible, and do her bidding with all the strength I possess."